The Fourth Leonaur Book
of
Great Ghost and Horror
Stories

The Fourth Leonaur Book
of
Great Ghost and Horror
Stories

Twenty-Two Short Stories of the Strange and
Unusual Including 'The Shadow of a Midnight',
'Green Branches', 'Our Last Walk', 'The Shell of
Sense', 'The Vengeance of a Tree', 'A Phantom Toe',
and 'La Morte Amoureuse'

Compiled by

Eunice Hetherington

LEONAUR

The Fourth Leonaur Book of
Great Ghost and Horror Stories
Twenty-Two Short Stories of the Strange and Unusual
Including 'The Shadow of a Midnight', 'Green Branches', '
Our Last Walk', 'The Shell of Sense', 'The Vengeance of a Tree', 'A Phantom Toe'and 'La
Morte Amoureuse'
Compiled by Eunice Hetherington

Leonaur is an imprint of Oakpast Ltd

Copyright in this form © 2022 Oakpast Ltd

ISBN: 978-1-915234-78-0 (hardcover)
ISBN: 978-1-915234-79-7 (softcover)

http://www.leonaur.com

Publisher's Notes

The views expressed in this book are not necessarily
those of the publisher.

Contents

A Bewitched Ship

W. Clark Russell

'About ten years ago,' began my friend, Captain Green, 'I went as second mate of a ship named the *Ocean King*. She'd been an old Indiaman in her time, and had a poop and topgallant forecastle, though alterations had knocked some of the dignity out of her. Her channels had been changed into plates with dead-eyes above the rail, and the eye missed the spread of the lower rigging that it naturally sought in looking at a craft with a square stern and windows in it, and chequered sides rounding out into curves that made a complete tub of the old hooker.

'Yet, spite of changes, the old-fashioned grace would break through. She looked like a lady who has seen better days, who has got to do work which servants did for her in the times when she was well off, but who, let her set her hand to what she will, makes you see that the breeding and the instincts are still there, and that she's as little to be vulgarised by poverty and its coarse struggles as she could be made a truer lady than she is by money. Ships, like human beings, have their careers, and the close of some of them is strange, and sometimes hard, I think.

'The *Ocean King* had been turned into a collier, and I went second mate of her when she was full up with coal for a South African port. Yet this ship, that was now carrying one of the dirtiest cargoes you could name, barring phosphate manure, had been reckoned in her day a fine passenger vessel, a noble Indiaman, indeed—her tonnage was something over eleven hundred—with a cuddy fitted up royally. Many a freight of soldiers had she carried round the Cape, many an old *nabob* had she conveyed—aye, and Indian potentates, who smoked out of jewelled *hookahs*, and who were waited upon by crowds of black servants in turbans and slippers.

'I used to moralise over her, just as I would over a tomb, when I had the watch, and was alone, and could let my thoughts run loose. The sumptuous cabin trappings were all gone, and I seemed to smell coal in the wind, even when my head was over the weather side, and when the breeze that blew along came fresh across a thousand miles of sea; but there was a good deal of the fittings left—fittings, which, I don't doubt, made the newspapers give a long account of this "fine great ship" when she was launched, quite enough of them to enable a man to reconstruct a picture of the cuddy of the *Ocean King* as it was in the days of her glory, when soft oil lamps shone bright on the draped tables and sparkled on silver and glass, when the old skipper, sitting with the mizzenmast behind him, would look, with his red face and white hair, down the rows of ladies and gentlemen eating and drinking, stewards running about, trays hanging from the deck above, and globes full of goldfish swinging to the roll of the vessel as she swung stately, with her stunsails hanging out, over the long blue swell wrinkled by the wind.

'The ship is still afloat. Where are the people she carried? The crews who have worked her? The captains who have commanded her? There is nothing that should be fuller of ghosts than an old ship; and I very well remember that when I first visited the *Victory* at Portsmouth, and descended into her cockpit, what I saw was not a well-preserved and cleanly length of massive deck, but groups of wounded and bleeding and dying men littering the dark floor, and the hatchway shadowed by groaning figures handed below, whilst the smell of English, French and Spanish gunpowder, even down there, was so strong—phew! I could have spat the flavour out.

'Well, the old *Ocean King* had once upon a time been said to be haunted. She had certainly been long enough afloat to own a hundred stories, and she was so staunch and true that if ever a

8

superstition got into her here was no chance of its getting out again. I only remember one of these yarns; it was told to me by the dockmaster, who had been at sea for many years, was an old man, and knew the history of all such craft as the *Ocean King*. He said that in '51, I think it was, there had been a row among the crew; an Italian sailor stabbed an Englishman, who bled to death.

'To avenge the Englishman's death, the rest of the crew, who were chiefly English, thrust the Italian into the forepeak and left him there in darkness. When he was asked for, they reported that he had fallen overboard, and this seems to have been believed. Whether the crew meant to starve him or not is not certain; but after he had been in the forepeak for three or four days, a fellow going behind the galley out of the way of the wind to light his pipe—it being then four bells in the first watch—came running into the forecastle with his hair on end, and the sweat pouring off his face, swearing he had seen the Italian lying there dead, with a score of rats upon him, which scampered off when the men dropped off below.

'During all the rest of the voyage his ghost was constantly seen, sometimes at the lee wheel, sometimes astride of the flying jibboom. What was the end of it—I mean, whether the men confessed the murder, and if so what became of them—the dockmaster said he didn't know. But be this as it may, I discovered shortly after we had begun our voyage that the crew had got to hear of this story, and the chief mate said it had been brought aboard by the carpenter, who had picked it up from some of the dockyard labourers.

'I well recollect two uncomfortable circumstances; we sailed on a Friday, and the able and ordinary seamen were thirteen in number, the idlers and ourselves aft bringing up the ship's company to nineteen souls! when, I suppose, in her prime, the *Ocean King* never left port short of seventy or eighty seamen, not to mention stewards, cooks, cooks' mates, butcher, butcher's mate, baker, and the rest of them. But double topsailyards were now in; besides, I understood that the vessel's masts had been reduced and her yards shortened, and we carried stump fore and mizzen topgallantmasts.

'All being ready, a tug got hold of our towrope, and we went down the river and out to sea.

'I don't believe myself that any stories which had been told the men about this ship impressed them much. Sailors are very superstitious, but they are not to be scared till something has happened to frighten them. Your merely telling them that there's a ghost aboard the ship they're in won't alarm them till they've caught sight of the ghost. But once let a man say to the others, "There's a bloomin' spehip. Lay your head agin the forehatch, and you'll hear him gnashing his teeth and rattlin' his chains," and then let another man go and listen, and swear, and perhaps very honestly, that he "heerd the noises plain," and you'll have all hands in a funk, talking in whispers, and going aloft in the dark nervously.

'In our ship nothing happened for some days. We were deep and slow, and rolled along solemnly, the sea falling away from the vessel's powerful round bows as from a rock. Pile what we could upon her, with tacks aboard, staysails drawing, and the wind hitting her best sailing points, we could seldom manage to get more than seven knots out of her. One night I had the first watch. It was about two bells. There was a nice wind, the sea smooth, and a red moon crawling up over the starboard beam. We were under all plain sail, leaning away from the wind a trifle, and the water washed along under the bends in lines through which the starlight ran glimmering.

'I was thinking over the five or six months' voyages which old waggons after the pattern of this ship took in getting to India, when seeing a squall coming along, I sung out for hands to stand by the main royal and mizzen topgallant halliards. It drove down dark, and not knowing what was behind I ordered the main royal to be clewed and furled. Two youngsters went aloft. By the time they were on the yard the squall thinned, but I fancied there was another bearing down, and thought it best to let the ordinary seamen roll the sail up. On a sudden down they both trotted hand over hand, leaving the sail flapping in the clutch of the clewlines.

'I roared out, "What d'ye mean by coming down before you've furled that sail?"

'They stood together in the main rigging, and one of them answered, "Please, sir, there's a ghost somewhere up aloft on the foretopsail-yard."

'"A ghost, you fool!" I cried.

'"Yes, sir," he answered. "He says, 'Jim your mother wants yer.' I says, 'What?' and he says, 'Your mother wants yer,' in the hollowest o' voices. Dick here heard it. There's no one aloft forrards, sir."

'I sung out to them to jump aloft again, and finding that they didn't move I made a spring, on which they dropped like lightning on deck, and began to beg and pray of me in the eagerest manner not to send them aloft, as they were too frightened to hold on. Indeed, the fellow named Jim actually began to shiver and cry when I threatened him; so, as the royal had to be furled, I sent an able seaman aloft, who, after rolling up the sail, came down and said that no voice had called to him, and that he reckoned it was a bit of skylarking on the part of the boys to get out of stowing the sail. However, I noticed that the man was wonderfully quick over the job, and that afterwards the watch on deck stood talking in low voices in the waist.

'Jim was a fool of a youth, but Dick was a smart lad, aged about nineteen, and good-looking, with a lively tongue, and I heard afterwards that he could spin a yarn to perfection all out of his imagination. I called him to me, and asked him if he had really heard a voice, and he swore he had.

'"Did it say," said I, "Jim, your mother wants you?"

'"Ay, sir," he answered, with a bit of a shudder, "as plain as you yourself say it. It seemed to come off the foretopgallant-yard, where I fancied I see something dark a-moving; but I was too frightened to take particular notice."

'Well, it was not long after this, about eleven o'clock in the morning, that, the captain being on deck, the cook steps out of the galley, comes walking along the poop, and going up to the skipper, touches his cap, and stands looking at him.

"'Didn't you call, sir?" says the cook.

"'Call!" cries the skipper. "Certainly not."

'The man looked stupid with surprise, and, muttering something to himself, went forward. Ten minutes after he came up again to the skipper, and says "Yes, sir!" as a man might who answers to a call. The skipper began to swear at him, and called him a lunatic, and so on; but the man, finding he was wrong again, grew white, and swore that if he was on his deathbed, he'd maintain that the captain had called him twice.

'The skipper, who was a rather nervous man, turned to me, and said, "What do you make of this, Mr Green? I can't doubt the cook's word. Who's calling him in my voice?"

"'Oh, it's some illusion, sir," said I, feeling puzzled for all that.

'But the cook, with the tears actually standing in his eyes, declared it was no illusion; he'd know the captain's voice if it was nine miles off. And then he walked in a dazed way towards the forecastle, singing out that whether the voice he had heard belonged to a ghost or a Christian man, it might go on calling "Cook!" for the next twenty years without his taking further notice of it. This thing coming so soon after the call to Jim that had so greatly alarmed the two ordinary seamen, made a great impression on the crew; and I never regret anything more than that my position should have prevented me from getting into their confidence, and learning their thoughts, for there is no doubt I should have stowed away memories enough to serve me for many a hearty laugh in after years.

'A few days rolled by without anything in particular happening. One night it came to my turn to have the first watch. It was a quiet night, with wind enough to keep the sails still whilst the old ship went drowsily along her course to the African port. Suddenly I heard a commotion forward, and, fearing that some accident had happened, I called out to know what the matter was. A voice answered, "Ghost or no ghost, there's somebody a-talking in the forehold; come and listen sir." The silence that followed suggested a good deal of alarm. I sang out as I approached the men, "Perhaps there's a stowaway below."

"'It's no living voice," was the reply; "it sounds as if it comes from a skeleton."

'I found a crowd of men standing in awed postures near the hatch, and the most frightened of all looked to me to be the ordinary seaman Dick, who had backed away on the other side of the hatch, and stood looking on, leaning with his hands on his knees, and staring as if was fascinated. I waited a couple or three minutes, which, in a business of this kind, seems a long time, and hearing nothing, I was going to ridicule the men for their nervousness, when a hollow voice under the hatch said distinctly, "It's a terrible thing to be a ghost and not be able to get out."

'I was greatly startled, and ran aft to tell the captain, who agreed with me that there must be a stowaway in the hold, and that he had gone mad. We both went forward and the hatch was lifted, and we looked on top of the coal; and I was then about to ask some of the men to join me in a search of the forepeak, for upon my word I had no taste single-handed for a job of that kind at such a moment, when the voice said, "There's no use looking, you'll never find me. I'm not to be seen."

"'Confound me!" cried the skipper, polishing his forehead with a pocket-handkerchief, "if ever I heard of such a thing. I'll tell you what this is," he shouted, looking into the hatch, "dead men can't talk, and so you're bound to be alive, you'd better come up out of that, and smartly too—d'ye hear?—or you'll find this the worst attempt at skylarking that was ever made."

'There was short silence, and you'd see all hands straining their ears, for there was light enough for that, given out by a lantern one of the men held.

"'You couldn't catch me because you couldn't see me," said the voice in a die-away tone, and this time it came from the direction of the main hatch, as though it had flitted aft.

"'Well," says the captain, "may I be jiggered!" and without another word he walked away on to the poop.

'I told the men to clap the hatches on again, and they did this in double-quick time, evidently afraid that the ghost might pop up out of the hold if they didn't mind their eye.

'All this made us very superstitious, from the captain down to the boys. We talked it over in the cabin, and the mate was incredulous, and disposed to ridicule me.

'"Anyway," said he, "it's strange that his voice is only heard in your watch. It's never favoured *me* with any remarks. The creaking and groaning of an old wooden ship is often like spoken words, and what you've been hearing may be nothing but a deception on the ear."

'"A deception in your eye!" cried the skipper. "The timber of an old wooden ship may strain and creak in the Dutch language, but hang me if they ever talked good sensible English. However, I'm not going to worry. For my part," said he, with a nervous glance around him, "I don't believe in ghosts; whatever it is that's talking in the hold may go on jawing, so long as he sticks to that, and don't frighten the men with an ugly mug, nor come upon us for a man's allowance."

'"If it's anybody's ghost," said I, "it must be the Italian's, the chap that was starved in the forepeak."

'"I doubt that," said the skipper. "I didn't detect anything foreign in what he said. To my ear it sounded more like Whitechapel than Italian."

'Well, for another week we heard little more of the ghost. It's true that one middle watch a chap I had sent aloft to loose the mainroyal has hardly stepped out of the lower rigging, after lingering in the crosstrees to overhaul his clewlines, when he comes rushing up to me and cries out, "I've been hailed from aloft, sir! a voice has just sung out, 'Tommy, jump aloft again that I may have a good look at you!'"

'"Who's up there?" I asked him, staring into the gloom where the mast and yards were towering.

'"There's no one up there, sir; I'll swear it. I was bound to see him had anyone been there.," he answered, evidently very much frightened.

'It occurred to me that someone of the crew might be lying hid in the top, and that if I could catch him, I might find out who the ghost was. So, I jumped into the rigging and trotted aloft, keeping my eye on the lee rigging, to make sure that no one descended by it. I gained the top, but nobody was there. I mounted to the crosstrees, but the deuce a sign of anyone could I see. I came down, feeling both foolish and scared; for you see I had heard the voice myself in the hold, there was no question that there was a voice, belonging to nobody knew what, knocking about the ship, and consequently it was now impossible to help believing a man when he said he heard it.

'However, it was necessary to keep the men in heart, and this was not to be done by captain and mates appearing scared; so, I reasoned a bit with the man, told him that there were no such things as ghosts, that a voice was bound to come from a live person, because a spectre couldn't possibly have lungs, those organs being of a perishable nature, and then sent him forward, but no easier in his mind, I suspect, than I was. Anyhow I was glad when eight bells were struck and it was my turn to go below.

'But as I have said, nothing much came of this—at least, nothing that reached my ears. But not many nights following the ship lay becalmed—there wasn't a breath of fresh air, and the sea lay smooth as polished jet. This time I had the middle watch again. I was walking quietly up and down the poop, on the lookout for a deeper shadow upon the sea to indicate the approach of wind, when a man came to the ladder and said, "There's someone a-talking to the ship under the bows."

'"Are you awake?" said I.

'"Heaven help me, as I stand here, sir," exclaimed the fellow, solemnly, "if that there voice which talked in the hold t'other day ain't now over the side."

'I ran forward, and found most of the watch huddled together near the starboard cathead. I peered over, and there was a dead silence.

'"What are you looking over the side for? I'm here!" said a thin, faint voice, that seemed more in the air than in the sea.

'"There!" exclaimed one of the seamen, in a hoarse whisper, "That's the third time. Whichever side we look, he's on the other."

"'But there must be someone in the water," said another man. "Anybody see his outline? Cuss me if I couldn't swear I see a chap swimmin' just now."

"'No, no," answered someone gruffly, "nothing but phosphorus, Joe, and the right ort o' stuff too, for if this ain't Old Nick—"

"'You're a liar, Sam!" came the voice clear and as one could swear, plain from over the side.

'There was a general recoil, and a sort of groan ran among the men.

'At the same moment I collared a figure standing near me, and slewed him round to bring his face fair to the starlight, clear of the staysail. "Come you along with me, Master Dick," said I; and I marched him off the forecastles, along the main deck, and up on to the poop. "So, you're the ghost, eh?" said I. "Why, to have kept your secret you should have given my elbow a wider berth. No wonder the Voice only makes observations in my watch. You're too lazy, I suppose to leave your hammock to try your wonderful power on the mate, eh? Now, see here," said I, finding him silent, and noticing how white his face glimmered to the stars, "I know you're the man, so you'd better confess. Own the truth, and I'll keep your secret, providing you belay all further tricks of this same kind, deny that you're the ghost and I'll speak to the captain and set the men upon you."

'This fairly frightened him. "Well, sir, it's true; I'm the Voice, sir; but for God's sake keep the secret, sir. The men 'ud have my life if they found out that it was me as scared them."

'This confession was what I needed, for though when standing pretty close to him on the forecastle I could have sworn that it was he who uttered the words which perplexed and awed the sailors, yet so perfect was the deception, so fine, in short, was his skill as a ventriloquist that, had he stoutly denied and gone on denying that he was the "voice," I should have believed him and continued sharing in the wonder and superstition of the crew. I kept his secret as I promised; but, somehow or other, it leaked out in time that he could deceive the ear by apparently pitching his voice among the rigging, or under the deck, or over the side, though the discovery was not made until the "ghost" had for a long time ceased to trouble the ship's company, and until the men's superstitions had faded somewhat, and they had recovered their old cheerfulness.

'We then sent Dick to the cabin, where he gave real entertainment as a ventriloquist, imitating all sorts of animals and producing sounds as of women in distress and men singing out for help in the berths; indeed, such was the skill that I'd often see the skipper and mate turning startled to look in the direction whence the voice proceeded. He made his peace with the men by amusing them in the same way; so that, instead of getting the rope's-ending aft and the pummelling forward which he deserved, he ended as a real and general favourite, and one of the most amusing fellows that a man ever was shipmate with. I used to tell him that if he chose to perform ashore, he was sure to make plenty of money, since such ventriloquial powers as his were the rarest thing in the world; and I'd sometimes fancy he meant to take my advice. But whether he died or kept going to sea I don't know, for after he left the ship, I never saw nor heard of him again.'

Green Branches

Fiona Macleod

In the year that followed the death of Mànus MacCodrum, James Achanna saw nothing of his brother Gloom. He might have thought himself alone in the world, of all his people, but for a letter that came to him out of the west. True, he had never accepted the common opinion that his brothers had both been drowned on that night when Anne Gillespie left Eilanmore with Mànus. In the first place, he had nothing of that inner conviction concerning the fate of Gloom which he had concerning that of Marcus; in the next, had he not heard the sound of the *feadan*, which no one that he knew played, except Gloom; and, for further token, was not the tune that which he hated above all others— the Dance of the Dead—for who but Gloom would be playing that, he hating it so, and the hour being late, and no one else on Eilanmore? It was no sure thing that the dead had not come back; but the more he thought of it the more Achanna believed that his sixth brother was still alive. Of this, however, he said nothing to anyone.

It was as a man set free that, at last, after long waiting and patient trouble with the disposal of all that was left of the Achanna heritage, he left the island. It was a grey memory for him. The bleak moorland of it, the blight that had lain so long and so often upon the crops, the rains that had swept the isle for grey days and grey weeks and grey months, the sobbing of the sea by day and its dark moan by night, its dim relinquishing sigh in the calm of dreary ebbs, its hollow baffling roar when the storm-shadow swept up out of the sea, one and all oppressed him, even in memory. He had never loved the island, even when it lay green and fragrant in the green and white seas under white and blue skies, fresh and sweet as an Eden of the sea.

He had ever been lonely and weary, tired of the mysterious shadow that lay upon his folk, caring little for any of his brothers except the eldest—long since mysteriously gone out of the ken of man—and almost hating Gloom, who had ever borne him a grudge because of his beauty, and because of his likeness to and reverent heed for Alison. Moreover, ever since he had come to love Katreen Macarthur, the daughter of Donald Macarthur who lived in Sleat of Skye, he had been eager to live near her; the more eager as he knew that Gloom loved the girl also, and wished for success not only for his own sake, but so as to put a slight upon his younger brother.

So, when at last he left the island, he sailed southward gladly. He was leaving Eilanmore; he was bound to a new home in Skye, and perhaps he was going to his long-delayed, long dreamed-of happiness. True, Katreen was not pledged to him; he did not even know for sure if she loved him. He thought, hoped, dreamed, almost believed that she did; but then there was her cousin Ian, who had long wooed her, and to whom old Donald Macarthur had given his blessing. Nevertheless, his heart would have been lighter than it had been for long, but for two things. First, there was the letter. Some weeks earlier he had received it, not recognising the writing, because of the few letters he had ever seen, and, moreover, as it was in a feigned hand. With difficulty he had deciphered the Manuscript, plain printed though it was. It ran thus:—

"Well, Sheumais, my brother, it is wondering if I am dead, you will be. Maybe ay and maybe no. But I send you this writing to let you see that I know all you do and think of. So, you are going to leave Eilanmore without an Achanna upon it? And you will be going to Sleat in Skye? Well, let me be telling you this thing. *Do not go.* I see blood there. And there is this, too: neither you nor any man shall take Katreen away from me. You know that; and Ian Macarthur knows it; and Katreen knows it: and that holds whether I am alive or dead. I say to you: do not go. It will be better for you and for all. Ian Macarthur is away in the north-sea with the whaler-captain who came to us at Eilanmore, and will not be back for three months yet. It will be better for him not to come back.

"But if he comes back, he will have to reckon with the man who says that Katreen Macarthur is his. I would rather not have two men to speak to, and one my brother. It does not matter to you where I am. I want no money just now. But put aside my portion for me. Have it ready for me against the day I call for it. I will not be patient that day: so, have it ready for me. In the place that I am I am content. You will be saying: why is my brother away in a remote place (I will say this to you: that it is not farther north than St Kilda nor farther south than the Mull of Cantyre!), and for what reason? That is between me and silence. But perhaps you think of Anne sometimes. Do you know that she lies under the green grass?

"And of Mànus MacCodrum? They say that he swam out into the sea and was drowned; and they whisper of the seal-blood, though the minister is wroth with them for that. He calls it a madness. Well, I was there at that madness, and I played to it on my *feadan*. And now, Sheumais, can you be thinking of what the tune was that I played?

"Your brother, who waits his own day,

"Gloom."

"Do not be forgetting this thing: *I would rather not be playing the 'Damhsa-na-mairbh!'* It was an ill hour for Mànus when he heard the Dàn-nan-Ròn; it was the song of his soul, that; and yours is the Davsana-Mairv."

This letter was ever in his mind: this, and what happened in the gloaming when he sailed away for Skye in the herring-smack of two men who lived at Armadale in Sleat. For, as the boat moved slowly out of the haven, one of the men asked him if he was sure that no one was left upon the island; for he thought he had seen a figure on the rocks, waving a black scarf. Achanna shook his head, but just then his companion cried that at that moment he had seen the same thing. So, the smack was put about, and when she was moving slow through the haven again, Achanna sculled ashore in the little coggly punt.

In vain he searched here and there, calling loudly again and again. Both men could hardly have been mistaken, he thought. If there were no human creature on the island, and if their eyes had not played them false, who could it be? The wraith of Marcus, mayhap; or might it be the old man himself (his father), risen to bid farewell to his youngest son, or to warn him?

It was no use to wait longer; so, looking often behind him, he made his way to the boat again, and rowed slowly out towards the smack.

Jerk—jerk—jerk across the water came, low but only too loud for him, the opening bars of the Damhsa-na-Mairbh. A horror came upon him, and he drove the boat through the water so that the sea splashed over the bows. When he came on deck, he cried in a hoarse voice to the man next him to put up the helm, and let the smack swing to the wind.

"There is no one there, Callum Campbell," he whispered.

"And who is it that will be making that strange music?"

"What music?"

21

"Sure, it has stopped now, but I heard it clear, and so did Anndra MacEwan. It was like the sound of a reed-pipe, and the tune was an eerie one at that."

"It was the Dance of the Dead."

"And who will be playing that?" asked the man, with fear in his eyes.

"No living man."

"No living man?"

"No. I'm thinking it will be one of my brothers who was drowned here, and by the same token that it is Gloom, for he played upon the *feadan*; but if not, then . . . then . . ."

The two men waited in breathless silence, each trembling with superstitious fear; but at last, the elder made a sign to Achanna to finish.

"Then . . . it will be the *Kelpie*."

"Is there . . . is there one of the . . . the cavewomen here?"

"It is said; and you know of old that the *Kelpie* sings or plays a strange tune to wile seamen to their death."

At that moment, the fantastic jerking music came loud and clear across the bay. There was a horrible suggestion in it, as if dead bodies were moving along the ground with long jerks, and crying and laughing wild. It was enough; the men, Campbell and MacEwan, would not now have waited longer if Achanna had offered them all he had in the world. Nor were they, or he, out of their panic haste till the smack stood well out at sea, and not a sound could be heard from Eilanmore.

They stood watching, silent. Out of the dusky mass that lay in the seaward way to the north came a red gleam. It was like an eye staring after them with blood-red glances.

"What is that, Achanna?" asked one of the men at last.

"It looks as though a fire had been lit in the house up in the island. The door and the window must be open. The fire must be fed with wood, for no peats would give that flame; and there were none lit when I left. To my knowing, there was no wood for burning except the wood of the shelves and the bed."

"And who would be doing that?"

"I know of that no more than you do, Callum Campbell."

No more was said, and it was a relief to all when the last glimmer of the light was absorbed in the darkness.

At the end of the voyage Campbell and MacEwan were well pleased to be quit of their companion; not so much because he was moody and distraught, as because they feared that a spell was upon

22

him—a fate in the working of which they might become involved. It needed no vow of the one to the other for them to come to the conclusion that they would never land on Eilanmore, or, if need be, only in broad daylight, and never alone.

The days went well for James Achanna, where he made his home at Ranza-beag, on Ranza Water in the Sleat of Skye. The farm was small but good, and he hoped that with help and care he would soon have the place as good a farm as there was in all Skye.

Donald Macarthur did not let him see much of Katreen, but the old man was no longer opposed to him. Sheumais must wait till Ian Macarthur came back again, which might be any day now. For sure, James Achanna of Ranza-beag was a very different person from the youngest of the Achanna-folk who held by on lonely Eilanmore; moreover, the old man could not but think with pleasure that it would be well to see Katreen able to walk over the whole land of Ranza, from the cairn at the north of his own Ranza-Mòr to the burn at the south of Ranza-beag, and know it for her own.

But Achanna was ready to wait. Even before he had the secret word of Katreen he knew from her beautiful dark eyes that she loved him. As the weeks went by, they managed to meet often, and at last Katreen told him that she loved him too, and would have none but him; but that they must wait till Ian came back, because of the pledge given to him by her father. They were days of joy for him. Through many a hot noontide hour, through many a gloaming, he went as one in a dream. Whenever he saw a birch swaying in the wind, or a wave leaping upon Loch Liath, that was near his home, or passed a bush covered with wild roses, or saw the moonbeams lying white on the boles of the pines, he thought of Katreen: his fawn for grace, and so lithe and tall, with sun-brown face and wavy dark mass of hair and shadowy eyes and rowan-red lips.

It is said that there is a god clothed in shadow who goes to and fro among the human kind, putting silence between lovers with his waving hands, and breathing a chill out of his cold breath, and leaving a gulf of deep water flowing between them because of the passing of his feet. That shadow never came their way. Their love grew as a flower fed by rains and warmed by sunlight.

When midsummer came, and there was no sign of Ian Macarthur, it was already too late. Katreen had been won.

During the summer months, it was the custom for Katreen and two of the farm girls to go up Maol Ranza, to reside at the shealing of Cnoc-an-Fhraoch: and this because of the hill-pasture for the sheep. Cnoc-an-Fhraoch is a round, boulder studded hill covered with heather, which has a precipitous corrie on each side, and in front slopes down to Lochan Fraoch, a lochlet surrounded by dark woods. Behind the hill, or great hillock rather, lay the shealing. At each week-end Katreen went down to Ranza-Mor, and on every Monday morning at sunrise returned to her heather-girt eyrie. It was on one of these visits that she endured a cruel shock. Her father told her that she must marry someone else than Sheumais Achanna. He had heard words about him which made a union impossible, and, indeed, he hoped that the man would leave Ranza-beag.

In the end, he admitted that what he had heard was to the effect that Achanna was under a doom of some kind; that he was involved in a blood feud; and, moreover, that he was fey. The old man would not be explicit as to the person from whom his information came, but hinted that he was a stranger of rank, probably a laird of the isles. Besides this, there was word of Ian Macarthur. He was at Thurso, in the far north, and would be in Skye before long, and he—her father—had written to him that he might wed Katreen as soon as was practicable.

"Do you see that lintie yonder, father?" was her response to this.

"Ay, lass; and what about the birdeen?"

"Well, when she mates with a hawk, so will I be mating with Ian Macarthur, but not till then."

With that she turned, and left the house, and went back to Cnoc-an-Fhraoch. On the way she met Achanna.

It was that night that, for the first time, he swam across Lochan Fraoch to meet Katreen.

The quickest way to reach the shealing was to row across the lochlet, and then ascend by a sheep-path that wound through the hazel copses at the base of the hill. Fully half-an-hour was thus saved, because of the steepness of the precipitous corries to right and left. A boat was kept for this purpose, but it was fastened to a shore-boulder by a padlocked iron chain, the key of which was kept by Donald Macarthur. Latterly he had refused to let this key out of his possession. For one thing, no doubt, he believed he could thus restrain Achanna from visiting his daughter. The young man could not approach the shealing from either side without being seen.

But that night, soon after the moon was whitening slow in the dark, Katreen stole down to the hazel copse and awaited the coming of her lover. The lochan was visible from almost any point on Cnoc-

an-Fhraoch, as well as from the south side. To cross it in a boat unseen, if any watcher were near, would be impossible, nor could even a
swimmer hope to escape notice unless in the gloom of night, or, mayhap, in the dusk. When, however, she saw, half way across the water, a
spray of green branches slowly moving athwart the surface, she knew
that Sheumais was keeping his tryst. If, perchance, anyone else saw, he
or she would never guess that those derelict rowan-branches shrouded
Sheumais Achanna.

It was not till the estray had drifted close to the ledge, where, hid
among the bracken and the hazel undergrowth, she awaited him, that
Katreen descried the face of her lover, as with one hand he parted the
green sprays and stared longingly and lovingly at the figure he could
just discern in the dim fragrant obscurity.

And as it was this night, so was it on many of the nights that followed. Katreen spent the days as in a dream. Not even the news of her
cousin Ian's return disturbed her much.

One day the inevitable meeting came. She was at Ranza-Mòr, and
when a shadow came into the dairy where she was standing, she looked
up, and saw Ian before her. She thought he appeared taller and stronger
than ever, though still not so tall as Sheumais, who would appear slim
beside the Herculean Skye man. But as she looked at his close curling
black hair, and thick bull neck, and the sullen eyes in his dark wind-red
face, she wondered that she had ever tolerated him at all.

He broke the ice at once.

"Tell me, Katreen, are you glad to see me back again?"

"I am glad that you are home once more safe and sound."

"And will you make it my home for me by coming to live with
me, as I've asked you again and again."

"No, as I've told you again and again."

He gloomed at her angrily for a few moments before he resumed.

"I will be asking you this one thing, Katreen, daughter of my father's brother: do you love that man Achanna who lives at Ranza-
beag?"

"You may ask the wind why it is from the east or the west, but it
won't tell you. You're not the wind's master."

"If you think I will let this man take you away from me, you are
thinking a foolish thing."

"And you saying a foolisher."

"Ay?"

"Ay, sure. What could you do, Ian-mhic-Ian? At the worst, you could do no more than kill James Achanna. What then? I too would die. You cannot separate us. I would not marry you, now, though you were the last man on the world and I the last woman."

"You're a fool, Katreen Macarthur. Your father has promised you to me, and I tell you this: if you love Achanna you'll save his life only by letting him go away from here. I promise you he will not be here long."

"Ay, you promise *me*; but you will not say that thing to James Achanna's face. You are a coward."

With a muttered oath the man turned on his heel.

"Let him beware o' me, and you, too, Katreen-mo-nighean-donn. I swear it by my mother's grave and by St Martin's Cross that you will be mine by hook or by crook."

The girl smiled scornfully. Slowly she lifted a milk-pail.

"It would be a pity to waste the good milk, *Ian-gorach*; but if you don't go, it is I that will be emptying the pail on you, and then you'll be as white without as your heart is within."

"So, you call me witless, do you? Ian-gorach! Well, we shall be seeing as to that; and as for the milk, there will be more than milk spilt because of *you*, Katreen-donn."

From that day, though neither Sheumais nor Katreen knew of it, a watch was set upon Achanna.

It could not be long before their secret was discovered; and it was with a savage joy overmastering his sullen rage that Ian Macarthur knew himself the discoverer, and conceived his double vengeance. He dreamed, gloatingly, on both the black thoughts that roamed like ravenous beasts through the solitudes of his heart. But he did not dream that another man was filled with hate because of Katreen's lover—another man who had sworn to make her his own; the man who, disguised, was known in Armadale as Donald McLean, and in the north isles would have been hailed as Gloom Achanna.

There had been steady rain for three days, with a cold raw wind. On the fourth the sun shone, and set in peace. An evening of quiet beauty followed, warm, fragrant, dusky from the absence of moon or star, though the thin veils of mist promised to disperse as the night grew.

There were two men that eve in the undergrowth on the south side of the lochlet. Sheumais had come earlier than his wont. Impatient for the dusk, he could scarce await the waning of the afterglow. Surely, he thought, he might venture. Suddenly his ears caught the sound of cautious footsteps. Could it be old Donald, perhaps, with some inkling of the way in which his daughter saw her lover, in despite of all; or, mayhap, might it be Ian Macarthur tracking him, as a hunter stalking a stag by the water-pools? He crouched, and waited. In a few minutes he saw Ian carefully picking his way. The man stooped as he descried the green branches; smiled as, with a low rustling, he raised them from the ground.

Meanwhile, yet another man watched and waited, though on the farther side of the lochan, where the hazel copses were. Gloom Achanna half hoped, half feared the approach of Katreen. It would be sweet to see her again, sweet to slay her lover before her eyes, brother to him though he was. But there was the chance that she might descry him, and, whether recognisingly or not, warn the swimmer. So it was that he had come there before sundown, and now lay crouched among the bracken underneath a projecting mossy ledge close upon the water, where it could scarce be that she or any should see him.

As the gloaming deepened, a great stillness reigned. There was no breath of wind. A scarce audible sigh prevailed among the spires of the heather. The churring of a nightjar throbbed through the darkness. Somewhere a corncrake called its monotonous *crék-craik*—the dull harsh sound emphasising the utter stillness. The pinging of the gnats hovering over and among the sedges made an incessant rumour through the warm sultry air.

There was a splash once as of a fish; then silence. Then a lower but more continuous splash, or rather wash of water. A slow susurrus rustled through the dark.

Where he lay among the fern Gloom Achanna slowly raised his head, stared through the shadows, and listened intently. If Katreen were waiting there she was not near.

Noiselessly he slid into the water. When he rose, it was under a clump of green branches. These he had cut and secured three hours before. With his left hand he swam slowly, or kept his equipoise in the water; with his right he guided the heavy rowan bough. In his mouth were two objects, one long and thin and dark, the other with an occasional glitter as of a dead fish.

His motion was scarce perceptible. None the less he was nigh the middle of the loch almost as soon the other clump of green branches. Doubtless the swimmer beneath it was confident that he was now safe from observation.

The two clumps of green branches drew nearer. The smaller

seemed a mere estray—a spray blown down by the recent gale. But all at once the larger clump jerked awkwardly and stopped. Simultaneously a strange low strain of music came from the other.

The strain ceased. The two clumps of green branches remained motionless. Slowly at last the larger moved forward. It was too dark for the swimmer to see if any one lay hid behind the smaller. When he reached it he thrust aside the leaves.

It was as though a great salmon leaped. There was a splash, and a narrow dark body shot through the gloom. At the end of it something gleamed. Then suddenly there was a savage struggle. The inanimate green branches tore this way and that, and surged and swirled. Gasping cries came from the leaves. Again, and again the gleaming thing leaped. At the third leap an awful scream shrilled through the silence. The echo of it wailed thrice with horrible distinctness in the corrie beyond Cnoc-an-Fhraoch. Then, after a faint splashing, there was silence once more. One clump of green branches drifted loosely up the lochlet. The other moved steadily towards the place whence, a brief while before, it had stirred.

Only one thing lived in the heart of Gloom Achanna—the joy of his exultation. He had killed his brother Sheumais. He had always hated him because of his beauty; of late he had hated him because he had stood between him, Gloom, and Katreen Macarthur, because he had become her lover. They were all dead now except himself—all the Achannas. He was "Achanna." When the day came that he would go back to Galloway there would be a magpie on the first birk, and a screaming jay on the first rowan, and a croaking raven on the first fir. Ay, he would be their suffering, though they knew nothing of him meanwhile! He would be Achanna of Achanna again. Let those who would stand in his way beware. As for Katreen: perhaps he would take her there, perhaps not. He smiled.

These thoughts were the wandering fires in his brain while he slowly swam shoreward under the floating green branches, and as he disengaged himself from them, and crawled upward through the bracken. It was at this moment that a third man entered the water from the farther shore.

Prepared as he was to come suddenly upon Katreen, Gloom was startled when, in a place of dense shadow, a hand touched his shoulder, and her voice whispered, "*Sheumais, Sheumais!*"

The next moment she was in his arms. He could feel her heart beating against his side.

"What was it, Sheumais? What was that awful cry?" she whispered.

For answer he put his lips to hers, and kissed her again and again.

The girl drew back. Some vague instinct warned her.

"What is it, Sheumais? Why don't you speak? "

He drew her close again.

"Pulse of my heart, it is I who love you—I who love you best of all. It is I, Gloom Achanna!"

With a cry, she struck him full in the face. He staggered, and in that moment, she freed herself.

"You *coward!*"

"Katreen, I . . . ."

"Come no nearer. If you do, it will be the death of you!"

"The death o' me! Ah, bonnie fool that you are, and is it you that will be the death o' me? "

"Ay, Gloom Achanna, for I have but to scream and Sheumais will be here, an' he would kill you like a dog if he knew you did me harm."

"Ah, but if there were no James, or any man, to come between me an' my will!"

"Then there would be a woman! Ay, if you overbore me, I would strangle you with my hair, or fix my teeth in your false throat!"

"I was not for knowing you were such a wild-cat! But I'll tame you yet, my lass! Aha, wild-cat!" and, as he spoke, he laughed low.

"It is a true word, Gloom of the black heart. I *am* a wild-cat, and like a wild-cat I am not to be seized by a fox, and that you will be finding to your cost, by the holy St Bridget! But now, off with you, brother of my man!"

"Your man . . . ha! ha! . . . ."

"Why do you laugh?"

"Sure, I am laughing at a warm white lass like yourself having a dead man as your lover!"

"A . . . dead . . . man?"

No answer came. The girl shook with a new fear. Slowly she drew closer till her breath fell warm against the face of the other. He spoke at last.

"Ay, a dead man."

"It is a lie."

"Where would you be that you were not hearing his goodbye? I'm thinking it was loud enough!"

"It is a lie . . . it is a lie!"

"No, it is no lie. Sheumais is cold enough now. He's low among the weeds by now. Ay, by now; down there in the lochan."

"*What* . . . you, *you devil!* Is it for killing your own brother you would be!"

"I killed no one. He died his own way. Maybe the cramp took him. Maybe . . . maybe a *kelpie* gripped him. I watched. I saw him beneath the green branches. He was dead before he died. I saw it in the white face o' him. Then he sank. He's dead—James is dead. Look here, girl, I've always loved you. I swore the oath upon you—you're mine. Sure, you're mine now, Katreen! It is loving you I am! It will be a south wind for you from this day, *muir-nean mochree!* See here, I'll show you how I . . . ."

"Back . . . back . . . *murderer!*"

"Be stopping that foolishness now, Katreen Macarthur! By the Book, I am tired of it! I am loving you, and it's having you for mine I am! And if you won't come to me like the dove to its mate, I'll come to you like the hawk to the dove!"

With a spring he was upon her. In vain she strove to beat him back. His arms held her as a stoat grips a rabbit.

He pulled her head back, and kissed her throat till the strangulating breath sobbed against his ear. With a last despairing effort she screamed the name of the dead man—"*Sheumais! Sheumais! Sheumais!*" The man who struggled with her laughed.

"Ay, call away! The herrin' will be coming through the bracken as soon as Sheumais comes to your call! Ah, it is mine you are now, Katreen! He's dead an' cold, . . . an' you'd best have a living man . . . an'. . . ."

She fell back, her balance lost in the sudden releasing. What did it mean? Gloom still stood there, but as one frozen. Through the darkness she saw at last that a hand gripped his shoulder—behind him a black mass vaguely obtruded.

For some moments there was absolute silence. Then a hoarse voice came out of the dark.

"You will be knowing now who it is, Gloom Achanna!"

The voice was that of Sheumais, who lay dead in the lochan. The murderer shook as in a palsy. With a great effort, slowly he turned his head. He saw a white splatch—the face of the corpse. In this white splatch flamed two burning eyes, the eyes of the soul of the brother whom he had slain.

He reeled, staggered as a blind man, and, free now of that awful clasp, swayed to and fro as one drunken.

Slowly Sheumais raised an arm, and pointed downward through

the wood towards the lochan. Still pointing, he moved swiftly forward. With a cry like a beast, Gloom Achanna swung to one side, stumbled, rose, and leaped into the darkness.

For some minutes Sheumais and Katreen stood, silent, apart, listening to the crashing sound of his flight—the race of the murderer against the pursuing shadow of the Grave.

La Morte Amoureuse

Theopile Gautier

Chapter 1: A Strange Story

Brother, you ask me if I have ever loved. Yes. My story is a strange and terrible one; and though I am sixty−six years of age, I scarcely dare even now to disturb the ashes of that memory. To you I can refuse nothing; but I should not relate such a tale to any less experienced mind. So strange were the circumstances of my story, that I can scarcely believe myself to have ever actually been a party to them. For more than three years I remained the victim of a most singular and diabolical illusion. Poor country priest though I was, I led every night in a dream—would to God it had been all a dream!—a most worldly life, a damning life, a life of a Sardanapalus. One single look too freely cast upon a woman well−nigh caused me to lose my soul; but finally, by the grace of God and the assistance of my patron saint, I succeeded in casting out the evil spirit that possessed me. My daily life was long interwoven with a nocturnal life of a totally different character.

By day I was a priest of the Lord, occupied with prayer and sacred things; by night, from the instant that I closed my eyes I became a young nobleman, a fine connoisseur in women, dogs, and horses; gambling, drinking, and blaspheming; and when I awoke at early daybreak, it seemed to me, on the other hand, that I had been sleeping, and had only dreamed that I was a priest. Of this somnambulistic life there now remains to me only the recollection of certain scenes and words which I cannot banish from my memory; but although I never actually left the walls of my presbytery, one would think to hear me speak that I were a man who, weary of all worldly pleasures, had become a religious, seeking to end a tempestuous life in the service of God, rather than an humble seminarist who has grown old in this obscure curacy, situated in the depths of the woods and even isolated from the life of the century.

Yes, I have loved as none in the world ever loved—with an insensate and furious passion—so violent that I am astonished it did not cause my heart to burst asunder. Ah, what nights—what nights!

From my earliest childhood I had felt a vocation to the priesthood, so that all my studies were directed with that idea in view. Up to the age of twenty-four my life had been only a prolonged novitiate. Having completed my course of theology, I successively received all the minor orders, and my superiors judged me worthy, despite my youth, to pass the last awful degree. My ordination was fixed for Easter week.

I had never gone into the world. My world was confined by the walls of the college and the seminary. I knew in a vague sort of a way that there was something called Woman, but I never permitted my thoughts to dwell on such a subject, and I lived in a state of perfect innocence. Twice a year only I saw my infirm and aged mother, and in those visits were comprised my sole relations with the outer world.

I regretted nothing; I felt not the least hesitation at taking the last irrevocable step; I was filled with joy and impatience. Never did a betrothed lover count the slow hours with more feverish ardour; I slept only to dream that I was saying mass; I believed there could be nothing in the world more delightful than to be a priest; I would have refused to be a king or a poet in preference. My ambition could conceive of no loftier aim.

I tell you this in order to show you that what happened to me could not have happened in the natural order of things, and to enable you to understand that I was the victim of an inexplicable fascination.

At last, the great day came. I walked to the church with a step so light that I fancied myself sustained in air, or that I had wings upon my shoulders. I believed myself an angel, and wondered at the sombre and thoughtful faces of my companions, for there were several of us. I had passed all the night in prayer, and was in a condition wellnigh bordering on ecstasy. The bishop, a venerable old man, seemed to me God the Father leaning over his Eternity, and I beheld Heaven through the vault of the temple.

You well know the details of that ceremony—the benediction, the communion under both forms, the anointing of the palms of the hands with the Oil of Catechumens, and then the holy sacrifice offered in concert with the bishop.

Ah, truly spake Job when he declared that the imprudent man is one who hath not made a covenant with his eyes! I accidentally lifted my head, which until then I had kept down, and beheld before me, so close that it seemed that I could have touched her—although she was actually a considerable distance from me and on the further side of the sanctuary railing—a young woman of extraordinary beauty, and attired with royal magnificence. It seemed as though scales had suddenly fallen from my eyes. I felt like a blind man who unexpectedly recovers his sight. The bishop, so radiantly glorious but an instant before, suddenly vanished away, the tapers paled upon their golden candlesticks like stars in the dawn, and a vast darkness seemed to fill the whole church. The charming creature appeared in bright relief against the background of that darkness, like some angelic revelation. She seemed herself radiant, and radiating light rather than receiving it.

I lowered my eyelids, firmly resolved not to again open them, that I might not be influenced by external objects, for distraction had gradually taken possession of me until I hardly knew what I was doing.

In another minute, nevertheless, I reopened my eyes, for through my eyelashes I still beheld her, all sparkling with prismatic colours, and surrounded with such a purple penumbra as one beholds in gazing at the sun.

Oh, how beautiful she was! The greatest painters, who followed ideal beauty into heaven itself, and thence brought back to earth the true portrait of the Madonna, never in their delineations even approached that wildly beautiful reality which I saw before me. Neither the verses of the poet nor the palette of the artist could convey any conception of her. She was rather tall, with a form and bearing of a goddess. Her hair, of a soft blonde hue, was parted in the midst and flowed back over her temples in two rivers of rippling gold; she seemed a diademed queen. Her forehead, bluish-white in its transparency, extended its calm breadth above the arches of her eyebrows, which by a strange singularity were almost black, and admirably relieved the effect of sea-green eyes of unsustainable vivacity and brilliancy.

What eyes! With a single flash they could have decided a man's destiny. They had a life, a limpidity, an ardour, a humid light which I have never seen in human eyes; they shot forth rays like arrows, which I could distinctly *see* enter my heart. I know not if the fire which illumined them came from heaven or from hell, but assuredly it came from one or the other. That woman was either an angel or a demon, perhaps both. Assuredly she never sprang from the flank of Eve, our common mother. Teeth of the most lustrous pearl gleamed in her ruddy smile, and at every inflection of her lips little dimples appeared in the satiny rose of her adorable cheeks.

There was a delicacy and pride in the regal outline of her nostrils bespeaking noble blood. Agate gleams played over the smooth lustrous skin of her half-bare shoulders, and strings of great blonde pearls—almost equal to her neck in beauty of colour—descended upon her bosom.

From time to time, she elevated her head with the undulating grace of a startled serpent or peacock, thereby imparting a quivering motion to the high lace ruff which surrounded it like a silver trelliswork.

She wore a robe of orange-red velvet, and from her wide ermine-lined sleeves there peeped forth patrician hands of infinite delicacy, and so ideally transparent that, like the fingers of Aurora, they permitted the light to shine through them.

All these details I can recollect at this moment as plainly as though they were of yesterday, for notwithstanding I was greatly troubled at the time, nothing escaped me; the faintest touch of shading, the little dark speck at the point of the chin, the imperceptible down at the corners of the lips, the velvety floss upon the brow, the quivering shadows of the eyelashes upon the cheeks—I could notice everything with astonishing lucidity of perception.

And gazing, I felt opening within me gates that had until then remained closed; vents long obstructed became all clear, permitting glimpses of unfamiliar perspectives within; life suddenly made itself visible to me under a totally novel aspect. I felt as though I had just been born into a new world and a new order of things. A frightful anguish commenced to torture my heart as with red-hot pincers. Every successive minute seemed to me at once but a second and yet a century. Meanwhile the ceremony was proceeding, and I shortly found myself transported far from that world of which my newly born desires were furiously besieging the entrance.

Nevertheless, I answered "Yes" when I wished to say "No," though all within me protested against the violence done to my soul by my tongue. Some occult power seemed to force the words from my throat against my will. Thus, it is, perhaps, that so many young girls walk to the altar firmly resolved to refuse in a startling manner the husband imposed upon them, and that yet not one ever fulfils her intention. Thus, it is, doubtless, that so many poor novices take the veil, though they have resolved to tear it into shreds at the moment when called upon to utter the vows. One dares not thus cause so great a scandal to all present, nor deceive the expectation of so many people. All those eyes, all those wills seem to weigh down upon you like a cope of lead; and, moreover, measures have been so well taken, everything has been so thoroughly arranged beforehand and after a fashion so evidently irrevocable, that the will yields to the weight of circumstances and utterly breaks down.

As the ceremony proceeded the features of the fair unknown changed their expression. Her look had at first been one of caressing tenderness; it changed to an air of disdain and of mortification, as though at not having been able to make itself understood.

With an effort of will sufficient to have uprooted a mountain, I strove to cry out that I would not be a priest, but I could not speak; my tongue seemed nailed to my palate, and I found it impossible to express my will by the least syllable of negation. Though fully awake, I felt like one under the influence of a nightmare, who vainly strives to shriek out the one word upon which life depends.

She seemed conscious of the martyrdom I was undergoing, and, as though to encourage me, she gave me a look replete with divinest promise. Her eyes were a poem; their every glance was a song.

She said to me:

"If thou wilt be mine, I shall make thee happier than God Himself in His paradise. The angels themselves will be jealous of thee. Tear off that funeral shroud in which thou art about to wrap thyself. I am Beauty, I am Youth, I am Life. Come to me! Together we shall be Love. Can Jehovah offer thee aught. in exchange? Our lives will flow on like a dream, in one eternal kiss.

"Fling forth the wine of that chalice, and thou art free. I will conduct thee to the Unknown Isles. Thou shalt sleep in my bosom upon a bed of massy gold under a silver pavilion, for I love thee and would take thee away from *thy* God, before whom so many noble hearts pour forth floods of love which never reach even the steps of His throne!"

These words seemed to float to my ears in a rhythm of infinite sweetness, for her look was actually sonorous, and the utterances of her eyes were re-echoed in the depths of my heart as though living lips had breathed them into my life. I felt myself willing to renounce God, and yet my tongue mechanically fulfilled all the formalities of the ceremony.

The fair one gave me another look, so beseeching, so despairing the keen blades seemed to pierce my heart, and I felt my bosom transfixed by more swords than those of Our Lady of Sorrows.

CHAPTER 2: ROOT IMPERISHABLE

All was consummated: I had become a priest.

Never was deeper anguish painted on human face than upon hers. The maiden who beholds her affianced lover suddenly fall dead at her side, the mother bending over the empty cradle of her child, Eve seated at the threshold of the gate of Paradise, the miser who finds a stone substituted for his stolen treasure, the poet who accidentally permits the only manuscript of his finest work to fall into the fire, could not wear a look so despairing, so inconsolable. All the blood had abandoned her charming face, leaving it whiter than marble; her beautiful arms hung lifelessly on either side of her body as though their muscles had suddenly relaxed, and she sought the support of a pillar, for her yielding limbs almost betrayed her. As for myself, I staggered toward the door of the church, livid as death, my forehead bathed with a sweat bloodier than that of Calvary; I felt as though I were being strangled; the vault seemed to have flattened down upon my shoulders, and it seemed to me that my head alone sustained the whole weight of the dome.

As I was about to cross the threshold a hand suddenly caught mine—a woman's hand! I had never till then touched the hand of any woman. It was cold as a serpent's skin, and yet its impress remained upon my wrist, burnt there as though branded by a glowing iron. It was she. "Unhappy man! Unhappy man! What hast thou done?" she exclaimed in a low voice, and immediately disappeared in the crowd.

The aged bishop passed by. He cast a severe and scrutinising look upon me. My face presented the wildest aspect imaginable; I blushed and turned pale alternately; dazzling lights flashed before my eyes. A companion took pity on me. He seized my arm and led me out. I could not possibly have found my way back to the seminary unassisted. At the corner of a street, while the young priest's attention was momentarily turned in another direction, a negro page, fantastically garbed, approached me, and without pausing on his way slipped into my hand a little pocketbook with gold-embroidered corners, at the same time giving me a sign to hide it.

I concealed it in my sleeve, and there kept it until I found myself alone in my cell. Then I opened the clasp. There were only two leaves within, bearing the words, "Clarimonde. At the Concini Palace." So little acquainted was I at that time with the things of this world that I had never heard of Clarimonde, celebrated as she was, and I had no idea as to where the Concini Palace was situated. I hazarded a thousand conjectures, each more extravagant than the last; but, in truth, I cared little whether she were a great lady or a courtesan, so that I could but see her once more.

My love, although the growth of a single hour, had taken imperishable root. I did not even dream of attempting to tear it up, so fully was I convinced such a thing would be impossible. That woman had completely taken possession of me. One look from her had sufficed to change my very nature. She had breathed her will into my life, and I no longer lived in myself, but in her and for her. I gave myself up to a thousand extravagancies. I kissed the place upon my hand which she had touched, and I repeated her name over and over again for hours in succession. I only needed to close my eyes in order to see her distinctly as though she were actually present; and I reiterated to myself the words she had uttered in my ear at the church porch: "Unhappy man! Unhappy man! What hast thou done?"

I comprehended at last the full horror of my situation, and the funereal and awful restraints of the state into which I had just entered became clearly revealed to me. To be a priest!—that is, to be chaste, to never love, to observe no distinction of sex or age, to turn from the sight of all beauty, to put out one's own eyes, to hide forever crouching in the chill shadows of some church or cloister, to visit none but the dying, to watch by unknown corpses, and ever bear about with one the black *soutane* as a garb of mourning for one's self, so that your very dress might serve as a pall for your coffin.

And I felt life rising within me like a subterranean lake, expanding and overflowing; my blood leaped fiercely through my arteries; my long–restrained youth suddenly burst into active being, like the aloe which blooms but once in a hundred years, and then bursts into blossom with a clap of thunder.

What could I do in order to see Clarimonde once more? I had no pretext to offer for desiring to leave the seminary, not knowing any person in the city. I would not even be able to remain there but a short time, and was only waiting my assignment to the curacy which I must thereafter occupy. I tried to remove the bars of the window; but it was at a fearful height from the ground, and I found that as I had no ladder it would be useless to think of escaping thus. And, furthermore, I could descend thence only by night in any event, and afterward how should I be able to find my way through the inextricable labyrinth of streets? All these difficulties, which to many would have appeared altogether insignificant, were gigantic to me, a poor seminarist who had fallen in love only the day before for the first time, without experience, without money, without attire.

"Ah!" cried I to myself in my blindness, "were I not a priest I could have seen her every day; I might have been her lover, her spouse. Instead of being wrapped in this dismal shroud of mine I would have had garments of silk and velvet, golden chains, a sword, and fair plumes like other handsome young cavaliers. My hair, instead of being dishonoured by the tonsure, would flow down upon my neck in waving curls; I would have a fine waxed moustache; I would be a gallant." But one hour passed before an altar, a few hastily articulated words, had forever cut me off from the number of the living, and I had myself sealed down the stone of my own tomb; I had with my own hand bolted the gate of my prison!

I went to the window. The sky was beautifully blue; the trees had donned their spring robes; nature seemed to be making parade of an ironical joy. The *Place* was filled with people, some going, others coming; young *beaux* and young beauties were sauntering in couples toward the groves and gardens; merry youths passed by, cheerily trolling refrains of drinking songs—it was all a picture of vivacity, life, animation, gayety, which formed a bitter contrast with my mourning and my solitude.

On the steps of the gate sat a young mother playing with her child. She kissed its little rosy mouth still impearled with drops of milk, and performed, in order to amuse it, a thousand divine little puerilities such as only mothers know how to invent. The father standing at a little distance smiled gently upon the charming group, and with folded arms seemed to hug his joy to his heart. I could not endure that spectacle.

I closed the window with violence, and flung myself on my bed, my heart filled with frightful hate and jealousy, and gnawed my fingers and my bedcovers like a tiger that has passed ten days without food.

I know not how long I remained in this condition, but at last, while writhing on the bed in a fit of spasmodic fury, I suddenly perceived the Abbé Serapion, who was standing erect in the centre of the room, watching me attentively. Filled with shame of myself, I let my head fall upon my breast and covered my face with my hands.

"Romuald, my friend, something very extraordinary is transpiring within you," observed Serapion, after a few moments' silence; "your conduct is altogether inexplicable. You—always so quiet, so pious, so gentle—you to rage in your cell like a wild beast! Take heed, brother—do not listen to the suggestions of the devil. The Evil Spirit, furious that you have consecrated yourself forever to the Lord, is prowling around you like a ravening wolf and making a last effort to obtain possession of you. Instead of allowing yourself to be conquered, my dear Romuald, make to yourself a *cuirass* of prayers, a buckler of mortifications, and combat the enemy like a valiant man; you will then assuredly overcome him. Virtue must be proved by temptation, and gold comes forth purer from the hands of the assayer. Fear not. Never allow yourself to become discouraged. The most watchful and steadfast souls are at moments liable to such temptation. Pray, fast, meditate, and the Evil Spirit will depart from you."

The words of the Abbé Serapion restored me to myself, and I became a little more calm. "I came," he continued, "to tell you that you have been appointed to the curacy of C——. The priest who had charge of it has just died, and *Monseigneur* the Bishop has ordered me to have you installed there at once. Be ready, therefore, to start tomorrow."

I responded with an inclination of the head, and the *abbé* retired. I opened my missal and commenced reading some prayers, but the letters became confused and blurred under my eyes, the thread of the ideas entangled itself hopelessly in my brain, and the volume at last fell from my hands without my being aware of it.

To leave tomorrow without having been able to see her again, to add yet another barrier to the many already interposed between us, to lose forever all hope of being able to meet her, except, indeed, through a miracle! Even to write her, alas! would be impossible, for by whom could I despatch my letter? With my sacred character of priest, to whom could I dare unbosom myself, in whom could I confide? I became a prey to the bitterest anxiety.

Then suddenly recurred to me the words of the Abbé Serapion regarding the artifices of the devil; and the strange character of the adventure, the supernatural beauty of Clarimonde, the phosphoric light of her eyes, the burning imprint of her hand, the agony into which she had thrown me, the sudden change wrought within me when all my piety vanished in a single instant—these and other things clearly testified to the work of the Evil One, and perhaps that satiny hand was but the glove which concealed his claws. Filled with terror at these fancies, I again picked up the missal which had slipped from my knees and fallen upon the floor, and once more gave myself up to prayer.

Next morning Serapion came to take me away. Two mules freighted with our miserable valises awaited us at the gate. He mounted one, and I the other as well as I knew how.

As we passed along the streets of the city, I gazed attentively at all the windows and balconies in the hope of seeing Clarimonde, but it was yet early in the morning, and the city had hardly opened its eyes. Mine sought to penetrate the blinds and window–curtains of all the palaces before which we were passing. Serapion doubtless attributed this curiosity to my admiration of the architecture, for he slackened the pace of his animal in order to give me time to look around me.

At last, we passed the city gates and commenced to mount the hill beyond. When we arrived at its summit, I turned to take a last look at the place where Clarimonde dwelt. The shadow of a great cloud hung, over all the city; the contrasting colours of its blue and red roofs were lost in the uniform half-tint, through which here and there floated upward, like white flakes of foam, the smoke of freshly kindled fires. By a singular optical effect one edifice, which surpassed in height all the neighbouring buildings that were still dimly veiled by the vapours, towered up, fair and lustrous with the gilding of a solitary beam of sunlight—although actually more than a league away it seemed quite near. The smallest details of its architecture were plainly distinguishable—the turrets, the platforms, the window–casements, and even the swallow–tailed weather–vanes.

"What is that palace I see over there, all lighted up by the sun?" I asked Serapion. He shaded his eyes with his hand, and having looked in the direction indicated, replied: "It is the ancient palace which the Prince Concini has given to the courtesan Clarimonde. Awful things are done there!"

At that instant, I know not yet whether it was a reality or an illusion, I fancied I saw gliding along the terrace a shapely white figure, which gleamed for a moment in passing and as quickly vanished. It was Clarimonde.

Oh, did she know that at that very hour, all feverish and restless—from the height of the rugged road which separated me from her and which, alas! I could never more descend—I was directing my eyes upon the palace where she dwelt, and which a mocking beam of sunlight seemed to bring nigh to me, as though inviting me to enter therein as its lord? Undoubtedly, she must have known it, for her soul was too sympathetically united with mine not to have felt its least emotional thrill, and that subtle sympathy it must have been which prompted her to climb—although clad only in her nightdress—to the summit of the terrace, amid the icy dews of the morning.

The shadow gained the palace, and the scene became to the eye only a motionless ocean of roofs and gables, amid which one mountainous undulation was distinctly visible. Serapion urged his mule forward, my own at once followed at the same gait, and a sharp angle in the road at last hid the city of S—— forever from my eyes, as I was destined never to return thither. At the close of a weary three–days' journey through dismal country fields, we caught sight of the cock upon the steeple of the church which I was to take charge of, peeping above the trees, and after having followed some winding roads fringed with thatched cottages and little gardens, we found ourselves in front of the facade, which certainly possessed few features of magnificence.

A porch ornamented with some mouldings, and two or three pillars rudely hewn from sandstone; a tiled roof with counterforts of the same sandstone as the pillars—that was all. To the left lay the cemetery overgrown with high weeds, and having a great iron cross rising up in its centre; to the right stood the presbytery, under the shadow of the church. It was a house of the most extreme simplicity and frigid cleanliness. We entered the enclosure. A few chickens were picking up some oats scattered upon the ground; accustomed, seemingly, to the black habit of ecclesiastics, they showed no fear of our presence and scarcely troubled themselves to get out of our way. A hoarse, wheezy barking fell upon our ears, and we saw an aged dog running toward us.

It was my predecessor's dog. He had dull bleared eyes, grizzled hair, and every mark of the greatest age to which a dog can possibly attain. I patted him gently, and he proceeded at once to march along beside me with an air of satisfaction unspeakable. A very old woman, who had been the housekeeper of the former *curé*, also came to meet us, and after having invited me into a little back parlour, asked whether I intended to retain her. I replied that I would take care of her, and the dog, and the chickens, and all the furniture her master had bequeathed her at his death. At this she became fairly transported with joy, and the Abbé Serapion at once paid her the price which she asked for her little property.

As soon as my installation was over, the Abbé Serapion returned to the seminary. I was, therefore, left alone, with no one but myself to look to for aid or counsel. The thought of Clarimonde again began to haunt me, and in spite of all my endeavours to banish it, I always found

43

it present in my meditations. One evening while promenading in my little garden along the walks bordered with box—plants, I fancied that I saw through the elm-trees the figure of a woman, who followed my every movement, and that I beheld two sea-green eyes gleaming through the foliage; but it was only an illusion, and on going round to the other side of the garden, I could find nothing except a footprint on the sanded walk—a footprint so small that it seemed to have been made by the foot of a child.

The garden was enclosed by very high walls. I searched every nook and corner of it, but could discover no one there. I have never succeeded in fully accounting for this circumstance, which, after all, was nothing compared with the strange things which happened to me afterward.

For a whole year I lived thus, filling all the duties of my calling with the most scrupulous exactitude, praying and fasting, exhorting and lending ghostly aid to the sick, and bestowing alms even to the extent of frequently depriving myself of the very necessaries of life.

But I felt a great aridness within me, and the sources of grace seemed closed against me. I never found that happiness which should spring from the fulfilment of a holy mission: my thoughts were far away, and the words of Clarimonde were ever upon my lips like an involuntary refrain. Oh, brother, meditate well on this! Through having but once lifted my eyes to look upon a woman, through one fault apparently so venial, I have for years remained a victim to the most miserable agonies, and the happiness of my life has been destroyed forever.

I will not longer dwell upon those defeats, or on those inward victories invariably followed by yet more terrible falls, but will at once proceed to the facts of my story. One night my doorbell was long and violently rung. The aged housekeeper arose and opened to the stranger, and the figure of a man, whose complexion was deeply bronzed, and who was richly clad in a foreign costume, with a poniard at his girdle, appeared under the rays of Barbara's lantern. Her first impulse was one of terror, but the stranger reassured her, and stated that he desired to see me at once on matters relating to my holy calling. Barbara invited him upstairs, where I was on the point of retiring. The stranger told me that his mistress, a very noble lady, was lying at the point of death, and desired to see a priest. I replied that I was prepared to follow him, took with me the sacred articles necessary for extreme unction, and descended in all haste.

Two horses black as the night itself stood without the gate, pawing

44

the ground with impatience, and veiling their chests with long streams of smoky vapor exhaled from their nostrils. He held the stirrup and aided me to mount upon one; then, merely laying his hand upon the pummel of the saddle, he vaulted on the other, pressed the animal's sides with his knees, and loosened rein.

The horse bounded forward with the velocity of an arrow. Mine, of which the stranger held the bridle, also started off at a swift gallop, keeping up with his companion. We devoured the road. The ground flowed backward beneath us in a long streaked line of pale grey, and the black silhouettes of the trees seemed fleeing by us on either side like an army in rout. We passed through a forest so profoundly gloomy that I felt my flesh creep in the chill darkness with superstitious fear.

The showers of bright sparks which flew from the stony road under the irons both feet of our horses remained glowing in our wake like a fiery trail; and had any one at that hour of the night beheld us both—my guide and myself—he must have taken us for two spectres riding upon nightmares. Witch-fires ever and *anon* flitted across the road before us, and the night-birds shrieked fearsomely in the depth of the woods beyond, where we beheld at intervals glow the phosphorescent eyes of wildcats. The manes of the horses became more and more dishevelled, the sweat streamed over their flanks, and their breath came through their nostrils hard and fast. But when he found them slacking pace, the guide reanimated them by uttering a strange, guttural, unearthly cry, and the gallop recommenced with fury.

At last, the whirlwind race ceased; a huge black mass pierced through with many bright points of light suddenly rose before us, the hoofs of our horses echoed louder upon a great vaulted archway which darkly yawned between two enormous towers. Some great excitement evidently reigned in the castle. Servants with torches were crossing the courtyard in every direction, and above, lights were ascending and descending from landing to landing. I obtained a confused glimpse of vast masses of architecture—columns, arcades, flights of steps, stairways—a royal voluptuousness and elfin magnificence of construction worthy of fairyland.

A negro page—the same who had before brought me the tablet from Clarimonde, and whom I instantly recognised—approached to aid me in dismounting, and the *major-domo*, attired in black velvet with a gold chain about his neck, advanced to meet me, supporting himself upon an ivory cane. Large tears were falling from his eyes and streaming over his cheeks and white beard. "Too late!" he cried, sorrowfully shaking his venerable head. "Too late, sir priest! But if you have not been able to save the soul, come at least and watch by the poor body."

He took my arm and conducted me to the death chamber. I wept not less bitterly than he, for I had learned that the dead one was none other than that Clarimonde whom I had so deeply and so wildly loved. A *prie-dieu* stood at the foot of the bed; a bluish flame flickering in a bonze patera filled all the room with a wan, deceptive light, here and there bringing out in the darkness at intervals some projection of furniture or cornice. In a chiselled urn upon the table there was a faded white rose, whose leaves—excepting one that still held—had all fallen, like odorous tears, to the foot of the vase. A broken black mask, a fan, and disguises of every variety, which were lying on the armchairs, bore witness that death had entered suddenly and unannounced into that sumptuous dwelling.

Without daring to cast my eyes upon the bed, I knelt down and commenced to repeat the Psalms for the Dead, with exceeding fervour, thanking God that he had placed the tomb between me and the memory of this woman, so that I might thereafter be able to utter her name in my prayers as a name forever sanctified by death. But my fervour gradually weakened, and I fell insensibly into a reverie. That chamber bore no semblance to a chamber of death. In lieu of the fetid and cadaverous odours which I had been accustomed to breathe during such funereal vigils, a languorous vapor of Oriental perfume—I know not what amorous odour of woman—softly floated through the tepid air. That pale light seemed rather a twilight gloom contrived for voluptuous pleasure than a substitute for the yellow–flickering watch tapers which shine by the side of corpses.

I thought upon the strange destiny which enabled me to meet Clarimonde again at the very moment when she was lost to me forever, and a sigh of regretful anguish escaped from my breast. Then it seemed to me that someone behind me had also sighed, and I turned round to look. It was only an echo. But in that moment my eyes fell upon the bed of death which they had till then avoided. The red damask curtains, decorated with large flowers worked in embroidery, and looped up with gold bullion, permitted me to behold the fair dead, lying at full length, with hands joined upon her bosom.

She was covered with a linen wrapping of dazzling whiteness, which formed a strong contrast with the gloomy purple of the hangings, and was of so fine a texture that it concealed nothing of her body's charming form, and allowed the eye to follow those beautiful outlines—undulating like the neck of a swan—which even death had not robbed of their supple grace. She seemed an alabaster statue executed by some skilful sculptor to place upon the tomb of a queen, or rather, perhaps, like a slumbering maiden over whom the silent snow had woven a spotless veil.

I could no longer maintain my constrained attitude of prayer. The air of the alcove intoxicated me, that febrile perfume of half-faded roses penetrated my very brain, and I commenced to pace restlessly up and down the chamber, pausing at each turn before the bier to contemplate the graceful corpse lying beneath the transparency of its shroud. Wild fancies came thronging to my brain. I thought to myself that she might not, perhaps, be really dead; that she might only have feigned death for the purpose of bringing me to her castle, and then declaring her love. At one time I even thought I saw her foot move under the whiteness of the coverings, and slightly disarrange the long, straight folds of the winding-sheet.

And then I asked myself: "Is this indeed Clarimonde? What proof have I that it is she? Might not that black page have passed into the service of some other lady? Surely, I must be going mad to torture and afflict myself thus!" But my heart answered with a fierce throbbing: "It is she; it is she indeed!" I approached the bed again, and fixed my eyes with redoubled attention upon the object of my incertitude. Ah, must I confess it? That exquisite perfection of bodily form, although purified and made sacred by the shadow of death, affected me more voluptuously than it should have done, and that repose so closely resembled slumber that one might well have mistaken it for such.

I forgot that I had come there to perform a funeral ceremony; I fancied myself a young bridegroom entering the chamber of the bride, who all modestly hides her fair face, and through coyness seeks to keep herself wholly veiled. Heartbroken with grief, yet wild with hope, shuddering at once with fear and pleasure, I bent over her and grasped the corner of the sheet. I lifted it back, holding my breath all the while through fear of waking her. My arteries throbbed with such violence that I felt them hiss through my temples, and the sweat poured from my forehead in streams, as though I had lifted a mighty slab of marble.

There, indeed, lay Clarimonde, even as I had seen her at the church on the day of my ordination. She was not less charming than then. With her, death seemed but a last *coquetry*. The pallor of her cheeks, the less brilliant carnation of her lips, her long eyelashes lowered and relieving their dark fringe against that white skin, lent her an unspeakably seductive aspect of melancholy chastity and metal suffering; her long loose hair, still intertwined with some little blue flowers, made a shining pillow for her head, and veiled the nudity of her shoulders with its thick ringlets; her beautiful hands, purer, more diaphanous than the Host, were crossed on her bosom in an attitude of pious rest and silent prayer, which served to counteract all that might have proven otherwise too alluring—even after death—in the exquisite roundness and ivory polish of her bare arms from which the pearl bracelets had not yet been removed.

I remained long in mute contemplation, and the more I gazed, the less could I persuade myself that life had really abandoned that beautiful body forever. I do not know whether it was an illusion or a reflection of the lamplight, but it seemed to me that the blood was again commencing to circulate under that lifeless pallor, although she remained all motionless. I laid my hand lightly on her arm; it was cold, but not colder than her hand on the day when it touched mine at the portals of the church.

I resumed my position, bending my face above her, and bathing her cheeks with the warm dew of my tears. Ah, what bitter feelings of despair and helplessness, what agonies unutterable did I endure in that long watch! Vainly did I wish that I could have gathered all my life into one mass that I might give it all to her, and breathe into her chill remains the flame which devoured me.

The night advanced, and feeling the moment of eternal separation approach, I could not deny myself the last sad sweet pleasure of imprinting a kiss upon the dead lips of her who had been my only love. . . . .Oh, miracle! A faint breath mingled itself with my breath, and the mouth of Clarimonde responded to the passionate pressure of mine. Her eyes unclosed, and lighted up with something of their former brilliancy; she uttered a long sigh, and uncrossing her arms, passed them around my neck with a look of ineffable delight. "Ah, it is thou, Romuald!" she murmured in a voice languishingly sweet as the last vibrations of a harp. "What ailed thee, dearest? I waited so long for thee that I am dead; but we are now betrothed; I can see thee and visit thee. *Adieu*, Romuald, *adieu!* I love thee. That is all I wished to tell thee, and I give thee back the life which thy kiss for a moment recalled. We shall soon meet again."

Her head fell back, but her arms yet encircled me, as though to retain me still. A furious whirlwind suddenly burst in the window, and entered the chamber. The last remaining leaf of the white rose for a moment palpitated at the extremity of the stalk like a butterfly's wing, then it detached itself and flew forth through the open casement, bearing with it the soul of Clarimonde. The lamp was extinguished, and I fell, insensible upon the bosom of the beautiful dead.

CHAPTER 4: A VICTIM

When I came to myself again, I was lying on the bed in my little room at the presbytery, and the old dog of the former *curé* was licking my hand which had been hanging down outside of the covers. Barbara, all trembling with age and anxiety, was busying herself about the room, opening and shutting drawers, and emptying powders into glasses. On seeing me open my eyes, the old woman uttered a cry of joy, the dog yelped and wagged his tail, but I was still so weak that I could not speak a single word or make the slightest motion. Afterward I learned that I had lain thus for three days, giving no evidence of life beyond the faintest respiration. Those three days do not reckon in my life, nor could I ever imagine whither my spirit had departed during those three days; I have no recollection of aught relating to them.

Barbara told me that the same coppery-complexioned man who came to seek me on the night of my departure from the presbytery, had brought me back the next morning in a close litter, and departed immediately afterward. When I became able to collect my scattered thoughts, I reviewed within my mind all the circumstances of that fateful night. At first, I thought I had been the victim of some magical illusion, but ere long the recollection of other circumstances, real and palpable in themselves, came to forbid that supposition. I could not believe that I had been dreaming, since Barbara as well as myself had seen the strange man with his two black horses, and described with exactness every detail of his figure and apparel. Nevertheless, it appeared that none knew of any castle in the neighbourhood answering to the description of that in which I had again found Clarimonde.

One morning I found the Abbé Serapion in my room. Barbara had advised him that I was ill, and he had come with all speed to see me. Although this haste on his part testified to an affectionate interest in me, yet his visit did not cause me the pleasure which it should have done. The Abbé Serapion had something penetrating and inquisitorial in his gaze which made me feel very ill at ease. His presence filled me with embarrassment and a sense of guilt. At the first glance he divined my interior trouble, and I hated him for his clairvoyance. While he inquired after my health in hypocritically honeyed accents, he constantly kept his two great yellow lion−eyes fixed upon me, and plunged his look into my soul like a sounding lead.

Then he asked me how I directed my parish, if I was happy in it, how I passed the leisure hours allowed me in the intervals of pastoral duty, whether I had become acquainted with many of the inhabitants of the place, what was my favourite reading, and a thousand other such questions. I answered these inquiries as briefly as possible, and he, without ever waiting for my answers, passed rapidly from one subject of query to another. That conversation had evidently no connection with what he actually wished to say.

At last, without any premonition, but as though repeating a piece of news which he had recalled on the instant, and feared might otherwise be forgotten subsequently, he suddenly said, in a clear vibrant voice, which rang in my ears like the trumpets of the Last Judgment:

"The great courtesan Clarimonde died a few days ago, at the close of an orgy which lasted eight days and eight nights. It was something infernally splendid. The abominations of the banquets of Belshazzar and Cleopatra were re-enacted there. Good God, what age are we living in? The guests were served by swarthy slaves who spoke an unknown tongue, and who seemed to me to be veritable demons. The livery of the very least among them would have served for the gala-dress of an emperor. There have always been very strange stories told of this Clarimonde, and all her lovers came to a violent or miserable end.

"They used to say that she was a ghoul, a female vampire; but I believe she was none other than Beelzebub himself."

He ceased to speak and commenced to regard me more attentively than ever, as though to observe the effect of his words on me. I could not refrain from starting when I heard him utter the name of Clarimonde, and this news of her death, in addition to the pain it caused me by reason of its coincidence with the nocturnal scenes I had witnessed, filled me with an agony and terror which my face betrayed, despite my utmost endeavours to appear composed. Serapion fixed an anxious and severe look upon me, and then observed: "My son, I must warn you that you are standing with foot raised upon the brink of an abyss; take heed lest you fall therein. Satan's claws are long, and tombs are not always true to their trust. The tombstone of Clarimonde should be sealed down with a triple seal, for, if report be true, it is not the first time she has died. May God watch over you, Romuald!"

And with these words the *abbé* walked slowly to the door. I did not see him again at that time, for he left for S———— almost immediately.

I became completely restored to health and resumed my accustomed duties. The memory of Clarimonde and the words of the old Abbé were constantly in my mind; nevertheless, no extraordinary event had occurred to verify the funereal predictions of Serapion, and I had commenced to believe that his fears and my own terrors were overexaggerated, when one night I had a strange dream. I had hardly fallen asleep when I heard my bedcurtains drawn apart, as their rings slid back upon the curtain rod with a sharp sound. I rose up quickly upon my elbow, and beheld the shadow of a woman standing erect before me. I recognised Clarimonde immediately.

She bore in her hand a little lamp, shaped like those which are placed in tombs, and its light lent her fingers a rosy transparency, which extended itself by lessening degrees even to the opaque and milky whiteness of her bare arm. Her only garment was the linen winding-sheet which had shrouded her when lying upon the bed of death. She sought to gather its folds over her bosom as though ashamed of being so scantily clad, but her little hand was not equal to the task.

She was so white that the colour of the drapery blended with that of her flesh under the pallid rays of the lamp. Enveloped with this subtle tissue which betrayed all the contours of her body, she seemed rather the marble statue of some fair antique bather than a woman endowed with life. But dead or living, statue or woman, shadow or body, her beauty was still the same, only that the green light of her eyes was less brilliant, and her mouth, once so warmly crimson, was only tinted with a faint tender rosiness, like that of her cheeks. The little blue flowers which I had noticed entwined in her hair were withered and dry, and had lost nearly all their leaves, but this did not prevent her from being charming—so charming that notwithstanding the strange character of the adventure, and the unexplainable manner in which she had entered my room, I felt not even for a moment the least fear.

She placed the lamp on the table and seated herself at the foot of my bed; then bending toward me, she said, in that voice at once silvery clear and yet velvety in its sweet softness, such as I never heard from any lips save hers:

"I have kept thee long in waiting, dear Romuald, and it must have seemed to thee that I had forgotten thee. But I come from afar off, very far off, and from a land whence no other has ever yet returned. There is neither sun nor moon in that land whence I come: all is but space and shadow; there is neither road nor pathway: no earth for the foot, no air for the wing; and nevertheless, behold me here, for Love is stronger than Death and must conquer him in the end. Oh, what sad faces and fearful things I have seen on my way hither! What difficulty my soul, returned to earth through the power of will alone, has had in finding its body and reinstating itself therein! What terrible efforts I had to make ere I could lift the ponderous slab with which they had covered me! See, the palms of my poor hands are all bruised! Kiss them, sweet love, that they may be healed!"

She laid the cold palms of her hands upon my mouth, one after the other. I kissed them, indeed, many times, and she the while watched me with a smile of ineffable affection.

I confess to my shame that I had entirely forgotten the advice of the Abbé Serapion and the sacred office wherewith I had been invested. I had fallen without resistance, and at the first assault. I had not even made the least effort to repel the tempter. The fresh coolness of Clarimonde skin penetrated my own, and I felt voluptuous tremors pass over my whole body. Poor child! in spite of all I saw afterward, I can hardly yet believe she was a demon; at least she had no appearance of being such, and never did Satan so skilfully conceal his claws and horns. She had drawn her feet up beneath her, and squatted down on the edge of the couch in an attitude full of negligent *coquetry*.

From time to time, she passed her little hand through my hair and twisted it into curls, as though trying how a new style of wearing it would become my face. I abandoned myself to her hands with the most guilty pleasure, while she accompanied her gentle play with the prettiest prattle. The most remarkable fact was that I felt no astonishment whatever at so extraordinary an adventure, and as in dreams one finds no difficulty in accepting the most fantastic events as simple facts, so all these circumstances seemed to me perfectly natural in themselves.

"I loved thee long ere I saw thee, dear Romuald, and sought thee everywhere. Thou wast my dream, and I first saw thee in the church at the fatal moment. I said at once, 'It is he!' I gave thee a look into which I threw all the love I ever had, all the love I now have, all the love I shall ever have for thee—a look that would have damned a cardinal or brought a king to his knees at my feet in view of all his court. Thou remainedst unmoved, preferring thy God to me!

"Ah, how jealous I am of that God whom thou didst love and still lovest more than me!

"Woe is me, unhappy one that I am! I can never have thy heart all to myself, I whom thou didst recall to life with a kiss—dead Clarimonde, who for thy sake bursts asunder the gates of the tomb, and comes to consecrate to thee a life which she has resumed only to make thee happy!"

All her words were accompanied with the most impassioned caresses, which bewildered my sense and my reason to such an extent, that I did not fear to utter a frightful blasphemy for the sake of consoling her, and to declare that I loved her as much as God.

Her eyes rekindled and shone like chrysoprases. "In truth?—in very truth?—as much as God!" she cried, flinging her beautiful arms around me. "Since it is so, thou wilt come with me; thou wilt follow me whithersoever I desire. Thou wilt cast away thy ugly black habit. Thou shalt be the proudest and most envied of cavaliers; thou shalt be my lover! To be the acknowledged lover of Clarimonde, who has refused even a Pope; that will be something to feel proud of! Ah, the fair, unspeakably happy existence, the beautiful golden life we shall live together! And when shall we depart, my fair sir?"

"Tomorrow! Tomorrow!" I cried in my delirium.

"Tomorrow, then, so let it be!" she answered. "In the meanwhile, I shall have opportunity to change my toilet, for this is a little too light and in nowise suited for a voyage. I must also forthwith notify all my friends who believe me dead, and mourn for me as deeply as they are capable of doing. The money, the dresses, the carriages—all will be ready. I shall call for thee at this same hour. *Adieu*, dear heart!' And she lightly touched my forehead with her lips. The lamp went out, the curtains closed again, and all became dark; a leaden, dreamless sleep fell on me and held me unconscious until the morning following.

CHAPTER 5: SERAPION'S MATTOCK

I awoke later than usual, and the recollection of this singular adventure troubled me during the whole day. I finally persuaded myself that it was a mere vapor of my heated imagination. Nevertheless, its sensations had been so vivid that it was difficult to persuade myself that they were not real, and it was not without some presentiment of what was going to happen that I got into bed at last, after having prayed God to drive far from me all thoughts of evil, and to protect the chastity of my slumber.

I soon fell into a deep sleep, and my dream was continued. The curtains again parted, and I beheld Clarimonde, not as on the former occasion, pale in her pale winding-sheet, with the violets of death upon her cheeks, but gay, sprightly, jaunty, in a superb traveling dress of green velvet, trimmed with gold lace, and looped up on either side to allow a glimpse of satin petticoat. Her blonde hair escaped in thick ringlets from beneath a broad black felt hat, decorated with white feathers whimsically twisted into various shapes. In one hand she held a little riding whip terminated by a golden whistle. She tapped me lightly with it, and exclaimed: "Well, my fine sleeper, is this the way you make your preparations? I thought I would find you up and dressed. Arise quickly, we have no time to lose."

I leaped out of bed at once.

"Come, dress yourself, and let us go," she continued, pointing to a little package she had brought with her. "The horses are becoming impatient of delay and champing their bits at the door. We ought to have been by this time at least ten leagues distant from here."

I dressed myself hurriedly, and she handed me the articles of apparel herself one by one, bursting into laughter from time to time at my awkwardness, as she explained to me the use of a garment when I had made a mistake. She hurriedly arranged my hair, and this done, held up before me a little pocket mirror of Venetian crystal, rimmed with silver filigree-work, and playfully asked: "How dost find thyself now? Wilt engage me for thy *valet de chambre?*"

I was no longer the same person, and I could not even recognise myself. I resembled my former self no more than a finished statue resembles a block of stone. My old face seemed but a coarse daub of the one reflected in the mirror. I was handsome, and my vanity was sensibly tickled by the metamorphosis. That elegant apparel, that richly embroidered vest had made of me a totally different personage, and I marvelled at the power of transformation owned by a few yards of cloth cut after a certain pattern. The spirit of my costume penetrated my very skin, and within ten minutes more I had become something of a coxcomb.

In order to feel more at ease in my new attire, I took several turns up and down the room. Clarimonde watched me with an air of maternal pleasure, and appeared well satisfied with her work. "Come, enough of this child's play! Let us start, Romuald, dear. We have far to go, and we may not get there in time." She took my hand and led me forth. All the doors opened before her at a touch, and we passed by the dog without awaking him.

At the gate we found Margheritone waiting, the same swarthy groom who had once before been my escort. He held the bridles of three horses, all black like those which bore us to the castle—one for me, one for him, one for Clarimonde. Those horses must have been Spanish *genets* born of mares fecundated by a zephyr, for they were fleet as the wind itself, and the moon, which had just risen at our departure to light us on the way, rolled over the sky like a wheel detached from her own chariot. We beheld her on the right leaping from tree to tree, and putting herself out of breath in the effort to keep up with us.

Soon we came upon a level plain where, hard by a clump of trees, a carriage with four vigorous horses awaited us. We entered it, and the postilions urged their animals into a mad gallop. I had one arm around Clarimonde's waist, and one of her hands clasped in mine; her head leaned upon my shoulder, and I felt her bosom, half bare, lightly pressing against my arm. I had never known such intense happiness. In that hour I had forgotten everything, and I no more remembered having ever been a priest than I remembered what I had been doing in my mother's womb, so great was the fascination which the evil spirit exerted upon me. From that night my nature seemed in some sort to have become halved, and there were two men within me, neither of whom knew the other.

At one moment I believed myself a priest who dreamed nightly that he was a gentleman, at another that I was a gentleman who dreamed he was a priest. I could no longer distinguish the dream from the reality, nor could I discover where the reality began or where ended the dream. The exquisite young lord and libertine railed at the priest, the priest loathed the dissolute habits of the young lord. Two spirals entangled and confounded the one with the other, yet never touching, would afford a fair representation of this bucolic life which I lived. Despite the strange character of my condition, I do not believe that I ever inclined, even for a moment, to madness.

I always retained with extreme vividness all the perceptions of my two lives. Only there was one absurd fact which I could not explain to myself—namely, that the consciousness of the same individuality existed in two men so opposite in character. It was an anomaly for which I could not account—whether I believed myself to be the *curé* of the little village of C——, or *Il Signor Romualdo,* the titled lover of Clarimonde. Be that as it may, I lived, at least I believed that I lived, in

Venice. I have never been able to discover rightly how much of illusion and how much of reality there was in this fantastic adventure. We dwelt in a great palace on the Canaleio, filled with *frescoes* and statues, and containing two Titians in the noblest style of the great master, which were hung in Clarimonde's chamber.

It was a palace well worthy of a king. We had each our gondola, our *barcarolli* in family livery, our music hall, and our special poet. Clarimonde always lived upon a magnificent scale; there was something of Cleopatra in her nature. As for me, I had the retinue of a prince's son, and I was regarded with as much reverential respect as though I had been of the family of one of the twelve Apostles or the four Evangelists of the Most Serene Republic. I would not have turned aside to allow even the *Doge* to pass, and I do not believe that since Satan fell from heaven, any creature was ever prouder or more insolent than I. I went to the Ridotto, and played with a luck which seemed absolutely infernal.

I received the best of all society—the sons of ruined families, women of the theatre, shrewd knaves, parasites, hectoring swashbucklers. But notwithstanding the dissipation of such a life, I always remained faithful to Clarimonde. I loved her wildly. She would have excited satiety itself, and chained inconstancy. To have Clarimonde was to have twenty mistresses; aye, to possess all women; so mobile, so varied of aspect, so fresh in new charms was she all in herself—a very chameleon of a woman, in sooth. She made you commit with her the infidelity you would have committed with another, by donning to perfection the character, the attraction, the style of beauty of the woman who appeared to please you. She returned my love a hundredfold, and it was in vain that the young patricians and even the Ancients of the Council of Ten made her the most magnificent proposals. A Foscari even went so far as to offer to espouse her. She rejected all his overtures.

Of gold she had enough. She wished no longer for anything but love —a love youthful, pure, evoked by herself, and which should be a first and last passion. I would have been perfectly happy but for a cursed nightmare which recurred every night, and in which I believed myself to be a poor village *curé*, practicing mortification and penance for my excesses during the day. Reassured by my constant association with her, I never thought further of the strange manner in which I had become acquainted with Clarimonde. But the words of the Abbé Serapion concerning her recurred often to my memory, and never ceased to cause me uneasiness.

For some time, the health of Clarimonde had not been so good as usual; her complexion grew paler day by day. The physicians who were summoned could not comprehend the nature of her malady and knew not how to treat it. They all prescribed some insignificant remedies, and never called a second time. Her paleness, nevertheless, visibly increased, and she became colder and colder, until she seemed almost as white and dead as upon that memorable night in the unknown castle. I grieved with anguish unspeakable to behold her thus slowly perishing; and she, touched by my agony, smiled upon me sweetly and sadly with the fateful smile of those who feel that they must die.

One morning I was seated at her bedside, and breakfasting from a little table placed close at hand, so that I might not be obliged to leave her for a single instant. In the act of cutting some fruit I accidentally inflicted rather a deep gash on my finger. The blood immediately gushed forth in a little purple jet, and a few drops spurted upon Clarimonde. Her eyes flashed, her face suddenly assumed an expression of savage and ferocious joy such as I had never before observed in her. She leaped out of her bed with animal agility—the agility, as it were, of an ape or a cat—and sprang upon my wound, which she commenced to suck with an air of unutterable pleasure. She swallowed the blood in little mouthfuls, slowly and carefully, like a connoisseur tasting a wine from Xeres or Syracuse. Gradually her eyelids half closed, and the pupils of her green eyes became oblong instead of round.

From time to time, she paused in order to kiss my hand, then she would recommence to press her lips to the lips of the wound in order to coax forth a few more ruddy drops. When she found that the blood would no longer come, she arose with eyes liquid and brilliant, rosier than a May dawn; her face full and fresh, her hand warm and moist—in fine, more beautiful than ever, and in the most perfect health.

"I shall not die! I shall not die!" she cried, clinging to my neck, half mad with joy. "I can love thee yet for a long time. My life is thine, and all that is of me comes from thee. A few drops of thy rich and noble blood, more precious and more potent than all the elixirs of the earth, have given me back life."

This scene long haunted my memory, and inspired me with strange doubts in regard to Clarimonde; and the same evening, when slumber had transported me to my presbytery, I beheld the Abbé Serapion, graver and more anxious of aspect than ever. He gazed attentively at me, and sorrowfully exclaimed: "Not content with losing your soul, you now desire also to lose your body. Wretched young man, into how terrible a plight have you fallen!" The tone in which he uttered these words powerfully affected me, but in spite of its vividness even that impression was soon dissipated, and a thousand other cares erased it from my mind. At last, one evening, while looking into a mirror whose traitorous position she had not taken into account, I saw Clarimonde in the act of emptying a powder into the cup of spiced wine which she had long been in the habit of preparing after our repasts.

I took the cup, feigned to carry it to my lips, and then placed it on the nearest article of furniture as though intending to finish it at my leisure. Taking advantage of a moment when the fair one's back was turned, I threw the contents under the table, after which I retired to my chamber and went to bed, fully resolved not to sleep, but to watch and discover what should come of all this mystery. I did not have to wait long. Clarimonde entered in her nightdress, and having removed her apparel, crept into bed and lay down beside me. When she felt assured that I was asleep, she bared my arm, and drawing a gold pin from her hair, commenced to murmur in a low voice:

"One drop, only one drop! One ruby at the end of my needle! Since thou lovest me yet, I must not die! . . . Ah, poor love! His beautiful blood, so brightly purple, I must drink it. Sleep, my only treasure! Sleep, my god, my child! I will do thee no harm; I will only take of thy life what I must to keep my own from being forever extinguished. But that I love thee so much, I could well resolve to have other lovers whose veins I could drain; but since I have known thee all other men have become hateful to me. . . . Ah, the beautiful arm! How round it is! How white it is! How shall I ever dare to prick this pretty blue vein!"

And while thus murmuring to herself she wept, and I felt her tears raining on my arm as she clasped it with her hands. At last, she took the resolve, slightly punctured me with her pin, and commenced to suck up the blood which oozed from the place. Although she swallowed only a few drops, the fear of weakening me soon seized her, and she carefully tied a little band around my arm, afterward rubbing the wound with an unguent which immediately cicatrized it.

Further doubts were impossible. The Abbé Serapion was right. Notwithstanding this positive knowledge, however, I could not cease to love Clarimonde, and I would gladly of my own accord have, given her all the blood she required to sustain her factitious life. Moreover, I felt but little fear of her. The woman seemed to plead with me for the vampire, and what I had already heard and seen sufficed to reassure me completely. In those days I had plenteous veins, which would not have been so easily exhausted as at present; and I would not have thought of bargaining for my blood, drop by drop. I would rather have opened myself the veins of my arm and said to her: "Drink, and may my love infiltrate itself throughout thy body together with my blood!" I carefully avoided ever making the least reference to the narcotic drink she had prepared for me, or to the incident of the pin, and we lived in the most perfect harmony.

Yet my priestly scruples commenced to torment me more than ever, and I was at a loss to imagine what new penance I could invent in order to mortify and subdue my flesh. Although these visions were involuntary, and though I did not actually participate in anything relating to them, I could not dare to touch the body of Christ with hands so impure and a mind defiled by such debauches whether real or imaginary. In the effort to avoid falling under the influence of these wearisome hallucinations, I strove to prevent myself from being overcome by sleep.

I held my eyelids open with my fingers, and stood for hours together leaning upright against the wall, fighting sleep with all my might; but the dust of drowsiness invariably gathered upon my eyes at last, and finding all resistance useless, I would have to let my arms fall in the extremity of despairing weariness, and the current of slumber would again bear me away to the perfidious shores. Serapion addressed me with the most vehement exhortations, severely reproaching me for my softness and want of fervour. Finally, one day when I was more wretched than usual, he said to me:

"There is but one way by which you can obtain relief from this continual torment, and though it is an extreme measure it must be made use of; violent diseases require violent remedies. I know where Clarimonde is buried. It is necessary that we shall disinter her remains, and that you shall behold in how pitiable a state the object of your love is. Then you will no longer be tempted to lose your soul for the sake of an unclean corpse devoured by worms, and ready to crumble into dust. That will assuredly restore you to yourself."

For my part, I was so tired of this double life that I at once consented, desiring to ascertain beyond a doubt whether a priest or a gentleman had been the victim of delusion. I had become fully resolved either to kill one of the two men within me for the benefit of the other, or else to kill both, for so terrible an existence could not last long and be endured. The Abbé Serapion provided himself with a mattock, a lever, and a lantern, and at midnight we wended our way to the cemetery of ——, the location and place of which were perfectly familiar to him. After having directed the rays of the dark lantern upon the inscriptions of several tombs, we came at last upon a great slab, half concealed by huge weeds and devoured by mosses and parasitic plants, whereupon we deciphered the opening lines of the epitaph:

Here lies Clarimonde
Who was famed in her lifetime
As the fairest of women.

"It is here without a doubt," muttered Serapion, and placing his lantern on the ground, he forced the point of the lever under the edge of the stone and commenced to raise it. The stone yielded, and he proceeded to work with the mattock. Darker and more silent than the night itself, I stood by and watched him do it, while he, bending over his dismal toil, streamed with sweat, panted, and his hard-coming breath seemed to have the harsh tone of a death rattle. It was a weird scene, and had any persons from without beheld us, they would assuredly have taken us rather for profane wretches and shroud-stealers than for priests of God. There was something grim and fierce in Serapion's zeal which lent him the air of a demon rather than of an apostle or an angel, and his great aquiline face, with all its stern features brought out in strong relief by the lantern-light, had something fearsome in it which enhanced the unpleasant fancy.

I felt an icy sweat come out upon my forehead in huge beads, and my hair stood up with a hideous fear. Within the depths of my own heart, I felt that the act of the austere Serapion was an abominable sacrilege; and I could have prayed that a triangle of fire would issue from the entrails of the dark clouds, heavily rolling above us, to reduce him to cinders. The owls which had been nestling in the cypress-trees, startled by the gleam of the lantern, flew against it from time to time, striking their dusty wings against its panes, and uttering plaintive cries of lamentation; wild foxes yelped in the far darkness, and a thousand sinister noises detached themselves from the silence.

At last, Serapion's mattock struck the coffin itself, making its planks re-echo with a deep sonorous sound, with that terrible sound nothingness utters when stricken. He wrenched apart and tore up the lid, and I beheld Clarimonde, pallid as a figure of marble, with hands joined; her white winding-sheet made but one fold from her head to her feet. A little crimson drop sparkled like a speck of dew at one corner of her colourless mouth. Serapion, at this spectacle, burst into fury: "Ah, thou art here, demon! Impure courtesan! Drinker of blood and gold!" And he flung holy water upon the corpse and the coffin, over which he traced the sign of the cross with the sprinkler. Poor Clarimonde had no sooner been touched by the blessed spray than her beautiful body crumbled into dust, and became only a shapeless and frightful mass of cinders and half-calcined bones.

"Behold your mistress, my Lord Romuald!" cried the inexorable priest, as he pointed to these sad remains. "Will you be easily tempted after this to promenade on the Lido or at Fusina with your beauty?" I covered my face with my hands, a vast ruin had taken place within me. I returned to my presbytery, and the noble Lord Romuald, the lover of Clarimonde, separated himself from the poor priest with whom he had kept such strange company so long.

But once only, the following night, I saw Clarimonde. She said to me, as she had said the first time at the portals of the church: "Unhappy man! Unhappy man! What hast thou done? Wherefore have hearkened to that imbecile priest? Wert thou not happy? And what harm had I ever done thee that thou shouldst violate my poor tomb, and lay bare the miseries of my nothingness? All communication between our souls and our bodies is henceforth forever broken. *Adieu!* Thou wilt yet regret me!" She vanished in air as smoke, and I never saw her more.

Alas! she spoke truly indeed. I have regretted her more than once, and I regret her still. My soul's peace has been very dearly bought. The love of God was not too much to replace such a love as hers. And this, brother, is the story of my youth. Never gaze upon a woman, and walk abroad only with eyes ever fixed upon the ground; for however chaste and watchful one may be, the error of a single moment is enough to make one lose eternity.

Lazarus

Leonid Andreyev

1

When Lazarus left the grave, where, for three days and three nights he had been under the enigmatical sway of death, and returned alive to his dwelling, for a long time no one noticed in him those sinister oddities, which, as time went on, made his very name a terror. Gladdened unspeakably by the sight of him who had been returned to life, those near to him caressed him unceasingly, and satiated their burning desire to serve him, in solicitude for his food and drink and garments.

And they dressed him gorgeously, in bright colours of hope and laughter, and when, like to a bridegroom in his bridal vestures, he sat again among them at the table, and again ate and drank, they wept, overwhelmed with tenderness. And they summoned the neighbours to look at him who had risen miraculously from the dead. These came and shared the serene joy of the hosts. Strangers from far-off towns and hamlets came and adored the miracle in tempestuous words. Like to a beehive was the house of Mary and Martha.

Whatever was found new in Lazarus' face and gestures was thought to be some trace of a grave illness and of the shocks recently experienced. Evidently, the destruction wrought by death on the corpse was only arrested by the miraculous power, but its effects were still apparent; and what death had succeeded in doing with Lazarus' face and body, was like an artist's unfinished sketch seen under thin glass. On Lazarus' temples, under his eyes, and in the hollows of his cheeks, lay a deep and cadaverous blueness; cadaverously blue also were his long fingers, and around his fingernails, grown long in the grave, the blue had become purple and dark.

On his lips the skin, swollen in the grave, had burst in places, and thin, reddish cracks were formed, shining as though covered with transparent mica. And he had grown stout. His body, puffed up in the

63

grave, retained its monstrous size and showed those frightful swellings, in which one sensed the presence of the rank liquid of decomposition. But the heavy corpse-like odour which penetrated Lazarus' graveclothes and, it seemed, his very body, soon entirely disappeared, the blue spots on his face and hands grew paler, and the reddish cracks closed up, although they never disappeared altogether. That is how Lazarus looked when he appeared before people, in his second life, but his face looked natural to those who had seen him in the coffin.

In addition to the changes in his appearance, Lazarus' temper seemed to have undergone a transformation, but this circumstance startled no one and attracted no attention. Before his death Lazarus had always been cheerful and carefree, fond of laughter and a merry joke. It was because of this brightness and cheerfulness, with not a touch of malice and darkness, that the Master had grown so fond of him. But now Lazarus had grown grave and taciturn, he never jested, himself, nor responded with laughter to other people's jokes; and the words which he uttered, very infrequently, were the plainest, most ordinary, and necessary words, as deprived of depth and significance, as those sounds with which animals express pain and pleasure, thirst and hunger. They were the words that one can say all one's life, and yet they give no indication of what pains and gladdens the depths of the soul.

Thus, with the face of a corpse which for three days had been under the heavy sway of death, dark and taciturn, already appallingly transformed, but still unrecognised by anyone in his new self, he was sitting at the feasting table, among friends and relatives, and his gorgeous nuptial garments glittered with yellow gold and bloody scarlet. Broad waves of jubilation, now soft, now tempestuously sonorous surged around him; warm glances of love were reaching out for his face, still cold with the coldness of the grave; and a friend's warm palm caressed his blue, heavy hand. And music played the tympanum and the pipe, the cithara and the harp. It was as though bees hummed, grasshoppers chirped and birds warbled over the happy house of Mary and Martha.

2

One of the guests incautiously lifted the veil. By a thoughtless word he broke the serene charm and uncovered the truth in all its naked ugliness. Ere the thought formed itself in his mind, his lips uttered with a smile:

"Why dost thou not tell us what happened yonder?"

And all grew silent, startled by the question. It was as if it occurred to them only now that for three days Lazarus had been dead, and they looked at him, anxiously awaiting his answer. But Lazarus kept silence.

"Thou dost not wish to tell us,"—wondered the man, "is it so terrible yonder?"

And again his thought came after his words. Had it been otherwise, he would not have asked this question, which at that very moment oppressed his heart with its insufferable horror. Uneasiness seized all present, and with a feeling of heavy weariness they awaited Lazarus' words, but he was silent, sternly and coldly, and his eyes were lowered. And as if for the first time, they noticed the frightful blueness of his face and his repulsive obesity. On the table, as though forgotten by Lazarus, rested his bluish-purple wrist, and to this all eyes turned, as if it were from it that the awaited answer was to come. The musicians were still playing, but now the silence reached them too, and even as water extinguishes scattered embers, so were their merry tunes extinguished in the silence. The pipe grew silent; the voices of the sonorous tympanum and the murmuring harp died away; and as if the strings had burst, the cithara answered with a tremulous, broken note. Silence.

"Thou dost not wish to say?" repeated the guest, unable to check his chattering tongue. But the stillness remained unbroken, and the bluish-purple hand rested motionless. And then he stirred slightly and everyone felt relieved. He lifted up his eyes, and lo! straightway embracing everything in one heavy glance, fraught with weariness and horror, he looked at them—Lazarus who had arisen from the dead.

It was the third day since Lazarus had left the grave. Ever since then many had experienced the pernicious power of his eye, but neither those who were crushed by it forever, nor those who found the strength to resist in it the primordial sources of life—which is as mysterious as death—never could they explain the horror which lay motionless in the depth of his black pupils. Lazarus looked calmly and simply with no desire to conceal anything, but also with no intention to say anything; he looked coldly, as he who is infinitely indifferent to those alive.

Many carefree people came close to him without noticing him, and only later did they learn with astonishment and fear who that calm stout man was, that walked slowly by, almost touching them with his gorgeous and dazzling garments. The sun did not cease shining, when he was looking, nor did the fountain hush its murmur, and the sky overhead remained cloudless and blue. But the man under the spell of his enigmatical look heard no more the fountain and saw not the sky overhead. Sometimes, he wept bitterly, sometimes he tore his hair and in frenzy called for help; but more often it came to pass that apathetically and quietly he began to die, and so he languished many years, before everybody's very eyes, wasted away, colourless, flabby, dull, like a tree, silently drying up in a stony soil. And of those who gazed at him, the ones who wept madly, sometimes felt again the stir of life; the others never.

"So, thou dost not wish to tell us what thou hast seen yonder?" repeated the man. But now his voice was impassive and dull, and deadly grey weariness showed in Lazarus' eyes. And deadly grey weariness covered like dust all the faces, and with dull amazement the guests stared at each other and did not understand wherefore they had gathered here and sat at the rich table. The talk ceased. They thought it was time to go home, but could not overcome the flaccid lazy weariness which glued their muscles, and they kept on sitting there, yet apart and torn away from each other, like pale fires scattered over a dark field.

But the musicians were paid to play and again they took their instruments and again tunes full of studied mirth and studied sorrow began to flow and to rise. They unfolded the customary melody but the guests hearkened in dull amazement. Already they knew not wherefore is it necessary, and why is it well, that people should pluck strings, inflate their cheeks, blow in thin pipes, and produce a bizarre, many-voiced noise.

"What bad music," said someone.

The musicians took offense and left. Following them, the guests left one after another, for night was already come. And when placid darkness encircled them and they began to breathe with more ease, suddenly Lazarus' image loomed up before each one in formidable radiance: the blue face of a corpse, grave-clothes gorgeous and resplendent, a cold look, in the depths of which lay motionless an unknown horror. As though petrified, they were standing far apart, and darkness enveloped them, but in the darkness blazed brighter and brighter the supernatural vision of him who for three days had been under the enigmatical sway of death.

For three days had he been dead: thrice had the sun risen and set, but he had been dead; children had played, streams murmured over pebbles, the wayfarer had lifted up hot dust in the highroad—but he had been dead. And now he is again among them—touches them,— looks at them—looks at them! and through the black discs of his pupils, as through darkened glass, stares the unknowable Yonder.

3

No one was taking care of Lazarus, for no friends no relatives were left to him, and the great desert which encircled the holy city, came near the very threshold of his dwelling. And the desert entered his house, and stretched on his couch, like a wife and extinguished the fires. No one was taking care of Lazarus. One after the other, his sisters—Mary and Martha—forsook him. For a long while Martha was loath to abandon him, for she knew not who would feed him and pity him, she wept and prayed. But one night, when the wind was roaming in the desert and with a hissing sound the cypresses were bending over the roof, she dressed noiselessly and secretly left the house.

Lazarus probably heard the door slam; it banged against the side-post under the gusts of the desert wind, but he did not rise to go out and to look at her that was abandoning him. All the night long the cypresses hissed over his head and plaintively thumped the door, letting in the cold, greedy desert.

Like a leper he was shunned by everyone, and it was proposed to tie a bell to his neck, as is done with lepers, to warn people against sudden meetings. But someone remarked, growing frightfully pale, that it would be too horrible if by night the moaning of Lazarus' bell were suddenly heard under the windows—and so the project was abandoned.

And since he did not take care of himself, he would probably have starved to death, had not the neighbours brought him food in fear of something that they sensed but vaguely. The food was brought to him by children; they were not afraid of Lazarus, nor did they mock him with naive cruelty, as children are wont to do with the wretched and miserable. They were indifferent to him, and Lazarus answered them with the same coldness; he had no desire to caress the black little curls, and to look into their innocent shining eyes. Given to Time and to the Desert, his house was crumbling down, and long since had his famishing, lowing goats wandered away to the neighbouring pastures. And his bridal garments became threadbare. Ever since that happy day, when the musicians played, he had worn them unaware of the difference of the new and the worn. The bright colours grew dull and faded; vicious dogs and the sharp thorn of the Desert turned the tender fabric into rags.

By day, when the merciless sun slew all things alive, and even scor-

67

pions sought shelter under stones and writhed there in a mad desire to sting, he sat motionless under the sunrays, his blue face and the uncouth, bushy beard lifted up, bathing in the fiery flood.

When people still talked to him, he was once asked:

"Poor Lazarus, does it please thee to sit thus and to stare at the sun?"

And he had answered:

"Yes, it does."

So strong, it seemed, was the cold of his three days' grave, so deep the darkness, that there was no heat on earth to warm Lazarus, nor a splendour that could brighten the darkness of his eyes. That is what came to the mind of those who spoke to Lazarus, and with a sigh they left him.

And when the scarlet, flattened globe would lower, Lazarus would set out for the desert and walk straight toward the sun, as though striving to reach it. He always walked straight toward the sun and those who tried to follow him and to spy upon what he was doing at night in the desert, retained in their memory the black silhouette of a tall stout man against the red background of an enormous flattened disc. Night pursued them with her horrors, and so they did not learn of Lazarus' doings in the desert, but the vision of the black on red was forever branded on their brain. Just as a beast with a splinter in its eye furiously rubs its muzzle with its paws, so they too foolishly rubbed their eyes, but what Lazarus had given was indelible, and Death alone could efface it.

But there were people who lived far away, who never saw Lazarus and knew of him only by report. With daring curiosity, which is stronger than fear and feeds upon it, with hidden mockery, they would come to Lazarus who was sitting in the sun and enter into conversation with him. By this time Lazarus' appearance had changed for the better and was not so terrible. The first minute they snapped their fingers and thought of how stupid the inhabitants of the holy city were; but when the short talk was over and they started homeward, their looks were such that the inhabitants of the holy city recognized them at once and said:

"Look, there is one more fool on whom Lazarus has set his eye,"— and they shook their heads regretfully, and lifted up their arms.

There came brave, intrepid warriors, with tinkling weapons; happy youths came with laughter and song; busy tradesmen, jingling their money, ran in for a moment, and haughty priests leaned their crosiers against Lazarus' door, and they were all strangely changed, as they came back. The same terrible shadow swooped down upon their souls and gave a new appearance to the old familiar world.

Those who still had the desire to speak, expressed their feelings thus:

"All things tangible and visible grew hollow, light, and transparent—similar to lightsome shadows in the darkness of night;

"For, that great darkness, which holds the whole cosmos, was dispersed neither by the sun or by the moon and the stars, but like an immense black shroud enveloped the earth and, like a mother, embraced it;

"It penetrated all the bodies, iron and stone—and the particles of the bodies, having lost their ties, grew lonely; and it penetrated into the depth of the particles, and the particles of particles became lonely;

"For that great void, which encircles the cosmos, was not filled by things visible: neither by the sun, nor by the moon and the stars, but reigned unrestrained, penetrating everywhere, severing body from body, particle from particle;

"In the void hollow trees spread hollow roots threatening a fantastic fall; temples, palaces, and horses loomed up and they were hollow; and in the void men moved about restlessly but they were light and hollow like shadows;

"For, Time was no more, and the beginning of all things came near their end: the building was still being built, and builders were still hammering away, and its ruins were already seen and the void in its place; the man was still being born, but already funeral candles were burning at his head, and now they were extinguished, and there was the void in place of the man and of the funeral candles.

"And wrapped by void and darkness the man in despair trembled in the face of the Horror of the Infinite."

Thus, spake the men who had still a desire to speak. But surely, much more could have told those who wished not to speak, and died in silence.

4

At that time there lived in Rome a renowned sculptor. In clay, marble, and bronze he wrought bodies of gods and men, and such was their beauty, that people called them immortal. But he himself was discontented and asserted that there was something even more beautiful, that he could not embody either in marble or in bronze. "I have not yet gathered the glimmers of the moon, nor have I my fill of sunshine," he was wont to say, "and there is no soul in my marble, no life in my beautiful bronze." And when on moonlight nights he slowly walked along the road, crossing the black shadows of cypresses, his white tunic glittering in the moonshine, those who met him would laugh in a friendly way and say:

"Art thou going to gather moonshine, Aurelius? Why then didst thou not fetch baskets?"

And he would answer, laughing and pointing to his eyes:

"Here are the baskets wherein I gather the sheen of the moon and the glimmer of the sun."

And so it was: the moon glimmered in his eyes and the sun sparkled therein. But he could not translate them into marble and therein lay the serene tragedy of his life.

He was descended from an ancient patrician race, had a good wife and children, and suffered from no want.

When the obscure rumour about Lazarus reached him, he consulted his wife and friends and undertook the far journey to Judea to see him who had miraculously risen from the dead. He was somewhat weary in those days and he hoped that the road would sharpen his blunted senses. What was said of Lazarus did not frighten him: he had pondered much over Death, did not like it, but he disliked also those who confused it with life.

In this life—life and beauty;
beyond—Death, the enigmatical—

. . . . thought he, and there is no better thing for a man to do than to delight in life and in the beauty of all things living. He had even a vainglorious desire to convince Lazarus of the truth of his own view and restore his soul to life, as his body had been restored. This seemed so much easier because the rumours, shy and strange, did not render the whole truth about Lazarus and but vaguely warned against something frightful.

Lazarus had just risen from the stone in order to follow the sun which was setting in the desert, when a rich Roman attended by an armed slave, approached him and addressed him in a sonorous tone of voice:

"Lazarus!"

And Lazarus beheld a superb face, lit with glory, and arrayed in fine clothes, and precious stones sparkling in the sun. The red light lent to the Roman's face and head the appearance of gleaming bronze—that also Lazarus noticed. He resumed obediently his place and lowered his weary eyes.

"Yes, thou art ugly, my poor Lazarus,"—quietly said the Roman, playing with his golden chain; "thou art even horrible, my poor friend; and Death was not lazy that day when thou didst fall so heedlessly into his hands. But thou art stout, and, as the great Caesar used to say, fat people are not ill-tempered; to tell the truth, I don't understand why men fear thee. Permit me to spend the night in thy house; the hour is late, and I have no shelter."

Never had anyone asked Lazarus' hospitality.

"I have no bed," said he.

"I am somewhat of a soldier and I can sleep sitting," the Roman answered. "We shall build a fire."

"I have no fire."

"Then we shall have our talk in the darkness, like two friends. I think thou wilt find a bottle of wine."

"I have no wine."

The Roman laughed.

"Now I see why thou art so sombre and dislikest thy second life. No wine! Why, then we shall do without it: there are words that make the head go round better than the Falernian."

By a sign he dismissed the slave, and they remained all alone. And again, the sculptor started speaking, but it was as if, together with the setting sun, life had left his words; and they grew pale and hollow, as if they staggered on unsteady feet, as if they slipped and fell down, drunk with the heavy lees of weariness and despair. And black chasms grew up between the words—like far-off hints of the great void and the great darkness.

"Now I am thy guest, and thou wilt not be unkind to me, Lazarus!"—said he. "Hospitality is the duty even of those who for three days were dead. Three days, I was told, thou didst rest in the grave. There it must be cold . . . and that is whence comes thy ill habit of going without fire and wine. As to me, I like fire; it grows dark here so rapidly. . . . The lines of thy eyebrows and forehead are quite, quite interesting: they are like ruins of strange palaces, buried in ashes after an earthquake. But why dost thou wear such ugly and queer garments? I have seen bridegrooms in thy country, and they wear such clothes—

are they not funny—and terrible.... But art thou a bridegroom?"

The sun had already disappeared, a monstrous black shadow came running from the east—it was as if gigantic bare feet began rumbling on the sand, and the wind sent a cold wave along the backbone.

"In the darkness thou seemest still larger, Lazarus, as if thou hast grown stouter in these moments. Dost thou feed on darkness, Lazarus? I would fain have a little fire—at least a little fire, a little fire. I feel somewhat chilly, your nights are so barbarously cold.... Were it not so dark, I should say that thou wert looking at me, Lazarus. Yes, it seems to me, thou art looking. ... Why, thou art looking at me, I feel it—but there thou art smiling."

Night came, and filled the air with heavy blackness.

"How well it will be, when the sun will rise tomorrow anew. ... I am a great sculptor, thou knowest; that is how my friends call me. I create. Yes, that is the word . . . but I need daylight. I give life to the cold marble, I melt sonorous bronze in fire, in bright hot fire. ... Why didst thou touch me with thy hand?"

"Come"—said Lazarus—"Thou art my guest."

And they went to the house. And a long night enveloped the earth.

The slave, seeing that his master did not come, went to seek him, when the sun was already high in the sky. And he beheld his master side by side with Lazarus: in profound silence were they sitting right under the dazzling and scorching sunrays and looking upward. The slave began to weep and cried out:

"My master, what has befallen thee, master?"

The very same day the sculptor left for Rome. On the way Aurelius was pensive and taciturn, staring attentively at everything—the men, the ship, the sea, as though trying to retain something. On the high sea a storm burst upon them, and all through it Aurelius stayed on the deck and eagerly scanned the seas looming near and sinking with a thud.

At home his friends were frightened at the change which had taken place in Aurelius, but he calmed them, saying meaningly:

"I have found it."

And without changing the dusty clothes he wore on his journey, he fell to work, and the marble obediently resounded under his sonorous hammer. Long and eagerly worked he, admitting no one, until one morning he announced that the work was ready and ordered his friends to be summoned, severe critics and connoisseurs of art. And to meet them he put on bright and gorgeous garments, that glittered with yellow gold—and—scarlet *byssus*.

"Here is my work," said he thoughtfully.

His friends glanced and a shadow of profound sorrow covered their faces. It was something monstrous, deprived of all the lines and shapes familiar to the eye, but not without a hint at some new, strange image.

On a thin, crooked twig, or rather on an ugly likeness of a twig rested askew a blind, ugly, shapeless, outspread mass of something utterly and inconceivably distorted, a mad leap of wild and bizarre fragments, all feebly and vainly striving to part from one another. And, as if by chance, beneath one of the wildly-rent salients a butterfly was chiselled with divine skill, all airy loveliness, delicacy, and beauty, with transparent wings, which seemed to tremble with an impotent desire to take flight.

"Wherefore this wonderful butterfly, Aurelius?" said somebody falteringly.

"I know not"—was the sculptor's answer.

But it was necessary to tell the truth, and one of his friends who loved him best said firmly:

"This is ugly, my poor friend. It must be destroyed. Give me the hammer."

And with two strokes he broke the monstrous man into pieces, leaving only the infinitely delicate butterfly untouched.

From that time on Aurelius created nothing. With profound indifference he looked at marble and bronze, and on his former divine works, where everlasting beauty rested. With the purpose of arousing his former fervent passion for work and, awakening his deadened soul, his friends took him to see other artists' beautiful works—but he remained indifferent as before, and the smile did not warm up his tightened lips. And only after listening to lengthy talks about beauty, he would retort wearily and indolently:

"But all this is a lie."

And by the day, when the sun was shining, he went into his magnificent, skilfully built garden and having found a place without shadow, he exposed his bare head to the glare and heat. Red and white butterflies fluttered around; from the crooked lips of a drunken satyr, water streamed down with a splash into a marble cistern, but he sat motionless and silent—like a pallid reflection of him who, in the far-off distance, at the very gates of the stony desert, sat under the fiery sun.

5

And now it came to pass that the great, deified Augustus himself summoned Lazarus. The imperial messengers dressed him gorgeously, in solemn nuptial clothes, as if Time had legalized them, and he was to remain until his very death the bridegroom of an unknown bride. It was as though an old, rotting coffin had been gilt and furnished with new, gay tassels. And men, all in trim and bright attire, rode after him, as if in bridal procession indeed, and those foremost trumpeted loudly, bidding people to clear the way for the emperor's messengers. But Lazarus' way was deserted: his native land cursed the hateful name of him who had miraculously risen from the dead, and people scattered at the very news of his appalling approach. The solitary voice of the brass trumpets sounded in the motionless air, and the wilderness alone responded with its languid echo.

Then Lazarus went by sea. And his was the most magnificently arrayed and the most mournful ship that ever mirrored itself in the azure waves of the Mediterranean Sea. Many were the travellers aboard, but like a tomb was the ship, all silence and stillness, and the despairing water sobbed at the steep, proudly curved prow. All alone sat Lazarus exposing his head to the blaze of the sun, silently listening to the murmur and splash of the wavelets, and afar seamen and messengers were sitting, a vague group of weary shadows. Had the thunder burst and the wind attacked the red sails, the ships would probably have perished, for none of those aboard had either the will or the strength to struggle for life. With a supreme effort some mariners would reach the board and eagerly scan the blue, transparent deep, hoping to see a *naiad's* pink shoulder flash in the hollow of an azure wave, or a drunken gay centaur dash along and in frenzy splash the wave with his hoof. But the sea was like a wilderness, and the deep was dumb and deserted.

With utter indifference did Lazarus set his feet on the street of the eternal city. As though all her wealth, all the magnificence of her palaces built by giants, all the resplendence, beauty, and music of her refined life were but the echo of the wind in the wilderness, the reflection of the desert quicksand. Chariots were dashing, and along the streets were moving crowds of strong, fair, proud builders of the eternal city and haughty participants in her life; a song sounded; fountains and women laughed a pearly laughter; drunken philosophers harangued, and the sober listened to them with a smile; hoofs struck the stone pavements. And surrounded by cheerful noise, a stout, heavy man was moving, a cold spot of silence and despair, and on his way, he sowed disgust, anger, and vague, gnawing weariness. Who dares to be sad in Rome, wondered indignantly the citizens, and frowned. In two days, the entire city already knew all about him who had miraculously risen from the dead, and shunned him shyly.

But some daring people there were, who wanted to test their strength, and Lazarus obeyed their imprudent summons. Kept busy by state affairs, the emperor constantly delayed the reception, and seven days did he who had risen from the dead go about visiting others.

And Lazarus came to a cheerful Epicurean, and the host met him with laughter on his lips:

"Drink, Lazarus, drink!"—shouted he. "Would not Augustus laugh to see thee drunk!"

And half-naked drunken women laughed, and rose petals fell on Lazarus' blue hands. But then the Epicurean looked into Lazarus' eyes, and his gaiety ended forever. Drunkard remained he for the rest of his life; never did he drink, yet forever was he drunk. But instead of the gay reverie which wine brings with it, frightful dreams began to haunt him, the sole food of his stricken spirit. Day and night he lived in the poisonous vapours of his nightmares, and death itself was not more frightful than her raving, monstrous forerunners.

And Lazarus came to a youth and his beloved, who loved each other and were most beautiful in their passions. Proudly and strongly embracing his love, the youth said with serene regret:

"Look at us, Lazarus, and share our joy. Is there anything stronger than love?"

And Lazarus looked. And for the rest of their life, they kept on loving each other, but their passion grew gloomy and joyless, like those funeral cypresses whose roots feed on the decay of the graves and whose black summits in a still evening hour seek in vain to reach the sky. Thrown by the unknown forces of life into each other's embraces, they mingled tears with kisses, voluptuous pleasures with pain, and they felt themselves doubly slaves, obedient slaves to life, and patient servants of the silent Nothingness. Ever united, ever severed, they blazed like sparks and like sparks lost themselves in the boundless Dark.

And Lazarus came to a haughty sage, and the sage said to him:

"I know all the horrors thou canst reveal to me. Is there anything thou canst frighten me with?"

But before long the sage felt that the knowledge of horror was far from being the horror itself, and that the vision of Death, was not

Death. And he felt that wisdom and folly are equal before the face of Infinity, for Infinity knows them not. And it vanished, the dividing-line between knowledge and ignorance, truth and falsehood, top and bottom, and the shapeless thought hung suspended in the void. Then the sage clutched his grey head and cried out frantically:

"I cannot think! I cannot think!"

Thus, under the indifferent glance for him, who miraculously had risen from the dead, perished everything that asserts life, its significance and joys. And it was suggested that it was dangerous to let him see the emperor, that it was better to kill him and, having buried him secretly, to tell the emperor that he had disappeared no one knew whither. Already swords were being whetted and youths devoted to the public welfare prepared for the murder, when Augustus ordered Lazarus to be brought before him next morning, thus destroying the cruel plans.

If there was no way of getting rid of Lazarus, at least it was possible to soften the terrible impression his face produced. With this in view, skilful painters, barbers, and artists were summoned, and all night long they were busy over Lazarus' head. They cropped his beard, curled it, and gave it a tidy, agreeable appearance. By means of paints they concealed the corpse-like blueness of his hands and face. Repulsive were the wrinkles of suffering that furrowed his old face, and they were puttied, painted, and smoothed; then, over the smooth background, wrinkles of good-tempered laughter and pleasant, carefree mirth were skilfully painted with fine brushes.

Lazarus submitted indifferently to everything that was done to him. Soon he was turned into a becomingly stout, venerable old man, into a quiet and kind grandfather of numerous offspring. It seemed that the smile, with which only a while ago he was spinning funny yarns, was still lingering on his lips, and that in the corner of his eye serene tenderness was hiding, the companion of old age. But people did not dare change his nuptial garments, and they could not change his eyes, two dark and frightful glasses through which looked at men, the unknowable Yonder.

6

Lazarus was not moved by the magnificence of the imperial palace. It was as though he saw no difference between the crumbling house, closely pressed by the desert, and the stone palace, solid and fair, and indifferently he passed into it. And the hard marble of the floors under his feet grew similar to the quicksand of the desert, and the multitude of richly dressed and haughty men became like void air under his glance. No one looked into his face, as Lazarus passed by, fearing to fall under the appalling influence of his eyes; but when the sound of his heavy footsteps had sufficiently died down, the courtiers raised their heads and with fearful curiosity examined the figure of a stout, tall, slightly bent old man, who was slowly penetrating into the very heart of the imperial palace.

Were Death itself passing, it would be faced with no greater fear: for until then the dead alone knew Death, and those alive knew Life only—and there was no bridge between them. But this extraordinary man, although alive, knew Death, and enigmatical, appalling, was his cursed knowledge. "Woe," people thought, "he will take the life of our great, deified Augustus," and they sent curses after Lazarus, who meanwhile kept on advancing into the interior of the palace.

Already did the emperor know who Lazarus was, and prepared to meet him. But the monarch was a brave man, and felt his own tremendous, unconquerable power, and in his fatal duel with him who had miraculously risen from the dead he wanted not to invoke human help. And so, he met Lazarus face to face:

"Lift not thine eyes upon me, Lazarus," he ordered. "I heard thy face is like that of Medusa and turns into stone whomsoever thou lookest at. Now, I wish to see thee and to have a talk with thee, before I turn into stone,"—added he in a tone of kingly jesting, not devoid of fear.

Coming close to him, he carefully examined Lazarus' face and his strange festal garments. And although he had a keen eye, he was deceived by his appearance.

"So, Thou dost not appear terrible, my venerable old man. But the worse for us, if horror assumes such a respectable and pleasant air. Now let us have a talk."

Augustus sat, and questioning Lazarus with his eye as much as with words, started the conversation:

"Why didst thou not greet me as thou enteredst?"

Lazarus answered indifferent:

"I knew not it was necessary."

"Art thou a Christian?"

"No."

Augustus approvingly shook his head.

"That is good. I do not like Christians. They shake the tree of life before it is covered with fruit, and disperse its odorous bloom to the winds. But who art thou?"

With a visible effort Lazarus answered:

"I was dead."

"I had heard that. But who art thou now?"

Lazarus was silent, but at last repeated in a tone of weary apathy:

"I was dead."

"Listen to me, stranger," said the emperor, distinctly and severely giving utterance to the thought that had come to him at the beginning, "my realm is the realm of Life, my people are of the living, not of the dead. Thou art here one too many. I know not who thou art and what thou sawest there; but, if thou liest, I hate thy lies, and if thou tellst the truth, I hate thy truth. In my bosom I feel the throb of life; I feel strength in my arm, and my proud thoughts, like eagles, pierce the space. And yonder in the shelter of my rule, under the protection of laws created by me, people live and toil and rejoice. Dost thou hear the battle-cry, the challenge men throw into the face of the future?"

Augustus, as in prayer, stretched forth his arms and exclaimed solemnly:

"Be blessed, O great and divine Life!"

Lazarus was silent, and with growing sternness the emperor went on:

"Thou art not wanted here, miserable remnant, snatched from under Death's teeth, thou inspirest weariness and disgust with life; like a caterpillar in the fields, thou gloatest on the rich ear of joy and belchest out the drivel of despair and sorrow. Thy truth is like a rusty sword in the hands of a nightly murderer—and as a murderer thou shalt be executed. But before that, let me look into thine eyes. Perchance, only cowards are afraid of them, but in the brave, they awake the thirst for strife and victory; then thou shalt be rewarded, not executed. . . . Now, look at me, Lazarus."

At first it appeared to the deified Augustus that a friend was looking at him—so soft, so tenderly fascinating was Lazarus' glance. It promised not horror, but sweet rest and the Infinite seemed to him a tender mistress, a compassionate sister, a mother. But stronger and stronger grew its embraces, and already the mouth, greedy of hissing kisses, interfered with the monarch's breathing, and already to the surface of the soft tissues of the body came the iron of the bones and tightened its merciless circle—and unknown fangs, blunt and cold, touched his heart and sank into it with slow indolence.

"It pains," said the deified Augustus, growing pale. "But look at me, Lazarus, look."

It was as though some heavy gates, ever closed, were slowly moving apart, and through the growing interstice the appalling horror of the Infinite poured in slowly and steadily. Like two shadows there entered the shoreless void and the unfathomable darkness; they extinguished the sun, ravished the earth from under the feet, and the roof from over the head. No more did the frozen heart ache.

"Look, look, Lazarus," ordered Augustus tottering.

Time stood still, and the beginning of each thing grew frightfully near to its end. Augustus' throne just erected, crumbled down, and the void was already in the place of the throne and of Augustus. Noiselessly did Rome crumble down, and a new city stood on its site and it too was swallowed by the void. Like fantastic giants, cities, states, and countries fell down and vanished in the void darkness—and with uttermost indifference did the insatiable black womb of the Infinite swallow them.

"Halt!"—ordered the emperor.

In his voice sounded already a note of indifference, his hands dropped in languor, and in the vain struggle with the onrushing darkness his fiery eyes now blazed up, and now went out.

"My life thou hast taken from me, Lazarus,"—said he in a spiritless, feeble voice.

And these words of hopelessness saved him. He remembered his people, whose shield he was destined to be, and keen salutary pain pierced his deadened heart. "They are doomed to death," he thought wearily. "Serene shadows in the darkness of the Infinite," thought he, and horror grew upon him. "Frail vessels with living seething blood with a heart that knows sorrow and also great joy," said he in his heart, and tenderness pervaded it.

Thus, pondering and oscillating between the poles of Life and Death, he slowly came back to life, to find in its suffering and in its joys a shield against the darkness of the void and the horror of the Infinite.

"No, thou hast not murdered me, Lazarus," said he firmly, "but I will take thy life. Be gone."

That evening the deified Augustus partook of his meats and drinks with particular joy. Now and then his lifted hand remained suspended in the air, and a dull glimmer replaced the bright sheen of his fiery eye. It was the cold wave of Horror that surged at his feet. Defeated, but not undone, ever awaiting its hour, that Horror stood at the emperor's bedside, like a black shadow all through his life; it swayed his nights, but yielded the days to the sorrows and joys of life.

The following day, the hangman with a hot iron burned out Lazarus' eyes. Then he was sent home. The deified Augustus dared not kill him.

★★★★★★★★

Lazarus returned to the desert, and the wilderness met him with hissing gusts of wind and the heat of the blazing sun. Again, he was sitting on a stone, his rough, bushy beard lifted up; and the two black holes in place of his eyes looked at the sky with an expression of dull terror. Afar-off the holy city stirred noisily and restlessly, but around him everything was deserted and dumb. No one approached the place where lived he who had miraculously risen from the dead, and long since his neighbours had forsaken their houses. Driven by the hot iron into the depth of his skull, his cursed knowledge hid there in an ambush. As though leaping out from an ambush it plunged its thousand invisible eyes into the man—and no one dared look at Lazarus.

And in the evening, when the sun, reddening and growing wider, would come nearer and nearer the western horizon, the blind Lazarus would slowly follow it. He would stumble against stones and fall, stout and weak as he was; would rise heavily to his feet and walk on again; and on the red screen of the sunset his black body and outspread hands would form a monstrous likeness of a cross.

And it came to pass that once he went out and did not come back. Thus, seemingly ended the second life of him who for three days had been under the enigmatical sway of death, and rose miraculously from the dead.

Our Last Walk

Hugh Conway

If I wished to tell a love-tale, I should begin this with the sweet-est memories of my life, and relate when and where Walter Linton and I first met; should describe my pride and happiness when I knew that he wished me to become his wife. The love we bore each other through life—aye, even after life—may be made manifest as I write these lines, but it is not because I loved him, I have this tale to tell. Other women have loved as I love, and have mourned as I mourn: my life, so far as the joy and grief of it go, is but the life of thousands.

Had Walter Linton, when first he asked me for the heart which was already his own, been but a poor struggling man, I should have given him all as freely as I did then. If need had been, I could have waited patiently for years, or until fortune smiled upon him. Feeling this, I had no false sentiment as to sharing the worldly good that was his, although I was a penniless girl and brought nothing in my hands. Of course, kind friends around wondered why Walter did not choose a wife who would bring him wealth as well as love. Ah, no one could have given him more love than I could give him: that was all he wanted or asked for. He was twenty-three, and his own master; I was twenty, and utterly alone in the world. So, we were married—just six weeks after that happy spring-day on which he told me I was dearest to him.

Our home—a dear, grey old house, full of pleasant corners—was Draycot Hall, Somersetshire, not far from the Mendip Hills. Walter had recently inherited the house and the estate of Draycot, and when we took possession of our kingdom, which was almost as new to Walter as it was to me, life seemed to hide all that could be desired. Walter's income was sufficient for the life of a quiet country gentleman—a life to which he settled down, and appeared to find every wish gratified in that happy existence. Shooting, fishing, and hunting gave him plenty

81

of amusement, and the land, part of which he farmed himself, brought occupation and interest enough to make him feel that his life was not altogether an idle or useless one.

Then, to make our happiness complete, the children came—a girl, then one, two, three bonny boys. How merry and busy the old house grew with them, the sturdy rogues! How proud Walter was of them!

We were not very rich people. Compared to that of some of our county neighbours, our income was insignificant. Draycot Hall, although not such an imposing pile as the name might suggest, was by no means a small house; and, like all rambling old places, cost a good deal of money to keep up. Even when we began life together, we found, at the end of the year, that our expenditure and income nearly tallied, and as expenses increased with an increasing family, we felt that a few hundreds added to our revenue would be a very welcome addition. But in spite of this our lot was too happy for us to think of grumbling.

We sat one summer's evening on the lawn. The air was cooled by late fallen rain, and sweet with fragrance rising from the freshened flowers—for days were long and petals not yet closed. Our latest given child slept on my knee; and, as we watched the sun sink slowly down behind the Mendip Hills, my husband said:

'Helena, how shall we manage to start all these boys in life?'

I laughed at such a distant obligation. We were still young, and it seemed that so many years must pass before the baby on my knee would want a starting hand. I kissed the child's little white fingers.

'Why, Walter. I said, 'you are looking a long, long way into the future.'

'Yes, my girl; but days happy as ours, pass very quickly. It will not seem so long before we shall be obliged to think about it. What shall we do then? We save no money even now, you know. By-and-by we must send these babies to school; after that they will want money to help them on in professions. How are we to do all this? Our income won't increase.'

'We must try and economise. I answered, impressed by the really serious view he took.

'But how? As it is, we can scarcely make both ends meet. I am afraid I am selfish in living as I do. I have serious thoughts of going into some business and trying to make a fortune.'

I begged, beseeched him to dismiss the wild idea. Were we not happy enough with all we now possessed? Why change our mode of life, which was so peaceful and sweet? Besides, in my heart of hearts I doubted if my good, easy-going Walter was suite fitted for a commercial careen He kissed me as I pleaded eloquently for a continuation of our present happiness, and for a time the subject dropped. 'Yet I could see, from remarks he now and again made, that the thought lingered in his mind, and I began to fear lest, some day, he might put it into practical shape, when the anxieties attendant on money-making or money-losing might be ours.

It was some months after our conversation that old Reuben Dyke, a well-known character in the village of Draycot, came to the Hall. He wanted to see the master on important business, he said. This old Reuben was the greatest gossip of the place—the ale-house oracle— meddler in everyone's business, and unsolicited adviser-in-general to the little world around him. He was a great authority among the villagers, many of whom would have backed his opinion against the united wisdom of a Daniel and a Solomon. His talk and broad Somerset accent always amused us, and, it may be, ensured him a better reception than his virtues merited.

Today he entered the room with an indescribable look of mystery and secrecy on his shrewd old face. He carefully closed the door after him and bade us a respectful good-day. Then, drawing quite close to us, he spoke in guarded whispers.

'I be jest come, zur, to tell 'ee as ther' have a-bin a chap a staayin' at the Blue Boar for the last two or dree daays. Mebby, zur, as you ve a zeed un about—a darkish, picket-noased zort of a chap!

'Yes, I saw him. answered Walter. 'What about him?'

'Now, look here, zur. None o' we couldn't at vust miake out what a wer' up to. He yent one o' them outrides, you zee He werdn't lookin' aater shopkippers. He were a ferrettin' about aater land. Zo we up and ax'd un what farm a wer' aater, or if a did want to buy any land hereabouts? He laughed and zed, zes he, "We be gwain to make a raailroad right up droo theese yer valley." Zes I, "I hoap my head won't yache till we do get a raailwaay on Mendip, for that is a devilish poor country." "True," zes he; "but there be a lot o' coal jest under—along Havyat Green and Upper Langford." Zes I, "Zo I've a-heerd;" and then I zeed in a minute which waay the cat wer' jumpin'. He werdn't gwain to make nar a raailwaay; he wanted to zenk a coalpit, and get howld o' zome land under false pertences. Zo, if I wer' you, zur, and if I wer' Mr. Llewellyn, I should jest keep my eyes open; for I shouldn't wonder if, one o' thease here daays, he won't be along and offer 'ee a hundred and fifty a yacre for zome o' your poorest land. But my advice to you, zur, is—doan't 'ee zell it—not for double the money.'

After this important communication, Reuben bowed himself out; retiring probably to the kitchen, in order that he might regale himself with meat and drink and our servants with the latest village gossip. Walter and I sat digesting his news.

'I wonder if there can be any truth in it,' said Walter. 'I'll go down tomorrow and see that fellow at the inn, and ask him point-blank about it.'

But on the morrow the fellow at the inn was there no longer. He had departed and left no address. The landlord only knew him as plain Mr. Smith. We never saw or heard of him again—whatever his errand may have been, it was not revealed to us; but, nevertheless, old Reuben's conjecture as to the object of his sojourn at the Blue Boar quite unsettled Walter's mind. The thought that untold wealth might be lying under our very feet was always present to it, and at last he resolved to employ experts who were competent to give an opinion on the matter, and settle our hopes and doubts.

So, very soon, we were visited by Captain Thomas Davies of Aberfellteg, and Captain Davies Thomas of Cwmtygwyn, two gentlemen whose strangely accented English, redundant with such words as 'Inteet' and 'Inteet to coodness,' was a source of great amusement and enjoyment to each of us. They inspected, diagnosed, experimented, and then reported. My poor dear love! shall I ever forget your excitement, your joy, as we perused together that glowing joint production? What wealth you dreamed of and counted up! Not, I know, that you wished for riches for your own sake—if was for the sake of wife and children that the desire of acquiring a large fortune obtained such a hold on you.

Ah me! how certain, how clear and straightforward it all seemed! Had not the mining captains calculated, with an accuracy that seemed infallible, every ton of coal that lay hidden beneath our green fields? Did not their figures prove beyond dispute the profit each ton raised must bring? After every contingency had been guarded against, what read like Aladdin's wealth lay waiting for us to stoop down, take, and enjoy. Why should we not do so?

Then other gentlemen came to our quiet home—legal gentlemen—gentlemen who were called financiers—gentlemen learned, very learned, it seemed to me, in acreages, crops, and soils. Old safes were unlocked, old plans and musty deeds extracted from their recesses. I heard the word 'Mortgage' frequently; and Walter told me he had resolved to share his promised wealth with no one. He would work the projected mines solely on his own account; but, in order to begin operations, money was needful: so, he had arranged with the two financial gentlemen, Messrs. Leach and Vincent, of Bristol, that such sums of money as were necessary should be advanced to him upon the security of his estate. And these gentlemen applauded Walter's courageous resolution, and everything went so pleasantly.

Then the digging began!

Oh, how I hated it! From the very first I hated it! Not only did it spoil one of our prettiest fields—the one where the children gathered earliest cowslips—but it brought strange faces and rough forms to the quiet, sleepy little village. Men and women of at very different type to that of labourers round about. Slatternly untidy women and strong surly men who knew not the traditions of the land. Men who were supposed to beat their wives once a week, and who, we knew, played havoc with our neighbours' costly preserves. Men who worked hard—very hard—and insisted upon that work being highly paid for—who spent so large a proportion of those hard-earned wages in drink, that the landlords of the opposition village inns actually shook hands in their unexpected prosperity; whilst our kind, old, easy-going Rector fairly cried at the way in which his new and unwelcome parishioners were demoralising the old ones, and old Reuben? Dyke seemed to look almost patronisingly upon us, as two deserving young people helped to fortune by his great sagacity and wisdom.

So, it went on, month after month; yet I saw no signs of the advent of that promised wealth. So far as I could understand it, the seam of coal hit upon by those clever captains was a failure. It broke, or dipped, or something else; so, the continuation had to be sought elsewhere. Thereupon Captains Thomas Davies and Davies Thomas came over again, inspected again, and reported so cheerfully that Walter's face lost that look of anxiety which I had lately seen upon it, and he pushed on the work more briskly than before.

Then they told me the right seam had been found—Walter was radiant. Out of the first money gained he would send Thomas Davies and Davies Thomas a hundred pounds apiece, as an extra recognition due to their skill and good counsel. Larger sums than before were furnished by our financial friends, who came to the Hall once or twice, and were, I thought, very rude and familiar in their manner. Machinery and engines were erected, more men engaged, and in time, great black heaps began to accumulate, and grimy black faces met me at every turn. Our peaceful and beautiful home was so changed that I began almost to loathe what had once been the dearest spot on earth to me, and to long for change of air and scene.

Money seemed always being paid away—large sums that frightened me. But was I not only a woman, who knew nothing of business?

Yet all these grievances were nothing to the grief I felt at seeing the change in my darling's face. Every week I noticed an alteration. Gradually, a cloud of care seemed settling down on his once gay nature, and I knew his mind was anxious and ill at ease. He grew thinner: his dark hair showed signs of premature greyness: his sleep was often restless and unrefreshing. Though now, as he ever had been, kind and gentle to me, at times with others he was moody, silent, and evidently worried. All the brightness of youth appeared to be leaving him, so much so, that my heart ached to see him, and I felt I could bear it no longer. I would learn the worst he had to tell me, claiming my right as a true wife to share trouble as well as joy with my husband.

The confidence I was resolved to claim came unasked for. One evening Walter returned home and threw himself into a chair, apparently utterly broken down. He covered his eyes with his hands and sobbed bitterly.

I knelt at his side and my arms were round him. Then he told me all—I need not give the details. The bare truth was this: After all the money spent, the coal raised was of such a poor quality that every ton sold was sold at a loss. And more money than I had ever imagined had been expended. Of course, he had been cheated—I knew he was being cheated the moment I saw the faces of the men who had lent him the money he wanted; but there was no help for it, now. Messrs. Leach and Vincent claimed, for advances, costs and interest, the enormous sum of close upon ten thousand pounds. Walter had just come from Bristol, where these men carried on business, and after a stormy interview with them, had been informed that unless the amount was paid by Saturday, house, lands, and everything would be at once advertised for sale—and today was Wednesday!

I knew nothing of law, but, even to my ignorance, this sudden demand and swift procedure seemed unusual.

'But can they do it?' I asked.

'Yes, I am afraid they can. Months ago, when they made me a large advance, they gave me notice to pay the mortgage off. It was a mere matter of form, they said; but now they will act upon it. They are thoroughgoing rogues, and I believe have some scheme in their heads by which they fancy it possible to get absolute possession of the whole estate.'

'But, Walter dear, the estate must be worth thousands more than that amount'

'Oh yes, I can get the money easily enough. But not in three days. It will cut me to the heart even to see it all advertised, although doubtless the sale may be stopped.'

'Why not go to that nice old gentleman, Mr. Mainwaring?' I suggested. 'You always call him your family solicitor. He will help you, I am sure.'

'That is just what I intend doing. I shall go to London tomorrow, and show him exactly how I stand, and beg as a great favour that I may have the money at once. When I return, I will give orders for all the men to be discharged and the machinery sold. There shall be an end of it before it makes an end of me.'

I was almost hysterical with joy as I heard his last words.

'Oh, my love!' I cried. 'It will all come right with us yet. We are after all only half ruined. We can let the Hall and go abroad for several years. Don't trouble about it anymore. If you could only know how happy I am to think I shall have you back once again, all to myself as of old, you would be happy too. We will live in some quiet French or Swiss town, and be everything to one another again.'

So, I talked to him and comforted him, until he grew more composed, and, kissing me, owned that life was still worth having, even if shorn of half its wealth.

That night I slept more happily than I had slept for months.

The morning's post brought a letter from Leach and Vincent. It was couched in legal terms, and stated that unless the amount due was paid in notes or gold by Saturday at noon, they would take the threatened steps. Walter at once despatched a telegram, saying the money would be paid, and requesting that the necessary release might be prepared in order to avoid any delay. Then he started for London, in quest of ten thousand pounds.

I had little fear as to the result of his expedition. I can read faces; and long ago I had read in Mr. Mainwaring's face the kindness of his disposition. I knew he was rich, and that his clients were also rich men; moreover, he had a high opinion of Walter, and held him in what might almost be termed affection. When he congratulated me upon my marriage, he told me, in unmistakable words, what he thought of my husband. So, I was not surprised when, on the Friday evening, Walter returned with a semblance of the old joyous smile on his face; and, after locking a pocketful of banknotes in the safe, sat down by me, and for the rest of the evening built airy castles, or rather cottages, full of peacefulness and love.

When I awoke, next morn, my heart was light; trouble, it seemed, had been, but passed away so swiftly that its traces scarce remained. I threw the window open, and the fresh sweet air of spring brought gladness on its wings. The honeysuckle, old and great, that clothed the wall beneath my window, just gave signs of breaking into blossom; leaning out, I plucked some sprays and pinned them in my dress. A thrush sang from a bush below; my heart kept echoing his notes of love and joy. What cared I for the money, or its loss? Should I not have my own love back again, and watch his face regain its old bright look of health and happiness? Passed by his side, and with our children round, would not my life be pleasant in some quaint old town of France? And we would live so carefully, and save money as years went on, until someday might bring us to the dear old Hall again. Unhappy?—no! few moments in my life had happier been than these.

And Walter was cheerful. He would soon be out of the clutches of his obliging friends. The shock was over. He had told me what had been gnawing at his heart for so long; he was now looking his troubles fairly in the face, and, as usually happens, found them not so terrible in aspect as he had imagined. He buttoned his banknotes in his breast-pocket and started for the railway station. He felt better and stronger today, and, as the morning was so beautifully fine, was tempted to walk the five miles, instead of driving, as he usually did.

We were early risers, so he had plenty of time, and I thought the walk would do him good. Perhaps it was the feeling of newly restored confidence—perfect and true—which now existed between us that made his farewell to me that morning even more affectionate than it was wont to be—made him insist upon having all the children brought down, and taking many a kiss from those little rosy pursed-up lips—made him pause when he reached the furthest point to which my eyes could follow him, and turning, waft me one more farewell.

I should have walked with him, at any rate, part of the way; but household duties had to be attended to; so, after watching his tall figure disappear at the turning of the drive, I re-entered the house, hoping that the day would pass quickly, and hasten the evening which would bring him back again.

Months and months ago I had promised a friend, who sighed in far-away lands for English fields again, to make, this spring, a little collection of dried ferns and send it to her. The anxiety of the last few months had driven the promise from my mind, but as, this morning, I pictured our own projected emigration, my thoughts turned to my distant friend, and my broken promise came back to me. I determined that on the first opportunity I would make amends for my neglect.

Ferns, many of them scarce ones, grew plentifully in our pleasant country; but on the road that Walter must take on his way to the station they flourished in unusual abundance. I could obtain many varieties close at hand, but some few grew further off; so, I asked Walter, if he should chance to meet with any specimens of these particular sorts, to pick a frond or two, which he could place between the leaves of the book he carried. I wanted, especially, a specimen of the Northern Shield Fern, which even here is not very common, growing as it does in little patches, sometimes miles apart. He laughed at my idle request, but promised to attend to it.

The day wore on, and the sun got low. It was time to send the dog-cart to meet the train. Long, long before the time had elapsed in which, by any chance, it could return, I was waiting' at the window to welcome Walter home again. I waited and waited, until so many weary minutes crawled away that I was fain to conclude he had been detained in Bristol until the next and last train.

I nursed my disappointment, and killed the time as best I could. The hour when I might surely expect him came and passed. The train must be late. I opened the window, and waited and listened for the sound of his coming.

At last, I heard the ring of the horse's hoofs, and saw the approaching dog-cart dimly, by the light of the stars. I ran to the door, eager to greet my husband; but, as the horse drew up on the gravel, I could see only one figure in the dogcart—that of James, our groom. He told me that his master had come by neither train, so, after waiting, he had driven back alone.

I turned away, very miserable and sad at heart, but, strange to say, felt no fear of evil. Business had, of course, detained him. It seemed unkind not to have let me know in some way, but perhaps he could find no means of doing so. There was not the slightest chance of his returning tonight, the distance being far too great for driving. I must wait until tomorrow.

It was only when I went to bed—alone, for almost the first time since we were married—that fear fell upon me, and fancy brought horrid ideas to my mind—that the possibility of evil having befallen my husband came to me. The large sum of money he carried, the lonely road, the black-faced colliers about the neighbourhood—all combined to fill me with a nameless dread—a terror which I could scarcely put into thoughts, much less into words. Yet I strove with my fears, trying to strangle each one as it was born.

'I shall see him tomorrow. Tomorrow I shall see him.' I repeated over and over again; and as that morning at last dawned, I fell into a restless sleep.

But morning brought him not: noon brought him not— neither letter nor message. So, my heart died within me; and taking a maid with me, I started for Bristol by the afternoon train. It was Sunday: the streets of the large town looked dreary and deserted as we passed through them. Knowing Mr. Leach's private address, we drove straight to his house. After some delay I was shown into a room.

By-and-by Mr. Leach entered, with his fat forefinger closed in a book of sermons which, I felt instinctively, he had been engaged in reading for the benefit of his young vultures. His smooth face was full of gentle astonishment that anyone should wish to confer with him on business matters on that particular evening in the week. As I looked at him and read through his mask of hypocrisy, I knew that the man was a rogue and capable of committing any crime. When he saw who his visitor was, his astonished look changed to one of annoyance. He closed his book entirely, laying it on the table with the edifying title turned towards me.

It seems childish to mention such trivial incidents; but during that terrible time every word, every detail, seems graven upon my memory in deep lines that will never be effaced.

'I have called, Mr. Leach 'I began.

'My dear Mrs. Linton, I know why you have called. But I am sorry to be obliged to say that your errand is useless—utterly useless. Mr. Linton made a promise he has not kept. He cannot blame us for the steps we have taken.'

'A promise not kept?' I echoed.

'Certainly not. He undertook to pay us a large sum of money yesterday' He has not been near us—I conclude he is ill,' he added, with an approach to a sneer.

I sank back in the wildest grief. Then, all my fears of the night, all my forebodings. of the day, were true! I knew that never—never again should I look on Walter's face. He had been murdered—but by whom?

Mr. Leach endeavoured, after the manner of his kind, to comfort me. He placed his fat hand in a soothing way upon my arm. This action restored my senses to me.

'My husband left me only yesterday morning with the money you claim in his pocket. I know it for certain. He was going straight to you. Where is he? Tell me!'

Mr. Leach gave a start of surprise, but said nothing. I waited for his answer.

'Where is he?' I reiterated. 'Tell me!' Mr. Leach placed his fingertips together, and looked at me with an expression almost like placid amusement.

'Mrs. Linton. he said slowly, 'I am a man of business, and have seen strange things in my time, so you mustn't be, offended if I ask you a question. Mr. Linton had the money ready for us, you say. In what form was it?'

'In notes, sir,' I replied. 'He told me you declined taking anything else.'

'Yes, yes—except gold. So, we did. We are bound to be careful. Now, Mrs. Linton—mind, I mean no offence—do you know that your husband was much embarrassed?'

'I know he could pay all just debts—and unjust ones, too,' I answered, with rising indignation.

'Yes, of course. All just and unjust debts. All unjust debts—very good. Now, do you think it possible—ten thousand is a lot of money—do you think it possible that Mr. Linton may have—well, in plain English, decamped with it?'

I heard no more. My face was flaming. I rose and, without another word, left the room. I was in the cab before Mr. Leach had recovered from his surprise, and in another minute was sobbing my poor heart out on the shoulder of my maid—a faithful, good girl who loved me.

I cannot tell you of the next few days. The uncertainty of everything, yet, to me, the utter hopelessness. The dread of what any moment might make known to me. The searchers searching and hoping to find—what? For I knew that the success of their quest could only bring me the dead body of my darling— murdered, perhaps, for the sake of the money he carried. Yet hardest of all to bear was the knowledge that the sorrow manifested by those around me was only assumed out of respect to me; that no one believed Walter to be dead;

that the wicked, cruel slander which had framed itself in Mr. Leach's mind had entered into the minds of others. I could read the thought in the faces of all who came near me during those days. I knew that the paid seekers performed their task with a smile on their lips—that the word went round among them that, in order to be successful, the search should be, not for a dead, but for a living man, to find whom it was needful to look farther away. How was it I did not go mad?

I cared nothing when someone told me that the property, house, and all were advertised for sale in a few weeks' time. I thought of nothing, saw nothing but the cold, still face of the one I loved. I wished for nothing now but to see his name cleared from the stain thrown upon it—a stain he would have heeded more than death; this done, I wished to die—that was all. The wild thought which had at first entered my head, that the men to whom he owed the money had taken it and made away with him, was at last dispelled; for proof was positive that Walter had not gone to Bristol on that fatal morning: The passengers from the station were too few, and Walter too well known not to have been noticed.

Indeed, no ticket for the class by which he would certainly have travelled had been issued that day. No one had met him that morning, and he had disappeared without leaving a trace; for people told me that every inch of the country near had been scoured.

But I knew they deceived me, and that the wicked thought was in every hearty although no one dared to speak it in words to me, who knew him and loved him.

Mr. Mainwaring, whom I had almost forgotten in my grief, came down in the course of a few days. Unfit as I was for business, I was compelled to see him. The kind old man was in great distress and anxiety, but he was very good to me. He started when he saw that I had already put on mourning.

'It is dreadful,' he said, with tears in his eyes, and taking both my hands in his. 'Not that I care for the money so much—although, of course, I must make up any deficiency myself, having been guilty of such an irregularity. It is dreadful to think that I, who tried to help Walter, must now strip his wife and children of their last shilling. I trusted him so that I let him have my client's agony simply on his note-of-hand, bearing, of course, all responsibility myself. It was most irregular; but he was so urgent, and I wanted to help him. Poor girl! I will do what I can for you, but I am afraid it can be but little.'

I begged him not to think of us, and thanked him again and again for his great kindness.

'I would, if only in my own interests, pay the money again and stop the sale; but no one has the power to mortgage the property to me. We do not even know that Walter is dead. It cannot, cannot be true, what everyone seems to hint at?' he added, almost shamefacedly.

I burst into a flood of tears and almost fell at his feet.

'Not you, Mr. Mainwaring! Not you!' I sobbed out 'You, who knew him, and knew that dishonour was not in him! Let me think that one, at least, believes in my dead love. Would to God, for my sake, it were as people think, so that I might someday see him again.'

The kind old friend raised me.

'No,' he said; 'I don't believe it I have known him from a boy, and I knew his father before him. They lie who say Walter Linton could have done such a thing. But it is all very, very dreadful.'

Mr. Mainwaring slept at Draycot Half that night, but I could not bring myself to spend the evening in his company. We could but think or speak of one subject, and I felt I had no right to inflict my grief upon him. I should be better alone. I watched the children sink to sleep, and for some hours sat by their little white beds listening to their regular breathing. Then I kissed them all gently and very quickly, lest my hot tears, falling on their upturned faces, should awake them; and, near midnight, retired to what with me would wrongly be called rest I locked the door of my room, undressed myself, and sat in my dressing-gown over the fire; for the night being damp and cold, my good maid had kindled a fire for me.

And there I sat, not seeking rest. I knew that sleep and I must strangers be for hours r that not until my strength was quite worn out would sad thoughts cease and change to sadder dreams: not till at last from sheer fatigue they fell, would weary eyelids curtail tearful eyes. And so, I sat, till slowly died the fire, and morning air stole chilly through the room—thinking of all the joy and. sweetness life so lately promised, all it gave me now. It seemed so hard to lose the one I loved—lost, as it were, in darkest night, with none to say where he had wandered.

'Oh,' I cried, 'if I could see you once and say farewell, although your words came but from dying lips! I should not grieve so much, and for the sake of children dear to both might live, and even not go mad.'

The wind had risen with the night, and gusts now and again bore heavy rain that beat against my window; whilst the tall trees round moaned as the gale went tearing through their boughs. The world seemed full of dismal sounds and grief, and I the saddest in the world. At last sleep conquered sorrow, so I threw myself down on the bed and slept. How long it was I slept I cannot tell, for all the while I seemed awake and seeing fearful sights. Cruel voices whispered words that stabbed my heart, so that in dreams I longed for wakefulness. Then I awoke and heard the wind and rain, louder and fiercer, whilst the room looked strange, as morning dawned in cheerless grey, and crept in through the half turned blind.

I felt dazed. For a moment I could scarcely realize where I was, or quite recall what had happened. I even turned, from force of habit, to see if Walter, who should be by my side, was also awake. Then, as I saw the vacant pillow by mine, all came back to me—came back with such a reflux of sorrow, that, in my despair, I threw out my arms, and sobbing bitterly, called on the one who could not hear me. My right hand lay as it had fallen, outside the coverlid, and, in a minute, I almost shrieked with horror and alarm; for I felt another hand seek it, touch it; and I experienced the sensation of fingers closing round my own. Hastily I tore my hand away from that clasp—if what held without restraining, made itself distinctly felt without offering resistance, can be called a clasp—and sprang from the bed.

Courageous as I am by nature, I trembled like a leaf, and had it been dark when that unknown hand sought mine, my horror must have vented itself in screams. But the room was nearly light; so, in a few moments I conquered that overpowering fright, and looked around for the intruder. I peered into every nook in which one might possibly hide, but detected no one. The door was as firmly locked as I left it. I was alone, for no one could have entered either by door or window.

Then I sat down and reasoned with myself on my folly. It was fancy from a mind upset and overwrought with grief It was the lingering impression left by one of those dreams—those dreadful dreams which sleep had brought me! It was a pure delusion, a creation of my own, and I wondered if, as I feared at times, I was going out of my senses.

Although, I was able to persuade myself that this reasoning was correct, I dared not return to my bed, but, sitting once more in my chair, longed for broad daylight. My thoughts soon wandered away from my recent fright, and took that path which they always followed. My arm dropped to my side, and my fingers relaxed themselves. And then, once more, I felt that hand creep to mine, take it, and hold it. Again, I felt the unmistakable sensation of fingers that closed round mine. I felt that there was no hand in mine that my hand could clasp in return, but the sensation of a palm against my palm—fingers twining my fingers—was indisputable. The sensation of pressure was there—faintly, it is true, but it was there. It was no fancy, no dream, this time. Whether mortal or not, a hand, or the semblance of a hand, was holding mine. Again, the horror overcame me, again I strove to tear my hand away from this invisible clasp.

My blood curdled as I found the result of my efforts failed on this second occasion—found that the fingers which fastened on my own could not be shaken off, do what I would. As I moved my hand, even so the band that held it moved with it. If I clenched my own, I could yet feel the strange pressure of those unseen fingers. If I grasped my right hand in my left, there was still the sensation of another hand between my own. Do what I would, move how I would, that clasp, or phantom of a clasp, was ever on my hand.

Yet I struggled with fear until the awful thought flashed through my brain that this was the aura, the forerunner of paralysis or epilepsy. Then I could bear it no longer. Whether that grasp was the result of bodily or mental ailment, I could bear it no longer—I felt my mind was going. I rushed to the door, tore it open, and my screams rang through the house—Remember, I was but a woman, and alone.

As the sound of hurrying feet drew near, that hand or hand-clasp lying on my own quitted it. Then, as the strange sensation ceased, did I hear a mournful sound, like a sigh, or was it only the wind outside? Did the phantom fingers draw themselves away from mine soothingly, even, it seemed, reluctantly, or was that fancy too? As the servants with frightened looks drew near me, could that wild and joyful thought that flashed through my brain be more than the thought of a madwoman? What could it mean?

Except for this I was myself again. I had been frightened, I told all who came to me—frightened by dreams, by shadows, by solitude, and my own thoughts. No one wondered at it; what flesh and blood could stand, unmoved, the anxiety I had borne during the last week?

I was overwrought and suffering from sleeplessness, so Mr. Mainwaring insisted upon giving me an opiate. I swallowed it reluctantly, and my maid sat with me, until, in due time, dull sleep told of the potency and efficacy of the drug which I had been made to take.

This artificial sleep lasted without a break until late in the afternoon. Then I awoke refreshed, and in full possession of my senses. I arose and prayed, as I had never prayed before, that my hand might again feel that unseen touch which had nearly driven me mad in the night. 'Will it come again? O, let it come again! was the constant cry of my heart; and I longed ardently for the night, which, perhaps, might bring that hand seeking my own again. For, incredible as it seems, I knew, when those fingers last left mine, that love had in part conquered death—that Walter had been with me. Now I feared nothing. Why should I fear? He had loved me living—he loved me now. Whether he came to me in body or in spirit, should he not be welcome? Oh, that he might come again!

And he came again. Mr. Mainwaring, who would not leave Draycot that day on account of the apparently strange state of my health, that evening insisted upon my taking a turn in the garden. I obeyed him, although every plant, every blossom around, seemed breathing sadness. I was too tired to walk for longer than a few minutes, but sat on my favourite seat, and watched the sun sink behind the hills. Even then and there—in broad daylight—I felt his hand seek my own, and my heart leapt with joy. I shunned or strove to avoid it no longer.

I let my hand lie still, and again I felt the touch, or the spirit of the touch, of the one I loved. So naturally those fingers closed round mine; so familiar seemed that clasps to me, that could I have forgotten the last week, I might have closed my eyes, and, lying there with my hand in his, have thought I had only to open them to happiness once more. If I could but forget!

Even if I had not known in whose hand mine was resting, the caress those fingers gave me would have told me. I wondered why I feared and repulsed them at first If only I could sometimes sit as I sat then, and know and feel that Walter was beside me, I thought that life might even be happy. So, I turned my head towards him, and said, softly—so softly:

'Dearest love, you will come often and often, will you not? You will be always, with me; then I shall not be unhappy.'

He answered not, but I felt a change in the clasp of his hand, and I pondered as to what its meaning could be. Then I fancied that faintly, very faintly, that touch was endeavouring to make me understand something which my grosser earthly faculties failed to grasp—to direct, to lead me somewhere for some purpose. For it left me and came again, left and came again, till at last I learnt its meaning.

Then and there I rose. 'I come, my love,' I said. And once more Walter Linton and his wife walked, as they had walked many a time before, hand-in-hand down the broad garden path; past the rustic lodge, covered with rosebuds and woodbine; through the gateway; out into the high road. I feared nothing: the hand of the one I loved was in mine, and guiding me whither he chose; moreover, it was yet daylight, and I was not dreaming.

I even knew that Mr. Mainwaring followed us as we walked down the path. I saw him come to my side and look at me with wonder, I wanted no one to be near my husband and myself, so I waved him back imperiously. 'Follow if you like. I said, 'but do not speak to us.' Perhaps he thought I was mad, perhaps that I was walking in my sleep, and, if so, feared to awake me. Any way, he followed us silently, and that was all I knew or cared about him, or about anything else. For were not my love and I walking, once more, hand-in-hand, and it was not in a dream?

Along and along the road, each side of which is beautiful with its green banks and hedges, and every inch of which we know, even keeping to that side we always choose because the flowers grow thickest there. How fresh and green everything looks this evening! The swallows are flying here and there. Every blade of grass is washed clean from dust by the heavy rain of the morning. No. I am not dreaming. I am walking with my husband. A nightingale breaks into song near us, as we walk. We stop—who could help stopping to listen? Now its melody ceases, and Walter leads me on. It is like in the old days when we were first wed; before we thought or wished for more wealth. Those days when all the country round was fresh and new to me.

Never did the wild-flowers, I think, look gayer than they look this evening, although they are closing fast. I would stop, my darling, and gather a bunch for the children; but they have so many flowers at home, and I fear to loose your hand for a moment Besides, you wish to lead me further yet; we have somewhere to go to this evening. I forget whither it was you told me, Walter. Is it to the lily-pond, to see if we can find any snow-white cups floating, buoyed up by the broad green leaves? Is it to climb the hill that lies in front of us, and see the very last of the glorious sun; to catch the crimson sparkle of its rays on the distant windows of our dear home?

That sun which will rise tomorrow, and waken us both so early— for you will never leave me again, Walter—promise me, my darling—I have been so unhappy. Is it further yet? To the ruins of the grey old abbey where the poet's ivy grows so freely? Shall we wait there, as once before, and see the full moon shine through the rose of the east windows? Shall we wander arm-in-arm through the dim shades, laughing at the foolish monks who chose to live and die there, knowing not love, nor the sweetness of life when two share its joys. and troubles?

But our troubles are over now, are they not, dearest? No matter, lead me whither you will: I care not—you are with me, your hand is in mine, and I am happy. But wherever we go, we will walk back by moonlight, and, then creep up quietly and kiss the children just once before we go to bed. Tomorrow we will wake and love again. No, I am not dreaming. But why do you not speak to me and tell me where you have been—why you left me so long? Oh, how I have wept and waited for you! Dearest, you will never leave me again?

This is the spot you wished to lead me to—the place where the ferns grow? Ah, you remembered what I wanted. Are there any of that sort up there? Let us go and see, although the day is flying fast. Through the hazel bushes—deep, deep into the underwood—on and on—up and up—brambles and stones I did not know it was so steep here. Hold my hand firmer and help me. More bushes, more under-growth; and how the twilight fades! My darling, we shall find no ferns tonight. May we not go back and come again tomorrow?

Yet, on and on! Love, where you lead, I follow and fear not! Is not your hand in mine, and you will never leave me again! Still on! My darling, you have brought me to the very edge of a rock! Don't leave me here! Don't draw your hand from mine! Stay one minute—one moment longer! I cannot see you; it is dark and cold! I cannot feel you, and the world seems filling again with grief. Come back! Come back! Walter! Walter!

★★★★★★★★★★★★★★★★

They told me I dreamed it—that I walked in my sleep. Clever and learned men said so, and I am only a woman, neither clever nor learned. Mr. Mainwaring, who had with great difficulty followed us—for I say 'us', in spite of all that wisdom can urge—found me lying life-less at the brink of the rocky depth to which Walter had led me, and where he had left me. Down below me lay something that I, thank God, never saw. They bore it home and told me it was all that was left of Walter Linton, my husband. But I knew better, for had he not that evening walked hand in hand with me for miles?

They told me, also, that he had fallen from the top of the rock—that it was not a great height, but high enough for the fall to kill him instantaneously—that most likely he was led to that fatal place, seek-ing some rare plant; as a root and withered leaves were clenched in his hand—that the notes he had placed in his pocket when he left his home were still there—that Draycot was still mine and his children's. But they believe me not when I tell them that my love, my husband, through the power of the love he bore me, could come from the dead—could take my hand in his and lead me with him, on and on, till he showed me where and how he died—till he saved those he loved from utter ruin and a life of penury—till, more than all, he cleared his own dear memory from stain and dishonour. Yet these things were!

The Deserted House

Ernst Theodor Amadeus Hoffmann

They were all agreed in the belief that the actual facts of life are often far more wonderful than the invention of even the liveliest imagination can be.

"It seems to me," spoke Lelio," that history gives proof sufficient of this. And that is why the so-called historical romances seem so repulsive and tasteless to us, those stories wherein the author mingles the foolish fancies of his meagre brain with the deeds of the great powers of the universe."

Franz took the word. "It is the deep reality of the inscrutable secrets surrounding us that oppresses us with a might wherein we recognise the Spirit that rules, the Spirit out of which our being springs."

"Alas," said Lelio, "it is the most terrible result of the fall of man, that we have lost the power of recognising the eternal verities."

"Many are called, but few are chosen," broke in Franz. "Do you not believe that an understanding of the wonders of our existence is given to some of us in the form of another sense? But if you would allow me to drag the conversation up from the dark regions where we are in danger of losing our path altogether up into the brightness of light-hearted merriment, I would like to make the scurrilous suggestion that those mortals to whom this gift of seeing the Unseen has been given remind me of bats. You know the learned anatomist Spallanzani has discovered a sixth sense in those little animals which can do not only the entire work of other senses, but work of his own besides."

"Oho," laughed Edward, "according to that, the bats would be the only natural-born clairvoyants. But I know someone who possesses that gift of insight, of which you were speaking, in a remarkable degree. Because of it he will often follow for days some unknown person who has happened to attract his attention by an oddity in manner, appearance, or garb; he will ponder to melancholy over some trifling incident, some lightly told story; he will combine the antipodes and raise up relationships in his imagination which are unknown to everyone else."

"Wait a bit," cried Lelio. "It is our Theodor of whom you are speaking now. And it looks to me as if he were having some weird vision at this very moment. See how strangely he gazes out into the distance."

Theodor had been sitting in silence up to this moment. Now he spoke: "If my glances are strange, it is because they reflect the strange things that were called up before my vision by your conversation, the memories of a most remarkable adventure."

"Oh, do tell us," interrupted his friends.

"Gladly," continued Theodor. "But first, let me set right a slight confound in your ideas on the subject of the mysterious. You appear to be confusing what is merely odd and what unusual with what is really mysterious or marvellous; that which surpasses comprehension or belief. The odd and the unusual, it is true, spring often from the truly marvellous, and the twigs and flowers hide the parent stem from our eyes. Both the odd and the unusual and truly marvellous are mingled in the adventure which I am about to narrate to you, mingled in a manner which is striking and even awesome."

With these words Theodor drew from his pocket a notebook in which, as his friends knew, he had written down the impressions of his late journeyings. Refreshing his memory by a look at its pages now and then, he narrated the following story:

★★★★★★★★★★★★★★★★★

You know already that I spent the greater part of last summer in X——, began Theodore. The many old friends and acquaintances I found there, the free, jovial life, the manifold artistic and intellectual interests—all these combined to keep me in that city. I was happy as never before, and found rich nourishment for my old fondness for wandering alone through the streets, stopping to enjoy every picture in the shop windows, every placard on the walls, or watching the passers-by and choosing some one or the other of them to cast his horoscope secretly to myself.

There is one broad avenue leading to the —— Gate and lined with handsome buildings of all descriptions, which is the meeting place of the rich and fashionable world. The shops which occupy the ground floor of the tall palaces are devoted to the trade in articles of luxury, and the apartments above are the dwellings of people of wealth and position. The aristocratic hotels are to be found in this avenue, the palaces of the foreign ambassadors are there, and you can easily imagine that such a street would be the centre of the city's life and gaiety.

I had wandered through the avenue several tunes, when one day my attention was caught by a house which contrasted strangely with the others surrounding it. Picture to yourselves a low building but four windows broad, crowded in between two tall, handsome structures. Its one upper storey was a little higher than the tops of the ground-floor windows of its neighbours, its roof was dilapidated, its windows patched with paper, its discoloured walls spoke of years of neglect. You can imagine how strange such a house must have looked in this street of wealth and fashion.

Looking at it more attentively I perceived that the windows of the upper storey were tightly closed and curtained, and that a wall had been built to hide the windows of the ground floor. The entrance gate, a little to one side, served also as a doorway for the building, but I could find no sign of latch, lock, or even a bell on this gate. I was convinced that the house must be unoccupied, for at whatever hour of the day I happened to be passing I had never seen the faintest signs of life about it. An unoccupied house in this avenue was indeed an odd sight.

But I explained the phenomenon to myself by saying that the owner was doubtless absent upon a long journey, or living upon his country estates, and that he perhaps did not wish to sell or rent the property, preferring to keep it for his own use in the eventuality of a visit to the city.

You all, the good comrades of my youth, know that I have been prone to consider myself a sort of clairvoyant, claiming to have glimpses of a strange world of wonders, a world which you, with your hard common sense, would attempt to deny or laugh away. I confess that I have often lost myself in mysteries which after all turned out to be no mysteries at all. And it looked at first as if this was to happen to me in the matter of the deserted house, that strange house which drew my steps and my thoughts to itself with a power that surprised me. But the point of my story will prove to you that I am right in asserting that I know more than you do. Listen now to what I am about to tell you.

One day, at the hour in which the fashionable world is accustomed to promenade up and down the avenue, I stood as usual before the deserted house, lost in thought. Suddenly I felt, without looking up, that someone had stopped beside me, fixing his eyes on me. It was Count P——, who told me that the old house contained nothing more mysterious than a cake bakery belonging to the pastrycook whose handsome shop adjoined the old structure. The windows of the ground floor were walled up to give protection to the ovens, and the heavy curtains of the upper storey were to keep the sunlight from the wares laid out there.

When the count informed me of this I felt as if a bucket of cold water had been suddenly thrown over me. But I could not believe in this story of the cake and candy factory. Through some strange freak of the imagination, I felt as a child feels when some fairy tale has been told it to conceal the truth it suspects. I scolded myself for a silly fool; the house remained unaltered in its appearance, and the visions faded in my brain, until one day a chance incident woke them to life again.

I was wandering through the avenue as usual, and as I passed the deserted house, I could not resist a hasty glance at its close-curtained upper windows. But as I looked at it, the curtain on the last window near the pastry shop began to move. A hand, an arm, came out from between its folds. I took my opera glass from my pocket and saw a beautifully formed woman's hand, on the little finger of which a large diamond sparkled in unusual brilliancy; a rich bracelet glittered on the white, rounded arm. The hand set a tall, oddly formed crystal bottle on the window ledge and disappeared again behind the curtain.

I stopped as if frozen to stone; a weirdly pleasurable sensation, mingled with awe, streamed through my being with the warmth of an electric current. I stared up at the mysterious window and a sigh of longing arose from the very depths of my heart. When I came to myself again, I was angered to find that I was surrounded by a crowd which stood gazing up at the window with curious faces. I stole away inconspicuously, and the demon of all things prosaic whispered to me that what I had just seen was the rich pastrycook's wife, in her Sunday adornment, placing an empty bottle, used for rose-water or the like, on the window sill. Nothing very weird about this.

Suddenly a most sensible thought came to me. I turned and entered the shining, mirror-walled shop of the pastrycook. Blowing the steaming foam from my cup of chocolate, I remarked: "You have a very useful addition to your establishment next door." The man leaned over his counter and looked at me with a questioning smile, as if he did not understand me. I repeated that in my opinion he had been very clever to set his bakery in the neighbouring house, although the deserted appearance of the building was a strange sight in its contrasting surroundings.

"Why, sir," began the pastrycook, "who told you that the house next door belongs to us? Unfortunately, every attempt on our part to acquire it has been in vain, and I fancy it is all the better so, for there is something queer about the place."

You can imagine, dear friends, how interested I became upon hearing these words, and that I begged the man to tell me more about the house.

"I do not know anything very definite, sir," he said. "All that we know for a certainty is that the house belongs to the Countess S——, who lives on her estates and has not been to the city for years. This house, so they tell me, stood in its present shape before any of the handsome buildings were raised which are now the pride of our avenue, and in all these years there has been nothing done to it except to keep it from actual decay. Two living creatures alone dwell there, an aged misanthrope of a steward and his melancholy dog, which occasionally howls at the moon from the back courtyard.

"According to the general story the deserted house is haunted. In very truth my brother, who is the owner of this shop, and myself have often, when our business kept us awake during the silence of the night, heard strange sounds from the other side of the walls. There was a rumbling and a scraping that frightened us both. And not very long ago we heard one night a strange singing which I could not describe to you. It was evidently the voice of an old woman, but the tones were so sharp and clear, and ran up to the top of the scale in cadences and long trills, the like of which I have never heard before, although I have heard many singers in many lands.

"It seemed to be a French song, but I am not quite sure of that, for I could not listen long to the mad, ghostly singing, it made the hair stand erect on my head. And at times, after the street noises are quiet, we can hear deep sighs, and sometimes a mad laugh, which seem to come out of the earth. But if you lay your ear to the wall in our back room, you can hear that the noises come from the house next door."

He led me into the back room and pointed through the window. "And do you see that iron chimney coming out of the wall there? It smokes so heavily sometimes, even in summer when there are no fires used, that my brother has often quarrelled with the old steward about it, fearing danger. But the old man excuses himself by saying that he was cooking his food. Heaven knows what the queer creature may eat, for often, when the pipe is smoking heavily, a strange and queer smell can be smelled all over the house."

The glass doors of the shop creaked in opening. The pastrycook hurried into the front room, and when he had nodded to the figure now entering, he threw a meaning glance at me. I understood him perfectly. Who else could this strange guest be, but the steward who had charge of the mysterious house! Imagine a thin little man with a face the colour of a mummy, with a sharp nose, tight-set lips, green cat's eyes, and a crazy smile; his hair dressed in the old-fashioned style with a high toupee and a bag at the back, and heavily powdered. He wore a faded old brown coat which was carefully brushed, grey stockings, and broad, flat-toed shoes with buckles.

And imagine further, that in spite of his meagreness this little person is robustly built, with huge fists and long, strong fingers, and that he walks to the shop counter with a strong, firm step, smiling his imbecile smile, and whining out: "A couple of candied oranges—a couple of macaroons—a couple of sugared chestnuts."

The pastrycook smiled at me and then spoke to the old man. "You do not seem to be quite well. Yes, yes, old age, old age! It takes the strength from our limbs." The old man's expression did not change, but his voice went up: "Old age?—Old age?—Lose strength?—Grow weak?—Oho!" And with this he clapped his hands together until the joints cracked, and sprang high up into the air until the entire shop trembled and the glass vessels on the walls and counters rattled and shook. But in the same moment a hideous screaming was heard; the old man had stepped on his black dog, which, creeping in behind him, had laid itself at his feet on the floor, "Devilish beast—dog of hell!" groaned the old man in his former miserable tone, opening his bag and giving the dog a large macaroon.

The dog, which had burst out into a cry of distress that was truly human, was quiet at once, sat down on its haunches, and gnawed at the macaroon like a squirrel. When it had finished its titbit, the old man had also finished the packing up and putting away of his purchases. "Goodnight, honoured neighbour," he spoke, taking the hand of the pastrycook and pressing it until the latter cried aloud in pain. "The weak old man wishes you a goodnight, most honourable Sir Neighbour," he repeated, and then walked from the shop, followed closely by his black dog. The old man did not seem to have noticed me at all. I was quite dumfounded in my astonishment.

"There, you see," began the pastrycook. "This is the way he acts when he comes in here, two or three times a month, it is. But I can get nothing out of him except the fact that he was a former valet of

Count S——, that he is now in charge of this house here, and that every day—for many years now—he expects the arrival of his master's family." The hour was now come when fashion demanded that the elegant world of the city should assemble in this attractive shop. The doors opened incessantly, the place was thronged, and I could ask no further questions.

This much I knew, that Count P——'s information about the ownership and the use of the house were not correct; also, that the old steward, in spite of his denial, was not living alone there, and that some mystery was hidden behind its discoloured walls. How could I combine the story of the strange and gruesome singing with the appearance of the beautiful arm at the window? That arm could not be part of the wrinkled body of an old woman; the singing, according to the pastrycook's story, could not come from the throat of a blooming and youthful maiden. I decided in favour of the arm, as it was easy to explain to myself that some trick of acoustics had made the voice sound sharp and old, or that it had appeared so only in the pastry-cook's fear-distorted imagination.

Then I thought of the smoke, the strange odours, the oddly formed crystal bottle that I had seen, and soon the vision of a beautiful creature held enthralled by fatal magic stood as if alive before my mental vision. The old man became a wizard who, perhaps quite independently of the family he served, had set up his devil's kitchen in the deserted house. My imagination had begun to work, and in my dreams that night I saw clearly the hand with the sparkling diamond on its finger, the arm with the shining bracelet. From out thin, grey mists there appeared a sweet face with sadly imploring blue eyes, then the entire exquisite figure of a beautiful girl. And I saw that what I had thought was mist was the fine steam flowing out in circles from a crystal bottle held in the hands of the vision.

"Oh, fairest creature of my dreams," I cried in rapture, "reveal to me where thou art, what it is that enthrals thee. Ah, I know it! It is black magic that holds thee captive—thou art the unhappy slave of that malicious devil who wanders about brown-clad and bewigged in pastry shops, scattering their wares with his unholy springing and feeding his demon dog on macaroons, after they have howled out a Satanic measure in five-eighth time. Oh, I know it all, thou fair and charming vision. The diamond is the reflection of the fire of thy heart. But that bracelet about thine arm is a link of the chain which the brown-clad one says is a magnetic chain. Do not believe it, O glorious

107

one! See how it shines in the blue fire from the retort. One moment more and thou art free. And now, O maiden, open thy rosebud mouth and tell me—" In this moment a gnarled fist leaped over my shoulder and clutched at the crystal bottle, which sprang into a thousand pieces in the air. With a faint, sad moan, the charming vision faded into the blackness of the night.

When morning came to put an end to my dreaming I hurried through the avenue, seeking the deserted house as usual and I saw something glistening in the last window of the upper storey. Coming nearer I noticed that the outer blind had been quite drawn up and the inner curtain slightly opened. The sparkle of a diamond met my eye. O kind Heaven! The face of my dream looked at me, gently imploring, from above the rounded arm on which her head was resting. But how was it possible to stand still in the moving crowd without attracting attention? Suddenly I caught sight of the benches placed in the gravel walk in the centre of the avenue, and I saw that one of them was directly opposite the house.

I sprang over to it, and leaning over its back, I could stare up at the mysterious window undisturbed. Yes, it was she, the charming maiden of my dream! But her eye did not seem to seek me as I had at first thought; her glance was cold and unfocused, and had it not been for an occasional motion of the hand and arm, I might have thought that I was looking at a cleverly painted picture.

I was so lost in my adoration of the mysterious being in the window, so aroused and excited throughout all my nerve centres, that I did not hear the shrill voice of an Italian street hawker, who had been offering me his wares for some time. Finally, he touched me on the arm; I turned hastily and commanded him to let me alone. But he did not cease his entreaties, asserting that he had earned nothing today, and begging me to buy some small trifle from him. Full of impatience to get rid of him I put my hand in my pocket. With the words: "I have more beautiful things here," he opened the under drawer of his box and held out to me a little, round pocket mirror. In it, as he held it up before my face, I could see the deserted house behind me, the window, and the sweet face of my vision there.

I bought the little mirror at once, for I saw that it would make it possible for me to sit comfortable and inconspicuously, and yet watch the window. The longer I looked at the reflection in the glass, the more I fell captive to a weird and quite indescribable sensation, which I might almost call a waking dream. It was as if a lethargy had lamed my eyes, holding them fastened on the glass beyond my power to loosen them. And now at last the beautiful eyes of the fair vision looked at me, her glance sought mine and shone deep down into my heart.

"You have a pretty little mirror there," said a voice beside me. I awoke from my dream, and was not a little confused when I saw smiling faces looking at me from either side. Several persons had sat down upon the bench, and it was quite certain that my staring into the window, and my probably strange expression, had afforded them great cause for amusement.

"You have a pretty little mirror there," repeated the man, as I did not answer him. His glance said more, and asked without words the reason of my staring so oddly into the little glass. He was an elderly man, neatly dressed, and his voice and eyes were so full of good nature that I could not refuse him my confidence. I told him that I had been looking in the mirror at the picture of a beautiful maiden who was sitting at a window of the deserted house. I went even farther; I asked the old man if he had not seen the fair face himself. "Over there? In the old house—in the last window" He repeated my questions in a tone of surprise.

"Yes, yes," I exclaimed.

The old man smiled and answered: "Well, well, that was a strange delusion. My old eyes—thank Heaven for my old eyes! Yes, yes, sir. I saw a pretty face in the window there, with my own eyes; but it seemed to me to be an excellently well-painted oil portrait."

I turned quickly and looked toward the window; there was no one there, and the blind had been pulled down. "Yes," continued the old man, "yes sir. Now it is too late to make sure of the matter, for just now the servant, who, as I know, lives there alone in the house of the Countess S——, took the picture away from the window after he had dusted it, and let down the blinds."

"Was it, then, surely a picture?" I asked again, in bewilderment.

"You can trust my eyes," replied the old man. "The optical delusion was strengthened by your seeing only the reflection in the mirror. And when I was in your years it was easy enough for my fancy to call up the picture of a beautiful maiden."

"But the hand and arm moved," I exclaimed. "Oh, yes, they moved, indeed they moved," said the old man smiling, as he patted me on the shoulder. Then he arose to go, and bowing politely, closed his remarks with the words, "Beware of mirrors which can lie so vividly. Your obedient servant, sir."

You can imagine how I felt when I saw that he looked upon me as a foolish fantast. I began to be convinced that the old man was right, and that it was only my absurd imagination which insisted on raising up mysteries about the deserted house.

I hurried home full of anger and disgust, and promised myself that I would not think of the mysterious house, and would not even walk through the avenue for several days. I kept my vow, spending my days working at my desk, and my evenings in the company of jovial friends, leaving myself no time to think of the mysteries which so enthralled me. And yet, it was just in these days that I would start up out of my sleep as if awakened by a touch, only to find that all that had aroused me was merely the *thought* of that mysterious being whom I had seen in my vision and in the window of the deserted house.

Even during my work, or in the midst of a lively conversation with my friends, I felt the same thought shoot through me like an electric current. I condemned the little mirror in which I had seen the charming picture to a prosaic daily use. But I placed the mirror on my dressing-table that I might bind my cravat before it, and thus it happened one day, when I was about to utilise it for this important business, that its glass seemed dull, and that I took it up and breathed on it to rub it bright again. My heart seemed to stand still, every fibre in me trembled in delightful awe.

Yes, that is all the name I can find for the feeling that come over me, when, as my breath clouded the little mirror, I saw the beautiful face of my dreams arise and smile at me through blue mists. You laugh at me? You look upon me as an incorrigible dreamer? Think what you will about it—the fair face looked at me from out of the mirror! But as soon as the clouding vanished, the face vanished in the brightened glass.

I will not weary you with a detailed recital of my sensations the next few days, I will only say that I repeated again the experiments with the mirror, sometimes with success, sometimes without. When I had not been able to call up the vision, I would run to the deserted house and stare up at the windows; but I saw no human being anywhere about the building. I lived only in thoughts of my vision; everything else seemed indifferent to me. I neglected my friends and my studies. The tortures in my soul passed over into, or rather mingled with, physical sensations which frightened me, and which at last made me fear for my reason.

One day, after an unusually severe attack, I put my little mirror in my pocket and hurried to the home of Dr. K——, who was noted for his treatment of those diseases of the mind out of which physical diseases so often grow. I told him my story; I did not conceal the slightest incident from him, and I implored him to save me from the terrible fate which seemed to threaten me. He listened to me quietly, but I read astonishment in his glance. Then he said: "The danger is not as near as you believe, and I think that I may say that it can be easily prevented. You are undergoing an unusual psychical disturbance, beyond a doubt.

"But the fact that you understand that some evil principle seems to be trying to influence you, gives you a weapon by which you can combat it. Leave your little mirror here with me, and force yourself to take up with some work which will afford scope for all your mental energy. Do not go to the avenue; work all day, from early to late, then take a long walk, and spend your evenings in the company of your friends. Eat heartily, and drink heavy, nourishing wines. You see I am endeavouring to combat your fixed idea of the face in the window of the deserted house and in the mirror, by diverting your mind to other things, and by strengthening your body. You yourself must help me in this."

I was very reluctant to part with my mirror. The physician, who had already taken it, seemed to notice my hesitation. He breathed upon the glass and holding it up to me, he asked: "Do you see anything?"

"Nothing at all," I answered, for so it was.

"Now breathe on the glass yourself," said the physician, laying the mirror in my hands.

I did as he requested. There was the vision even more clearly than ever before.

"There she is!" I cried aloud.

The physician looked into the glass, and then said: "I cannot see anything. But I will confess to you that when I looked into this glass, a queer shiver overcame me, passing away almost at once. Now do it once more."

I breathed upon the glass again and the physician laid his hand upon the back of my neck. The face appeared again, and the physician, looking into the mirror over my shoulder, turned pale. Then he took the little glass from my hands, looked at it attentively, and locked it into his desk, returning to me after a few moments' silent thought.

"Follow my instructions strictly," he said. "I must confess to you that I do not yet understand those moments of your vision. But I hope to be able to tell you more about it very soon."

Difficult as it was to me, I forced myself to live absolutely according to the doctor's orders. I soon felt the benefit of the steady work and the nourishing diet, and yet I was not free from those terrible attacks, which would come either at noon, or, more intensely still, at midnight. Even in the midst of a merry company, in the enjoyment of wine and song, glowing daggers seemed to pierce my heart, and all the strength of my intellect was powerless to resist their might over me. I was obliged to retire, and could not return to my friends until I had recovered from my condition of lethargy.

It was in one of these attacks, an unusually strong one, that such an irresistible, mad longing for the picture of my dreams came over me, that I hurried out into the street and ran toward the mysterious house. While still at a distance from it, I seemed to see lights shining out through the fast-closed blinds, but when I came nearer, I saw that all was dark. Crazy with my desire I rushed to the door; it fell back before the pressure of my hand. I stood in the dimly lighted vestibule, enveloped in a heavy, close atmosphere. My heart beat in strange fear and impatience.

Then suddenly a long, sharp tone, as from a woman's throat, shrilled through the house, I know not how it happened that I found myself suddenly in a great hall brilliantly lighted and furnished in old-fashioned magnificence of golden chairs and strange Japanese ornaments. Strongly perfumed incense arose in blue clouds about me. "Welcome—welcome, sweet bridegroom! the hour has come, our bridal hour!" I heard these words in a woman's voice, and as little as I can tell, how I came into the room, just so little do I know how it happened that suddenly a tall, youthful figure, richly dressed, seemed to arise from the blue mists. With the repeated shrill cry: "Welcome, sweet bridegroom!" she came toward me with outstretched arms— and a yellow face, distorted with age and madness, stared into mine!

I fell back in terror, but the fiery, piercing glance of her eyes, like the eyes of a snake, seemed to hold me spellbound. I did not seem able to turn my eyes from this terrible old woman, I could not move another step. She came still nearer, and it seemed to me suddenly as if her hideous face were only a thin mask, beneath which I saw the features of the beautiful maiden of my vision. Already I felt the touch of her hands, when suddenly she fell at my feet with a loud scream, and a voice behind me cried:

"Oho, is the devil playing his tricks with your grace again? To bed, to bed, Your Grace. Else there will be blows, mighty blows!"

I turned quickly and saw the old steward in his nightclothes, swinging a whip above his head. He was about to strike the screaming figure at my feet when I caught at his arm. But he shook me from him, exclaiming: "The devil, sir! That old Satan would have murdered you if I had not come to your aid. Get away from here at once!"

I rushed from the hall, and sought in vain in the darkness for the door of the house. Behind me I heard the hissing blows of the whip and the old woman's screams. I drew breath to call aloud for help, when suddenly the ground gave way under my feet; I fell down a short flight of stairs, bringing up with such force against a door at the bottom that it sprang open, and I measured my length on the floor of a small room. From the hastily vacated bed, and from the familiar brown coat hanging over a chair, I saw that I was in the bedchamber of the old steward.

There was a trampling on the stair, and the old man himself entered hastily, throwing himself at my feet. "By all the saints, sir," he entreated with folded hands, "whoever you may be, and however her grace, that old Satan of a witch has managed to entice you to this house, do not speak to any one of what has happened here. It will cost me my position. Her crazy excellency has been punished, and is bound fast in her bed. Sleep well, good sir, sleep softly and sweetly. It is a warm and beautiful July night. There is no moon, but the stars shine brightly. A quiet goodnight to you." While talking, the old man had taken up a lamp, had led me out of the basement, pushed me out of the house door, and locked it behind me.

I hurried home quite bewildered, and you can imagine that I was too much confused by the gruesome secret to be able to form any explanation of it in my own mind for the first few days. Only this much was certain, that I was now free from the evil spell that had held me captive so long. All my longing for the magic vision in the mirror had disappeared, and the memory of the scene in the deserted house was like the recollection of an unexpected visit to a madhouse. It was evident beyond a doubt that the steward was the tyrannical guardian of a crazy woman of noble birth, whose condition was to be hidden from the world. But the mirror? and all the other magic? Listen, and I will tell you more about it.

Some few days later I came upon Count P—— at an evening

entertainment. He drew me to one side and said, with a smile, "Do you know that the secrets of our deserted house are beginning to be revealed?" I listened with interest; but before the count could say more the doors of the dining-room were thrown open, and the company proceeded to the table. Quite lost in thought at the words I had just heard, I had given a young lady my arm, and had taken my place mechanically in the ceremonious procession.

I led my companion to the seats arranged for us, and then turned to look at her for the first time. The vision of my mirror stood before me, feature for feature, there was no deception possible! I trembled to my innermost heart, as you can imagine; but I discovered that there was not the slightest echo even, in my heart, of the mad desire which had ruled me so entirely when my breath drew out the magic picture from the glass.

My astonishment, or rather my terror, must have been apparent in my eyes. The girl looked at me in such surprise that I endeavoured to control myself sufficiently to remark that I must have met her somewhere before. Her short answer, to the effect that this could hardly be possible, as she had come to the city only yesterday for the first time in her life, bewildered me still more and threw me into an awkward silence. The sweet glance from her gentle eyes brought back my courage, and I began a tentative exploring of this new companion's mind. I found that I had before me a sweet and delicate being, suffering from some psychic trouble.

At a particularly merry turn of the conversation, when I would throw in a daring word like a dash of pepper, she would smile, but her smile was pained, as if a wound had been touched. "You are not very merry tonight, countess. Was it the visit this morning?" An officer sitting near us had spoken these words to my companion, but before he could finish his remarks his neighbour had grasped him by the arm and whispered something in his ear, while a lady at the other side of the table, with glowing cheeks and angry eyes, began to talk loudly of the opera she had heard last evening.

Tears came to the eyes of the girl sitting beside me. "Am I not foolish?" She turned to me. A few moments before she had complained of headache.

"Merely the usual evidences of a nervous headache," I answered in an easy tone, "and there is nothing better for it than the merry spirit which bubbles in the foam of this poet's nectar." With these words I filled her champagne glass, and she sipped at it as she threw me a look of gratitude. Her mood brightened, and all would have been well had I not touched a glass before me with unexpected strength, arousing from it a shrill, high tone. My companion grew deadly pale, and I myself felt a sudden shiver, for the sound had exactly the tone of the mad woman's voice in the deserted house.

While we were drinking coffee, I made an opportunity to get to the side of Count P——. He understood the reason for my movement. "Do you know that your neighbour is Countess Edwina S——? And do you know also that it is her mother's sister who lives in the deserted house, incurably mad for many years? This morning both mother and daughter went to see the unfortunate woman. The old steward, the only person who is able to control the countess in her outbreaks, is seriously ill, and they say that the sister has finally revealed the secret to Dr. K——. This eminent physician will endeavour to cure the patient, or if this is not possible, at least to prevent her terrible outbreaks of mania. This is all that I know yet."

Others joined us and we were obliged to change the subject. Dr. K—— was the physician to whom I had turned in my own anxiety, and you can well imagine that I hurried to him as soon as I was free, and told him all that had happened to me in the last days. I asked him to tell me as much as he could about the mad woman, for my own peace of mind; and this is what I learned from him under promise of secrecy.

"Angelica, Countess Z——," thus the doctor began, "had already passed her thirtieth year, but was still in full possession of great beauty, when Count S——, although much younger than she, became so fascinated by her charm that he wooed her with ardent devotion and followed her to her father's home to try his luck there. But scarcely had the count entered the house, scarcely had he caught sight of Angelica's younger sister, Gabrielle, when he awoke as from a dream. The elder sister appeared faded and colourless beside Gabrielle, whose beauty and charm so enthralled the count that he begged her hand of her father.

"Count Z—— gave his consent easily, as there was no doubt of Gabrielle's feelings toward her suitor. Angelica did not show the slightest anger at her lover's faithlessness. 'He believes that he has forsaken me, the foolish boy! He does not perceive that he was but my toy, a toy of which I had tired.' Thus, she spoke in proud scorn, and not a look or an action on her part belied her words. But after the ceremonious betrothal of Gabrielle to Count S——, Angelica was seldom seen by the members of her family. She did not appear at the dinner table, and it was said that she spent most of her time walking alone in the neighbouring wood.

"A strange occurrence disturbed the monotonous quiet of life in the castle. The hunters of Count Z——, assisted by peasants from the village, had captured a band of gipsies who were accused of several robberies and murders which had happened recently in the neighbourhood. The men were brought to the castle courtyard, fettered together on a long chain, while the women and children were packed on a cart. Noticeable among the last was a tall, haggard old woman of terrifying aspect, wrapped from head to foot in a red shawl. She stood upright in the cart, and in an imperious tone demanded that she should be allowed to descend. The guards were so awed by her manner and appearance that they obeyed her at once.

"Count Z—— came down to the courtyard and commanded that the gang should be placed in the prisons under the castle. Suddenly Countess Angelica rushed out of the door, her hair all loose, fear and anxiety in her pale face. Throwing herself on her knees, she cried in a piercing voice, 'Let these people go! Let these people go! They are innocent! Father, let these people go! If you shed one drop of their blood, I will pierce my heart with this knife!'

"The countess swung a shining knife in the air and then sank swooning to the ground. 'Yes, my beautiful darling—my golden child—I knew you would not let them hurt us,' shrilled the old woman in red. She cowered beside the countess and pressed disgusting kisses to her face and breast, murmuring crazy words. She took from out the recesses of her shawl a little vial in which a tiny goldfish seemed to swim in some silver-clear liquid. She held the vial to the countess's heart. The latter regained consciousness immediately. When her eyes fell on the gipsy woman, she sprang up, clasped the old creature ardently in her arms, and hurried with her into the castle.

"Count Z——, Gabrielle, and her, lover, who had come out during this scene, watched it in astonished awe. The gipsies appeared quite indifferent. They were loosed from their chains and taken separately to the prisons. Next morning Count Z—— called the villagers together. The gipsies were led before them and the count announced that he had found them to be innocent of the crimes of which they were accused, and that he would grant them free passage through his domains. To the astonishment of all present, their fetters were struck off and they were set at liberty. The red-shawled woman was not among them. It was whispered that the gipsy captain, recognisable from the golden chain about his neck and the red feather in his high Spanish hat, had paid a secret visit to the count's room the night before. But it was discovered, a short time after the release of the gipsies, that they were indeed guiltless of the robberies and murders that had disturbed the district.

"The date set for Gabrielle's wedding approached. One day, to her great astonishment, she saw several large wagons in the courtyard being packed high with furniture, clothing, linen, with everything necessary for a complete household outfit. The wagons were driven away, and the following day Count Z—— explained that, for many reasons, he had thought it best to grant Angelica's odd request that she be allowed to set up her own establishment in his house in X——. He had given the house to her, and had promised her that no member of the family, not even he himself should enter it without her express permission. He added also, that, at her urgent request, he had permitted his own valet to accompany her, to take charge of her household.

"When the wedding festivities were over, Count S—— and his bride departed for their home, where they spent a year in cloudless happiness. Then the count's health failed mysteriously. It was as if some secret sorrow gnawed at his vitals, robbing him of joy and strength. All efforts of his young wife to discover the source of his trouble were fruitless. At last, when the constantly recurring fainting spells threatened to endanger his very life, he yielded to the entreaties of his physicians and left his home, ostensibly for Pisa. His young wife was prevented from accompanying him by the delicate condition of her own health.

"And now," said the doctor, "the information given me by Countess S—— became, from this point on, so rhapsodical that a keen observer only could guess at the true coherence of the story. Her baby, a daughter, born during her husband's absence, was spirited away from the house, and all search for it was fruitless. Her grief at this loss deepened to despair, when she received a message from her father stating that her husband, whom all believed to be in Pisa, had been found dying of heart trouble in Angelica's home in X——, and that Angelica herself had become a dangerous maniac. The old count added that all this horror had so shaken his own nerves that he feared he would not long survive it.

"As soon as Gabrielle was able to leave her bed, she hurried to her father's castle. One night, prevented from sleeping by visions of the loved ones she had lost, she seemed to hear a faint crying, like that of an infant, before the door of her chamber. Lighting her candle, she opened the door. Great Heaven! there cowered the old gipsy woman, wrapped in her red shawl, staring up at her with eyes that seemed already glazing in death. In her arms she held a little child, whose crying had aroused the countess. Gabrielle's heart beat high with joy—it was her child—her lost daughter! She snatched the infant from the gipsy's arms, just as the woman fell at her feet lifeless. The countess's screams awoke the house, but the gipsy was quite dead and no effort to revive her met with success.

"The old count hurried to X—— to endeavour to discover something that would throw light upon the mysterious disappearance and reappearance of the child. Angelica's madness had frightened away all her female servants; the valet alone remained with her. She appeared at first to have become quite calm and sensible. But when the count told her the story of Gabrielle's child, she clapped her hands and laughed aloud, crying: 'Did the little darling arrive? You buried her you say? How the feathers of the gold pheasant shine in the sun! Have you seen the green lion with the fiery blue eyes?' Horrified the count perceived that Angelica's mind was gone beyond a doubt, and he resolved to take her back with him to his estates, in spite of the warnings of his old valet. At the mere suggestion of removing her from the house Angelica's ravings increased to such an extent as to endanger her own life and that of the others.

"When a lucid interval came again Angelica entreated her father, with many tears, to let her live and die in the house she had chosen. Touched by her terrible trouble he granted her request, although he believed the confession which slipped from her lips during this scene to be a fantasy of her madness. She told him that Count S—— had returned to her arms, and that the child which the gipsy had taken to her father's house was the fruit of their love. The rumour went abroad in the city that Count Z—— had taken the unfortunate woman to his home; but the truth was that she remained hidden in the deserted house under the care of the valet. Count Z—— died a short time ago, and Countess Gabrielle came here with her daughter Edwina to arrange some family affairs.

"It was not possible for her to avoid seeing her unfortunate sister. Strange things must have happened during this visit, but the countess has not confided anything to me, saying merely that she had found it necessary to take the mad woman away from the old valet. It had been discovered that he had controlled her outbreaks by means of force and physical cruelty; and that also, allured by Angelica's assertions that she could make gold, he had allowed himself to assist her in her weird operations.

"It would be quite unnecessary," thus the physician ended his story, "to say anything more to you about the deeper inward relationship of all these strange things. It is clear to my mind that it was you who brought about the catastrophe, a catastrophe which will mean recovery or speedy death for the sick woman. And now I will confess to you that I was not a little alarmed, horrified even, to discover that— when I had set myself in magnetic communication with you by placing my hand on your neck—I could see the picture in the mirror with my own eyes. We both know now that the reflection in the glass was the face of Countess Edwina."

I repeat Dr. K——'s words in saying that, to my mind also, there is no further comment that can be made on all these facts. I consider it equally unnecessary to discuss at any further length with you now the mysterious relationship between Angelica, Edwina, the old valet, and myself—a relationship which seemed the work of a malicious demon who was playing his tricks with us. I will add only that I left the city soon after all these events, driven from the place by an oppression I could not shake off. The uncanny sensation left me suddenly a month or so later, giving way to a feeling of intense relief that flowed through all my veins with the warmth of an electric current. I am convinced that this change within me came about in the moment when the mad woman died.

The Haunted Orchard

Richard Le Gallienne

Spring was once more in the world. As she sang to herself in the faraway woodlands her voice reached even the ears of the city, weary with the long winter. Daffodils flowered at the entrances to the Subway, furniture removing vans blocked the side streets, children clustered like blossoms on the doorsteps, the open cars were running, and the cry of the "cash clo'" man was once more heard in the land.

Yes, it was the spring, and the city dreamed wistfully of lilacs and the dewy piping of birds in gnarled old apple-trees, of dogwood lighting up with sudden silver the thickening woods, of water-plants unfolding their glossy scrolls in pools of morning freshness.

On Sunday mornings, the outbound trains were thronged with eager pilgrims, hastening out of the city, to behold once more the ancient marvel of the spring; and, on Sunday evenings, the railway termini were aflower with banners of blossom from rifled woodland and orchard carried in the hands of the returning pilgrims, whose eyes still shone with the spring magic, in whose ears still sang the fairy music.

And as I beheld these signs of the vernal equinox, I knew that I, too, must follow the music, forsake awhile the beautiful siren we call the city, and in the green silences meet once more my sweetheart Solitude.

As the train drew out of the Grand Central, I hummed to myself, "I've a neater, sweeter maiden, in a greener, cleaner land" and so, I said goodbye to the city, and went forth with beating heart to meet the spring.

I had been told of an almost forgotten corner on the south coast of Connecticut, where the spring and I could live in an inviolate loneliness—a place uninhabited save by birds and blossoms, woods and thick grass, and an occasional silent farmer, and pervaded by the breath and shimmer of the Sound.

Nor had rumour lied, for when the train set me down at my destination I stepped out into the most wonderful green hush, a leafy Sabbath silence through which the very train, as it went farther on its way, seemed to steal as noiselessly as possible for fear of breaking the spell.

After a winter in the town, to be dropped thus suddenly into the intense quiet of the country-side makes an almost ghostly impression upon one, as of an enchanted silence, a silence that listens and watches but never speaks, finger on lip. There is a spectral quality about everything upon which the eye falls: the woods, like great green clouds, the wayside flowers, the still farmhouses half lost in orchard bloom—all seem to exist in a dream.

Everything is so still, everything so supernaturally green. Nothing moves or talks, except the gentle susurrus of the spring wind swaying the young buds high up in the quiet sky, or a bird now and again, or a little brook singing softly to itself among the crowding rushes.

Though, from the houses one notes here and there, there are evidently human inhabitants of this green silence, none are to be seen. I have often wondered where the countryfolk hide themselves, as I have walked hour after hour, past farm and croft and lonely door-yards, and never caught sight of a human face. If you should want to ask the way, a farmer is as shy as a squirrel, and if you knock at a farmhouse door, all is as silent as a rabbit-warren.

As I walked along in the enchanted stillness, I came at length to a quaint old farmhouse—"old Colonial" in its architecture—embowered in white lilacs, and surrounded by an orchard of ancient apple-trees which cast a rich shade on the deep spring grass. The orchard had the impressiveness of those old religious groves, dedicated to the strange worship of sylvan gods, gods to be found now only in Horace or Catullus, and in the hearts of young poets to whom the beautiful antique Latin is still dear.

The old house seemed already the abode of Solitude. As I lifted the latch of the white gate and walked across the forgotten grass, and up on to the veranda already festooned with wistaria, and looked into the window, I saw Solitude sitting by an old piano, on which no composer later than Bach had ever been played.

In other words, the house was empty; and going round to the back, where old barns and stables leaned together as if falling asleep, I found a broken pane, and so climbed in and walked through the echoing rooms. The house was very lonely. Evidently no one had lived in it for a long time. Yet it was all ready for some occupant, for whom it seemed to be waiting. Quaint old four-poster bedsteads stood in three rooms—dimity curtains and spotless linen—old oak chests and mahogany presses; and, opening drawers in Chippendale sideboards, I came upon beautiful frail old silver and exquisite china that set me thinking of a beautiful grandmother of mine, made out of old lace and laughing wrinkles and mischievous old blue eyes.

There was one little room that particularly interested me, a tiny bedroom all white, and at the window the red roses were already in bud. But what caught my eye with peculiar sympathy was a small bookcase, in which were some twenty or thirty volumes, wearing the same forgotten expression—forgotten and yet cared for—which lay like a kind of memorial charm upon everything in the old house. Yes, everything seemed forgotten and yet everything, curiously—even religiously—remembered. I took out book after book from the shelves, once or twice flowers fell out from the pages—and I caught sight of a delicate handwriting here and there and frail markings.

It was evidently the little intimate library of a young girl. What surprised me most was to find that quite half the books were in French— French poets and French romancers: a charming, very rare edition of Ronsard, a beautifully printed edition of Alfred de Musset, and a copy of Théophile Gautier's *Mademoiselle de Maupin*. How did these exotic books come to be there alone in a deserted New England farmhouse?

This question was to be answered later in a strange way. Meanwhile I had fallen in love with the sad, old, silent place, and as I closed the white gate and was once more on the road, I looked about for someone who could tell me whether or not this house of ghosts might be rented for the summer by a comparatively living man.

I was referred to a fine old New England farmhouse shining white through the trees a quarter of a mile away. There I met an ancient couple, a typical New England farmer and his wife; the old man, lean, chin-bearded, with keen grey eyes flickering occasionally with a shrewd humour, the old lady with a kindly old face of the withered-apple type and ruddy. They were evidently prosperous people, but their minds—for some reason I could not at the moment divine— seemed to be divided between their New England desire to drive a hard bargain and their disinclination to let the house at all.

Over and over again they spoke of the loneliness of the place. They feared I would find it very lonely. No one had lived in it for a long time, and so on. It seemed to me that afterwards I understood their curious hesitation, but at the moment only regarded it as a part of the circuitous New England method of bargaining. At all events, the rent I offered finally overcame their disinclination, whatever its cause, and so I came into possession—for four months—of that silent old house, with the white lilacs, and the drowsy barns, and the old piano, and the strange orchard; and, as the summer came on, and the year changed its name from May to June, I used to lie under the apple-trees in the afternoons, dreamily reading some old book, and through half-sleepy eyelids watching the silken shimmer of the Sound.

I had lived in the old house for about a month, when one afternoon a strange thing happened to me. I remember the date well. It was the afternoon of Tuesday, June 13th. I was reading, or rather dipping here and there, in Burton's *Anatomy of Melancholy*. As I read, I remember that a little unripe apple, with a petal or two of blossom still clinging to it, fell upon the old yellow page. Then I suppose I must have fallen into a dream, though it seemed to me that both my eyes and my ears were wide open, for I suddenly became aware of a beautiful young voice singing very softly somewhere among the leaves. The singing was very frail, almost imperceptible, as though it came out of the air. It came and went fitfully, like the elusive fragrance of sweetbrier—as though a girl was walking to and fro, dreamily humming to herself in the still afternoon. Yet there was no one to be seen. The orchard had never seemed more lonely.

And another fact that struck me as strange was that the words that floated to me out of the aerial music were French, half sad, half gay snatches of some long-dead singer of old France, I looked about for the origin of the sweet sounds, but in vain. Could it be the birds that were singing in French in this strange orchard? Presently the voice seemed to come quite close to me, so near that it might have been the voice of a dryad singing to me out of the tree against which I was leaning. And this time I distinctly caught the words of the sad little song:

Chante, rossignol, chante,
Toi qui as le cœur gai;
Tu as le cœur à rire,
Moi, je l'ai-t-à pleurer.

But though the voice was at my shoulder, I could see no one, and then the singing stopped with what sounded like a sob; and a moment or two later I seemed to hear a sound of sobbing far down the orchard. Then there followed silence, and I was left to ponder on the strange occurrence. Naturally, I decided that it was just a day-dream between sleeping and waking over the pages of an old book; yet when next day and the day after the invisible singer was in the orchard again, I could not be satisfied with such mere matter-of-fact explanation.

A la claire fontaine

... .went the voice to and fro through the thick orchard boughs,

M'en allant promener,
J'ai trouvé l'eau si belle
Que je m'y suis baigné,
Lui y a longtemps que je t'aime,
Jamais je ne t'oubliai.

It was certainly uncanny to hear that voice going to and fro the orchard, there somewhere amid the bright sun-dazzled boughs—yet not a human creature to be seen—not another house even within half a mile. The most materialistic mind could hardly but conclude that here was something "not dreamed of in our philosophy." It seemed to me that the only reasonable explanation was the entirely irrational one—that my orchard was haunted: haunted by some beautiful young spirit, with some sorrow of lost joy that would not let her sleep quietly in her grave.

And next day I had a curious confirmation of my theory. Once more I was lying under my favourite apple-tree, half reading and half watching the Sound, lulled into a dream by the whir of insects and the spices called up from the earth by the hot sun. As I bent over the page, I suddenly had the startling impression that someone was leaning over my shoulder and reading with me, and that a girl's long hair was falling over me down on to the page. The book was the Ronsard I had found in the little bedroom. I turned, but again there was nothing there. Yet this time I knew that I had not been dreaming, and I cried out:

"Poor child! tell me of your grief—that I may help your sorrowing heart to rest."

But, of course, there was no answer; yet that night I dreamed a strange dream. I thought I was in the orchard again in the afternoon and once again heard the strange singing—but this time, as I looked up, the singer was no longer invisible. Coming toward me was a young girl with wonderful blue eyes filled with tears and gold hair that fell to her waist. She wore a straight, white robe that might have been a shroud or a bridal dress. She appeared not to see me, though she came directly to the tree where I was sitting. And there she knelt and buried her face in the grass and sobbed as if her heart would break.

Her long hair fell over her like a mantle, and in my dream, I stroked it pityingly and murmured words of comfort for a sorrow I did not understand. . . . Then I woke suddenly as one does from dreams. The moon was shining brightly into the room. Rising from my bed, I looked out into the orchard. It was almost as bright as day. I could plainly see the tree of which I had been dreaming, and then a fantastic notion possessed me. Slipping on my clothes, I went out into one of the old barns and found a spade. Then I went to the tree where I had seen the girl weeping in my dream and dug down at its foot.

I had dug little more than a foot when my spade struck upon some hard substance, and in a few more moments I had uncovered and exhumed a small box, which, on examination, proved to be one of those pretty old-fashioned Chippendale work-boxes used by our grandmothers to keep their thimbles and needles in, their reels of cotton and skeins of silk. After smoothing down the little grave in which I had found it, I carried the box into the house, and under the lamp-light examined its contents.

Then at once I understood why that sad young spirit went to and fro the orchard singing those little French songs—for the treasure-trove I had found under the apple-tree, the buried treasure of an unquiet, suffering soul, proved to be a number of love-letters written mostly in French in a very picturesque hand—letters, too, written but some five or six years before. Perhaps I should not have read them— yet I read them with such reverence for the beautiful, impassioned love that animated them, and literally made them "smell sweet and blossom in the dust," that I felt I had the sanction of the dead to make myself the confidant of their story. Among the letters were little songs, two of which I had heard the strange young voice singing in the orchard, and, of course, there were many withered flowers and such like remembrances of bygone rapture.

Not that night could I make out all the story, though it was not difficult to define its essential tragedy, and later on a gossip in the neighbourhood and a headstone in the churchyard told me the rest. The unquiet young soul that had sung so wistfully to and fro the orchard was my landlord's daughter. She was the only child of her parents, a beautiful, wilful girl, exotically unlike those from whom she was sprung and among whom she lived with a disdainful air of exile. She was, as a child, a little creature of fairy fancies, and as she grew up it was plain to her father and mother that she had come from another world than theirs. To them she seemed like a child in an old fairy-tale strangely found on his hearth by some shepherd as he returns from the fields at evening—a little fairy girl swaddled in fine linen, and dowered with a mysterious bag of gold.

Soon she developed delicate spiritual needs to which her simple parents were strangers. From long truancies in the woods, she would come home laden with mysterious flowers, and soon she came to ask for books and pictures and music, of which the poor souls that had given her birth had never heard. Finally, she had her way, and went to study at a certain fashionable college; and there the brief romance of her life began. There she met a romantic young Frenchman who had read Ronsard to her and written her those picturesque letters I had found in the old mahogany workbox. And after a while the young Frenchman had gone back to France, and the letters had ceased.

Month by month went by, and at length one day, as she sat wistful at the window, looking out at the foolish sunlit road, a message came. He was dead. That headstone in the village churchyard tells the rest. She was very young to die—scarcely nineteen years; and the dead who have died young, with all their hopes and dreams still like unfolded buds within their hearts, do not rest so quietly in the grave as those who have gone through the long day from morning until evening and are only too glad to sleep.

★★★★★★★★★★★★★★★★

Next day I took the little box to a quiet corner of the orchard, and made a little pyre of fragrant boughs—for so I interpreted the wish of that young, unquiet spirit—and the beautiful words are now safe, taken up again into the aerial spaces from which they came.

But since then, the birds sing no more little French songs in my old orchard.

The Interval

Vincent O'Sullivan

Mrs. Wilton passed through a little alley leading from one of the gates which are around Regent's Park, and came out on the wide and quiet street. She walked along slowly, peering anxiously from side to side so as not to overlook the number. She pulled her furs closer round her; after her years in India this London damp seemed very harsh. Still, it was not a fog today. A dense haze, grey and tinged ruddy, lay between the houses, sometimes blowing with a little wet kiss against the face. Mrs. Wilton's hair and eyelashes and her furs were powdered with tiny drops. But there was nothing in the weather to blur the sight; she could see the faces of people some distance off and read the signs on the shops.

Before the door of a dealer in antiques and second-hand furniture she paused and looked through the shabby uncleaned window at an unassorted heap of things, many of them of great value. She read the Polish name fastened on the pane in white letters.

"Yes; this is the place."

She opened the door, which met her entrance with an ill-tempered jangle. From somewhere in the black depths of the shop the dealer came forward, he had a clammy white face, with a sparse black beard, and wore a skull cap and spectacles. Mrs. Wilton spoke to him in a low voice.

A look of complicity, of cunning, perhaps of irony, passed through the dealer's cynical and sad eyes. But he bowed gravely and respectfully.

"Yes, she is here, madam. Whether she will see you or not I do not know. She is not always well; she has her moods. And then, we have to be so careful. The police—Not that they would touch a lady like you. But the poor alien has not much chance these days."

Mrs. Wilton followed him to the back of the shop, where there was a winding staircase. She knocked over a few things in her passage and stooped to pick them up, but the dealer kept muttering, "It does not matter—surely it does not matter." He lit a candle.

"You must go up these stairs. They are very dark; be careful. When you come to a door, open it and go straight in."

He stood at the foot of the stairs holding the light high above his head as she ascended.

The room was not very large, and it seemed very ordinary. There were some flimsy, uncomfortable chairs in gilt and red. Two large palms were in corners. Under a glass cover on the table was a view of Rome. The room had not a business-like look, thought Mrs. Wilton; there was no suggestion of the office or waiting-room where people came and went all day; yet you would not say that it was a private room which was lived in. There were no books or papers about; every chair was in the place it had been placed when the room was last swept; there was no fire and it was very cold.

To the right of the window was a door covered with a plush curtain. Mrs. Wilton sat down near the table and watched this door. She thought it must be through it that the soothsayer would come forth. She laid her hands listlessly one on top of the other on the table. This must be the tenth seer she had consulted since Hugh had been killed. She thought them over. No, this must be the eleventh. She had forgotten that frightening man in Paris who said he had been a priest. Yet of them all it was only he who had told her anything definite. But even he could do no more than tell the past. He told of her marriage; he even had the duration of it right—twenty-one months. He told too of their time in India—at least, he knew that her husband had been a soldier, and said he had been on service in the "colonies."

On the whole, though, he had been as unsatisfactory as the others. None of them had given her the consolation she sought. She did not want to be told of the past. If Hugh was gone forever, then with him had gone all her love of living, her courage, all her better self. She wanted to be lifted out of the despair, the dazed aimless drifting from day to day, longing at night for the morning, and in the morning for the fall of night, which had been her life since his death. If somebody could assure her that it was not all over, that he was somewhere, not too far away, unchanged from what he had been here, with his crisp hair and rather slow smile and lean brown face, that he saw her sometimes, that he had not forgotten her. . . .

"Oh, Hugh, darling!"

When she looked up again the woman was sitting there before her. Mrs. Wilton had not heard her come in. With her experience, wide enough now, of seers and fortune-tellers of all kinds, she saw at once that this woman was different from the others. She was used to the quick appraising look, the attempts, sometimes clumsy, but often cleverly disguised, to collect some fragments of information whereupon to erect a plausible vision. But this woman looked as if she took it out of herself.

Not that her appearance suggested intercourse with the spiritual world more than the others had done; it suggested that, in fact, considerably less. Some of the others were frail, yearning, evaporated creatures, and the ex-priest in Paris had something terrible and condemned in his look. He might well sup with the devil, that man, and probably did in some way or other.

But this was a little fat, weary-faced woman about fifty, who only did not look like a cook because she looked more like a sempstress. Her black dress was all covered with white threads. Mrs. Wilton looked at her with some embarrassment. It seemed more reasonable to be asking a woman like this about altering a gown than about intercourse with the dead. That seemed even absurd in such a very commonplace presence.

The woman seemed timid and oppressed; she breathed heavily and kept rubbing her dingy hands, which looked moist, one over the other; she was always wetting her lips, and coughed with a little dry cough. But in her these signs of nervous exhaustion suggested overwork in a close atmosphere, bending too close over the sewing-machine. Her uninteresting hair, like a rat's pelt, was eked out with a false addition of another colour. Some threads had got into her hair too.

Her harried, uneasy look caused Mrs. Wilton to ask compassionately: "Are you much worried by the police?"

"Oh, the police! Why don't they leave us alone? You never know who comes to see you. Why don't they leave me alone? I'm a good woman. I only think. What I do is no harm to anyone." . . .

She continued in an uneven querulous voice, always rubbing her hands together nervously. She seemed to the visitor to be talking at random, just gabbling, like children do sometimes before they fall asleep.

"I wanted to explain—" hesitated Mrs. Wilton.

But the woman, with her head pressed close against the back of the chair, was staring beyond her at the wall. Her face had lost whatever little expression it had; it was blank and stupid. When she spoke, it was very slowly and her voice was guttural.

"Can't you see him? It seems strange to me that you can't see him. He is so near you. He is passing his arm round your shoulders."

This was a frequent gesture of Hugh's. And indeed, at that moment she felt that somebody was very near her, bending over her. She was enveloped in tenderness. Only a very thin veil, she felt, prevented her from seeing. But the woman saw. She was describing Hugh minutely, even the little things like the burn on his right hand.

"Is he happy? Oh, ask him does he love me?"

The result was so far beyond anything she had hoped for that she was stunned. She could only stammer the first thing that came into her head. "Does he love me?"

"He loves you. He won't answer, but he loves you. He wants me to make you see him; he is disappointed, I think, because I can't. But I can't unless you do it yourself."

After a while she said:

"I think you will see him again. You think of nothing else. He is very close to us now."

Then she collapsed, and fell into a heavy sleep and lay there motionless, hardly breathing. Mrs. Wilton put some notes on the table and stole out on tiptoe.

She seemed to remember that downstairs in the dark shop the dealer with the waxen face detained her to shew some old silver and jewellery and such like. But she did not come to herself, she had no precise recollection of anything, till she found herself entering a church near Portland Place. It was an unlikely act in her normal moments. Why did she go in there? She acted like one walking in her sleep.

The church was old and dim, with high black pews. There was nobody there. Mrs. Wilton sat down in one of the pews and bent forward with her face in her hands.

After a few minutes she saw that a soldier had come in noiselessly and placed himself about half-a-dozen rows ahead of her. He never turned round; but presently she was struck by something familiar in the figure. First, she thought vaguely that the soldier looked like her Hugh. Then, when he put up his hand, she saw who it was.

She hurried out of the pew and ran towards him. "Oh, Hugh, Hugh, have you come back?"

He looked round with a smile. He had not been killed. It was all a mistake. He was going to speak. . . .

Footsteps sounded hollow in the empty church. She turned and glanced down the dim aisle.

It was an old sexton or verger who approached. "I thought I heard you call," he said.

"I was speaking to my husband." But Hugh was nowhere to be seen.

"He was here a moment ago." She looked about in anguish. "He must have gone to the door."

"There's nobody here," said the old man gently. "Only you and me. Ladies are often taken funny since the war. There was one in here yesterday afternoon said she was married in this church and her husband had promised to meet her here. Perhaps you were married here?"

"No," said Mrs. Wilton, desolately. "I was married in India."

It might have been two or three days after that, when she went into a small Italian restaurant in the Bayswater district. She often went out for her meals now: she had developed an exhausting cough, and she found that it somehow became less troublesome when she was in a public, place looking at strange faces. In her flat there were all the things that Hugh had used; the trunks and bags still had his name on them with the labels of places where they had been together. They were like stabs. In the restaurant, people came and went, many soldiers too among them, just glancing at her in her corner.

This day, as it chanced, she was rather late and there was nobody there. She was very tired. She nibbled at the food they brought her. She could almost have cried from tiredness and loneliness and the ache in her heart.

Then suddenly he was before her, sitting there opposite at the table. It was as it was in the days of their engagement, when they used sometimes to lunch at restaurants. He was not in uniform. He smiled at her and urged her to eat, just as he used in those days. . . .

I met her that afternoon as she was crossing Kensington Gardens, and she told me about it.

"I have been with Hugh." She seemed most happy.

"Did he say anything?"

"N-no. Yes. I think he did, but I could not quite hear. My head was so very tired. The next time—"

I did not see her for some time after that. She found, I think, that by going to places where she had once seen him—the old church, the little restaurant—she was more certain to see him again. She never saw him at home. But in the street or the park he would often walk along beside her. Once he saved her from being run over. She said she actually felt his hand grabbing her arm, suddenly, when the car was nearly upon her.

She had given me the address of the clairvoyant; and it is through that strange woman that I know—or seem to know—what followed.

Mrs. Wilton was not exactly ill last winter, not so ill, at least, as to keep to her bedroom. But she was very thin, and her great handsome eyes always seemed to be staring at some point beyond, searching. There was a look in them that seamen's eyes sometimes have when they are drawing on a coast of which they are not very certain. She lived almost in solitude: she hardly ever saw anybody except when they sought her out. To those who were anxious about her she laughed and said she was very well.

One sunny morning she was lying awake, waiting for the maid to bring her tea. The shy London sunlight peeped through the blinds. The room had a fresh and happy look.

When she heard the door open, she thought that the maid had come in. Then she saw that Hugh was standing at the foot of the bed. He was in uniform this time, and looked as he had looked the day he went away.

"Oh, Hugh, speak to me! Will you not say just one word?"

He smiled and threw back his head, just as he used to in the old days at her mother's house when he wanted to call her out of the room without attracting the attention of the others. He moved towards the door, still signing to her to follow him. He picked up her slippers on his way and held them out to her as if he wanted her to put them on. She slipped out of bed hastily. . . .

It is strange that when they came to look through her things after her death the slippers could never be found.

The Mass of Shadows

Anatole France

1

This tale the sacristan of the church of St. Eulalie at Neuville
d'Aumont told me, as we sat under the arbour of the White Horse,
one fine summer evening, drinking a bottle of old wine to the health
of the dead man, now very much at his ease, whom that very morning
he had borne to the grave with full honours, beneath a pall powdered
with smart silver tears.

"My poor father who is dead" (it is the sacristan who is speaking,)
"was in his lifetime a grave-digger. He was of an agreeable disposition,
the result, no doubt, of the calling he followed, for it has often been
pointed out that people who work in cemeteries are of a jovial turn.
Death has no terrors for them; they never give it a thought. I, for in-
stance, *monsieur*, enter a cemetery at night as little perturbed as though
it were the arbour of the White Horse. And if by chance I meet with
a ghost, I don't disturb myself in the least about it, for I reflect that he
may just as likely have business of his own to attend to as I.

"I know the habits of the dead, and I know their character. Indeed,
so far as that goes, I know things of which the priests themselves are
ignorant. If I were to tell you all I have seen, you would be astounded.
But a still tongue makes a wise head, and my father, who, all the same,
delighted in spinning a yarn, did not disclose a twentieth part of what
he knew. To make up for this he often repeated the same stories, and
to my knowledge he told the story of Catherine Fontaine at least a
hundred times.

"Catherine Fontaine was an old maid whom he well remembered
having seen when he was a mere child. I should not be surprised if
there were still, perhaps, three old fellows in the district who could remember having heard folks speak of her, for she was very well known
and of excellent reputation, though poor enough. She lived at the

135

corner of the Rue aux Nonnes, in the turret which is still to be seen there, and which formed part of an old half-ruined mansion looking on to the garden of the Ursuline nuns. On that turret can still be traced certain figures and half-obliterated inscriptions. The late *curé* of St. Eulalie, Monsieur Levasseur, asserted that there are the words in Latin, *Love is stronger than death*, 'which is to be understood,' so he would add, 'of divine love.'

2

"Catherine Fontaine lived by herself in this tiny apartment. She was a lace-maker. You know, of course, that the lace made in our part of the world was formerly held in high esteem. No one knew anything of her relatives or friends. It was reported that when she was eighteen years of age, she had loved the young Chevalier d'Aumont-Cléry, and had been secretly affianced to him. But decent folk didn't believe a word of it, and said it was nothing but a tale concocted because Catherine Fontaine's demeanour was that of a lady rather than that of a working woman, and because, moreover, she possessed beneath her white locks the remains of great beauty. Her expression was sorrowful, and on one finger she wore one of those rings fashioned by the goldsmith into the semblance of two tiny hands clasped together. In former days folks were accustomed to exchange such rings at their betrothal ceremony. I am sure you know the sort of thing I mean.

"Catherine Fontaine lived a saintly life. She spent a great deal of time in churches, and every morning, whatever might be the weather, she went to assist at the six o'clock Mass at St. Eulalie.

"Now one December night, whilst she was in her little chamber, she was awakened by the sound of bells, and nothing doubting that they were ringing for the first Mass, the pious woman dressed herself, and came downstairs and out into the street. The night was so obscure that not even the walls of the houses were visible, and not a ray of light shone from the murky sky.

"And such was the silence amid this black darkness, that there was not even the sound of a distant dog barking, and a feeling of aloofness from every living creature was perceptible. But Catherine Fontaine knew well every single stone she stepped on, and, as she could have found her way to the church with her eyes shut, she reached without difficulty the corner of the Rue aux Nonnes and the Rue de la Paroisse, where the timbered house stands with the tree of Jesse carved on one of its massive beams.

"When she reached this spot, she perceived that the church doors were open, and that a great light was streaming out from the wax tapers. She resumed her journey, and when she had passed through the porch, she found herself in the midst of a vast congregation which entirely filled the church. But she did not recognise any of the worshipers and was surprised to observe that all of these people were dressed in velvets and brocades, with feathers in their hats, and that they wore swords in the fashion of days gone by. Here were gentlemen who carried tall canes with gold knobs, and ladies with lace caps fastened with coronet-shaped combs.

"Chevaliers of the Order of St. Louis extended their hands to these ladies, who concealed behind their fans painted faces, of which only the powdered brow and the patch at the corner of the eye were visible! All of them proceeded to take their places without the slightest sound, and as they moved neither the sound of their footsteps on the pavement, nor the rustle of their garments could be heard. The lower places were filled with a crowd of young artisans in brown jackets, dimity breeches, and blue stockings, with their arms round the waists of pretty blushing girls who lowered their eyes.

"Near the holy water stoups peasant women, in scarlet petticoats and laced bodices, sat upon the ground as immovable as domestic animals, whilst young lads, standing up behind them, stared out from wide-open eyes and twirled their hats round and round on their fingers, and all these sorrowful countenances seemed centred irremovably on one and the same thought, at once sweet and sorrowful.

"On her knees, in her accustomed place, Catherine Fontaine saw the priest advance toward the altar, preceded by two servers. She recognised neither priest nor clerks. The Mass began. It was a silent Mass, during which neither the sound of the moving lips nor the tinkle of the bell was audible. Catherine Fontaine felt that she was under the observation and the influence also of her mysterious neighbour, and when, scarcely turning her head, she stole a glance at him, she recognised the young Chevalier d'Aumont-Cléry, who had once loved her, and who had been dead for five and forty years.

"She recognised him by a small mark which he had over the left ear, and above all by the shadow which his long black eyelashes cast upon his cheeks. He was dressed in his hunting clothes, scarlet with gold lace, the very clothes he wore that day when he met her in St. Leonard's Wood, begged of her a drink, and stole a kiss. He had preserved his youth and good looks.

When he smiled, he still displayed magnificent teeth. Catherine said to him in an undertone:

3

"'*Monseigneur*, you who were my friend, and to whom in days gone by I gave all that a girl holds most dear, may God keep you in His grace! O, that He would at length inspire me with regret for the sin I committed in yielding to you; for it is a fact that, though my hair is white and I approach my end, I have not yet repented of having loved you. But, dear dead friend and noble *seigneur*, tell me, who are these folk, habited after the antique fashion, who are here assisting at this silent Mass?'

"The Chevalier d'Aumont-Cléry replied in a voice feebler than a breath, but none the less crystal clear:

"'Catherine, these men and women are souls from purgatory who have grieved God by sinning as we ourselves sinned through love of the creature, but who are not on that account cast off by God, inasmuch as their sin, like ours, was not deliberate.

"'Whilst separated from those whom they loved upon earth, they are purified in the cleansing fires of purgatory, they suffer the pangs of absence, which is for them the most cruel of tortures. They are so unhappy that an angel from heaven takes pity upon their love-torment. By the permission of the Most High, for one hour in the night, he reunites each year lover to loved in their parish church, where they are permitted to assist at the Mass of Shadows, hand clasped in hand. These are the facts. If it has been granted to me to see thee before thy death, Catherine, it is a boon which is bestowed by God's special permission.'

"And Catherine Fontaine answered him:

"'I would die gladly enough, dear, dead lord, if I might recover the beauty that was mine when I gave you to drink in the forest.'

"Whilst they thus conversed under their breath, a very old canon was taking the collection and proffering to the worshipers a great copper dish, wherein they let fall, each in his turn, ancient coins which have long since ceased to pass current: *écus* of six *livres*, florins, *ducats* and *ducatoons*, *jacobuses* and rose-nobles, and the pieces fell silently into the dish.

"When at length it was placed before the *chevalier*, he dropped into it a *louis* which made no more sound than had the other pieces of gold and silver.

"Then the old canon stopped before Catherine Fontaine, who fumbled in her pocket without being able to find a farthing. Then, being unwilling to allow the dish to pass without an offering from herself, she slipped from her finger the ring which the *chevalier* had given her the day before his death, and cast it into the copper bowl. As the golden ring fell, a sound like the heavy clang of a bell rang out, and on the stroke of this reverberation the *chevalier*, the canon, the celebrant, the servers, the ladies and their cavaliers, the whole assembly vanished utterly; the candles guttered out, and Catherine Fontaine was left alone in the darkness."

Having concluded his narrative after this fashion, the sacristan drank a long draught of wine, remained pensive for a moment, and then resumed his talk in these words:

"I have told you this tale exactly as my father has told it to me over and over again, and I believe that it is authentic, because it agrees in all respects with what I have observed of the manners and customs peculiar to those who have passed away. I have associated a good deal with the dead ever since my childhood, and I know that they are accustomed to return to what they have loved.

"It is on this account that the miserly dead wander at night in the neighbourhood of the treasures they conceal during their life time. They keep a strict watch over their gold; but the trouble they give themselves, far from being of service to them, turns to their disadvantage; and it is not a rare thing at all to come upon money buried in the ground on digging in a place haunted by a ghost. In the same way deceased husbands come by night to harass their wives who have made a second matrimonial venture, and I could easily name several who have kept a better watch over their wives since death than they ever did while living.

"That sort of thing is blameworthy, for in all fairness the dead have no business to stir up jealousies. Still, I do but tell you what I have observed myself. It is a matter to take into account if one marries a widow. Besides, the tale I have told you is vouchsafed for in the manner following:

"The morning after that extraordinary night Catherine Fontaine was discovered dead in her chamber. And the beadle attached to St. Eulalie found in the copper bowl used for the collection a gold ring with two clasped hands. Besides, I'm not the kind of man to make jokes. Suppose we order another bottle of wine?. . ."

The Shadow of a Midnight

Maurice Baring

It was nine o'clock in the evening. Sasha, the maid, had brought in the *samovar* and placed it at the head of the long table. Marie Nikolaevna, our hostess, poured out the tea. Her husband was playing Vindt with his daughter, the doctor, and his son-in-law in another corner of the room. And Jameson, who had just finished his Russian lesson—he was working for the Civil Service examination—was reading the last number of the *Rouskoe Slovo*.

"Have you found anything interesting, Frantz Frantzovitch?" said Marie Nikolaevna to Jameson, as she handed him a glass of tea.

"Yes, I have," answered the Englishman, looking up. His eyes had a clear dreaminess about them, which generally belongs only to fanatics or visionaries, and I had no reason to believe that Jameson, who seemed to be common sense personified, was either one or the other. "At least," he continued, "it interests me. And it's odd—very odd."

"What is it?" asked Marie Nikolaevna.

"Well, to tell you what it is would mean a long story which you wouldn't believe," said Jameson; "only it's odd—very odd."

"Tell us the story," I said.

"As you won't believe a word of it," Jameson repeated, "it's not much use my telling it."

We insisted on hearing the story, so Jameson lit a cigarette, and began:—

"Two years ago," he said, "I was at Heidelberg, at the University, and I made friends with a young fellow called Braun. His parents were German, but he had lived five or six years in America, and he was practically an American. I made his acquaintance by chance at a lecture, when I first arrived, and he helped me in a number of ways. He was an energetic and kind-hearted fellow, and we became great friends. He was a student, but he did not belong to any *Korps* or *Bur-*

141

senschaft, he was working hard then. Afterwards he became an engineer. When the summer *Semester* came to an end, we both stayed on at Heidelberg. One day Braun suggested that we should go for a walking tour and explore the country. I was only too pleased, and we started. It was glorious weather, and we enjoyed ourselves hugely.

"On the third night after we had started, we arrived at a village called Salzheim. It was a picturesque little place, and there was a curious old church in it with some interesting tombs and relics of the Thirty Years War. But the inn where we put up for the night was even more picturesque than the church. It had been a convent for nuns, only the greater part of it had been burnt, and only a quaint gabled house, and a kind of tower covered with ivy, which I suppose had once been the belfry, remained.

"We had an excellent supper and went to bed early. We had been given two bedrooms, which were airy and clean, and altogether we were satisfied. My bedroom opened into Braun's, which was beyond it, and had no other door of its own. It was a hot night in July, and Braun asked me to leave the door open. I did—we opened both the windows. Braun went to bed and fell asleep almost directly, for very soon I heard his snores.

"I had imagined that I was longing for sleep, but no sooner had I got into bed than all my sleepiness left me. This was odd, because we had walked a good many miles, and it had been a blazing hot day, and up till then I had slept like a log the moment I got into bed. I lit a candle and began reading a small volume of Heine I carried with me. I heard the clock strike ten, and then eleven, and still I felt that sleep was out of the question. I said to myself: 'I will read till twelve and then I will stop.' My watch was on a chair by my bedside, and when the clock struck eleven, I noticed that it was five minutes slow, and set it right. I could see the church tower from my window, and every time the clock struck—and it struck the quarters—the noise boomed through the room.

"When the clock struck a quarter to twelve, I yawned for the first time, and I felt thankful that sleep seemed at last to be coming to me. I left off reading, and taking my watch in my hand I waited for midnight to strike. This quarter of an hour seemed an eternity. At last, the hands of my watch showed that it was one minute to twelve. I put out my candle and began counting sixty, waiting for the clock to strike. I had counted a hundred and sixty, and still the clock had not struck. I counted up to four hundred; then I thought I must have made a mistake. I lit my candle again, and looked at my watch: it was two minutes past twelve. And still the clock had not struck!

"A curious uncomfortable feeling came over me, and I sat up in bed with my watch in my hand and longed to call Braun, who was peacefully snoring, but I did not like to. I sat like this till a quarter past twelve; the clock struck the quarter as usual. I made up my mind that the clock must have struck twelve, and that I must have slept for a minute–at the same time I knew I had not slept–and I put out my candle. I must have fallen asleep almost directly.

"The next thing I remember was waking with a start. It seemed to me that someone had shut the door between my room and Braun's. I felt for the matches. The matchbox was empty. Up to that moment— I cannot tell why—something—an unaccountable dread—had prevented me looking at the door. I made an effort and looked. It was shut, and through the cracks and through the keyhole I saw the glimmer of a light. Braun had lit his candle. I called him, not very loudly: there was no answer. I called again more loudly: there was still no answer.

"Then I got out of bed and walked to the door. As I went, it was gently and slightly opened, just enough to show me a thin streak of light. At that moment I felt that someone was looking at me. Then it was instantly shut once more, as softly as it had been opened. There was not a sound to be heard. I walked on tiptoe towards the door, but it seemed to me that I had taken a hundred years to cross the room. And when at last I reached the door, I felt I could not open it. I was simply paralysed with fear. And still I saw the glimmer through the key-hole and the cracks.

"Suddenly, as I was standing transfixed with fright in front of the door, I heard sounds coming from Braun's room, a shuffle of footsteps, and voices talking low but distinctly in a language I could not understand. It was not Italian, Spanish, nor French. The voices grew all at once louder; I heard the noise of a struggle and a cry which ended in a stifled groan, very painful and horrible to hear. Then, whether I regained my self-control, or whether it was excess of fright which prompted me, I don't know, but I flew to the door and tried to open it. Someone or something was pressing with all its might against it. Then I screamed at the top of my voice, and as I screamed, I heard the cock crow.

"The door gave, and I almost fell into Braun's room. It was quite dark. But Braun was waked by my screams and quietly lit a match. He asked me gently what on earth was the matter. The room was empty and everything was in its place. Outside the first greyness of dawn was in the sky.

"I said I had had a nightmare, and asked him if he had not had one as well; but Braun said he had never slept better in his life.

"The next day we went on with our walking tour, and when we got back to Heidelberg Braun sailed for America. I never saw him again, although we corresponded frequently, and only last week I had a letter from him, dated Nijni Novgorod, saying he would be at Moscow before the end of the month.

"And now I suppose you are all wondering what this can have to do with anything that's in the newspaper. Well, listen," and he read out the following paragraph from the *Rouskoe Slovo*:—

Samara, II, ix. In the centre of the town, in the Hotel —— a band of armed swindlers attacked a German engineer named Braun and demanded money. On his refusal one of the robbers stabbed Braun with a knife. The robbers, taking the money which was on him, amounting to 500 *roubles*, got away. Braun called for assistance, but died of his wounds in the night. It appears that he had met the swindlers at a restaurant.

"Since I have been in Russia," Jameson added, "I have often thought that I knew what language it was that was talked behind the door that night in the inn at Salzheim, but now I know it was Russian."

The Shell of Sense

Olivia Howard Dunbar

It was intolerably unchanged, the dim, dark-toned room. In an agony of recognition my glance ran from one to another of the comfortable, familiar things that my earthly life had been passed among. Incredibly distant from it all as I essentially was. I noted sharply that the very gaps that I myself had left in my bookshelves still stood unfilled; that the delicate fingers of the ferns that I had tended were still stretched futilely toward the light; that the soft agreeable chuckle of my own little clock, like some elderly woman with whom conversation has become automatic, was undiminished.

Unchanged—or so it seemed at first. But there were certain trivial differences that shortly smote me. The windows were closed too tightly; for I had always kept the house very cool, although I had known that Theresa preferred warm rooms. And my work-basket was in disorder; it was preposterous that so small a thing should hurt me so. Then, for this was my first experience of the shadow-folded transition, the odd alteration of my emotions bewildered me.

For at one moment the place seemed so humanly familiar, so distinctly my own proper envelope, that for love of it I could have laid my cheek against the wall; while in the next I was miserably conscious of strange new shrillnesses. How could they be endured—and had I ever endured them?—those harsh influences that I now perceived at the window; light and colour so blinding that they obscured the form of the wind, tumult so discordant that one could scarcely hear the roses open in the garden below?

But Theresa did not seem to mind any of these things. Disorder, it is true, the dear child had never minded. She was sitting all this time at my desk—at *my* desk—occupied, I could only too easily surmise how. In the light of my own habits of precision it was plain that that sombre correspondence should have been attended to before; but I believe that I did not really reproach Theresa, for I knew that her notes, when she did write them, were perhaps less perfunctory than mine. She finished the last one as I watched her, and added it to the heap of black-bordered envelopes that lay on the desk. Poor girl! I saw now that they had cost her tears.

Yet, living beside her day after day, year after year, I had never discovered what deep tenderness my sister possessed. Toward each other it had been our habit to display only a temperate affection, and I remember having always thought it distinctly fortunate for Theresa, since she was denied my happiness, that she could live so easily and pleasantly without emotions of the devastating sort. . . . And now, for the first time, I was really to behold her. . . . Could it be Theresa, after all, this tangle of subdued turbulences? Let no one suppose that it is an easy thing to bear, the relentlessly lucid understanding that I then first exercised; or that, in its first enfranchisement, the timid vision does not yearn for its old screens and mists.

Suddenly, as Theresa sat there, her head, filled with its tender thoughts of me, held in her gentle hands, I felt Allan's step on the carpeted stair outside. Theresa felt it, too—but how? for it was not audible. She gave a start, swept the black envelopes out of sight, and pretended to be writing in a little book. Then I forgot to watch her any longer in my absorption in Allan's coming. It was he, of course, that I was awaiting.

It was for him that I had made this first lonely, frightened effort to return, to recover. . . . It was not that I had supposed he would allow himself to recognise my presence, for I had long been sufficiently familiar with his hard and fast denials of the invisible. He was so reasonable always, so sane—so blindfolded. But I had hoped that because of his very rejection of the ether that now contained me I could perhaps all the more safely, the more secretly, watch him, linger near him. He was near now, very near—but why did Theresa, sitting there in the room that had never belonged to her, appropriate for herself his coming? It was so manifestly I who had drawn him, I whom he had come to seek.

The door was ajar. He knocked softly at it "Are you there, Theresa?" he called. He expected to find her, then, there in my room? I shrank back, fearing, almost, to stay.

"I shall have finished in a moment," Theresa told him, and he sat down to wait for her.

No spirit still unreleased can understand the pang that I felt with

Allan sitting almost within my touch. Almost irresistibly the wish beset me to let him for an instant feel my nearness. Then I checked myself, remembering—oh, absurd, piteous human fears!—that my too unguarded closeness might alarm him. It was not so remote a time that I myself had known them, those blind, uncouth timidities. I came, therefore, somewhat nearer—but I did not touch him. I merely leaned toward him and with incredible softness whispered his name. That much I could not have forborne; the spell of life was still too strong in me.

But it gave him no comfort, no delight. "Theresa!" he called, in a voice dreadful with alarm—and in that instant the last veil fell, and desperately, scarce believingly, I beheld how it stood between them, those two.

She turned to him that gentle look of hers.

"Forgive me," came from him hoarsely. "But I had suddenly the most—unaccountable sensation. Can there be too many windows open? There is such a—chill—about."

"There are no windows open," Theresa assured him. "I took care to shut out the chill. You are not well, Allan!"

"Perhaps not." He embraced the suggestion. "And yet I feel no illness apart from this abominable sensation that persists—persists. . . . Theresa, you must tell me: do I fancy it, or do you, too, feel—something—strange here?"

"Oh, there is something very strange here," she half sobbed. "There always will be."

"Good heavens, child, I didn't mean that!" He rose and stood looking about him. "I know, of course, that you have your beliefs, and I respect them, but you know equally well that I have nothing of the sort! So—don't let us conjure up anything inexplicable."

I stayed impalpably, imponderably near him. Wretched and bereft though I was, I could not have left him while he stood denying me.

"What I mean," he went on, in his low, distinct voice, "is a special, an almost ominous sense of cold. Upon my soul, Theresa,"—he paused—"if I *were* superstitious, if I *were* a woman, I should probably imagine it to seem—a presence!"

He spoke the last word very faintly, but Theresa shrank from it nevertheless.

"*Don't* say that, Allan!" she cried out. "Don't think it, I beg of you! I've tried so hard myself not to think it—and you must help me. You know it is only perturbed, uneasy spirits that wander. With her it is quite different. She has always been so happy—she must still be."

I listened, stunned, to Theresa's sweet dogmatism. From what blind distances came her confident misapprehensions, how dense, both for her and for Allan, was the separating vapor!

Allan frowned. "Don't take me literally, Theresa," he explained; and I, who a moment before had almost touched him, now held myself aloof and heard him with a strange untried pity, new born in me. "I'm not speaking of what you call—spirits. It's something much more terrible." He allowed his head to sink heavily on his chest. "If I did not positively know that I had never done her any harm, I should suppose myself to be suffering from guilt, from remorse. . . . Theresa, you know better than I, perhaps. Was she content, always? Did she believe in me?"

"Believe in you?—when she knew you to be so good!—when you adored her!"

"She thought that? She said it? Then what in Heaven's name ails me?—unless it is all as you believe, Theresa, and she knows now what she didn't know then, poor dear, and minds———"

"Minds what? What do you mean, Allan?"

I, who with my perhaps illegitimate advantage saw so clear, knew that he had not meant to tell her: I did him that justice, even in my first jealousy. If I had not tortured him so by clinging near him, he would not have told her. But the moment came, and overflowed, and he did tell her—passionate, tumultuous story that it was. During all our life together, Allan's and mine, he had spared me, had kept me wrapped in the white cloak of an unblemished loyalty.

But it would have been kinder, I now bitterly thought, if, like many husbands, he had years ago found for the story he now poured forth some clandestine listener; I should not have known. But he was faithful and good, and so he waited till I, mute and chained, was there to hear him. So well did I know him, as I thought, so thoroughly had he once been mine, that I saw it in his eyes, heard it in his voice, before the words came. And yet, when it came, it lashed me with the whips of an unbearable humiliation. For I, his wife, had not known how greatly he could love.

And that Theresa, soft little traitor, should, in her still way, have cared too! Where was the iron in her, I moaned within my stricken spirit, where the steadfastness? From the moment he bade her, she turned her soft little petals up to him—and my last delusion was spent. It was intolerable; and none the less so that in another moment she

148

had, prompted by some belated thought of me, renounced him. Allan was hers, yet she put him from her; and it was my part to watch them both.

Then in the anguish of it all I remembered, awkward, untutored spirit that I was, that I now had the Great Recourse. Whatever human things were unbearable, I had no need to bear. I ceased, therefore, to make the effort that kept me with them. The pitiless poignancy was dulled, the sounds and the light ceased, the lovers faded from me, and again I was mercifully drawn into the dim, infinite spaces.

★★★★★★★★★★★★★★★★

There followed a period whose length I cannot measure and during which I was able to make no progress in the difficult, dizzying experience of release. "Earth-bound" my jealousy relentlessly kept me. Though my two dear ones had forsworn each other, I could not trust them, for theirs seemed to me an affectation of a more than mortal magnanimity. Without a ghostly sentinel to prick them with sharp fears and recollections, who could believe that they would keep to it? Of the efficacy of my own vigilance, so long as I might choose to exercise it, I could have no doubt, for I had by this time come to have a dreadful exultation in the new power that lived in me. Repeated delicate experiment had taught me how a touch or a breath, a wish or a whisper, could control Allan's acts, could keep him from Theresa.

I could manifest myself as palely, as transiently, as a thought. I could produce the merest necessary flicker, like the shadow of a just-opened leaf, on his trembling, tortured consciousness. And these unrealised perceptions of me he interpreted, as I had known that he would, as his soul's inevitable penance. He had come to believe that he had done evil in silently loving Theresa all these years, and it was my vengeance to allow him to believe this, to prod him ever to believe it afresh.

I am conscious that this frame of mind was not continuous in me. For I remember, too, that when Allan and Theresa were safely apart and sufficiently miserable, I loved them as dearly as I ever had, more dearly perhaps. For it was impossible that I should not perceive, in my new emancipation, that they were, each of them, something more and greater than the two beings I had once ignorantly pictured them. For years they had practiced a selflessness of which I could once scarcely have conceived, and which even now I could only admire without entering into its mystery.

While I had lived solely for myself, these two divine creatures had lived exquisitely for me. They had granted me everything, themselves

nothing. For my undeserving sake their lives had been a constant torment of renunciation—a torment they had not sought to alleviate by
the exchange of a single glance of understanding. There were even
marvellous moments when, from the depths of my newly informed
heart, I pitied them—poor creatures, who, withheld from the infinite
solaces that I had come to know, were still utterly within that. . . .

Shell of sense
So frail, so piteously contrived for pain.

Within it, yes; yet exercising qualities that so sublimely transcended
it. Yet the shy, hesitating compassion that thus had birth in me was far
from being able to defeat the earlier, earthlier emotion. The two, I recognised, were in a sort of conflict; and I, regarding it, assumed that the
conflict would never end; that for years, as Allan and Theresa reckoned
time, I should be obliged to withhold myself from the great spaces and
linger suffering, grudging, shamed, where they lingered.

★★★★★★★★★★★★★★

It can never have been explained, I suppose, what, to devitalized
perception such as mine, the contact of mortal beings with each other
appears to be. Once to have exercised this sense-freed perception is to
realise that the gift of prophecy, although the subject of such frequent
marvel, is no longer mysterious. The merest glance of our sensitive and
uncloyed vision can detect the strength of the relation between two
beings, and therefore instantly calculate its duration. If you see a heavy
weight suspended from a slender string, you can know, without any
wizardry, that in a few moments the string will snap; well, such, if you
admit the analogy, is prophecy, is foreknowledge.

And it was thus that I saw it with Theresa and Allan. For it was perfectly visible to me that they would very little longer have the strength
to preserve, near each other, the denuded impersonal relation that
they, and that I, behind them, insisted on; and that they would have to
separate. It was my sister, perhaps the more sensitive, who first realised
this. It had now become possible for me to observe them almost constantly, the effort necessary to visit them had so greatly diminished; so
that I watched her, poor, anguished girl, prepare to leave him.

I saw each reluctant movement that she made. I saw her eyes, worn
from self-searching; I heard her step grown timid from inexplicable
fears; I entered her very heart and heard its pitiful, wild beating. And
still, I did not interfere.

For at this time, I had a wonderful, almost demoniacal sense of disposing of matters to suit my own selfish will. At any moment I could have checked their miseries, could have restored happiness and peace. Yet it gave me, and I could weep to admit it, a monstrous joy to know that Theresa thought she was leaving Allan of her own free intention, when it was I who was contriving, arranging, insisting. . . . And yet she wretchedly felt my presence near her; I am certain of that.

A few days before the time of her intended departure my sister told Allan that she must speak with him after dinner. Our beautiful old house branched out from a circular hall with great arched doors at either end; and it was through the rear doorway that always in summer, after dinner, we passed out into the garden adjoining. As usual, therefore, when the hour came, Theresa led the way. That dreadful daytime brilliance that in my present state I found so hard to endure was now becoming softer. A delicate, capricious twilight breeze danced inconsequently through languidly whispering leaves. Lovely pale flowers blossomed like little moons in the dusk, and over them the breath of mignonette hung heavily. It was a perfect place—and it had so long been ours, Allan's and mine. It made me restless and a little wicked that those two should be there together now.

For a little they walked about together, speaking of common, daily things. Then suddenly Theresa burst out:

"I am going away, Allan. I have stayed to do everything that needed to be done. Now your mother will be here to care for you, and it is time for me to go."

He stared at her and stood still. Theresa had been there so long, she so definitely, to his mind, belonged there. And she was, as I also had jealously known, so lovely there, the small, dark, dainty creature, in the old hall, on the wide staircases, in the garden. . . . Life there without Theresa, even the intentionally remote, the perpetually renounced Theresa—he had not dreamed of it, he could not, so suddenly, conceive of it.

"Sit here," he said, and drew her down beside him on a bench, "and tell me what it means, why you are going. Is it because of something that I have been—have done?"

She hesitated. I wondered if she would dare tell him. She looked out and away from him, and he waited long for her to speak.

The pale stars were sliding into their places. The whispering of the leaves was almost hushed. All about them it was still and shadowy and sweet. It was that wonderful moment when, for lack of a visible horizon, the not yet darkened world seems infinitely greater—a moment when anything can happen, anything be believed in. To me, watching, listening, hovering, there came a dreadful purpose and a dreadful courage. Suppose for one moment, Theresa should not only feel, but *see* me—would she dare to tell him then?

There came a brief space of terrible effort, all my fluttering, uncertain forces strained to the utmost. The instant of my struggle was endlessly long and the transition seemed to take place outside me—as one sitting in a train, motionless, sees the leagues of earth float by. And then, in a bright, terrible flash I knew I had achieved it—I had *attained visibility*. Shuddering, insubstantial, but luminously apparent, I stood there before them. And for the instant that I maintained the visible state I looked straight into Theresa's soul.

She gave a cry. And then, thing of silly, cruel impulses that I was, I saw what I had done. The very thing that I wished to avert I had precipitated. For Allan, in his sudden terror and pity, had bent and caught her in his arms. For the first time they were together; and it was I who had brought them.

Then, to his whispered urging to tell the reason of her cry, Theresa said:

"Frances was here. You did not see her, standing there, under the lilacs, with no smile on her face?"

"My dear, my dear!" was all that Allan said. I had so long now lived invisibly with them, he knew that she was right.

"I suppose you know what it means?" she asked him, calmly.

"Dear Theresa," Allan said, slowly, "if you and I should go away somewhere, could we not evade all this ghostliness? And will you come with me?"

"Distance would not banish her," my sister confidently asserted. And then she said, softly: "Have you thought what a lonely, awesome thing it must be to be so newly dead? Pity her, Allan. We who are warm and alive should pity her. She loves you still—that is the meaning of it all, you know—and she wants us to understand that for that reason we must keep apart. Oh, it was so plain in her white face as she stood there. And you did not see her?"

"It was your face that I saw," Allan solemnly told her—oh, how different he had grown from the Allan that I had known!—"and yours is the only face that I shall ever see." And again, he drew her to him.

She sprang from him. "You are defying her, Allan!" she cried. "And you must not. It is her right to keep us apart, if she wishes. It must be as she insists. I shall go, as I told you. And, Allan, I beg of you, leave me the courage to do as she demands!"

They stood facing each other in the deep dusk, and the wounds that I had dealt them gaped red and accusing. "We must pity her," Theresa had said. And as I remembered that extraordinary speech, and saw the agony in her face, and the greater agony in Allan's, there came the great irreparable cleavage between mortality and me. In a swift, merciful flame the last of my mortal emotions—gross and tenacious they must have been—was consumed. My cold grasp of Allan loosened and a new unearthly love of him bloomed in my heart.

I was now, however, in a difficulty with which my experience in the newer state was scarcely sufficient to deal. How could I make it plain to Allan and Theresa that I wished to bring them together, to heal the wounds that I had made?

Pityingly, remorsefully, I lingered near them all that night and the next day. And by that time had brought myself to the point of a great determination. In the little time that was left, before Theresa should be gone and Allan bereft and desolate, I saw the one way that lay open to me to convince them of my acquiescence in their destiny.

In the deepest darkness and silence of the next night I made a greater effort than it will ever be necessary for me to make again. When they think of me, Allan and Theresa, I pray now that they will recall what I did that night, and that my thousand frustrations and selfishnesses may shrivel and be blown from their indulgent memories.

Yet the following morning, as she had planned, Theresa appeared at breakfast dressed for her journey. Above in her room there were the sounds of departure. They spoke little during the brief meal, but when it was ended Allan said:

"Theresa, there is half an hour before you go. Will you come upstairs with me? I had a dream that I must tell you of."

"Allan!" She looked at him, frightened, but went with him. "It was of Frances you dreamed," she said, quietly, as they entered the library together.

"Did I say it was a dream? But I was awake—thoroughly awake. I had not been sleeping well, and I heard, twice, the striking of the clock. And as I lay there, looking out at the stars, and thinking—thinking of you, Theresa—she came to me, stood there before me, in my room. It was no sheeted spectre, you understand; it was Frances, literally she. In some inexplicable fashion I seemed to be aware that she wanted to make me know something, and I waited, watching her face. After a few moments it came. She did not speak, precisely. That is, I am

153

sure I heard no sound. Yet the words that came from her were definite enough. She said: 'Don't let Theresa leave you. Take her and keep her.' Then she went away. Was that a dream?"

"I had not meant to tell you," Theresa eagerly answered, "but now I must. It is too wonderful. What time did your clock strike, Allan?"

"One, the last time."

"Yes; it was then that I awoke. And she had been with me. I had not seen her, but her arm had been about me and her kiss was on my cheek. Oh. I knew; it was unmistakable. And the sound of her voice was with me."

"Then she bade you, too——"

"Yes, to stay with you. I am glad we told each other." She smiled tearfully and began to fasten her wrap.

"But you are not going—*now!*" Allan cried. "You know that you cannot, now that she has asked you to stay."

"Then you believe, as I do, that it was she?" Theresa demanded.

"I can never understand, but I know," he answered her. "And now you will not go?"

★★★★★★★★★★★★★★

I am freed. There will be no further semblance of me in my old home, no sound of my voice, no dimmest echo of my earthly self. They have no further need of me, the two that I have brought together. Theirs is the fullest joy that the dwellers in the shell of sense can know. Mine is the transcendent joy of the unseen spaces.

The Tree of Death

Barry Pain

1

In the cool of the evening, I always saw her. She came up from the river with the other women. That was a great moment when she, who all the day had been in my heart, came at last into the sight of my eyes. Sometimes she would be soon lost to me, going into her father's house. Sometimes she would crouch with the others on the steps by the wall of a brown hut listening to the old storyteller, and it was wonderful to see the story reflected in her eyes as she heard it, like the image of the palm-tree in the deep river. Sometimes even she would walk by my side and speak with me, and those were evenings to be long remembered for rapture and for sorrow.

And one day I went to the storyteller. He was dark-skinned and not of our race, and he had come from a far country, travelling for many months alongside the river. Some said that he had fled for his life.

"This evening," I said to him, "I beg that you will come out and tell your stories to us."

He waved his hand at me in refusal, saying that he would not. But when I showed him the gift, I had brought for him, then he consented. And I did this because my eyes ached for the sight of her, and I could not bear that this evening she should pass quickly by me.

And when the man began to draw with his stick in the sand, and tell stories of that distant country from which he had come, she was among those that gathered round to listen. And I gazed at her as one tortured with thirst who sees far off the water he would drink.

He told us of a tree that is called the tree of death. He said that the seed was like bright silver to look at and of the size of a man's fist. If you set that seed in the ground, for two years nothing would appear, and then came the miracle, for betwixt sunrise and sunset the tree

155

came to full maturity, growing with incredible rapidity to twice the height of a man, and died again. And in those short hours of life that tree sought to drink the blood of a man sending out a heavy fragrance that brought sleep and death, and lashing its victim with long, writhing tendrils. And each tendril was covered with sucking mouths like the mouth of a leech.

And thereon he told us a story of a faithless woman and of a man's deferred vengeance. Secretly, by night, the man planted the seed of the tree of death in the garden of his wife's lover. But when in two years the tree came to being, it slew the woman for whom the lover had deserted the wife.

They found her white body in the morning, buried beneath the dead and decaying ruin of the tree, and they found, moreover, the three silver seeds that the tree had produced.

"And in the whole earth," said the man, "there are but those three seeds left, and because the tree is so evil, those seeds have not yet been planted." Twice he stretched out the fingers of both hands and closed them again. "Yes, twenty times since then the river has risen and fallen. And for five years more the silver seed must be kept and guarded. And then the power of life, which is the power of evil, will have left those seeds and they will be harmless toys, and never any more will man or woman behold the great magic of the tree of death."

I give his story in a few words. He told it in many words, making it a living picture, so that we seemed to see all as it happened and to hear the very words that were spoken. And all the while my eyes were fixed upon the woman whom I loved in vain. She was as one entranced, breathing deeply, and her fingers tore to pieces the flowers of scarlet hibiscus that she carried, the petals dropping on the sand as drops of blood. The sunset, too, was blood-red that evening.

As he finished speaking, we heard a jackal far away in the desert. And then a boy, laughing, said that the man told many lies.

"Son of a dog, I lie not," said the man, with sudden fury. "I tell you what I have seen and known. In this hand—this very hand—I have held the silver seed of the tree of death. Yes, yes." He rose and stood erect, and his voice dropped to a whisper. "Was it not I, myself," he said, "who planted that seed in the garden of my wife's lover?"

We were all silent, and he turned and left us. And then for the first time that evening the woman looked at me and her hand made a little sign. So, I followed her down to the river bank, and there for a while we sat and talked in the light of a great burnished moon.

"You praise me and say that I am very beautiful," she said. "It may be and it may not be, but it is rather pleasant to hear. You bring many gifts to my father's house, and again it is pleasant to receive gifts. I think you paid the old storyteller, for clearly, he showed more deference to you than to others. And that is the best of all. For one day is as another, and we go the same round continuously, like the ox with bandaged eyes that draws up the water for the garden; but to the hearing of stories, we live many lives and are ever changing. But then—then—you pour out your love to me, and would have me give you mine. How can one give who has it not? Others also speak of love to me and have the same answer. It may be that I am still too young, for I am very young, and that one day the fire will burn up in me. But now, when you speak of love, it is as though I gazed at the writing of a scribe having no skill to read it. And yet—yet—there was something I would say."

"Speak on. Your voice is sweet to hear."

"It is of the story that we have heard. I think there is truth in it, even if it be not all true. I will tell you why, and I have told no other of this. Two years ago, an old woman lay dying in her house, and those that should have tended her had fled in fear. And I brought up water for her from the river. She drank eagerly of it, for the fever was on her. And then she bade me pour a little of the water in the hollowed palm of my left hand and hold it so that she might gaze into it. She looked long into it, so that my little hand shook. And then she said words that I have never forgotten and never yet told. These are the words: 'The eyes of the dying have seen beyond, and as I say it shall be. The man of your love shall come to you holding in his hand a ball that is not of silver but of the colour of silver, and in that ball, there shall be life and death.'

"Tonight, I knew that the ball must be the seed of the tree of death. I know not where the seed is. The old man said it was guarded. It may be that one must go a long and perilous journey, and that blood must be shed, and that a great price must be paid. But this I know—on the day that you come to me holding in your hand a seed of the tree of death, I shall be so filled with love for you that my head will droop and my eyes will faint, and my body and my soul will be yours."

And in a voice that had become suddenly hoarse I said: "And you have told no other of this?"

"Have I not said it? Also, if you swear you will get for me the silver seed, I shall tell no other until it is clear that you have failed. I chose you for many reasons. You are gentle, and when my beauty is gone and you cease to love me you will not then begin to beat me. You are not so wealthy as some of those that seek me, but neither do you hold your wealth with so hard a grip as they do. Did you not also pay the storyteller for my delight?"

"For your delight and for the delight of my eyes in you."

"It is as I thought. And without that I might never have heard of the tree of death or understood the secret of my future. And though I do not now love you—not in the very least—yet I come to you first. But if you think it too hard and hazardous for you, then—"

"Ah, wait!" I said. "Believe me that not for a moment has there been a doubt in my mind. If anywhere on earth there be that silver seed, I swear that I will find it, and bring it to you, and nothing save death shall stay me."

"It is enough," she said. "And when will you bring it?"

"I do not know how long it will be. Will you wait for me for a year if need be?"

"Yes, for a year. But I have seen love run away as water. If, when you hold the seed in your hand, you no longer love me, then bring it not to me, lest you bring sorrow with it."

I pointed to the river at our feet. "The river runs forever," I said, "but the river is ever there. So is my love for you."

And as we parted I said to her: "Then you wish to have this seed of the tree?"

"To me," she said, "it is no more than a sign of destiny. If you bring it, then I shall love you. But if you are not destined then another will bring it, and I shall love him. But for the seed itself, since it is evil, it shall be fuel for the fore. Or haply—" she looked at me with steady eyes—"I may keep it till it has no more power to harm, and then it may serve as a toy for the children that I bear."

That night I slept ill, my thoughts going backward and forward between joy and sorrow like a ball that is struck by the hands of the players. It was joy that she had spoken to me seated close by my side, that she had trusted me with a secret, that of her own will she had given me the chance to gain her love.

It was sorrow that she loved me not yet, and that if I failed in the adventure, she would never love me and would love another. Nay, the man had said that there were three seeds of the tree of death. It might be that if I found one of them, another man also might find one, and he, going more swiftly or by shorter road, might take from me my beloved.

Moreover, though in this adventure I might risk all, yet if I were not destined, I should fail; and if I were destined, then, though I sat quietly in my house and risked nothing, the unseen hand would place in mine the silver seed of the tree. And so, I came back to the wisdom that is old and strong and cruel as granite rock—that which is written, is written, and that which will be, will be.

And yet what pleasure could I have of gold dust and gems, of herds and fertile land, if I had not this woman? Without her, life itself was worthless. So, I was determined to risk all. Had I not seen this myself, and had I not heard of it in many stories—that he who of his own will makes a great sacrifice shall in the end have his reward?

3

I found the old man, as I had expected, stretched upon his bed, though for some hours the sun had been up. He was ever idle, though he still had strength to work. Those that by chance listened to his stories would bring him small gifts. But if one would command a story, as I had done, then the gift was greater; and so, he lived.

And at first, as I came in from the bright sunlight, the hut seemed dark. But presently I saw him well, and I knew who had given him the robe that he wore and who had given him the loose slippers that lay on the ground beside him.

And after our words of salutation, I said to him: "I have in my mind a great matter of which I would speak with you, desiring your help. If you can help me, then in return I will give many and very rich presents. Come into my garden, where we may talk quietly, and there is pleasant shade, and the fruit of last year still hangs upon my orange-tree."

So, he said courteously that I was without doubt of divine descent and that he was my servant. And, rising from the bed, he thrust his feet into his slippers and came shuffling after me.

Seated under the orange-tree, he sipped the coffee that was brought out to him, but the oranges that I gave him he wrapped in a fold of his robe for another time.

"Last night," I said, "you told us of the tree of death."

"And for that reason," he said, "a woman brought me this morning bread and coffee, but the coffee was less good than this."

"She was beautiful?"

"She was a song of love, but unfortunately I am now old. When I had eaten and drunk, I went out and found that son of a dog who said that I lied, and beat him with my slipper until he howled. For I had told him of things that have been and still are. True, I have also stories of things that might be, and these are more beautiful. What of it? Shall the young insult the old? But this matter in which you need my help, I beg you to tell me of it."

"I go to seek one of the three silver seeds of the tree of death. As beside that, my life and such wealth as I have are nothing. I must have that seed. You can tell me whither I must go and what I must do to attain it."

"If a man travel with the utmost rapidity and sparing nothing, he may make the journey in four months."

"Then in four months I will accomplish it."

"There are perils of the road—robbers and dangerous beasts."

"I fear them not." And I showed him the dagger that I carried.

"But you will come to a country where the stranger is suspect, and in the place where the silver seed lies guarded no stranger may enter at all; and the guard is threefold—a circle, and within it a second circle, and within that a third circle. You may stain your skin till it is as dark as mine, but you cannot speak in the tongue of that people, neither do you know their ways. And if you would attain your end by violence, you will be one man against a myriad of men. So, that if you go, two things are certain. The first is that you will never even see the silver seed, and the second is that you will die very soon."

"Have you no better help for me than this?"

"There may be another way. You said truly that this is a great matter. It is one that must be weighed well with long thought. I will, if you please, go back now and ponder upon it. And tomorrow at this time I will come again to you."

So, I gave him a present and let him go, his robe curiously swollen with many oranges that he carried.

And next day he came back to me and said: "There is one way, and one only. It may bring you what you seek but it is not sure. If you would take it, two things will be necessary. The first is that you must trust me utterly, more than most men will trust their brothers. Secondly, the cost will be great, so that of all your possessions there will be but little left to you."

"You are sure that it is the only way?"

"It is the only way."

"Then I will take it. Tell me of it."

"You cannot go, but I can go for you. Also, I am very willing to go. Twenty years have I been a stranger in this little place, and my own country calls me. I know the tongue of the people and all their ways. Moreover, I myself have been of the innermost guard of the temple, and know much which is hidden from most men of my race. If there is any man on earth who can get the seed of the tree of death, then I can get it. But I must be able to buy men, and they are such that a small present will not tempt them."

"When will you return?"

"In the ninth month from that day that I can start you should have the silver seed either at my hand or at the hand of a sure messenger."

"If I trust you whom at least I know, that may be well. Must I trust also as messenger whom I do not know?"

"You may do so without fear. For he will not receive the last half of his reward until he has delivered the seed into your hands. Moreover, he will know that if he is treacherous, his own life and the life of his dearest that he leaves behind him will be forfeited."

"It is a great journey, and you are old."

"I still have strength, not having spent myself with too much labour. Moreover, there are two that travel speedily—the young man that goes to his beloved and the old man that returns at last to his native country."

"You have no fear that you will be robbed? For you will carry with you much wealth."

"If I went with a train of laden camels, travelling as a rich merchant, then the danger would be great. But my wealth will be hidden in a belt about my body and I shall seem to be a poor man. There is indeed the chance that death one way or another may overtake me, but both you and I must take that chance."

"How do you know that you will find the silver seeds? Since it is known that they are evil, may not they have been destroyed?"

"No, for it is know that the evil must die of itself, and they who would destroy it will make yet worse evil that shall fall on their own heads."

"When you yourself planted that seed in the garden of your wife's lover, was it then guarded in the temple? And if that be so, how came you to be able to make these great gifts and so get possession of it?"

"The temple was triply guarded, and I myself was of the innermost guard. But the seed was not there then neither was the nature of it known—save to me only—until two years after I had planted it. In quite another way did I obtain that seed, and I beg that you will not ask of it, for it was shameful to me."

Many other questions did I ask of him, and to all he had a ready answer. But I showed little judgment, my mind being filled with thoughts of my beloved. And in all things, I did as he bade me.

Then for many days I sold my possessions until the man said: "It is enough," and afterwards I journeyed with him for three days to a town where there was a great bazaar, but our business was not in the bazaar, but at the house of the principal merchants. For we bought diamonds, emeralds, and pearls. And among the pearls there were two that were twins, being perfectly alike in size and shape, in weight and colour. And when he secured this treasure into the belt that he would wear, he left out one of these twin pearls and placed it in my hand, bidding me to keep it with the utmost care.

"For," he said, "I am an old man and it is more likely that I shall choose to die in the land of my fathers. The messenger that I send with the silver seed will take the great oath of my people, swearing that he will be guilty of no negligence, and no treachery, and no disobedience. If any man takes this oath and breaks it, then in the whole earth there is no place where he may hide from swift and terrible vengeance. For this reason, no man of my people will take this oath unless for a great reward."

"It is justice," I said.

"Therefore, I give him one of the twin pearls when he sets forth. And when he arrives and places in your hands the silver seed, you will give him the other. Then he will return and show me the two pearls, and that will be the sign that he has performed his oath, and I shall have written for him quittance of it. So, he will sell the pearls and get himself a wife and a house, and I myself may die in peace."

And he found a brown-sailed boat that went up with a favouring wind to the next village carrying sugarcane. And making a small payment to the owner of the boat, he stretched himself upon the sugarcane and so was carried out of my sight.

All the day he would sleep in the boat and at night he would leave the boat, and purchase an ass, swift and sure-footed, and ride all night. And so, he would go on, by this way and that, taking the best that chance offered or his wit could devise, until he came to his journey's end.

4

On the day that the man went I made my computation. My house and my walled garden were left to me, and there was enough for another month. All else—herds and fertile land, and the treasure that I had of my fathers—was changed into little stones and these stones were being carried away from me round the belly of a man whom I should never see again. In another month it seemed that I who had hired others to work for me must myself work for hire.

To most men these would have been black thoughts, and they would have rent their garments and cursed their own folly that had brought such ruin upon them. But to me all this was a source of joy. "Now truly," I said, "of mine own will have I made a great sacrifice, and in the end, I shall have my reward."

And that evening, as my custom was, I waited to see my beloved come up from the river. And as she passed me, she made a sign that I should wait. And having set the water-jar down in her father's house, she came back to me.

It was the first time she had spoken with me since the night when we heard of the tree of death and afterwards sat by the river together. True, I might have spoken to her, but I feared lest by being too importunate I should lose such favour as I had in her eyes.

"These last days," she said, "I have heard much foolish talk about you and about the old storyteller. Those that know a few things, yet have not the key of them, must always guess wrongly. But I have the key; would you hear what I know?"

"Your words are to me the sweetest music."

"Some say that the man has gone to tell his stories in other villages, that for one story he may receive many gifts. Others say he pays a visit to his own country, and others say that he goes to examine for you some house or land that you are minded to buy in place of that which you have sold. Certainly, he is gone, and another will sleep in his hut this night. It is true that he has gone to his own country, but I know that he goes to get for you the silver seed, though you declared to me that you would go yourself, even if it cost you your life, so great was love for me."

And then I told her all, as I have set it down, explaining that I had indeed been willing to go and why that could not be. And she said:

"If a man risk his life for a woman, that is his greatest praise of her. But if he buy another man to risk his life, that is a greater wisdom for him. Yet in other respects you have not acted wisely. For the old man may die, or he may be a thief; and even if he live and be worthy of trust, he may fail to get the silver seed; and even if he gets it, he may fail to render it to you. So that if the measure of your folly be the measure of your love for me, I am still commended, though with a lesser praise. Meanwhile, there will be none to tell me a story, making the cool evening pleasant for me. Moreover, that which you have given to get me you cannot give again to keep me. Also, my father has scolded me, and—"

Here she stayed, and her brow cleared, and she laughed.

"Take no heed of these words. If you are destined for me, I shall certainly love you very much. It is this heavy air that makes me say bitter things to you. Nor is it I alone who am troubled by it. The river itself is troubled—fretting and tossing—and there is anger in the setting sun. Somewhere tonight there will be havoc and great misery."

And therein she spoke the truth. For that night the earthquake came, awakening me from a deep sleep. Scarce can the fringe of it have touched the village. In my house two jars were shattered and I felt the earth move under me; but three mud-huts were brought down in ruins, so that there was much praying and screaming until the dawn came.

I judged that the full force of the earthquake had spent itself in the desert, so when the dawn came, I saddled an ass and rode into the desert to see what had befallen. And since the air was now fresh and serene, the ride was pleasant to me. And presently I saw that the outline of a great rock had changed from what it was aforetime. So, I rode up to it. And then I saw that the rock had split, revealing the entrance to a tomb.

I dismounted and went in a little way, but it was so dark within that I could distinguish nothing. And I went back to my house and said nothing of what I had seen, lest some others should forestall me.

And that night, when the village slept and all was at peace, again I rode out, taking with me a spade and a good lantern. And all the night I spent in the tomb.

I think it was the tomb of one of royal blood. It had many chambers with marvellous paintings on the walls, ranged on each side of the entrance hall, and from thence were fine wide steps that led downwards, but somewhat encumbered with sand and fallen fragments of the rock. And never had I seen such treasure—cups and platters, rings and figures, all of the purest gold. And there were also ornaments of precious stones.

Much of this treasure I had buried that night in another place, marking the spot in a way that none save he who set the mark could have the skill to see. And on many of the nights that followed I buried further treasure. And I had none to help me, for I could trust none.

So, once more it became necessary for me to go to that great town. By night I loaded two camels with treasure, hiding it so that it would appear that they carried forage only. And even so I travelled in great fear, with my dagger ever ready to my hand, and urging the camels to their greatest speed.

But it was appointed that I should arrive safely. And I was well received in the houses of the principal merchants with whom I had traded before, and so disposed of my treasure.

Thus, by chance all that which I had given up, in order that I might have the silver seed and thereby the heart of my beloved, was restored to me again, and at first, I was well content.

But afterwards my eyes were opened, and in great anguish I saw what had befallen me. For of my own free will had I made sacrifice and it had not been accepted, and that which I had given was returned into my hands again. What reward then, could I hope?

"Without doubt," I said, "the earthquake overtook the old story-teller as he went through the night and he is buried beneath fallen rocks or is drowned in the river. And the desire of my heart is taken from me."

And that very night I spoke with a man who, as he was travelling towards the village on the day of the earthquake, had met the old man. Thus, vainly do we fit our keys to the door that is ever locked. That which is written, is written, and that which will be, will be. So that now I no longer dared to forecast either my happiness or the manner of my suffering. I folded my hands and waited.

Once more in the evening my beloved spoke to me.

"They speak of you in the village after this manner," she said. "They say that you sold much and that now you buy much, and that in the difference of the price you have your advantage. This is the wisdom of fools who speak, not having the key. But I have the key. I know that, when you sold, the old man took it away with him, so that I even marvelled if my father would willingly give me to one who had become poor. Whence, then, have you the means now to buy so much? Either you lied to me, and the old man bore no wealth of precious stones in his belt, or you have worked some great magic. And if it be the first, then he will not send you the silver seed, for it was not his habit to do much for little, nor are you destined for me. But if it be

165

the second, then I beg that you will show me how to work the same magic, that I may make my father very content and also buy for myself a new robe and bracelet of gold."

"Neither have I lied to you, nor have I worked any magic. Since you gave me your secret, and have kept close in your own heart what I have told you so far, I will trust you yet again. It was destined that I should find a great treasure, making up for all that I had bestowed on the old man. Ask me no more of this now, but tell me why you wish for a new robe and a bracelet of gold?"

"I have a cousin, and she is beautiful, but not so beautiful as you think I am. Also, the time has come that she must be married. Neither she nor I know who her husband will be, but she is obedient and will leave the choice to her father. Undoubtedly, he will choose a rich man, and there will be a very great festival of the marriage, lasting all the night through, with music and dancing girls. Surely I shall be bidden to the festival, and I would not be ashamed there. But my father is not rich, neither does he ever find anything."

"Then it is you who must find."

"What shall I find?"

"A purse hidden in a basket of pomegranates. And this basket of pomegranates I will send to your father's house soon after the hour of sunrise tomorrow."

"Listen," she said. "Your love for me is as the desert, and my love for you is not even yet as one grain of sand. Will you still send this gift?"

"I will still send it."

She said that, if it were known, the tongues of the malicious would speak evil of her, and, therefore, it would be a secret. And she was pleased, just as a child may be pleased with a little gift. She had said truly that she was still very young. She laughed and played with the maidens of her age. And neither for me nor for any other man had she one thought of love.

Yet even then love slept deep in her calm eyes, as the fish with golden scales lies sleeping at the bottom of a deep pool. And the time of awakening was near.

5

He that enjoys knows how swift the passage of time may be. But at last, eight months had passed since the departure of the old storyteller, and he had said that in the next month—the great month of fruition—I should receive the silver seed of the tree of death—if, indeed, I ever received it.

So now in every footstep I seemed to hear the sound of an approaching messenger, and in every sound to hear my name called. My blood grew hot as with a fever and my sleep left me, so that for the greater part of the night I paced I my garden alone.

All night on the ninth night of the month I heard in the distance the sounds of music and revelry. It was the wedding of the cousin of my beloved, and there was a great festival. But towards dawn the sounds died away, and I paced to and fro in my garden. And suddenly, as I passed the door in the wall of the garden, I heard a little sound, and I was called by my name. But it was not the voice of any messenger that called. It was the voice of my beloved.

I opened the door and bade her enter. She came in without a word, wearing the new robe and the golden bracelet. And in the grey and awful light of dawn her face seemed still wondrous beautiful, and yet changed.

"You are weary?" I said.

She made a sign of assent.

"Yes," I said, "the marriage festival was long. All night I heard the music. Your eyes tell of your weariness." And I spread a silken carpet for her under a tree that she might rest, greatly wondering that she should come to me in this way.

She knelt on the carpet, bending her body and covering her face with her hands.

"I have not been at the festival," she said. "Oh, I have much to say and there is not one word of it that you can ever forgive. Yet promise to hear me to the end, and then—then do with me as you will."

Then my heart fainted and doom sang in my ears. And there was a long silence before I could say: "I will hear you to the end."

And now she stretched herself at full length on the rug, her hands clasped behind her head. And she spoke like a tired child that repeats a long lesson.

"Yesterday," she said, "at sunrise I went down to wash myself in the water of the river. And when I had put on my garment again and risen up, I was aware that a youth came towards me riding upon a white ass that was bedecked with silver ornaments. And he dismounted and looked long at me. He was darker than we are, yet not so dark as the old storyteller. And I read in his eyes that which I have read in yours and in the eyes of other men. I knew that he desired me. Every day a beautiful woman may read that language. Yet it moved me not, and it was as if there was a mist before my eyes.

"He named you and asked me where he might find you, speaking in our tongue but slowly, as one but newly accustomed to it.

"I said: 'If you follow me, I will take you to him.'

"'And afterwards?' he said. 'For you are more beautiful than any woman on this earth, and it is for you that my love has waited.'

"I laughed, for there was still the mist before my eyes. Besides, such a speech was daring and sudden, since he now saw me for the first time. 'Afterwards,' I said, 'will be as it will be. Meantime what seek you with this man?'

"He turned his eyes from me, as if he feared to look on me. 'It is forbidden to me,' he said, 'so much as to speak of it.'

"Now, whether you believe it or not, it is true that in the next words which I said I had no intent but to vex him a little. Was not the mist still before my eyes, so that I could not judge aright? Was I any more than the thistle-seed caught in the wind of destiny?

"I said, still laughing: 'You love me, and yet you refuse the first thing that I ask of you?'

"And now he looked long at me again, breathing deeply, and suddenly he thrust his hand into his robe and drew forth something that glistened.

"'Since you ask it,' he said, 'behold! I go to render this to him'

"And so he stood before me, holding in his hand a ball that was not of silver but of the colour of silver, and in the ball there was life and death. Thus, was it determined in the beginning, before the stars were set and before the earth was shaped. The mist passed from my eyes and I saw that there was no beauty like his beauty. And when he spoke his voice was dearer to me than any that I have ever heard. And never had there been such love as now burnt my whole being.

"'See!' he cried. 'I have broken the great oath, and for that death will come soon upon me. My hours are numbered, and yet if they be hours of love, the price is small. Do I not love you? Do I not worship you?'

"My head drooped and my eyes fainted and I sank down on my knees. 'Lord of my heart!' I said. 'Lord of my life.'"

And now she turned over on her face, and her whole body was shaken with weeping.

For a few moments I remained silent, and then I said: "Have you ended that which you would say to me?"

168

"No, no!" she cried. "No, no!"

"Speak on then," I said, "and I would beg you to speak quickly."

Now she rose to her feet, and thereafter she spoke standing, holding to the trunk of the tree as if for support.

"He had come by the way of the desert, and the night before he had come to the great rock. And finding a great tomb in the rock, he had rested there for the night, and there he had left his gear, setting forth with the white ass to find you, and so to complete his mission.

"Little thought had he now of that mission. And since already people were astir in the village, he took me back with him to the tomb in the rock. I rode and he ran by my side, and in less than an hour we were there alone with our love in the cool dusk of the tomb.

"And when it drew near to the evening, I was afraid lest my father should send out on all sides to seek me, and haply I should be found with my lover. So, I arose and went to my father's house, and when he demanded why I had been away so long, I said I had been helping in the preparation for my cousin's festival. Moreover, I put on my new robe and the gold bracelet on my arm, and said to him that I now went to her wedding. And he was content, and disposed himself to sleep, for he is old and feeble and unsuited to a night of revelry.

"And so, in breathless haste I went back to my lover, knowing that our hours were but few, and that eternity could scarce contain our love. Until an hour ago I was with him, and then it was necessary to see you. And I came near the latticed door of your garden, and, hearing your step, I called to you. And so, I come to the very heart of the matter."

Here, pausing, she looked intently at me. And presently she went on speaking.

"There is neither anger nor mercy in your eyes. They have become like the eyes of a stone image in a temple—eyes that change not and see not. Hear me now to the end.

"He has broken the great oath, and the punishment is sure. One will come to him—he knows not when, but it will be very soon—and will say to him: 'show me the twin pearls that are in all things alike, for this is the proof that you have fulfilled your oath.' And if he has them not, then must he be slain instantly. And, further in that far country from whence he came the life of his mother will be forfeited, for she was the surety for him in the great oath. And shall not his death be also mine?

"He has but one of the twin pearls, and the other is in your keeping. So that you now hold in your hand three lives.

"It may be that you will say to yourself that I was very young, and that when I tempted him to break his oath, I knew not what I did. And you may say further that your hatred is against destiny, and not with these thistle-seeds that the wind of destiny has swept together. If that were so, and you gave me the twin pearl and let us depart with it to his own country, then in all the words of praise there is none, that is worthy of such a great nobility.

"But in that I ask, it may be, more than any man can give. So, if you still desire me, I will remain here. And if you would have me as a wife or as a slave, I will be ever faithful and obedient. And I ask no reward but that by some instant messenger you will send the twin pearl to my lover, that he may go in peace. And I myself will see him no more at all. Do with me as you will, but let not his blood be upon my head. The fault was mine. Moreover, he has in part fulfilled his oath, for by me he sends to you the seed of the tree of death. I pray you to answer me."

It is very truth that until then I knew not what I would answer. But as she spoke, she drew from her garment that silver glistening ball, and held it out to me, and I took it. It was still warm with the warmth of her beautiful body.

In a moment I had buried my dagger deep in her body. She fell at my feet, and a shudder went through her, and she was dead.

I became quite calm again, and my mind was as clear water, and my heart beat steadily and quietly. I knew just what I would do.

I dug a deep grave for her in a corner of my garden. Then I drew forth the dagger, wrapped her in the silken carpet, and so buried her and the silver seed with her.

I made the earth smooth over her, and cleaned my dagger. And at last, it was all so ordered that the garden looked even as it looked the morning before, and there was no trace of that which had been done. Neither had any eye beheld it.

And then I rode forth to the tomb that I had found in the great rock, and that the woman's lover had also found. But there, even as I feared, I came too late, and my work had been done for me.

The man lay dead in the entrance to the tomb with a knife in his throat. The bundle of fodder that he had carried for the ass had been spread out like a couch, and beside it were a jar of water and a brass cup. But the white ass bedecked with silver ornaments was no longer there; and I supposed that the man who had slain him had taken it, but he had not taken the twin pearl, for that lay on the open hand of the dead man. There I left it. And I left the dead man to the vultures and jackals. And I saw that all the time the messenger journeyed from that far country another had travelled close behind him, watching to see if he fulfilled his oath, and with the power to slay him if he broke it.

And after that I went back to my own house and lay on my bed, preparing for myself that which I believed should be my last sleep, merging itself in the end in death. But the drug that I took failed me. Sleep, indeed, I obtained, but at noon on the following day I waked again. And in my sleep, it was revealed to me that not at this time, nor after this manner, should my death be. There were to be yet two years of waiting for me, while the silver seed woke to life where I had set it, even in the very heart of death.

6

It was said in the village that my beloved had fled with a man of another race—for the two had been seen together—thus bringing shame upon her father's house. It was also said by others that the river had taken her, for she was accustomed to wash herself in the water of the river. And some said one thing and some another, but none said the truth, nor did any accuse me.

And as the tale of the months grew, I became greatly changed. No longer could the beauty of any woman move me, nor could any enterprise attract me. Had fabulous wealth been within my reach I would not have put out my hand to it. I was almost without wishes, save the wish to be alone. Never was there a guest in my house, nor the sound of music, nor laughter. Long and sweet sleep at night had left me, and I slept fitfully at strange hours, haunted always by dreams that seemed so real, that waking I scarce knew whether I was awake or slept, nor which was the substance and which the shadow.

Waking or sleeping, the thought of her whom I loved was ever present with me. I longed to call her up from death that I might tell her how nearly I had come to forgiveness, and how slight a thing in the end had driven me to madness. It grieved me that she would never know that. There was no longer any jealousy or rancour in my heart towards her. She had been ever as she had said, as thistledown caught in the wind of destiny.

After the first year of waiting, I sometimes saw her as I walked in my garden in the cool of the evening. She came and vanished again, like smoke scattered by the wind. And as the second year drew on, the vision came more frequently and remained longer with me. Even I heard her speak. She stood beneath my orange-tree, and she opened her robe wide and pointed to the wound in her breast.

"You have hurt me," she said. "How could you hurt her whom you loved?"

And at last, the day came when the tree of death should rise to twice the height of a man, and should drink my blood, and should die again, and all betwixt a sunrise and a sunset.

The sun was not fully risen when I examined the earth over her grave. None other but myself was permitted to come into that part of the garden, and it was with my own hands that I had kept it free of all chance growth. And I saw now that there were in the earth crevices like the picture of the sun's rays, and through the centres of these something hard pushed its way. It was rounded at the top, and it was dark green and crimson intermingled, and on the surface of it were little drops of moisture as though it sweated with the struggle to get through.

Then I went back through the empty garden to the empty house, for on the day before I had sent forth those that waited on me. And I bathed myself and put on a white robe, and then I saw to it that the doors were securely locked, and came back to the tree of death. It had risen now to the height of my knee, and it was still a single shaft tapering upwards, and it seemed to me that a light vapour came from it. And sitting down I watched this great miracle.

When it was the height of a man many stems separated themselves from the main stem save at the base where they were joined to it, and these lolled outwards and grew no more. But from these side stems a shower of tendrils began to descend, writhing in the air as if they had been serpents. And looking closely I saw that each of them was covered with little mouths that opened and shut continuously. But the centre stem grew upwards tapering still, but carrying at the summit a curious mass. This increased in size, and I knew that from it would come the flower of the tree.

It was the hour of noon. I withdrew myself a little and watched. From the side stems the rain of tendrils descended continuously, and they covered the ground so that over the place where I had laid her here was a moving sea of green and crimson. And shortly after noon the heavy mass at the head of the stem separated into three pods; the skin of them was like clear, thin silk, and they had veins like the veins of a man. I could see them swelling more and more, and that something white seemed to be struggling within them, and the top of the stem rocked to and fro a little as if in agony.

So far all had gone on in silence. But suddenly the skin of one of these pods was rent fro end to end, and in the rending, it made a sound like a woman that is hurt. From the burst pod there leapt a white flower of gorgeous beauty, greater than I have ever seen, and from the flower there fell a cloud of gold dust, sparkling in the sunlight, and the perfume of it, even at the distance where I stood, was of almost intolerable richness.

Then I cried aloud the words that came to me:

"O tree of love!" I cried. "You whose roots have devoured and taken into your being all that I have loved on earth, now take me also, that at the last we may be mingled together, and after the anguish and evil of life there may be peace. O tree of love and death, I come to you!"

And I went forward slowly and knelt beside the tree, looking upwards. And twice I heard that cry as of a woman that is hurt as the second and third flower burst forth. The clouds of gold dust blinded my eyes, and the heavy scent suffocated me. I fell at full length among those ramping tendrils whose little mouths sought my blood. And the last sleep came.

★★★★★★★★★★★★

I have written this, I who have been long dead, so that my bones are dust and for countless years my name has been forgotten. And I have written in a strange language and in a strange land, and by the living hand of one whom I know not.

The Burned House

Vincent O'Sullivan

One night at the end of dinner, the last time I crossed the Atlantic, somebody in our group remarked that we were just passing over the spot where the Lusitania had gone down. Whether this was the case or not, the thought of it was enough to make us rather grave, and we dropped into some more or less serious discussion about the emotions of men and women who see all hope gone, and realise that they are going to sink with the vessel. From that the talk wandered to the fate of the drowned: was not theirs, after all, a fortunate end? Somebody related details from the narratives of those who had been all but drowned in the accidents of the war.

A Scotch lady inquired fancifully if the ghosts of those who are lost at sea ever appear above the waters and come aboard ships. Would there be danger of seeing one when the light was turned out in her cabin? This put an end to all seriousness, and most of us laughed. But a little tight-faced man from Fall River, bleak and iron-grey, who had been listening attentively, did not laugh. The lady noticed his decorum and appealed to him for support.

"You are like me—you believe in ghosts?" she asked lightly.

He hesitated, thinking it over.

"In ghosts?" he repeated slowly. "N-no; I don't know as I do. I've never had any personal experience that way.

I've never seen the ghost of any one I knew. Has anybody here?"

No one replied. Instead, most of us laughed again, a little uneasily, perhaps.

"Well, I guess not," resumed the man from Fall River. "All the same, strange enough things happen in life, even if you cut out ghosts, that you can't clear up by laughing. You laugh till you've had some experience big enough to shock you, and then you don't laugh any more. It's like being thrown out of a car—"

At this moment there was a blast on the whistle, and everybody rushed up on deck. As it turned out, we had only entered into a belt of fog. On the upper deck I fell in again with the New-Englander, smoking a cigar and walking up and down. We took a few turns together, and he referred to the conversation at dinner. Our laughter evidently rankled in his mind.

"So many damn' strange things happen in life that you can't account for," he protested. "You go on laughing at faith-healing and at dreams and this and that, and then something comes along that you just can't explain. You have got to throw up your hands and allow that it doesn't answer to any tests our experience has provided us with. Now, I guess I'm as matter of fact a man as any of those folks down there. I'm in the outfitting business. My favourite author is Ingersoll; whenever I go on a journey like this, I carry one of his books.

"If you read Ingersoll and *think* Ingersoll year in, year out, you don't have much use for wool-gathering. But once I had an experience which I had to conclude was out of the ordinary. Whether other people believe it or not, or whether they think they can explain it, don't matter; it happened to me, and I could no more doubt it than I could doubt having had a tooth pulled after the dentist had done it. I only wish Ingersoll was still alive; I'd like to put it up to him. If you will sit down here with me in this corner out of the wind, I'll tell you how it was.

"Some years ago, I had to be for several months in New York. I was before the courts; it does not signify now what for, and it is all forgotten by this time. But it was a long and worrying case, and it aged me by twenty years. Well, sir, all through the trial, in that grimy courtroom, I kept thinking and thinking of a fresh little place I knew in the Vermont hills; and I helped to get through the hours by thinking that if things went well with me I'd go there at once. And so it was that on the very next morning after I was acquitted, I stepped on the cars at the Grand Central station.

"It was the early fall; the days were closing in, and it was night and cold when I arrived. The village was very dark and deserted; they don't go out much after dark in those parts, anyhow, and the keen mountain wind was enough to quell any lingering desire. The hotel was not one of those modern places called inns from sentiment in America, which are equipped and upholstered like the great city hotels; it was one of the real old-fashioned New England taverns, about as uncomfortable places as there are on earth, where the idea is to show the traveller that traveling is a penitential state, and that morally and physically the best place for him is home.

"The landlord brought me a kind of supper, with his hat on and a pipe in his mouth. The room was chilly; but when I asked for a fire, he said he guessed he couldn't go out to the wood-pile till morning. There was nothing else to do when I had eaten my supper but to go outside, both to get the smell of the lamp out of my nose and to warm myself by a short walk.

"As I did not know the country well, I did not mean to go far. But although it was an overcast night, with a high northeast wind and an occasional flurry of rain, the moon was up, and even concealed by clouds as it was, it yet lit the night with a kind of twilight grey, not vivid, like the open moonlight, but good enough to see some distance. On account of this I prolonged my stroll, and kept walking on and on till I was a considerable way from the village, and in a region as lonely as anywhere in the State. Great trees and shrubs bordered the road, and many feet below was a mountain stream.

"What with the passion of the wind pouring through the high trees and the shout of the water racing among the boulders, it seemed to me sometimes like the noise of a crowd of people, and two or three times I turned to see if a crowd might be out after me, well as I knew that no crowd could be there. Sometimes the branches of the trees became so thick that I was walking as if in a black pit, unable to see my hand close to my face. Then, coming out from the tunnel of branches, I would step once more into a grey clearness which opened the road and surrounding country a good way on all sides.

"I suppose it might be some three quarters of an hour I had been walking when I came to a fork of the road. One branch ran downward, getting almost on a level with the bed of the torrent. The other mounted in a steep hill, and this, after a little idle debating, I decided to follow. After I had climbed for more than half a mile, thinking that if I should happen to lose track of one of the landmarks, I should be very badly lost, the path—for it was now no more than that—curved, and I came out on a broad plateau.

"There, to my astonishment, I saw a house. It was a good-sized wooden house, three stories high, with a *piazza* round two sides of it, and from the elevation on which it stood it commanded a far stretch of country. There were a few great trees at a little distance from the house, and behind it, a stone's-throw away, was a clump of bushes. Still, it looked lonely and stark, offering its four sides unprotected to the winds. For all that, I was very glad to see it. 'It does not matter now,' I thought, 'whether I have lost my way or not. The house people will set me right.'

"But when I came up to it, I found that it was, to all appearance, uninhabited. The shutters were closed on all the windows; there was not a spark of light anywhere. There was something about it, something sinister and barren, that gave me the kind of shiver you have at the door of a room where you know that a dead man lies inside, or if you get thinking hard about dropping over the rail into that black waste of writers out there. This feeling, you know, isn't altogether unpleasant; you relish all the better your present security. It was the same with me standing before that house.

"I was not *really* scared. I was alone up here, miles from any kind of help, at the mercy of whoever might be lurking behind the shutters of that sullen house; but I felt that by all the chances I was perfectly alone and safe. My sensation of the uncanny was due to the effect on the nerves produced by wild scenery and the unexpected sight of a house in such a very lonely situation. Thus, I reasoned, and instead of following the road farther, I walked over the grass till I came to a stone wall perhaps two hundred and fifty yards in front of the house, and rested my arms on it, looking forth at the scene.

"On the crests of the hills far away a strange light lingered, like the first touch of dawn in the sky on a rainy morning or the last glimpse of twilight before night comes. Between me and the hills was a wide stretch of open country. On my right hand was an apple-orchard, and I observed that a stile had been made in the wall of piled stones to enable the house people to go back and forth.

"Now, after I had been there leaning on the wall some considerable time, I saw a man coming toward me through the orchard. He was walking with a good, free stride, and as he drew nearer, I could see that he was a tall, sinewy fellow between twenty-five and thirty, with a shaven face, wearing the slouch-hat of that country, a dark woollen shirt, and high boots. When he reached the stile and began climbing over it, I bade him goodnight in neighbourly fashion. He made no reply, but he looked me straight in the face, and the look gave me a qualm.

"Not that it was an evil face, mind you—it was a handsome, serious face—but it was ravaged by some terrible passion: stealth was on it, ruthlessness, and a deadly resolution, and at the same time such a look as a man driven by some uncontrollable power might throw on surrounding things, asking for comprehension and mercy. It was impossible for me to resent his churlishness, his thoughts were so certainly elsewhere. I doubt if he even saw me.

"He could not have gone by more than a quarter of a minute when I turned to look after him. He had disappeared. The plateau lay bare before me, and it seemed impossible that even if he had sprinted like an athlete he could have got inside the house in so little time. But I have always made it a rule to attribute what I cannot understand to natural causes that I have failed to observe. I said to myself that no doubt the man had gone back into the orchard by some other opening in the wall lower down, or there might be some flaw in my vision owing to the uncertain and distorting light.

"But even as I continued to look toward the house, leaning my back now against the wall, I noticed that there were lights springing up in the windows behind the shutters. They were flickering lights, now bright, now dim, and had a ruddy glow like firelight. Before I had looked long, I became convinced that it was indeed firelight: the house was on fire. Black smoke began to pour from the roof; the red sparks flew in the wind. Then at a window above the roof of the *piazza* the shutters were thrown open, and I heard a woman shriek. I ran toward the house as hard as I could, and when I drew near, I could see her plainly.

"She was a young woman; her hair fell in disorder over her white nightgown. She stretched out her bare arms, screaming. I saw a man come behind and seize her. But they were caught in a trap. The flames were licking round the windows, and the smoke was killing them. Even now the part of the house where they stood was caving in.

"Appalled by this horrible tragedy, which had thus suddenly risen before me, I made my way still nearer the house, thinking that if the two could struggle to the side of the house not bounded by the *piazza* they might jump, and I might break the fall. I was shouting this at them; I was right up close to the fire; and then I was struck by—I noticed for the first time an astonishing thing—the flames had no heat in them!

"I was standing near enough to the fire to be singed by it, and yet I felt no heat. The sparks were flying about my head; some fell on my hands, and they did not burn. And now I perceived that although the smoke was rolling in columns, I was not choked by the smoke, and that there had been no smell of smoke since the fire broke out. Neither was there any glare against the sky.

"As I stood there stupefied, wondering how these things could be, the whole house was swept by a very tornado of flame, and crashed down in a red ruin.

"Stricken to the heart by this abominable catastrophe, I made my way uncertainly down the hill, shouting for help. As I came to a little wooden bridge spanning the torrent, just beyond where the roads forked, I saw what appeared to be a rope in loose coils lying there. I saw that part of it was fastened to the railing of the bridge and hung outside, and I looked over. There was a man's body swinging by the neck between the road and the stream. I leaned over still farther, and then I recognised him as the man I had seen coming out of the orchard. His hat had fallen off, and the toes of his boots just touched the water.

"It seemed hardly possible, and yet it was certain. That was the man, and he was hanging there. I scrambled down at the side of the bridge, and put out my hand to seize the body, so that I might lift it lip and relieve the weight on the rope. I succeeded in clutching hold of his loose shirt, and for a second I thought that it had come away in my hand. Then I found that my hand had closed on nothing; I had clutched nothing but air. And yet the figure swung by the neck before my eyes!

"I was suffocated with such horror that I feared for a moment I must lose consciousness. The next minute I was running and stumbling along that dark road in mortal anxiety, my one idea being to rouse the town and bring men to the bridge. That, I say, was my intention; but the fact is that when I came at last in sight of the village, I slowed down instinctively and began to reflect. After all, I was unknown there; I had just gone through a disagreeable trial in New York, and rural people were notoriously given to groundless suspicion. I had had enough of the law and of arrests without sufficient evidence. The wisest thing would be to drop a hint or two before the landlord and judge by his demeanour whether to proceed.

"I found him sitting where I had left him, smoking, in his shirt-sleeves, with his hat on.

"'Well,' he said slowly, 'I didn't know where the gosh-blamed blazes you had got to. Been to see the folks?'

"I told him I had been taking a walk. I went on to mention casually the fork in the road, the hill, and the plateau.

"'And who lives in that house,' I asked with a good show of indifference, 'on top of the hill?'

"He stared.

"'House? There ain't no house up there,' he said positively. 'Old Joe Snedeker, who owns the land, says he's going to build a house up there for his son to live in when he gets married; but he ain't begun yet, and some folks reckon he never will.'

"'I feel sure I *saw* a house,' I protested feebly. But I was thinking—no heat in the fire, no substance in the body. I had not the courage to dispute.

"The landlord looked at me not unkindly. 'You seem sort of sick,' he remarked. 'Guess you been doin' too much down in the city. What you want is to go to bed.'"

The man from Fall River paused, and for a moment we sat silent, listening to the pant of the machinery, the thrumming of the wind in the wire stays, and the lash of the sea. Some voices were singing on the deck below. I considered him with the shade of contemptuous superiority we feel, as a rule, toward those who tell us their dreams or what some fortune-teller has predicted.

"Hallucinations," I said at last, with reassuring indulgence. "Trick of the vision. toxic ophthalmia. After the long strain of your trial your nerves were shattered."

"That's what I thought myself," he replied shortly, "especially after I had been out to the plateau the next morning and saw no sign that a house had ever stood there."

"And no corpse at the bridge?" I said, and laughed.

"And no corpse at the bridge."

He tried to get a light for another cigar. This took him some little time, and when at last he managed it, he got out of his chair and stood looking down at me.

"Now listen here. I told you that the thing happened several years ago. I'd got almost to forget it; if you can only persuade yourself that a thing is a freak of imagination, it pretty soon gets dim inside your head. Delusions have no staying power once it is realized that they are delusions. Whenever it did come back to me, I used to think how near I had once been to going out of my mind. That was all.

"Well, last year I went up to that village again from Boston. I went to the same hotel and found the same landlord. He remembered me at once as 'The feller who come up from the city and thought he see a house. I believe you had the jim-jams,' he said.

"We laughed, and the landlord spat.

"'There's been a house there since, though.'

181

"'Has there?'

"'Why, yes; an' it ha' been as well if there never had been. Old man Snedeker built it for his son, a fine big house with a *piazza* on two sides. The son, young Joe, got courting Mamie Elting from here around. She'd gone down to work in a store somewhere in Connecticut—darned if I can remember where. New Haven or Danbury, maybe. Well, sir, she used to get carrying on with another young feller bout here, Jim Travers, and Jim was sure wild about her; used to save up his quarters to go down State to see her. But she turned him down in the end, and married Joe; I guess because Joe had the house, and the old man's money to expect. Well, poor Jim must ha' gone plumb crazy. What do you think he did? The very first night the new-wed pair spent in that house he burned it down. Burned the two of them in their bed, and he was as nice and quiet a feller as you want to see. He may ha' been full of whisky at the time.'

"'No, he wasn't,' I said.

"The landlord looked surprised.

"'I guess you've heard some about it?'

"'No; go on.'

"'Yes, sir, he burned them in their bed. And then what do you think he did? He hung himself at the little bridge half a mile below. Do you remember where the road divides? Well, it was there. I saw his body hanging there myself the next morning. The toes of his boots were just touching the water.'"

A Case of Eavesdropping

Algernon Blackwood

Jim Shorthouse was the sort of fellow who always made a mess of things. Everything with which his hands or mind came into contact issued from such contact in an unqualified and irremediable state of mess. His college days were a mess: he was twice rusticated. His schooldays were a mess: he went to half a dozen, each passing him on to the next with a worse character and in a more developed state of mess. His early boyhood was the sort of mess that copy-books and dictionaries spell with a big "M," and his babyhood—ugh! was the embodiment of howling, yowling, screaming mess.

At the age of forty, however, there came a change in his troubled life, when he met a girl with half a million in her own right, who consented to marry him, and who very soon succeeded in reducing his most messy existence into a state of comparative order and system.

Certain incidents, important and otherwise, of Jim's life would never have come to be told here but for the fact that in getting into his "messes" and out of them again he succeeded in drawing himself into the atmosphere of peculiar circumstances and strange happenings. He attracted to his path the curious adventures of life as unfailingly as meat attracts flies, and jam wasps. It is to the meat and jam of his life, so to speak, that he owes his experiences; his afterlife was all pudding, which attracts nothing but greedy children. With marriage the interest of his life ceased for all but one person, and his path became regular as the sun's instead of erratic as a comet's.

The first experience in order of time that he related to me shows that somewhere latent behind his disarranged nervous system there lay psychic perceptions of an uncommon order. About the age of twenty-two—I think after his second rustication—his father's purse and patience had equally given out, and Jim found himself stranded

183

high and dry in a large American city. High and dry! And the only clothes that had no holes in them safely in the keeping of his uncle's wardrobe.

Careful reflection on a bench in one of the city parks led him to the conclusion that the only thing to do was to persuade the city editor of one of the daily journals that he possessed an observant mind and a ready pen, and that he could "do good work for your paper, sir, as a reporter." This, then, he did, standing at a most unnatural angle between the editor and the window to conceal the whereabouts of the holes.

"Guess we'll have to give you a week's trial," said the editor, who, ever on the lookout for good chance material, took on shoals of men in that way and retained on the average one man per shoal. Anyhow it gave Jim Shorthouse the wherewithal to sew up the holes and relieve his uncle's wardrobe of its burden.

Then he went to find living quarters; and in this proceeding his unique characteristics already referred to—what theosophists would call his Karma—began unmistakably to assert themselves, for it was in the house he eventually selected that this sad tale took place.

There are no "diggings" in American cities. The alternatives for small incomes are grim enough—rooms in a boarding-house where meals are served, or in a room-house where no meals are served—not even breakfast. Rich people live in palaces, of course, but Jim had nothing to do with "sich-like." His horizon was bounded by boarding-houses and room-houses; and, owing to the necessary irregularity of his meals and hours, he took the latter.

It was a large, gaunt-looking place in a side street, with dirty windows and a creaking iron gate, but the rooms were large, and the one he selected and paid for in advance was on the top floor. The landlady looked gaunt and dusty as the house, and quite as old. Her eyes were green and faded, and her features large.

"Waal," she twanged, with her electrifying Western drawl, "that's the room, if you like it, and that's the price I said. Now, if you want it, why, just say so; and if you don't, why, it don't hurt me any."

Jim wanted to shake her, but he feared the clouds of long-accumulated dust in her clothes, and as the price and size of the room suited him, he decided to take it.

"Anyone else on this floor?" he asked.

She looked at him queerly out of her faded eyes before she answered.

"None of my guests ever put such questions to me before," she said; "but I guess you're different. Why, there's no one at all but an old gent that's stayed here every bit of five years. He's over thar," pointing to the end of the passage.

"Ah! I see," said Shorthouse feebly. "So I'm alone up here?"

"Reckon you are, pretty near," she twanged out, ending the conversation abruptly by turning her back on her new "guest," and going slowly and deliberately downstairs.

The newspaper work kept Shorthouse out most of the night. Three times a week he got home at 1 a.m., and three times at 3 a.m. The room proved comfortable enough, and he paid for a second week. His unusual hours had so far prevented his meeting any inmates of the house, and not a sound had been heard from the "old gent" who shared the floor with him. It seemed a very quiet house.

One night, about the middle of the second week, he came home tired after a long day's work. The lamp that usually stood all night in the hall had burned itself out, and he had to stumble upstairs in the dark. He made considerable noise in doing so, but nobody seemed to be disturbed. The whole house was utterly quiet, and probably everybody was asleep. There were no lights under any of the doors. All was in darkness. It was after two o'clock.

After reading some English letters that had come during the day, and dipping for a few minutes into a book, he became drowsy and got ready for bed. Just as he was about to get in between the sheets, he stopped for a moment and listened. There rose in the night, as he did so, the sound of steps somewhere in the house below. Listening attentively, he heard that it was somebody coming upstairs—a heavy tread, and the owner taking no pains to step quietly. On it came up the stairs, tramp, tramp, tramp—evidently the tread of a big man, and one in something of a hurry.

At once thoughts connected somehow with fire and police flashed through Jim's brain, but there were no sounds of voices with the steps, and he reflected in the same moment that it could only be the old gentleman keeping late hours and tumbling upstairs in the darkness. He was in the act of turning out the gas and stepping into bed, when the house resumed its former stillness by the footsteps suddenly coming to a dead stop immediately outside his own room.

With his hand on the gas, Shorthouse paused a moment before turning it out to see if the steps would go on again, when he was startled by a loud knocking on his door. Instantly, in obedience to

185

a curious and unexplained instinct, he turned out the light, leaving himself and the room in total darkness.

He had scarcely taken a step across the room to open the door, when a voice from the other side of the wall, so close it almost sounded in his ear, exclaimed in German, "Is that you, father? Come in."

The speaker was a man in the next room, and the knocking, after all, had not been on his own door, but on that of the adjoining chamber, which he had supposed to be vacant.

Almost before the man in the passage had time to answer in German, "Let me in at once," Jim heard someone cross the floor and unlock the door. Then it was slammed to with a bang, and there was audible the sound of footsteps about the room, and of chairs being drawn up to a table and knocking against furniture on the way. The men seemed wholly regardless of their neighbour's comfort, for they made noise enough to waken the dead.

"Serves me right for taking a room in such a cheap hole," reflected Jim in the darkness. "I wonder whom she's let the room to!"

The two rooms, the landlady had told him, were originally one. She had put up a thin partition—just a row of boards—to increase her income. The doors were adjacent, and only separated by the massive upright beam between them. When one was opened or shut the other rattled.

With utter indifference to the comfort of the other sleepers in the house, the two Germans had meanwhile commenced to talk both at once and at the top of their voices. They talked emphatically, even angrily. The words "Father" and "Otto" were freely used. Shorthouse understood German, but as he stood listening for the first minute or two, an eavesdropper in spite of himself, it was difficult to make head or tail of the talk, for neither would give way to the other, and the jumble of guttural sounds and unfinished sentences was wholly unintelligible. Then, very suddenly, both voices dropped together; and, after a moment's pause, the deep tones of one of them, who seemed to be the "father," said, with the utmost distinctness—

"You mean, Otto, that you refuse to get it?"

There was a sound of someone shuffling in the chair before the answer came. "I mean that I don't know how to get it. It is so much, father. It is *too* much. A part of it—"

"A part of it!" cried the other, with an angry oath, "a part of it, when ruin and disgrace are already in the house, is worse than useless. If you can get half you can get all, you wretched fool. Half-measures

186

only damn all concerned."

"You told me last time—" began the other firmly, but was not allowed to finish. A succession of horrible oaths drowned his sentence, and the father went on, in a voice vibrating with anger—

"You know she will give you anything. You have only been married a few months. If you ask and give a plausible reason you can get all we want and more. You can ask it temporarily. All will be paid back. It will re-establish the firm, and she will never know what was done with it. With that amount, Otto, you know I can recoup all these terrible losses, and in less than a year all will be repaid. But without it. . . . You must get it, Otto. Hear me, you must. Am I to be arrested for the misuse of trust moneys? Is our honoured name to be cursed and spat on?" The old man choked and stammered in his anger and desperation.

Shorthouse stood shivering in the darkness and listening in spite of himself. The conversation had carried him along with it, and he had been for some reason afraid to let his neighbourhood be known. But at this point he realised that he had listened too long and that he must inform the two men that they could be overheard to every single syllable. So he coughed loudly, and at the same time rattled the handle of his door. It seemed to have no effect, for the voices continued just as loudly as before, the son protesting and the father growing more and more angry. He coughed again persistently, and also contrived purposely in the darkness to tumble against the partition, feeling the thin boards yield easily under his weight, and making a considerable noise in so doing. But the voices went on unconcernedly, and louder than ever. Could it be possible they had not heard?

By this time Jim was more concerned about his own sleep than the morality of overhearing the private scandals of his neighbours, and he went out into the passage and knocked smartly at their door. Instantly, as if by magic, the sounds ceased. Everything dropped into utter silence. There was no light under the door and not a whisper could be heard within. He knocked again, but received no answer.

"Gentlemen," he began at length, with his lips close to the keyhole and in German, "please do not talk so loud. I can overhear all you say in the next room. Besides, it is very late, and I wish to sleep."

He paused and listened, but no answer was forthcoming. He turned the handle and found the door was locked. Not a sound broke the stillness of the night except the faint swish of the wind over the skylight and the creaking of a board here and there in the house below. The cold air of a very early morning crept down the passage, and made him shiver. The silence of the house began to impress him disagreeably. He looked behind him and about him, hoping, and yet fearing, that something would break the stillness. The voices still seemed to ring on in his ears; but that sudden silence, when he knocked at the door, affected him far more unpleasantly than the voices, and put strange thoughts in his brain—thoughts he did not like or approve.

Moving stealthily from the door, he peered over the banisters into the space below. It was like a deep vault that might conceal in its shadows anything that was not good. It was not difficult to fancy he saw an indistinct moving to-and-fro below him. Was that a figure sitting on the stairs peering up obliquely at him out of hideous eyes? Was that a sound of whispering and shuffling down there in the dark halls and forsaken landings? Was it something more than the inarticulate murmur of the night?

The wind made an effort overhead, singing over the skylight, and the door behind him rattled and made him start. He turned to go back to his room, and the draught closed the door slowly in his face as if there were someone pressing against it from the other side. When he pushed it open and went in, a hundred shadowy forms seemed to dart swiftly and silently back to their corners and hiding-places. But in the adjoining room the sounds had entirely ceased, and Shorthouse soon crept into bed, and left the house with its inmates, waking or sleeping, to take care of themselves, while he entered the region of dreams and silence.

Next day, strong in the common sense that the sunlight brings, he determined to lodge a complaint against the noisy occupants of the next room and make the landlady request them to modify their voices at such late hours of the night and morning. But it so happened that she was not to be seen that day, and when he returned from the office at midnight it was, of course, too late.

Looking under the door as he came up to bed he noticed that there was no light, and concluded that the Germans were not in. So much the better. He went to sleep about one o'clock, fully decided that if they came up later and woke him with their horrible noises he would not rest till he had roused the landlady and made her reprove them with that authoritative twang, in which every word was like the lash of a metallic whip.

However, there proved to be no need for such drastic measures, for Shorthouse slumbered peacefully all night, and his dreams—chiefly of the fields of grain and flocks of sheep on the far-away farms of his father's estate—were permitted to run their fanciful course unbroken.

Two nights later, however, when he came home tired out, after a difficult day, and wet and blown about by one of the wickedest storms he had ever seen, his dreams—always of the fields and sheep—were not destined to be so undisturbed.

He had already dozed off in that delicious glow that follows the removal of wet clothes and the immediate snuggling under warm blankets, when his consciousness, hovering on the borderland between sleep and waking, was vaguely troubled by a sound that rose indistinctly from the depths of the house, and, between the gusts of wind and rain, reached his ears with an accompanying sense of uneasiness and discomfort. It rose on the night air with some pretence of regularity, dying away again in the roar of the wind to reassert itself distantly in the deep, brief hushes of the storm.

For a few minutes Jim's dreams were coloured only—tinged, as it were, by this impression of fear approaching from somewhere insensibly upon him. His consciousness, at first, refused to be drawn back from that enchanted region where it had wandered, and he did not immediately awaken. But the nature of his dreams changed unpleasantly. He saw the sheep suddenly run huddled together, as though frightened by the neighbourhood of an enemy, while the fields of waving corn became agitated as though some monster were moving uncouthly among the crowded stalks. The sky grew dark, and in his dream an awful sound came somewhere from the clouds. It was in reality the sound downstairs growing more distinct.

Shorthouse shifted uneasily across the bed with something like a groan of distress. The next minute he awoke, and found himself sitting straight up in bed—listening. Was it a nightmare? Had he been dreaming evil dreams, that his flesh crawled and the hair stirred on his head?

The room was dark and silent, but outside the wind howled dismally and drove the rain with repeated assaults against the rattling windows. How nice it would be—the thought flashed through his mind—if all winds, like the west wind, went down with the sun! They made such fiendish noises at night, like the crying of angry voices. In the daytime they had such a different sound. If only——

Hark! It was no dream after all, for the sound was momentarily growing louder, and its *cause* was coming up the stairs. He found himself speculating feebly what this cause might be, but the sound was still too indistinct to enable him to arrive at any definite conclusion.

The voice of a church clock striking two made itself heard above the wind. It was just about the hour when the Germans had commenced their performance three nights before. Shorthouse made up his mind that if they began it again he would not put up with it for very long. Yet he was already horribly conscious of the difficulty he would have of getting out of bed. The clothes were so warm and comforting against his back. The sound, still steadily coming nearer, had by this time become differentiated from the confused clamour of the elements, and had resolved itself into the footsteps of one or more persons.

"The Germans, hang 'em!" thought Jim. "But what on earth is the matter with me? I never felt so queer in all my life."

He was trembling all over, and felt as cold as though he were in a freezing atmosphere. His nerves were steady enough, and he felt no diminution of physical courage, but he was conscious of a curious sense of malaise and trepidation, such as even the most vigorous men have been known to experience when in the first grip of some horrible and deadly disease. As the footsteps approached this feeling of weakness increased. He felt a strange lassitude creeping over him, a sort of exhaustion, accompanied by a growing numbness in the extremities, and a sensation of dreaminess in the head, as if perhaps the consciousness were leaving its accustomed seat in the brain and preparing to act on another plane. Yet, strange to say, as the vitality was slowly withdrawn from his body, his senses seemed to grow more acute.

Meanwhile the steps were already on the landing at the top of the stairs, and Shorthouse, still sitting upright in bed, heard a heavy body brush past his door and along the wall outside, almost immediately afterwards the loud knocking of someone's knuckles on the door of the adjoining room.

Instantly, though so far not a sound had proceeded from within, he heard, through the thin partition, a chair pushed back and a man quickly cross the floor and open the door.

"Ah! it's you," he heard in the son's voice. Had the fellow, then, been sitting silently in there all this time, waiting for his father's arrival? To Shorthouse it came not as a pleasant reflection by any means.

There was no answer to this dubious greeting, but the door was closed quickly, and then there was a sound as if a bag or parcel had been thrown on a wooden table and had slid some distance across it before stopping.

"What's that?" asked the son, with anxiety in his tone.

"You may know before I go," returned the other gruffly. Indeed his voice was more than gruff: it betrayed ill-suppressed passion.

Shorthouse was conscious of a strong desire to stop the conversation before it proceeded any further, but somehow or other his will was not equal to the task, and he could not get out of bed. The conversation went on, every tone and inflexion distinctly audible above the noise of the storm.

In a low voice the father continued. Jim missed some of the words at the beginning of the sentence. It ended with: " . . . but now they've all left, and I've managed to get up to you. You know what I've come for." There was distinct menace in his tone.

"Yes," returned the other; "I have been waiting."

"And the money?" asked the father impatiently.

No answer.

"You've had three days to get it in, and I've contrived to stave off the worst so far—but tomorrow is the end."

No answer.

"Speak, Otto! What have you got for me? Speak, my son; for God's sake, tell me."

There was a moment's silence, during which the old man's vibrating accents seemed to echo through the rooms. Then came in a low voice the answer—

"I have nothing."

"Otto!" cried the other with passion, "nothing!"

"I can get nothing," came almost in a whisper.

"You lie!" cried the other, in a half-stifled voice. "I swear you lie. Give me the money."

A chair was heard scraping along the floor. Evidently the men had been sitting over the table, and one of them had risen. Shorthouse heard the bag or parcel drawn across the table, and then a step as if one of the men was crossing to the door.

"Father, what's in that? I must know," said Otto, with the first signs of determination in his voice. There must have been an effort on the son's part to gain possession of the parcel in question, and on the father's to retain it, for between them it fell to the ground. A curious rattle followed its contact with the floor. Instantly there were sounds of a scuffle. The men were struggling for the possession of the box. The elder man with oaths, and blasphemous imprecations, the other with short gasps that betokened the strength of his efforts. It was of short duration, and the younger man had evidently won, for a minute later was heard his angry exclamation.

"I knew it. Her jewels! You scoundrel, you shall never have them. It is a crime."

The elder man uttered a short, guttural laugh, which froze Jim's blood and made his skin creep. No word was spoken, and for the space of ten seconds there was a living silence. Then the air trembled with the sound of a thud, followed immediately by a groan and the crash of a heavy body falling over on to the table. A second later there was a lurching from the table on to the floor and against the partition that separated the rooms. The bed quivered an instant at the shock, but the unholy spell was lifted from his soul and Jim Shorthouse sprang out of bed and across the floor in a single bound. He knew that ghastly murder had been done—the murder by a father of his son.

With shaking fingers but a determined heart he lit the gas, and the first thing in which his eyes corroborated the evidence of his ears was the horrifying detail that the lower portion of the partition bulged unnaturally into his own room. The glaring paper with which it was covered had cracked under the tension and the boards beneath it bent inwards towards him. What hideous load was behind them, he shuddered to think.

All this he saw in less than a second. Since the final lurch against the wall not a sound had proceeded from the room, not even a groan or a footstep. All was still but the howl of the wind, which to his ears had in it a note of triumphant horror.

Shorthouse was in the act of leaving the room to rouse the house and send for the police—in fact his hand was already on the doorknob—when something in the room arrested his attention. Out of the corner of his eyes he thought he caught sight of something moving. He was sure of it, and turning his eyes in the direction, he found he was not mistaken.

Something was creeping slowly towards him along the floor. It was something dark and serpentine in shape, and it came from the place where the partition bulged. He stooped down to examine it with feelings of intense horror and repugnance, and he discovered that it was moving toward him from the *other side* of the wall. His eyes were fascinated, and for the moment he was unable to move. Silently, slowly, from side to side like a thick worm, it crawled forward into the room beneath his frightened eyes, until at length he could stand it no longer and stretched out his arm to touch it. But at the instant of contact he withdrew his hand with a suppressed scream. It was sluggish—and it was warm! and he saw that his fingers were stained with living crimson.

A second more, and Shorthouse was out in the passage with his hand on the door of the next room. It was locked. He plunged forward with all his weight against it, and, the lock giving way, he fell headlong into a room that was pitch dark and very cold. In a moment he was on his feet again and trying to penetrate the blackness. Not a sound, not a movement. Not even the sense of a presence. It was empty, miserably empty!

Across the room he could trace the outline of a window with rain streaming down the outside, and the blurred lights of the city beyond. But the room was empty, appallingly empty; and so still. He stood there, cold as ice, staring, shivering listening. Suddenly there was a step behind him and a light flashed into the room, and when he turned quickly with his arm up as if to ward off a terrific blow he found himself face to face with the landlady. Instantly the reaction began to set in.

It was nearly three o'clock in the morning, and he was standing there with bare feet and striped pyjamas in a small room, which in the merciful light he perceived to be absolutely empty, carpetless, and without a stick of furniture, or even a window-blind. There he stood staring at the disagreeable landlady. And there she stood too, staring and silent, in a black wrapper, her head almost bald, her face white as chalk, shading a sputtering candle with one bony hand and peering over it at him with her blinking green eyes. She looked positively hideous.

"Waal?" she drawled at length, "I heard yer right enough. Guess you couldn't sleep! Or just prowlin' round a bit—is that it?"

The empty room, the absence of all traces of the recent tragedy, the silence, the hour, his striped pyjamas and bare feet—everything together combined to deprive him momentarily of speech. He stared at her blankly without a word.

"Waal?" clanked the awful voice.

"My dear woman," he burst out finally, "there's been something awful—" So far his desperation took him, but no farther. He positively stuck at the substantive.

"Oh! there hasn't been nothin'," she said slowly still peering at him. "I reckon you've only seen and heard what the others did. I never can keep folks on this floor long. Most of 'em catch on sooner or later—that is, the ones that's kind of quick and sensitive. Only you being an Englishman I thought you wouldn't mind. Nothin' really happens; it's only thinkin' like."

Shorthouse was beside himself. He felt ready to pick her up and drop her over the banisters, candle and all.

"Look there," he said, pointing at her within an inch of her blinking eyes with the fingers that had touched the oozing blood; "look there, my good woman. Is that only thinking?"

She stared a minute, as if not knowing what he meant.

"I guess so," she said at length.

He followed her eyes, and to his amazement saw that his fingers were as white as usual, and quite free from the awful stain that had been there ten minutes before. There was no sign of blood. No amount of staring could bring it back. Had he gone out of his mind? Had his eyes and ears played such tricks with him? Had his senses become false and perverted? He dashed past the landlady, out into the passage, and gained his own room in a couple of strides. Whew! ... the partition no longer bulged. The paper was not torn. There was no creeping, crawling thing on the faded old carpet.

"It's all over now," drawled the metallic voice behind him. "I'm going to bed again."

He turned and saw the landlady slowly going downstairs again, still shading the candle with her hand and peering up at him from time to time as she moved. A black, ugly, unwholesome object, he thought, as she disappeared into the darkness below, and the last flicker of her candle threw a queer-shaped shadow along the wall and over the ceiling.

Without hesitating a moment, Shorthouse threw himself into his clothes and went out of the house. He preferred the storm to the horrors of that top floor, and he walked the streets till daylight. In the evening he told the landlady he would leave next day, in spite of her assurances that nothing more would happen.

"It never comes back," she said—"that is, not after he's killed."

Shorthouse gasped.

"You gave me a lot for my money," he growled.

"Waal, it aren't my show," she drawled. "I'm no spirit medium. You take chances. Some'll sleep right along and never hear nothin'. Others, like yourself, are different and get the whole thing."

"Who's the old gentleman?—does he hear it?" asked Jim.

"There's no old gentleman at all," she answered coolly. "I just told you that to make you feel easy like in case you did hear anythin'. You were all alone on the floor."

"Say now," she went on, after a pause in which Shorthouse could think of nothing to say but unpublishable things, "say now, do tell, did you feel sort of cold when the show was on, sort of tired and weak, I mean, as if you might be going to die?"

"How can I say?" he answered savagely; "what I felt God only knows."

"Waal, but He won't tell," she drawled out. "Only I was wonderin' how you really did feel, because the man who had that room last was found one morning in bed—"

"In bed?"

"He was dead. He was the one before you. Oh! You don't need to get rattled so. You're all right. And it all really happened, they do say. This house used to be a private residence some twenty-five years ago, and a German family of the name of Steinhardt lived here. They had a big business in Wall Street, and stood 'way up in things."

"Ah!" said her listener.

"Oh yes, they did, right at the top, till one fine day it all bust and the old man skipped with the boodle—"

"Skipped with the boodle?"

"That's so," she said; "got clear away with all the money, and the son was found dead in his house, committed soocide it was thought. Though there was some as said he couldn't have stabbed himself and fallen in that position. They said he was murdered. The father died in prison. They tried to fasten the murder on him, but there was no motive, or no evidence, or no somethin'. I forget now."

"Very pretty," said Shorthouse.

"I'll show you somethin' mighty queer any-ways," she drawled, "if you'll come upstairs a minute. I've heard the steps and voices lots of times; they don't pheaze me any. I'd just as lief hear so many dogs barkin'. You'll find the whole story in the newspapers if you look it up—not what goes on here, but the story of the Germans. My house would be ruined if they told all, and I'd sue for damages."

They reached the bedroom, and the woman went in and pulled up the edge of the carpet where Shorthouse had seen the blood soaking in the previous night.

"Look thar, if you feel like it," said the old hag. Stooping down, he saw a dark, dull stain in the boards that corresponded exactly to the shape and position of the blood as he had seen it.

That night he slept in a hotel, and the following day sought new quarters. In the newspapers on file in his office after a long search he found twenty years back the detailed story, substantially as the woman had said, of Steinhardt & Co.'s failure, the absconding and subsequent arrest of the senior partner, and the suicide, or murder, of his son Otto. The landlady's room-house had formerly been their private residence.

The Devil of the Marsh

H. B. Marriott Watson

It was nigh upon dusk when I drew close to the Great Marsh, and already the white vapours were about, riding across the sunken levels like ghosts in a churchyard. Though I had set forth in a mood of wild delight, I had sobered in the lonely ride across the moor and was now uneasily alert. As my horse jerked down the grassy slopes that fell away to the jaws of the swamp, I could see thin streams of mist rise slowly, hover like wraiths above the long rushes, and then, turning gradually more material, go blowing heavily away across the flat. The appearance of the place at this desolate hour, so remote from human society and so darkly significant of evil presences, struck me with a certain wonder that she should have chosen this spot for our meeting. She was a familiar of the moors, where I had invariably encountered her; but it was like her arrogant caprice to test my devotion by some such dreary assignation.

The wide and horrid prospect depressed me beyond reason, but the fact of her neighbourhood drew me on, and my spirits mounted at the thought that at last she was to put me in possession of herself. Tethering my horse upon the verge of the swamp, I soon discovered the path that crossed it, and entering struck out boldly for the heart. The track could have been little used, for the reeds, which stood high above the level of my eyes upon either side, straggled everywhere across in low arches, through which I dodged, and broke my way with some inconvenience and much impatience. A full half hour I was solitary in that wilderness, and when at last a sound other than my own footsteps broke the silence the dusk had fallen.

I was moving very slowly at the time, with a mind half disposed to turn from the melancholy expedition, which it seemed to me now must surely be a cruel jest she had played upon me. While some such reluctance held me, I was suddenly arrested by a hoarse croaking which broke out upon my left, sounding somewhere from the reeds in the black mire. A little further it came again from close at hand, and when I had passed on a few more steps in wonder and perplexity, I heard it for the third time.

I stopped and listened, but the marsh was as a grave, and so taking the noise for the signal of some raucous frog, I resumed my way. But in a little the croaking was repeated, and coming quickly to a stand I pushed the reeds aside and peered into the darkness. I could see nothing, but at the immediate moment of my pause I thought I detected the sound of some body trailing through the rushes. My distaste for the adventure grew with this suspicion, and had it not been for my delirious infatuation I had assuredly turned back and ridden home. The ghastly sound pursued me at intervals along the track, until at last, irritated beyond endurance by the sense of this persistent and invisible company, I broke into a sort of run. This, it seemed, the creature (whatever it was) could not achieve, for I heard no more of it, and continued my way in peace.

My path at length ran out from among the reeds upon the smooth flat of which she had spoken, and here my heart quickened, and the gloom of the dreadful place lifted. The flat lay in the very centre of the marsh, and here and there in it a gaunt bush or withered tree rose like a spectre against the white mists. At the further end I fancied some kind of building loomed up; but the fog which had been gathering ever since my entrance upon the passage sailed down upon me at that moment and the prospect went out with suddenness.

As I stood waiting for the clouds to pass, a voice cried to me out of its centre, and I saw her next second with bands of mist swirling about her body, come rushing to me from the darkness. She put her long arms about me, and, drawing her close, I looked into her deep eyes. Far down in them, it seemed to me, I could discern a mystic laughter dancing in the wells of light, and I had that ecstatic sense of nearness to some spirit of fire which was wont to possess me at her contact.

"At last," she said, "at last, my beloved!" I caressed her.

"Why," said I, tingling at the nerves, "why have you put this dolorous journey between us? And what mad freak is your presence in this swamp?" She uttered her silver laugh, and nestled to me again.

"I am the creature of this place," she answered. "This is my home. I have sworn you should behold me in my native sin ere you ravished me away."

"Come, then," said I; "I have seen; let there be an end of this. I know you, what you are. This marsh chokes up my heart. God forbid you should spend more of your days here. Come."

"You are in haste," she cried. "There is yet much to learn. Look, my friend," she said, "you who know me, what I am. This is my prison, and I have inherited its properties. Have you no fear?"

For answer I pulled her to me, and her warm lips drove out the horrid humours of the night; but the swift passage of a flickering mockery over her eyes struck me as a flash of lightning, and I grew chill again.

"I have the marsh in my blood," she whispered: "the marsh and the fog of it. Think ere you vow to me, for I am the cloud in a starry night."

A lithe and lovely creature, palpable of warm flesh, she lifted her magic face to mine and besought me plaintively with these words. The dews of the nightfall hung on her lashes, and seemed to plead with me for her forlorn and solitary plight.

"Behold!" I cried, "witch or devil of the marsh, you shall come with me! I have known you on the moors, a roving apparition of beauty; nothing more I know, nothing more I ask. I care not what this dismal haunt means; not what these strange and mystic eyes. You have powers and senses above me; your sphere and habits are as mysterious and incomprehensible as your beauty. But that," I said, "is mine, and the world that is mine shall be yours also."

She moved her head nearer to me with an antic gesture, and her gleaming eyes glanced up at me with a sudden flash, the similitude (great heavens!) of a hooded snake. Starting, I fell away, but at that moment she turned her face and set it fast towards the fog that came rolling in thick volumes over the flat. Noiselessly the great cloud crept down upon us, and all dazed and troubled I watched her watching it in silence. It was as if she awaited some omen of horror, and I too trembled in the fear of its coming.

Then suddenly out of the night issued the hoarse and hideous croaking I had heard upon my passage. I reached out my arm to take her hand, but in an instant the mists broke over us, and I was groping in the vacancy. Something like panic took hold of me, and, beating through the blind obscurity, I rushed over the flat, calling upon her. In a little the swirl went by, and I perceived her upon the margin of the swamp, her arm raised as in imperious command. I ran to her, but stopped, amazed and shaken by a fearful sight. Low by the dripping reeds crouched a small squat thing, in the likeness of a monstrous frog, coughing and choking in its throat. As I stared, the creature rose upon its legs and disclosed a horrid human resemblance. Its face was white and thin, with long black hair; its body gnarled and twisted as with the ague of a thousand years. Shaking, it whined in a breathless voice, pointing a skeleton finger at the woman by my side.

"Your eyes were my guide," it quavered. "Do you think that after all these years I have no knowledge of your eyes? Lo, is there aught of evil in you I am not instructed in? This is the Hell you designed for me, and now you would leave me to a greater."

The wretch paused, and panting leaned upon a bush, while she stood silent, mocking him with her eyes, and soothing my terror with her soft touch.

"Hear!" he cried, turning to me, "hear the tale of this woman that you may know her as she is. She is the Presence of the marshes. Woman or Devil I know not, but only that the accursed marsh has crept into her soul and she herself is become its Evil Spirit; she herself, that lives and grows young and beautiful by it, has its full power to blight and chill and slay. I, who was once as you are, have this knowledge. What bones lie deep in this black swamp who can say but she? She has drained of health, she has drained of mind and of soul; what is between her and her desire that she should not drain also of life? She has made me a devil in her Hell, and now she would leave me to my solitary pain, and go search for another victim. But she shall not!" he screamed through his chattering teeth; "she shall not! My Hell is also hers! She shall not!"

Her smiling untroubled eyes left his face and turned to me: she put out her arms, swaying towards me, and so fervid and so great a light glowed in her face that, as one distraught of superhuman means, I took her into my embrace. And then the madness seized me.

"Woman or devil," I said, "I will go with you! Of what account this pitiful past? Blight me even as that wretch, so be only you are with me."

She laughed, and, disengaging herself, leaned, half-clinging to me, towards the coughing creature by the mire.

"Come," I cried, catching her by the waist. "Come!" She laughed again a silver-ringing laugh. She moved with me slowly across the flat to where the track started for the portals of the marsh. She laughed and clung to me.

But at the edge of the track, I was startled by a shrill, hoarse screaming; and behold, from my very feet, that loathsome creature rose up and wound his long black arms about her shrieking and crying in his pain. Stooping I pushed him from her skirts, and with one sweep of my arm drew her across the pathway; as her face passed mine her eyes were wide and smiling. Then of a sudden the still mist enveloped us once more; but ere it descended I had a glimpse of that contorted figure trembling on the margin, the white face drawn and full of desolate pain. At the sight an icy shiver ran through me. And then through the yellow gloom the shadow of her darted past me to the further side.

I heard the hoarse cough, the dim noise of a struggle, a swishing sound, a thin cry, and then the sucking of the slime over something in the rushes. I leapt forward: and once again the fog thinned, and I beheld her, woman or devil, standing upon the verge, and peering with smiling eyes into the foul and sickly bog. With a sharp cry wrung from my nerveless soul, I turned and fled down the narrow way from that accursed spot; and as I ran the thickening fog closed round me, and I heard far off and lessening still the silver sound of her mocking laughter.

A Fight with a Ghost
By Q. E. D.

"No, I never believed much in ghosts," said the doctor. "But I was always rather afraid of them."

"Have you ever seen one?" asked one of the other men.

The doctor took his cigar out of his mouth and contemplated the ash for a moment or two before replying. "I have had some rather startling experiences," he said, after a pause, during which the rest of us exchanged glances, for the doctor has seen many things and is not averse to talking about them in congenial company. "Would you care about hearing one of them? It gives me the cold shivers now to speak of it." We nodded, and the doctor, taking a sip as an antidote to the shivers, began:

"You remember George Carson, who played for the 'Varsity some years ago; big chap, with a light moustache? Well, I saw a good deal of him before he married, while he was reading for the bar in town. It was just after he became engaged to Miss Stonor, who is now Mrs. Carson, that he asked me to go down to a place which his people had taken in the country. Miss Stonor was to be there and he wanted me to meet her. I could not go down for Christmas Day, as I had promised to be with my people. But as I had been working a bit too hard, and wanted a few days' rest, I decided to run down for a few days about the New Year.

"Woodcote was a pleasant enough place to look at. There were two packs of hounds within easy distance, and it was not far enough from a station to cut you off completely from the morning papers. The Carsons had been lucky, I thought, in coming across such a good house at such a moderate figure. For, as George told me, the owner had been obliged to go abroad for his health, and was anxious not to leave the place empty all the winter. It was an old house, with big gables and preposterous corners all over the place, and you couldn't walk ten paces along any of the passages without tumbling up or down stairs. But it had been patched from time to time and, among other improvements, a big billiard-room had been built out at the back. A country house in the winter without a billiard-room, when the frost stops hunting, is just—well, not even a gilded prison. The party was a small one; besides George and his father and mother, there were only a couple of Misses Carson, who, being somewhere in the early teens, didn't count, and Miss Stonor, who, of course, counted a good deal, and, lastly, myself.

"Miss Stonor ought to have been happy, for George Carson, besides being an excellent fellow all around, was by no means a bad match, being an only son with considerable expectations. But, somehow or other, she did not strike me as looking either very well or very happy. She gave me the impression of having something on her mind, which made her alternately nervous and listless. George, I fancied, noticed it, and was puzzled by it, for I caught him several times watching her with an anxious and inquiring look, but, as I was not there as a doctor, of course it was no business of mine, though I discovered the reason before I left Woodcote.

"The second night after my arrival—we had been playing, I remember, a family pool; the rest had gone upstairs to bed—George and I adjourned to a sort of study, which he had arranged upstairs, for a final smoke and a chat before turning in. The study was next to his bedroom, and parted off from it by curtains. As we were settling down, I missed my pipe, and remembered that I had laid it down in the billiard-room. On principle I never smoke another man's pipe, so I lit a candle, the house being in darkness, and started away in search of my own. The house looked awfully weird by the flickering light of a solitary candle, and the stairs creaked in a particularly gruesome way behind me, just for all the world as though someone were following at my heels. I found my pipe where I had expected in the billiard-room, and came back in perhaps a little more hurry than was absolutely necessary. Which, perhaps, explains why I stumbled in the uncertain light over a couple of unforeseen stairs, and dropped my candle.

Of course, it went out, but after a little groping I found it. Having no matches with me I was obliged to feel my way along the banisters, for it was so dark that I could not see my hand in front of me. And as I slowly advanced, sliding my hand along the broad balustrade at my side, it suddenly slid over something cold and clammy, which was not balustrade at all; for, stopping dead, and closing my fingers round it for an instant, I felt that I was holding another hand, a skinny, bony hand, which writhed itself slowly from my grasp. And though I could hear nothing and see nothing, I was yet conscious that something was brushing past me and going up the stairs.

"'Hi—what's that? Who are you?' I called.

"There was no answer.

"I admit that I was in a regular funk. I must have shown it in my face.

"'What's the matter?' asked George, as I blundered into his study.

"'Oh, nothing,' I answered; 'dropped my candle and lost the way.'

"'But who were you talking to?'

"'I was only swearing at the candle,' I replied.

"'Oh! I thought perhaps you had seen—somebody,' replied George.

"Somehow, I did not like to tell him the truth, for fear he would laugh at my nervousness. But I determined to keep an eye on my liver, and take a couple of weeks' complete rest. That night I woke up several times with the feeling of that confounded hand under my own—a clammy hand which writhed as my fingers closed upon it.

"The next morning after breakfast I was in the billiard-room practicing strokes while Carson was over at the stables. Presently the door opened, and Miss Stonor looked in.

"'Come in,' I said; 'George will be back from the stables in a few minutes. Meanwhile we can have fifty up.'

"'I wanted to speak to you,' she said.

"She was looking very tired and ill, and I began to think I should not have an uninterrupted holiday after all.

"'Do you believe in ghosts?' she asked, having closed the door and come up to the table, where she stood leaning with both her hands upon it.

"'No,' I replied, missing an easy carrom as I remembered my experience of last night, 'but I believe in fancy.'

"'And, supposing then that a person fancied he saw things, is there any remedy?'

"'What do you mean, Miss Stonor?' I replied, looking at her in some surprise. 'Do you mean that you fancy——'

"I stopped, for Miss Stonor turned away, sat down on one of the easy-chairs by the wall, and burst into tears.

"'Oh! please help me' she sobbed; 'I believe I am going mad.'

"I laid down my cue and went over to her.

"'Look here, Miss Stonor,' I said, taking her hand, which was hot and feverish, 'I am a doctor, and a friend of George. Now tell me all about it, and I'll do my best to set it right.'

"She was in a more or less hysterical condition, and her words were freely punctuated by sobs. But gradually I managed to elicit from her that nearly every night since she came to Woodcote she had been awakened in some mysterious way, and had seen a horrible face looking at her from over the top of a screen which stood by the door of her bedroom. As soon as she moved the face disappeared, which convinced her that the apparition existed only in her imagination. That seemed to distress her even more than if she had believed it to be a genuine ghost, for she thought her brain was giving way.

"I told her that she was only suffering from a very common symptom of nervous disorder, as indeed it was, and promised to send a groom into the village to get a prescription made up for her. And, having made me promise to breathe no word to anyone on the subject, more especially to George, she went away relieved. Nevertheless, I was not quite certain that I had made a correct diagnosis of the case. You see I had been rather upset myself not many hours before. George was longer than I expected at the stable, and I was just going to find him when at the door I met Mrs. Carson.

"'Can you spare me one moment?' she said, as I held open the door for her. 'I wanted to find you alone.'

"'Certainly, Mrs. Carson, with pleasure; an hour, if you wish,' I replied.

"'It is so convenient, you know, to have a doctor in the house,' she said, with a nervous laugh. 'Now I want you to prescribe me a sleeping draught. My nerves are rather out of order, and—I don't sleep as I should.'

"'Ah,' I said, 'do you see faces—and such like things when you wake?'

"'How do you know?' she asked quickly.

"'Oh, I inferred from the other symptoms. We doctors have to observe all kinds of little things.'

"'Well, of course, I know it is only fancy; but it is just as bad as if it were real. I assure you it is making me quite ill; and I didn't like to mention it to Mr. Carson or to George. They would think I was losing my head.'

"I gave Mrs. Carson the same prescription as I had written for Miss Stonor, though by that time the conviction had grown upon me that there was something wrong which could not be cured by medicine. However, I decided to say nothing to George about the matter at present. For I could hardly utilize the confidence which had been placed in me by Miss Stonor and Mrs. Carson. And my own experience of the night before would scarcely have appeared convincing to him. But I determined that on the next day—which was Sunday—I would invent an excuse for staying at home from church and make some explorations in the house. There was obviously some mystery at work which wanted clearing up.

"We all sat up rather late that night. There seemed to be a general disinclination to go to bed. We stayed all together in the billiard-room until nearly midnight, and then loitered about in the hall, talking in an aimless sort of fashion. But at last, Mrs. Carson said goodnight, with a confidential nod to me, and Miss Stonor murmured, 'So many thanks; I've got it,' and they both went upstairs. George and I parted in the corridor above. Our rooms were opposite each other.

"I did not begin undressing at once, but sat down and tried to piece together some theory to account for the uncanniness of things. But the more I thought, the more perplexing it became. There was no doubt whatever that I had put my hand on something extremely alive and extremely unpleasant the night before. The bare recollection of it made me shudder. What living thing could possibly be creeping about the house in the dark? It was a man's hand. Of that I was certain from the size of it. George Carson was out of the question, for he was in his room all the time. Nor was it likely that Mr. Carson, senior, would steal about his own house in his socks and refuse to answer when spoken to. The only other man in the house was an eminently respectable-looking butler; and his hand, as I had noted particularly when he poured out my wine at dinner, was plump and soft, whereas the mysterious hand on the balustrade was thin and bony.

"And then, what was the real explanation of the face which had appeared to the two ladies? Indigestion might have explained either singly. Extraordinary coincidences do sometimes occur, but it seemed too extraordinary that a couple of ladies—one old and one young—should suffer from the same indigestion in the same house, at the same time, and with the same symptoms. On the whole, I did not feel at all comfortable, and looked carefully in all the cupboards and recesses, as well as under the bed, before starting to undress. Then I went to the door, intending to lock it. Just as my hand was upon the key, I heard a soft step in the corridor outside, accompanied by a sound which was something between a sigh and a groan. Very faint, but quite unmistakable, and, under the circumstances, discomposing. It might, of course, be George. Anyhow, I decided to look and see. I turned the handle gently and opened the door. There was nothing to be seen in the corridor. But on the opposite side I could see a door open, and George's head peeping round the corner.

"'Hullo!' he said.

"'Hullo!' I replied.

"'Was that you walking up the passage?' he asked.

"'No,' I answered, 'I thought it might be you.'

"'Then who the devil was it?' he said. 'I'll swear I heard someone.'

"There was silence for a few moments. I was wondering whether I had better tell him of the fright I had already had, when he spoke again:

"'I say, just come here for a bit, old fellow; I want to speak to you.'

"I stepped across the passage, and we went together into the little study which adjoined his bedroom.

"'Look here,' he said, poking up the fire, which was burning low, 'doesn't it strike you that there is something very odd about this house?'

"'You mean——'

"'Well, I wouldn't say anything about it to the master or Miss Stonor for fear of frightening them. All the same, scarcely a night passes but I hear curious footsteps on the stairs. You've heard them yourself, haven't you?'

"'Now you mention it,' I said, 'I confess I have.'

"'And, what is more,' he continued, 'I was sitting here two nights ago half asleep, and—it seems ridiculous, I know, but it's a fact—I suddenly saw a horrible face glaring at me from between those curtains behind you. It was gone in a moment, but I saw it as plainly as I see you.'

"I moved my seat uneasily.

"'Did you look in your bedroom or in the passage?' I asked.

"'Yes—at once,' he replied. 'There was nothing to be seen; but twice again that night I heard footsteps passing—good God!'

"He started up in his chair, staring straight over my shoulder. I turned quickly and saw the curtains which parted off the bedroom swing together.

"'What is it?' I asked, breathlessly.

"'I saw it again—the same face—between the curtains.'

"I tore the hangings aside, and rushed into the next room. It was empty. The lamp was burning upon a side table, and the door was open, just as George had left it. In the passage outside all was quiet. I came back into the study and found George running his fingers through his hair in perplexity.

"'There is clearly one person too many in the house,' I said. 'I think we ought to draw the place and find out who it is.'

"'All right,' said he, picking up the poker from the fireplace; 'if it's anything made of flesh and blood this will be useful, and if not——'

"He stopped short, for at that instant the most awful shriek of horror rang through the house—a shriek of wild, uncontrollable terror, such as I had never heard before and I never hope to hear again. One moment we stood staring at each other, dumbfounded. The next George Carson had dashed out of the room and down the corridor to the stairs. I followed close behind him. For we both knew that none but a woman in mortal fear would shriek like that, and that that woman was Miss Stonor.

"Down the stairs we tumbled pell-mell in the darkness. But before I reached the landing below, where Miss Stonor's room was, I felt, as I had felt the evening before, something brush swiftly past me. As I ran, I turned and caught at it in the dark. But my hand gripped only empty air. I was just about to turn back and follow it, when a cry from George arrested me, and, looking down, I saw him standing over the prostrate form of Miss Stonor. The door of her room was open, and by the moonlight which streamed into the room I could see her lying in her white nightdress across the threshold. What followed in the next few minutes I can scarcely recall with accuracy. The whole house was aroused by the poor girl's awful shriek. She was quite unconscious when we came upon her, but she revived more or less as soon as Mrs. Carson and one of the terrified servants had lifted her into bed again. Nothing intelligible could be gathered from her, however, as to the cause of her fright; she only repeated, hysterically, again and again:

"'Oh, the face; the face!'

"When I saw I could do her no further good for the present, I took George by the arm and led him out of the room.

"'Look here, George,' I said, 'we must find out the reason of this at once. I am certain I felt something go by me as I came downstairs. Now does that staircase lead anywhere but to our rooms?'

"George considered for a moment.

"'Yes,' he replied; 'there is a door at the end of the passage which leads up into a sort of lumber room.'

"'Then we'll explore it,' I said. 'For my part I can't go to sleep until I've got to the bottom of this. Get the man to bring a lantern along.'

"The butler looked as though he didn't half like the enterprise, and, to tell the truth, no more did I. It was the uncanniest job I ever undertook. However, we started, the three of us. First of all, we searched the rooms on the floor above, where George and I slept. Everything was just as we had left it. Then I pushed open the door at the end of the corridor. A crazy-looking staircase led up into darkness. We went cautiously up, I first with a candle, then George, and last of all the butler with a lantern.

"At the top we stepped into a big, rather low room, with beams across the ceiling, and a rough, uneven floor. Our lights threw strange shadows into the corners, and more than once I started at what looked like a crouching human figure. We searched every corner. There was nothing to be seen but a few old boxes, a roll or two of matting, and some broken chairs. But in the far corner George pointed out to me a rickety ladder which ended at a closed trapdoor. Just then I distinctly heard the curious, half groaning, half sighing sound which had already puzzled me in the corridor below. We stood still and looked at one another. We all heard the sound.

"'Whatever it is, it's up there,' I said. 'The question is, who is going up?'

"George put his candle down upon the floor and stepped upon the ladder. It cracked beneath his weight. He stopped.

"'Come down; it won't bear you,' I said. 'I shall have to go.'

"I don't know that I was ever in such a queer funk as I was while I slowly mounted that ladder, and pushed open the trapdoor. I had formed no clear idea of what I expected to find there. Certainly, I was not prepared for what happened. For no sooner was the trap-door fully open than there fell—literally fell—upon me from the darkness above a thing in human shape, which kicked and spat and tore at me as I stood clinging to the ladder. It lasted but a moment or so, but in that moment, I lived a lifetime of terror. The ladder swayed and cracked beneath me, and I fell to the floor with the thing gripping my throat like a vise. The next instant George had stunned it with a blow from the poker and dragged it off me. It lay upon its back on the floor—a ragged, hideous, loathsome shape. And the mystery was solved."

"But you haven't told us what it really was," said one of the listeners.

The doctor smiled.

"It was the owner of the house," he replied. "He had not gone abroad. He had gone to a private lunatic asylum with homicidal mania upon him. About a fortnight before this he had managed to escape; and, having made his way to his former home, had concealed himself, with a cunning often shown by lunatics, in the loft. I suppose he had found enough to eat in his nightly rambles about the house. The only wonder is that he didn't kill someone before he was caught."

Mrs. Davenport's Ghost

By Frederick P. Schrader.

Dear readers, do you agree with Hamlet? Do you believe that there is more between heaven and earth than we dream of in our philosophy? Does it seem possible to you that Eliphas Levy conjured up the shade of Apollonius of Tyana, the prophet of the *Magii*, in a London hotel, and that the great sage, William Crookes, drank his tea at breakfast several days a week, for months in succession, in the society of the materialised spirit of a young lady, attired in white linen, with a feather turban on her head?

Do not laugh! Panic would seize you in the presence even of a turbaned spirit, and the grotesque spectacle would but intensify your terror. As for me, I did not laugh last night on reading an account in a New York newspaper of a criminal trial that will probably terminate in the death penalty of the accused.

It is a sad case. I shudder as I transcribe the records of the trial from the testimony of the hotel waiter, who heard the conversation of the two confederates through a keyhole, and of forty thoroughly credible witnesses, who testified to the same facts. What would be my feelings if I had seen the beautiful victim with the gaping wound in her breast, into which she dipped her finger to mark the brow of her murderer?

1

About three o'clock on the afternoon of February 3, Professor Davenport and Miss Ida Soutchotte, a very pale and delicate young girl, who had submitted to the tests of Professor Davenport for a number of years, were finishing their dinner in their room in the second story of a New York hotel. Professor Benjamin Davenport was a celebrity, but it was said that he owed his fame to somewhat questionable means. The leading spiritualists did not repose the confidence in him that manifestly marked their regard for William Crookes or

Daniel Douglas Home.

"Greedy and unscrupulous mediums," the author of Spiritualism in America thinks, "are to blame for the most bitter attacks to which our cause has been exposed. When the materialisations do not take place as quickly as circumstances require, they resort to trickery and fraud to extricate themselves from a dilemma."

Professor Benjamin Davenport belonged to these "versatile" mediums. Aside from this, queer stories were afloat about him. He was secretly accused of highway robbery in South America, cheating at cards in the gambling houses of San Francisco, and the overhasty use of firearms toward persons who had never offended him. It was said almost openly, that the professor's wife had died from abuse and grief at his infidelity. But in spite of these annoying rumours, Mr. Davenport, by virtue of his skill as a fraud and *fakir*, continued to exercise a great deal of influence upon certain plain and simple-minded folks, whom it was impossible to convince that they had not touched the materialized spirits of their brothers, mothers, or sisters through the agency of his wonderful power. His professional success received material accession from his swarthy, Mephisto-like countenance, his deep, fiery eyes, his large curved nose, the cynical expression of his mouth, and the lofty, almost prophetic tone of his words.

When the waiter had made his last visit—he did not go far—the following conversation took place in the room:

"There is to be a *séance* this evening at the residence of Mrs. Harding," began the medium. "Quite a number of influential people will be there, and two or three millionaires. Conceal under your skirt the blonde woman's wig and the white material in which the spirits usually make their appearance."

"Very well," replied Ida Soutchotte, in a resigned tone.

The waiter heard her pace the room. After a pause, she asked:

"Whose spirit are you going to control this evening, Benjamin?"

The waiter heard a loud, brutal laugh and the chair groaning beneath the weight of the demonstrative professor.

"Guess."

"How should I know?" she asked.

"I am going to conjure up the spirit of my dead wife."

And another burst of laughter issued from the room, full of sinister levity. A cry of terror burst from Ida's lips. A muffled sound indicated to the eavesdropper at the door that she was dragging herself to the feet of the professor.

"Benjamin, Benjamin! don't do it," she sobbed.

"Why not? They say I broke Mrs. Davenport's heart. The story is damaging my reputation, but it will be forgotten if her spirit should address me in terms of endearment from the other shore in the presence of numerous witnesses. For you will speak to me tenderly, will you not, Ida?"

"No, no. You shall not do it; you shall not think of it. Listen to me, for God's sake. During the four years that I have been with you I have obeyed you faithfully and suffered patiently. I have lied and deceived, like you; I learned to imitate the sleep and symptoms of clairvoyants. Tell me, did I ever refuse to serve you, or utter a word of complaint, even when my shoulders bent with the weight of my burden, when you pierced the flesh of my arms with knitting needles? Worse than all this, I imitated distant voices behind curtains, and made mothers and wives believe that their sons and husbands had come from a better world to communicate with them.

"How often have I performed the most dangerous feats in parlours with the lamps turned low? Clothed in a shroud or white muslin I essayed to represent supernatural forms, whom tear-dimmed eyes recognised as those of departed dear ones. You do not know what I suffered at this unhallowed work. You scoff at the mysteries of eternity. I suffer the torments of an impending retribution.

"My God! if some time the dead whom I counterfeit should rise up before me with uplifted arms and dreadful imprecations! This constant terror has injured my heart—it will kill me. I am consumed by fever. Look how emaciated, how worn-out and downcast I am. But I am under your control. Do as you like with me; I am in your power, and I want it to be so.

"Have I ever complained? But do not force me to do this thing, Benjamin. Have pity on me for what I have done for you in the past, for what I am suffering. Do not attempt this mummery; do not compel me to play the role of your dead wife, who was so tender and beautiful. Oh, what put that thought into your mind? Spare me, Benjamin, I implore you!"

The professor did not laugh again. Amid the confusion of upturned articles of furniture, the eavesdropper distinguished the sound of a skull striking the floor. He concluded that Professor Davenport had knocked Miss Ida down with a blow of his fist, or had kicked her as she approached him. But the waiter did not enter the room, as no one rang for him.

2

That evening forty persons were assembled in Mrs. Joanne Harding's parlour, staring at the curtain where a spirit form was in process of materialising. One dark lantern in a corner of the room contributed the light that emphasized the darkness rather than relieved it. The room was pervaded by profound silence, save the quickened, suppressed breathing of the spectators. The fire in the grate cast mysterious rays of light, resembling fugitive spirits, upon the objects around, almost indistinguishable in the semi-gloom.

Professor Davenport was at his best this evening. The spirit world obeyed him without hesitation, like their lawful master. He was the mighty prince of souls. Hands that had no arms were seen picking flowers from the vases; the touch of an invisible spirit conjured sweet melodies from the keys of the piano; the furniture responded by intelligent rappings to the most unanticipated questions. The professor himself elevated his form in symbolical distortions from the floor to an altitude of three feet, indicated by Mrs. Harding, and remained suspended in the air for a quarter of an hour, holding live coals in his hands.

3

But the most interesting, as well as the most conclusive, test was to be the materialization of the spirit of Mrs. Arabella Davenport, which the professor had promised at the beginning of the *séance*.

"The hour has come," exclaimed the medium.

And while the hearts of all throbbed with anxious suspense, and their eyes distended with painful expectancy of the promised materialization, Benjamin Davenport stood before the curtain. In the twilight the tall man with the dishevelled hair and demon look, was really terrible and handsome.

"Appear, Arabella!" he exclaimed, in a commanding voice, with gestures of the Nazarene at the sepulchre of Lazarus.

All are waiting——

Suddenly a cry burst from behind the curtain—a piercing, shuddering, horrible shriek, the shriek of an expiring soul.

The spectators trembled. Mrs. Harding almost fainted. The medium himself appeared surprised.

But Benjamin recovered his composure on seeing the curtain move and admit the spirit.

The apparition was that of a young woman with long blonde tresses; she was beautiful and pale, clad in some light, whitish material. Her breast was bare, and on the left side appeared a bleeding wound, in which trembled a knife.

The spectators arose and retreated, pushing their chairs to the wall. Those who chanced to look at the medium noticed that a deathly pallor had overspread his face, and that he was cowering and trembling.

But the young woman, Mrs. Arabella, the real one, whom he so well remembered, she had come in response to his summons, and advanced in a direct line toward Benjamin, who in terror covered his eyes to shut out the ghastly sight, and with a cry fled behind the furniture. But she dipped the finger of her thin hand into the blood from her wound and traced it across the brow of the unconscious medium, the while repeating, in a slow, monotonous tone that sounded like the echo of a wail, again and again:

"You are my murderer! You are my murderer!"

And while he was rolling and tossing in deadly terror on the floor, they turned up the lights.

The spirit had vanished. But in the communicating room, behind the curtain, they found the body of poor Miss Ida Soutchotte with horribly distorted features. A physician who was present pronounced it heart stroke.

And that is the reason that Prof. Benjamin Davenport appeared alone in a New York courtroom to answer to the charge of having murdered his wife four years ago in San Francisco.

A Phantom Toe

Anonymous

I am not a superstitious man, far from it, but despite all my efforts to the contrary I could not help thinking, directly I had taken a survey of my chamber, that I should never quit it without going through a strange adventure. There was something in its immense size, heaviness and gloom that seemed to annihilate at one blow all my resolute scepticism as regards supernatural visitations. It appeared to me totally impossible to go into that room and disbelieve in ghosts.

The fact is, I had incautiously partaken at supper of that favourite Dutch dish, *sauerkraut*, and I suppose it had disagreed with me and put strange fancies into my head. Be this as it may I only know that after parting with my friend for the night I gradually worked myself up into such a state of fidgetiness that at last I wasn't sure whether I hadn't become a ghost myself.

"Supposing," ruminated I, "supposing the landlord himself should be a practical robber and should have taken the lock and bolt from off this door for the purpose of entering here in the dead of the night, abstracting all my property, and perhaps murdering me! I thought the dog had a very cutthroat air about him." Now, I had never had any such idea until that moment, for my host was a fat (all Dutchmen are fat), stupid-looking fellow, who I don't believe had sense enough to understand what a robbery or murder meant, but somehow or other, whenever we have anything really to annoy us (and it certainly was not pleasant to go to bed in a strange place without being able to fasten one's door), we are sure to aggravate it by myriads of chimeras of our own brain.

So, on the present occasion, in the midst of a thousand disagreeable reveries, some of the most wild absurdity, I jumped very gloomily into bed, having first put out my candle (for total darkness was far preferable to its flickering, ghostly light, which transformed rather than revealed objects), and soon fell asleep, perfectly tired out with my day's riding.

How long I lay asleep I don't know, but I suddenly awoke from a disagreeable dream of cutthroats, ghosts and long, winding passages in a haunted inn. An indescribable feeling, such as I never before experienced, hung upon me. It seemed as if every nerve in my body had a hundred spirits tickling it, and this was accompanied by so great a heat that, inwardly cursing mine host's *sauerkraut* and wondering how the Dutchmen could endure such poison, I was forced to sit up in bed to cool myself. The whole of the room was profoundly dark, excepting at one place, where the moonlight, falling through a crevice in the shutters, threw a straight line of about an inch or so thick upon the floor—clear, sharp and intensely brilliant against the darkness. I leave you to conceive my horror when, upon looking at this said line of light, I saw there a naked human toe—nothing more.

For the first instant I thought the vision must be some effect of moonlight, then that I was only half awake and could not see distinctly. So, I rubbed my eyes two or three times and looked again. Still there was the accursed thing—plain, distinct, immovable—marblelike in its fixedness and rigidity, but in everything else horribly human.

I am not an easily frightened man. No one who has travelled so much and seen so much and been exposed to so many dangers as I, can be, but there was something so mysterious and unusual in the appearance of this single toe that for a short time I could not think what to be at, so I did nothing but stare at it in a state of utter bewilderment.

At length, however, as the toe did not vanish under my steady gaze, I thought I might as well change my tactics, and remembering that all midnight invaders, be they thieves, ghosts or devils, dislike nothing so much as a good noise I shouted out in a loud voice:

"Who's there?"

The toe immediately disappeared in the darkness.

Almost simultaneously with my words I leaped out of bed and rushed toward the place where I had beheld the strange appearance. The next instant I ran against something and felt an iron grip round my body. After this I have no distinct recollection of what occurred, excepting that a fearful struggle ensued between me and my unseen opponent; that every now and then we were violently hurled to the floor, from which we always rose again in an instant, locked in a deadly embrace; that we tugged and strained and pulled and pushed, I in the convulsive and frantic energy of a fight for life, he (for by this time I had discovered that the intruder was a human being) actuated by some passion of which I was ignorant; that we whirled round and round, cheek to cheek and arm to arm, in fierce contest, until the room appeared to whiz round with us, and that at least a dozen people (my fellow traveller among them), roused, I suppose, by our repeated falls, came pouring into the room with lights and showed me struggling with a man having nothing on but a shirt, whose long, tangled hair and wild, unsettled eyes told me he was insane. And then, for the first time, I became aware that I had received in the conflict several gashes from a knife, which my opponent still held in his hand.

To conclude my story in a few words (for I daresay all of you by this time are getting very tired), it turned out that my midnight visitor was a madman who was being conveyed to a lunatic asylum at The Hague, and that he and his keeper had been obliged to stop at Delft on their way. The poor fellow had contrived during the night to escape from his keeper, who had carelessly forgotten to lock the door of his chamber, and with that irresistible desire to shed blood peculiar to many insane people had possessed himself of a pocketknife belonging to the man who had charge of him, entered my room, which was most likely the only one in the house unfastened, and was probably meditating the fatal stroke when I saw his toe in the moonlight, the rest of his body being hidden in the shade.

After this terrible freak of his he was watched with much greater strictness, but I ought to observe, as some excuse for the keeper's negligence, that this was the first act of violence he had ever attempted.

The Crown Derby Plate

By Marjorie Bowen

Martha Pym said that she had never seen a ghost and that she would very much like to do so, "particularly at Christmas, for you can laugh as you like, that is the correct time to see a ghost."

"I don't suppose you ever will," replied her cousin Mabel comfortably, while her cousin Clara shuddered and said that she hoped they would change the subject for she disliked even to think of such things.

The three elderly, cheerful women sat round a big fire, cosy and content after a day of pleasant activities; Martha was the guest of the other two, who owned the handsome, convenient country house; she always came to spend her Christmas with the Wyntons and found the leisurely country life delightful after the bustling round of London, for Martha managed an antique shop of the better sort and worked extremely hard. She was, however, still full of zest for work or pleasure, though sixty years old, and looked backwards and forwards to a succession of delightful days.

The other two, Mabel and Clara, led quieter but none the less agreeable lives; they had more money and fewer interests, but nevertheless enjoyed themselves very well.

"Talking of ghosts," said Mabel, "I wonder how that old woman at 'Hartleys' is getting on, for 'Hartleys,' you know, is supposed to be haunted."

"Yes, I know," smiled Miss Pym, "but all the years that we have known of the place we have never heard anything definite, have we?"

"No," put in Clara; "but there *is* that persistent rumour that the House is uncanny, and for myself, *nothing* would induce me to live there!"

"It is certainly very lonely and dreary down there on the marshes," conceded Mabel. "But as for the ghost—you never hear *what* it is supposed to be even."

"Who has taken it?" asked Miss Pym, remembering "Hartleys" as very desolate indeed, and long shut up.

"A Miss Lefain, an eccentric old creature—I think you met her here once, two years ago—"

"I believe that I did, but I don't recall her at all."

"We have not seen her since, 'Hartleys' is so un-get-at-able and she didn't seem to want visitors. She collects china, Martha, so really you ought to go and see her and talk 'shop.'"

With the word "china" some curious associations came into the mind of Martha Pym; she was silent while she strove to put them together, and after a second or two they all fitted together into a very clear picture.

She remembered that thirty years ago—yes, it must be thirty years ago, when, as a young woman, she had put all her capital into the antique business, and had been staying with her cousins (her aunt had then been alive) that she had driven across the marsh to "Hartleys," where there was an auction sale; all the details of this she had completely forgotten, but she could recall quite clearly purchasing a set of gorgeous china which was still one of her proud delights, a perfect set of Crown Derby save that one plate was missing.

"How odd," she remarked, "that this Miss Lefain should collect china too, for it was at 'Hartleys' that I purchased my dear old Derby service—I've never been able to match that plate—"

"A plate was missing? I seem to remember," said Clara. "Didn't they say that it must be in the house somewhere and that it should be looked for?"

"I believe they did, but of course I never heard any more and that missing plate has annoyed me ever since. Who had 'Hartleys'?"

"An old connoisseur, Sir James Sewell; I believe he was some relation to this Miss Lefain, but I don't know—"

"I wonder if she has found the plate," mused Miss Pym. "I expect she has turned out and ransacked the whole place—"

"Why not trot over and ask?" suggested Mabel. "It's not much use to her, if she has found it, one odd plate."

"Don't be silly," said Clara. "Fancy going over the marshes, this weather, to ask about a plate missed all those years ago. I'm sure Martha wouldn't think of it—"

But Martha did think of it; she was rather fascinated by the idea; how queer and pleasant it would be if, after all these years, nearly a lifetime, she should find the Crown Derby plate, the loss of which had always irked her! And this hope did not seem so altogether fantastical, it was quite likely that old Miss Lefain, poking about in the ancient house, had found the missing piece.

And, of course, if she had, being a fellow-collector, she would be quite willing to part with it to complete the set.

Her cousin endeavoured to dissuade her; Miss Lefain, she declared, was a recluse, an odd creature who might greatly resent such a visit and such a request.

"Well, if she does I can but come away again," smiled Miss Pym. "I suppose she can't bite my head off, and I rather like meeting these curious types—we've got a love for old china in common, anyhow."

"It seems so silly to think of it—after all these years—a plate!"

"A Crown Derby plate," corrected Miss Pym. "It is certainly strange that I didn't think of it before, but now that I have got it into my head, I can't get it out. Besides," she added hopefully, "I might see the ghost."

So full, however, were the days with pleasant local engagements that Miss Pym had no immediate chance of putting her scheme into practice; but she did not relinquish it, and she asked several different people what they knew about "Hartleys" and Miss Lefain.

And no one knew anything save that the house was supposed to be haunted and the owner "cracky."

"Is there a story?" asked Miss Pym, who associated ghosts with neat tales into which they fitted as exactly as nuts into shells.

But she was always told: "Oh, no, there isn't a story, no one knows anything about the place, don't know how the idea got about; old Sewell was half-crazy, I believe, he was buried in the garden and that gives a house a nasty name—"

"Very unpleasant," said Martha Pym, undisturbed.

This ghost seemed too elusive for her to track down; she would have to be content if she could recover the Crown Derby plate; for that at least she was determined to make a try and also to satisfy that faint tingling of curiosity roused in her by this talk about "Hartleys" and the remembrance of that day, so long ago, when she had gone to the auction sale at the lonely old house.

So, the first free afternoon, while Mabel and Clara were comfortably taking their afternoon repose, Martha Pym, who was of a more lively habit, got out her little governess cart and dashed away across the Essex flats.

She had taken minute directions with her, but she had soon lost her way.

Under the wintry sky, which looked as grey and hard as metal, the marshes stretched bleakly to the horizon, the olive-brown broken reeds were harsh as scars on the saffron-tinted bogs, where the sluggish waters that rose so high in winter were filmed over with the first stillness of a frost; the air was cold but not keen, everything was damp; faintest of mists blurred the black outlines of trees that rose stark from the ridges above the stagnant dykes; the flooded fields were haunted by black birds and white birds, gulls and crows, whining above the long ditch grass and wintry wastes.

Miss Pym stopped the little horse and surveyed this spectral scene, which had a certain relish about it to one sure to return to a homely village, a cheerful house and good company.

A withered and bleached old man, in colour like the dun landscape, came along the road between the sparse alders.

Miss Pym, buttoning up her coat, asked the way to "Hartley" as he passed her; he told her, straight on, and she proceeded, straight indeed across the road that went with undeviating length across the marshes.

"Of course," thought Miss Pym, "if you live in a place like this, you are bound to invent ghosts."

The house sprang up suddenly on a knoll ringed with rotting trees, encompassed by an old brick wall that the perpetual damp had overrun with lichen, blue, green, white colours of decay.

"Hartleys," no doubt, there was no other residence of human being in sight in all the wide expanse; besides, she could remember it, surely, after all this time, the sharp rising out of the marsh, the colony of tall trees, but then fields and trees had been green and bright—there had been no water on the flats, it had been summer-time.

"She certainly," thought Miss Pym, "must be crazy to live here. And I rather doubt if I shall get my plate."

She fastened up the good little horse by the garden gate which stood negligently ajar and entered; the garden itself was so neglected that it was quite surprising to see a trim appearance in the house, curtains at the window and a polish on the brass door knocker, which must have been recently rubbed there, considering the taint in the sea damp which rusted and rotted everything.

It was a square-built, substantial house with "nothing wrong with it but the situation," Miss Pym decided, though it was not very attractive, being built of that drab plastered stone so popular a hundred years ago, with flat windows and door, while one side was gloomily shaded by a large evergreen tree of the cypress variety which gave a blackish tinge to that portion of the garden.

There was no pretence at flower-beds nor any manner of cultivation in this garden where a few rank weeds and straggling bushes matted together above the dead grass; on the enclosing wall which appeared to have been built high as protection against the ceaseless winds that swung along the flats were the remains of fruit trees; their crucified branches, rotting under the great nails that held them up, looked like the skeletons of those who had died in torment.

Miss Pym took in these noxious details as she knocked firmly at the door; they did not depress her; she merely felt extremely sorry for anyone who could live in such a place.

She noticed, at the far end of the garden, in the corner of the wall, a headstone showing above the sodden colourless grass, and remembered what she had been told about the old antiquary being buried there, in the grounds of "Hartleys."

As the knock had no effect she stepped back and looked at the house; it was certainly inhabited—with those neat windows, white curtains and drab blinds all pulled to precisely the same level.

And when she brought her glance back to the door, she saw that it had been opened and that someone, considerably obscured by the darkness of the passage, was looking at her intently.

"Good afternoon," said Miss Pym cheerfully. "I just thought that I would call to see Miss Lefain—it is Miss Lefain, isn't it?"

"It's my house," was the querulous reply.

Martha Pym had hardly expected to find any servants here, though the old lady must, she thought, work pretty hard to keep the house so clean and tidy as it appeared to be.

"Of course," she replied. "May I come in? I'm Martha Pym, staying with the Wyntons, I met you there—"

"Do come in," was the faint reply. "I get so few people to visit me, I'm really very lonely."

"I don't wonder," thought Miss Pym; but she had resolved to take no notice of any eccentricity on the part of her hostess, and so she entered the house with her usual agreeable candour and courtesy.

The passage was badly lit, but she was able to get a fair idea of Miss Lefain; her first impression was that this poor creature was most dreadfully old, older than any human being had the right to be, why, she felt young in comparison—so faded, feeble, and pallid was Miss Lefain.

She was also monstrously fat; her gross, flaccid figure was shapeless and she wore a badly cut, full dress of no colour at all, but stained with earth and damp where Miss Pym supposed she had been doing futile gardening; this gown was doubtless designed to disguise her stoutness, but had been so carelessly pulled about that it only added to it, being rucked and rolled "all over the place" as Miss Pym put it to herself.

Another ridiculous touch about the appearance of the poor old lady was her short hair; decrepit as she was, and lonely as she lived, she had actually had her scanty relics of white hair cropped round her shaking head.

"Dear me, dear me," she said in her thin treble voice. "How very kind of you to come. I suppose you prefer the parlour? I generally sit in the garden."

"The garden? But not in this weather?"

"I get used to the weather. You've no idea how used one gets to the weather."

"I suppose so," conceded Miss Pym doubtfully. "You don't live here quite alone, do you?"

"Quite alone, lately. I had a little company, but she was taken away, I'm sure I don't know where. I haven't been able to find a trace of her anywhere," replied the old lady peevishly.

"Some wretched companion that couldn't stick it, I suppose," thought Miss Pym. "Well, I don't wonder—but someone ought to be here to look after her."

They went into the parlour, which, the visitor was dismayed to see, was without a fire but otherwise well kept.

And there, on dozens of shelves was a choice array of china at which Martha Pym's eyes glistened.

"Aha!" cried Miss Lefain. "I see you've noticed my treasures! Don't you envy me? Don't you wish that you had some of those pieces?"

Martha Pym certainly did and she looked eagerly and greedily round the walls, tables, and cabinets while the old woman followed her with little thin squeals of pleasure.

It was a beautiful little collection, most choicely and elegantly arranged, and Martha thought it marvellous that this feeble ancient creature should be able to keep it in such precise order as well as doing her own housework.

"Do you really do everything yourself here and live quite alone?" she asked, and she shivered even in her thick coat and wished that Miss Lefain's energy had risen to a fire, but then probably she lived in the kitchen, as these lonely eccentrics often did.

"There was someone," answered Miss Lefain cunningly, "but I had to send her away. I told you she's gone, I can't find her, and I am so glad. Of course," she added wistfully, "it leaves me very lonely, but then I couldn't stand her impertinence any longer. She used to say that it was *her* house and her collection of china! Would you believe it? She used to try to chase me away from looking at my own things!"

"How very disagreeable," said Miss Pym, wondering which of the two women had been crazy. "But hadn't you better get someone else."

"Oh, no," was the jealous answer. "I would rather be alone with my things, I daren't leave the house for fear someone takes them away—there was a dreadful time once when an auction sale was held here—"

"Were you here then?" asked Miss Pym; but indeed, she looked old enough to have been anywhere.

"Yes, of course," Miss Lefain replied rather peevishly and Miss Pym decided that she must be a relation of old Sir James Sewell. Clara and Mabel had been very foggy about it all. "I was very busy hiding all the china—but one set they got—a Crown Derby tea service—"

"With one plate missing!" cried Martha Pym. "I bought it, and do you know, I was wondering if you'd found it—"

"I hid it," piped Miss Lefain.

"Oh, you did, did you? Well, that's rather funny behaviour. Why did you hide the stuff away instead of buying it?"

"How could I buy what was mine?"

"Old Sir James left it to you, then?" asked Martha Pym, feeling very muddled.

"*She* bought a lot more," squeaked Miss Lefain, but Martha Pym tried to keep her to the point.

"If you've got the plate," she insisted, "you might let me have it—I'll pay quite handsomely, it would be so pleasant to have it after all these years."

"Money is no use to me," said Miss Lefain mournfully. "Not a bit of use. I can't leave the house or the garden."

"Well, you have to live, I suppose," replied Martha Pym cheerfully. "And, do you know, I'm afraid you are getting rather morbid and dull, living here all alone—you really ought to have a fire—why, it's just on Christmas and very damp."

"I haven't felt the cold for a long time," replied the other; she seated herself with a sigh on one of the horsehair chairs and Miss Pym noticed with a start that her feet were covered only by a pair of white stockings; "one of those nasty health fiends," thought Miss Pym, "but she doesn't look too well for all that."

"So, you don't think that you could let me have the plate?" she asked briskly, walking up and down, for the dark, neat, clean parlour was very cold indeed, and she thought that she couldn't stand this much longer; as there seemed no sign of tea or anything pleasant and comfortable she had really better go.

"I might let you have it," sighed Miss Lefain, "since you've been so kind as to pay me a visit. After all, one plate isn't much use, is it?"

"Of course not, I wonder you troubled to hide it—"

"I couldn't *bear*," wailed the other, "to see the things going out of the house!"

Martha Pym couldn't stop to go into all this; it was quite clear that the old lady was very eccentric indeed and that nothing very much could be done with her; no wonder that she had "dropped out" of everything and that no one ever saw her or knew anything about her, though Miss Pym felt that some effort ought really to be made to save her from herself.

"Wouldn't you like a run in my little governess cart?" she suggested. "We might go to tea with the Wyntons on the way back, they'd be delighted to see you, and I really think that you do want taking out of yourself."

"I was taken out of myself some time ago," replied Miss Lefain. "I really was, and I couldn't leave my things—though," she added with pathetic gratitude, "it is very, very kind of you—"

"Your things would be quite safe, I'm sure," said Martha Pym, humouring her. "Whoever would come up here, this hour of a winter's day?"

"They do, oh, they do! And *she* might come back, prying and nosing and saying that it was all hers, all my beautiful china, hers!"

Miss Lefain squealed in her agitation and rising up, ran round the wall fingering with flaccid yellow hands the brilliant glossy pieces on the shelves.

"Well, then, I'm afraid that I must go, they'll be expecting me, and it's quite a long ride; perhaps some other time you'll come and see us?"

"Oh, must you go?" quavered Miss Lefain dolefully. "I do like a little company now and then and I trusted you from the first—the others, when they do come, are always after my things and I have to frighten them away!"

"Frighten them away!" replied Martha Pym. "However, do you do that?"

"It doesn't seem difficult, people are so easily frightened, aren't they?"

Miss Pym suddenly remembered that "Hartleys" had the reputation of being haunted—perhaps the queer old thing played on that; the lonely house with the grave in the garden was dreary enough around which to create a legend.

"I suppose you've never seen a ghost?" she asked pleasantly. "I'd rather like to see one, you know—"

"There is no one here but myself," said Miss Lefain.

"So, you've never seen anything? I thought it must be all nonsense. Still, I do think it rather melancholy for you to live here all alone—"

Miss Lefain sighed:

"Yes, it's very lonely. Do stay and talk to me a little longer." Her whistling voice dropped cunningly. "And I'll give you the Crown Derby plate!"

"Are you sure you've really got it?" Miss Pym asked.

"I'll show you."

Fat and waddling as she was, she seemed to move very lightly as she slipped in front of Miss Pym and conducted her from the room, going slowly up the stairs—such a gross odd figure in that clumsy dress with the fringe of white hair hanging on to her shoulders.

The upstairs of the house was as neat as the parlour, everything well in its place; but there was no sign of occupancy; the beds were covered with dust sheets, there were no lamps or fires set ready. "I suppose," said Miss Pym to herself, "she doesn't care to show me where she really lives."

But as they passed from one room to another, she could not help saying:

"Where *do* you live, Miss Lefain?"

"Mostly in the garden," said the other.

Miss Pym thought of those horrible health huts that some people indulged in.

"Well, sooner you than I," she replied cheerfully.

In the most distant room of all, a dark, tiny closet, Miss Lefain opened a deep cupboard and brought out a Crown Derby plate which her guest received with a spasm of joy, for it was actually that missing from her cherished set.

"It's very good of you," she said in delight. "Won't you take something for it, or let me do something for you?"

"You might come and see me again," replied Miss Lefain wistfully.

"Oh, yes, of course I should like to come and see you again."

But now that she had got what she had really come for, the plate, Martha Pym wanted to be gone; it was really very dismal and depressing in the house and she began to notice a fearful smell—the place had been shut up too long, there was something damp rotting somewhere, in this horrid little dark closet no doubt.

"I really must be going," she said hurriedly.

Miss Lefain turned as if to cling to her, but Martha Pym moved quickly away.

"Dear me," wailed the old lady. "Why are you in such haste?"

"There's—a smell," murmured Miss Pym rather faintly.

She found herself hastening down the stairs, with Miss Lefain complaining behind her.

"How peculiar people are—*she* used to talk of a smell—"

"Well, you must notice it yourself."

Miss Pym was in the hall; the old woman had not followed her, but stood in the semi-darkness at the head of the stairs, a pale shapeless figure.

Martha Pym hated to be rude and ungrateful but she could not stay another moment; she hurried away and was in her cart in a moment—really—that smell—

"Goodbye!" she called out with false cheerfulness, "and thank you *so* much!"

There was no answer from the house.

Miss Pym drove on; she was rather upset and took another way than that by which she had come, a way that led past a little house raised above the marsh; she was glad to think that the poor old creature at "Hartleys" had such near neighbours, and she reined up the horse, dubious as to whether she should call someone and tell them that poor old Miss Lefain really wanted a little looking after, alone in a house like that, and plainly not quite right in her head.

A young woman, attracted by the sound of the governess cart, came to the door of the house and seeing Miss Pym called out, asking if she wanted the keys of the house?

"What house?" asked Miss Pym.

"'Hartleys,' mum, they don't put a board out, as no one is likely to pass, but it's to be sold. Miss Lefain wants to sell or let it—"

"I've just been up to see her—"

"Oh, no, mum—she's been away a year, abroad somewhere, couldn't stand the place, it's been empty since then, I just run in every day and keep things tidy—"

Loquacious and curious the young woman had come to the fence; Miss Pym had stopped her horse.

"Miss Lefain is there now," she said. "She must have just come back—"

"She wasn't there this morning, mum, 'tisn't likely she'd come, either—fair scared she was, mum, fair chased away, didn't dare move her china. Can't say I've noticed anything myself, but I never stay long—and there's a smell—"

"Yes," murmured Martha Pym faintly, "there's a smell. What—what—chased her away?"

The young woman, even in that lonely place, lowered her voice.

"Well, as you aren't thinking of taking the place, she got an idea in her head that old Sir James—well, he couldn't bear to leave 'Hartleys,' mum, he's buried in the garden, and she thought he was after her, chasing round them bits of china—"

"Oh!" cried Miss Pym.

"Some of it used to be his, she found a lot stuffed away, he said they were to be left in 'Hartleys,' but Miss Lefain would have the things sold, I believe—that's years ago—"

"Yes, yes," said Miss Pym with a sick look. "You don't know what he was like, do you?"

"No, mum—but I've heard tell he was very stout and very old—I wonder who it was you saw up at 'Hartleys'?"

Miss Pym took a Crown Derby plate from her bag.

"You might take that back when you go," she whispered. "I shan't want it, after all—"

Before the astonished young woman could answer Miss Pym had darted off across the marsh; that short hair, that earth-stained robe, the white socks, "I generally live in the garden—"

Miss Pym drove away, breakneck speed, frantically resolving to mention to no one that she had paid a visit to "Hartleys," nor lightly again to bring up the subject of ghosts.

She shook and shuddered in the damp, trying to get out of her clothes and her nostrils—that indescribable smell.

August Heat

By W. F. Harvey

Phenistone Road, Clapham. August 20th, 190—.

I have had what I believe to be the most remarkable day in my life, and while the events are still fresh in my mind, I wish to put them down on paper as clearly as possible.

Let me say at the outset that my name is James Clarence Withencroft.

I am forty years old, in perfect health, never having known a day's illness.

By profession I am an artist, not a very successful one, but I earn enough money by my black-and-white work to satisfy my necessary wants.

My only near relative, a sister, died five years ago, so that I am independent. I breakfasted this morning at nine, and after glancing through the morning paper I lighted my pipe and proceeded to let my mind wander in the hope that I might chance upon some subject for my pencil.

The room, though door and windows were open, was oppressively hot, and I had just made up my mind that the coolest and most comfortable place in the neighbourhood would be the deep end of the public swimming bath, when the idea came.

I began to draw. So intent was I on my work that I left my lunch untouched, only stopping work when the clock of St. Jude's struck four.

The final result, for a hurried sketch, was, I felt sure, the best thing I had done. It showed a criminal in the dock immediately after the judge had pronounced sentence. The man was fat—enormously fat. The flesh hung in rolls about his chin; it creased his huge, stumpy neck. He was clean shaven (perhaps I should say a few days before he must have been clean shaven) and almost bald. He stood in the dock, his short, clumsy fingers clasping the rail, looking straight in front of him. The feeling that his expression conveyed was not so much one of horror as of utter, absolute collapse.

There seemed nothing in the man strong enough to sustain that mountain of flesh.

I rolled up the sketch, and without quite knowing why, placed it in my pocket. Then with the rare sense of happiness which the knowledge of a good thing well done gives, I left the house.

I believe that I set out with the idea of calling upon Trenton, for I remember walking along Lytton Street and turning to the right along Gilchrist Road at the bottom of the hill where the men were at work on the new tram lines.

From there onwards I have only the vaguest recollection of where I went. The one thing of which I was fully conscious was the awful heat, that came up from the dusty asphalt pavement as an almost palpable wave. I longed for the thunder promised by the great banks of copper-coloured cloud that hung low over the western sky.

I must have walked five or six miles, when a small boy roused me from my reverie by asking the time.

It was twenty minutes to seven.

When he left me, I began to take stock of my bearings. I found myself standing before a gate that led into a yard bordered by a strip of thirsty earth, where there were flowers, purple stock and scarlet geranium. Above the entrance was a board with the inscription:—

Chs. Atkinson. Monumental Mason.
Worker in English and Italian Marbles

From the yard itself came a cheery whistle, the noise of hammer blows, and the cold sound of steel meeting stone.

A sudden impulse made me enter.

A man was sitting with his back towards me, busy at work on a slab of curiously veined marble. He turned round as he heard my steps and I stopped short.

It was the man I had been drawing, whose portrait lay in my pocket.

He sat there, huge and elephantine, the sweat pouring from his scalp, which he wiped with a red silk handkerchief. But though the face was the same, the expression was absolutely different.

He greeted me smiling, as if we were old friends, and shook my hand.

I apologised for my intrusion.

"Everything is hot and glary outside," I said. "This seems an oasis in the wilderness."

"I don't know about the oasis," he replied, "but it certainly is hot, as hot as hell. Take a seat, sir!"

He pointed to the end of the gravestone on which he was at work, and I sat down.

"That's a beautiful piece of stone you've got hold of," I said.

He shook his head. "In a way it is," he answered; "the surface here is as fine as anything you could wish, but there's a big flaw at the back, though I don't expect you'd ever notice it. I could never make really a good job of a bit of marble like that. It would be all right in the summer like this; it wouldn't mind the blasted heat. But wait till the winter comes. There's nothing quite like frost to find out the weak points in stone."

"Then what's it for?" I asked.

The man burst out laughing.

"You'd hardly believe me if I was to tell you it's for an exhibition, but it's the truth. Artists have exhibitions: so, do grocers and butchers; we have them too. All the latest little things in headstones, you know."

He went on to talk of marbles, which sort best withstood wind and rain, and which were easiest to work; then of his garden and a new sort of carnation he had bought. At the end of every other minute, he would drop his tools, wipe his shining head, and curse the heat.

I said little, for I felt uneasy. There was something unnatural, un-canny, in meeting this man.

I tried at first to persuade myself that I had seen him before, that his face, unknown to me, had found a place in some out-of-the-way corner of my memory, but I knew that I was practising little more than a plausible piece of self-deception.

Mr. Atkinson finished his work, spat on the ground, and got up with a sigh of relief.

"There! what do you think of that?" he said, with an air of evident pride. The inscription which I read for the first time was this—

SACRED TO THE MEMORY

OF

JAMES CLARENCE WITHENCROFT.

BORN JAN. 18TH, 1860.

He Passed Away Very Suddenly
On August 20th, 190—
"In the midst of life, we are in death."

For some time, I sat in silence. Then a cold shudder ran down my spine. I asked him where he had seen the name.

"Oh, I didn't see it anywhere," replied Mr. Atkinson. "I wanted some name, and I put down the first that came into my head. Why do you want to know?"

"It's a strange coincidence, but it happens to be mine." He gave a long, low whistle.

"And the dates?"

"I can only answer for one of them, and that's correct."

"It's a rum go!" he said.

But he knew less than I did. I told him of my morning's work. I took the sketch from my pocket and showed it to him. As he looked, the expression of his face altered until it became more and more like that of the man I had drawn.

"And it was only the day before yesterday," he said, "that I told Maria there were no such things as ghosts!"

Neither of us had seen a ghost, but I knew what he meant.

"You probably heard my name," I said.

"And you must have seen me somewhere and have forgotten it! Were you at Clacton-on-Sea last July?"

I had never been to Clacton in my life. We were silent for some time. We were both looking at the same thing, the two dates on the gravestone, and one was right.

"Come inside and have some supper," said Mr. Atkinson.

His wife was a cheerful little woman, with the flaky red cheeks of the country-bred. Her husband introduced me as a friend of his who was an artist. The result was unfortunate, for after the sardines and watercress had been removed, she brought out a *Doré Bible*, and I had to sit and express my admiration for nearly half an hour.

I went outside, and found Atkinson sitting on the gravestone smoking.

We resumed the conversation at the point we had left off. "You must excuse my asking," I said, "but do you know of anything you've done for which you could be put on trial?"

He shook his head. "I'm not a bankrupt, the business is prosperous enough. Three years ago, I gave turkeys to some of the guardians at

Christmas, but that's all I can think of. And they were small ones, too," he added as an afterthought.

He got up, fetched a can from the porch, and began to water the flowers. "Twice a day regular in the hot weather," he said, "and then the heat sometimes gets the better of the delicate ones. And ferns, good Lord! they could never stand it. Where do you live?"

I told him my address. It would take an hour's quick walk to get back home.

"It's like this," he said. "We'll look at the matter straight. If you go back home tonight, you take your chance of accidents. A cart may run over you, and there's always banana skins and orange peel, to say nothing of fallen ladders."

He spoke of the improbable with an intense seriousness that would have been laughable six hours before. But I did not laugh.

"The best thing we can do," he continued, "is for you to stay here till twelve o'clock. We'll go upstairs and smoke, it may be cooler inside."

To my surprise I agreed.

★★★★★★★★★★★★★★★★

We are sitting now in a long, low room beneath the eaves. Atkinson has sent his wife to bed. He himself is busy sharpening some tools at a little oilstone, smoking one of my cigars the while.

The air seems charged with thunder. I am writing this at a shaky table before the open window.

The leg is cracked, and Atkinson, who seems a handy man with his tools, is going to mend it as soon as he has finished putting an edge on his chisel.

It is after eleven now. I shall be gone in less than an hour.

But the heat is stifling.

It is enough to send a man mad.

The Vengeance of a Tree

By Eleanor F. Lewis.

Through the windows of Jim Daly's saloon, in the little town of
C——, the setting sun streamed in yellow patches, lighting up the
glasses scattered on the tables and the faces of several men who were
gathered near the bar. Farmers mostly they were, with a sprinkling
of shopkeepers, while prominent among them was the village editor, and all were discussing a startling piece of news that had spread
through the town and its surroundings. The tidings that Walter Stedman, a labourer on Albert Kelsey's ranch, had assaulted and murdered
his employer's daughter, had reached them, and had spread universal
horror among the people.

A farmer declared that he had seen the deed committed as he
walked through a neighbouring lane, and, having always been noted
for his cowardice, instead of running to the girl's aid, had hailed a party
of miners who were returning from their mid-day meal through a
field nearby. When they reached the spot, however, where Stedman
(as they supposed) had done his black deed, only the girl lay there,
in the stillness of death. Her murderer had taken the opportunity to
fly. The party had searched the woods of the Kelsey estate, and just as
they were nearing the house itself the appearance of Walter Stedman,
walking in a strangely unsteady manner toward it, made them quicken
their pace.

He was soon in custody, although he had protested his innocence
of the crime. He said that he had just seen the body himself on his
way to the station, and that when they had found him, he was going
to the house for help. But they had laughed at his story and had flung
him into the tiny, stifling calaboose of the town.

What were their proofs? Walter Stedman, a young fellow of about
twenty-six, had come from the city to their quiet town, just when
times were at their hardest, in search of work. The most of the men

living in the town were honest fellows, doing their work faithfully, when they could get it, and when they had socially asked Stedman to have a drink with them, he had refused in rather a scornful manner. "That infernal city chap," he was called, and their hate and envy increased in strength when Albert Kelsey had employed him in preference to any of themselves. As time went on, the story of Stedman's admiration for Margaret Kelsey had gone afloat, with the added information that his employer's daughter had repulsed him, saying that she would not marry a common labourer. So, Stedman, when this news reached his employer's ears, was discharged, and this, then, was his revenge! For them, these proofs were sufficient to pronounce him guilty.

Yet that afternoon, as Stedman, crouched on the floor of the calaboose, grew hopeless in the knowledge that no one would believe his story, and that his undeserved punishment would be swift and sure, a tramp, boarding a freight car several miles from the town, sped away from the spot where his crime had been committed, and knew that forever its shadow would follow him.

From the tiny window of his prison Walter Stedman could see the red glow of the heavens that betokened the setting of the sun. So, the red sun of his life was soon to set, a life that had been innocent of all crime, and that now was to be ended for a deed that he had never committed. Most prominent of all the visions that swept through his mind was that of Margaret Kelsey, lying as he had first found her, fresh from the hands of her murderer. But there was another of a more tender nature. How long he and Margaret had tried to keep their secret, until Walter could be promoted to a higher position, so that he could ask for her hand with no fear of the father's antagonism!

Then came the remembrance of an afternoon meeting between the two in the woods of the Kelsey estate—how, just as they were parting, Walter had heard footsteps near them, and, glancing sharply around, saw an evil, scowling, murderous face peering through the brush. He had started toward it, but the owner of the countenance had taken himself hurriedly off.

The gossiping townspeople had misconstrued this romance, and when Albert Kelsey had heard of this clandestine meeting from the man who was later on to appear as a leader of the mob, and that he had discharged Stedman, they had believed that the young man had formally proposed and had been rejected. But justice had gone wrong, as it had done innumerable times before, and will again. An innocent man was to be hanged, even without the comfort of a trial, while the man who was guilty was free to wander where he would.

That autumn night the darkness came quickly, and only the stars did their best to light the scene. A body of men, all masked, and having as a leader one who had ever since Stedman's arrival in town, cherished a secret hatred of the young man, dragged Stedman from the calaboose and tramped through the town, defying all, defying even God himself. Along the highway, and into Farmer Brown's "cross cut," they went, vigilantly guarding their prisoner, who, with the lanterns lighting up his haggard face, walked among them with the lagging step of utter hopelessness.

"That's a good tree," their leader said, presently, stopping and pointing out a spreading oak; when the slipknot was adjusted and Stedman had stepped on the box, he added: "If you've got anything to say, you'd better say it now."

"I am innocent, I swear before God," the doomed man answered; "I never took the life of Margaret Kelsey."

"Give us your proof," jeered the leader, and when Stedman kept a despairing silence, he laughed shortly.

"Ready, men!" he gave the order. The box was kicked aside, and then—only a writhing body swung to and fro in the gloom.

In front of the men stood their leader, watching the contortions of the body with silent glee. "I'll tell you a secret, boys," he said suddenly. "I was after that poor murdered girl myself. A d—— little chance I had; but, by ——, he had just as little!"

A pause—then: "He's shunted this earth. Cut him down, you fellows!"

★★★★★★★★★★★★★★★★★

"It's no use, son. I'll give up the blasted thing as a bad job. There's something queer about that there tree. Do you see how its branches balance it? We have cut the trunk nearly in two, but it won't come down. There's plenty of others around; we'll take one of them. If I'd a long rope with me I'd get that tree down, and yet the way the thing stands it would be risking a fellow's life to climb it. It's got the devil in it, sure."

So old Farmer Brown shouldered his axe and made for another tree, his son following. They had sawed and chopped and chopped and sawed, and yet the tall white oak, with its branches jutting out almost as regularly as if done by the work of a machine, stood straight and firm.

Farmer Brown, well known for his weak, cowardly spirit, who in beholding the murder of Albert Kelsey's daughter, had in his fright mistaken the criminal, now in his superstition let the oak stand, because its well-balanced position saved it from falling, when other trees would have been down. And so, this tree, the same one to which an innocent man had been hanged, was left—for other work.

It was a bleak, rainy night—such a night as can be found only in central California. The wind howled like a thousand demons, and lashed the trees together in wild embraces. Now and then the weird "hoot, hoot!" of an owl came softly from the distance in the lulls of the storm, while the barking of coyotes woke the echoes of the hills into sounds like fiendish laughter.

In the wind and rain a man fought his path through the bush and into Farmer Brown's "cross cut," as the shortest way home. Suddenly he stopped, trembling, as if held by some unseen impulse. Before him rose the white oak, wavering and swaying in the storm.

"Good God! it's the tree I swung Stedman from!" he cried, and a strange fear thrilled him.

His eyes were fixed on it, held by some undefinable fascination. Yes, there on one of the longest branches a small piece of rope still dangled. And then, to the murderer's excited vision, this rope seemed to lengthen, to form at the end into a slipknot, a knot that encircled a purple neck, while below it writhed and swayed the body of a man!

"Damn him!" he muttered, starting toward the hanging form, as if about to help the rope in its work of strangulation; "will he forever follow me? And yet he deserved it, the black-hearted villain! He took her life——"

He never finished the sentence. The white oak, towering above him in its strength, seemed to grow like a frenzied, living creature. There was a sudden splitting sound, then came a crash, and under the fallen tree lay Stedman's murderer, crushed and mangled.

From between the broken trunk and the stump that was left, a grey, dim shape sprang out, and sped past the man's still form, away into the wild blackness of the night.

Railhead

By Perceval Landon

This story was told me in Rangoon by a man whose name, I think, was Torrens, but I cannot remember very clearly, if indeed I ever knew. Really, I hardly know anything about the man except that he was obviously convinced of its truth. He said that John Silbermeister told him the story himself, and I have no doubt that he did. So far as Torrens could recall the man, Silbermeister was an ordinary lanky man, of a singular directness of speech, and totally unable to see a joke. So, for that matter, was Torrens. He said that he had verified the story to this extent, that at the date that Silbermeister mentioned, the NP Railway would have reached Enderton; nor is it apparent what motive there could be for Silbermeister lying in the matter. Torrens hadn't the imagination of a '*rickshaw-wallah*', so it isn't his lie either. At any rate, I give it for what it is worth.

Torrens was a little man who had taken up Christian Science somewhat earnestly a little beyond middle life. He was really a person of some importance on the railway, and I believe one of the company's most efficient servants. To listen to him sometimes one would hardly believe that an accident could possibly occur on the railway, except as a mere delusion of the senses. I believe he died about two years after he told me the story, and for his own sake I hope that he was able to maintain his Christian Science doctrines to the end, for he had sore need of them. He died of cholera at Bhamo in 1904.

He had shown me round the curiosity-shops of Rangoon, and with his help I had disentangled one or two interesting pieces of work from the mass of modern substitutes—it is unfair to call them forgeries—which fill up the curio-shelves of Rangoon dealers. One of them was a little bronze serpent, which sat on its rounded tail and blinked at me with ruby eyes as he told the story in the billiard-room of the "Strand"; and I remember that the Calcutta boat was coming in from

245

the Hastings shoal at the time, and from time to time wailed like a lost spirit up the river. The heat was intense. They have not in the Rangoon the mosquito antidotes to which one is used in India. One buzzing electric fan supplied the entire room, but its sphere of influence was entirely monopolized by a pair of German diamond merchants and their jet-clad wives.

"Some years ago," said Torrens, "a man called Silbermeister came to me with excellent references, and asked if there was any chance of his being employed on the new construction towards the Yunnan frontier. That was before Curzon had put a stopper on the whole project. I dare say Curzon was right. The railway to the North-East, both on this side and on the other side of the frontier, would have been extremely expensive and possibly impracticable. There are deep ravines, "canyons", Silbermeister called them, across which our line had to be thrown. To zigzag down to the bottom by reversing stations and then up again seemed to be the only possible means of crossing them, and with such enormous initial expenditure it was doubtful whether the traffic would ever pay one *per cent* upon the capital.

But we in Rangoon wanted to establish a definite connection with China for political reasons, and if the Indian Government had been willing to guarantee half the cost, the Burmah Railways would have gone on with the business. Silbermeister who had had a good deal of pioneer railway experience, would have been just the man for the job. While the matter was being decided in Calcutta he remained here, and I saw a good deal of him. One evening Silbermeister told me this story, and, so far as I can judge the man at all, I should say that he was telling me the truth.

★★★★★★★★★★★★★★★★

Some years ago, when the big New York Syndicate that employed Silbermeister, among thirty thousand others, was pushing forward the construction of the NP Railway in Nebraska, he was for about three months in charge of the railhead station at Enderton. This was merely a solidly built wooden hut by the side of the Line. Trains ran up to it and nominally carried passengers, but as a matter of fact very few wanted to go further than Castleton, a raw pioneer dump of houses, which had already blossomed out into half a dozen stores, seven "hotels", an electric generating shed, and thirty or forty pretentiously named wooden houses. Beyond Enderton the railway was at this time actually in course of construction. The navvies were chiefly Italian. It was a difficult piece of work, and about eight miles on matters had temporarily come to a standstill owing to a persistent subsidence along the edge of a small half-dry river.

On one Thursday morning a piece of the embankment had given way, and an Italian workman had been killed. This was a matter of no great importance; all engineers know that their lives must be sacrificed to carry out any important work, and on the whole the loss of life on this section of the NP line had been less than might have been expected. There were the usual police guards in the navvies' camp, which contained between three to four hundred workmen.

On a Friday evening, between six and seven o'clock, Silbermeister was sitting in his station-house at Enderton running over the week's wages' account, when a light engine ran up from Castleton. Silbermeister was expecting the money with which to pay the navvies' weekly wages on the following day, and a sub-inspector got off the footplate carrying a canvas bag which contained the money that was needed. It was the usual weekend routine. At the same time, a couple of railwaymen took off the tender half a dozen large packing-cases containing materials that had been requisitioned for the work, and put them into the baggage-room, which composed one-half of the station-house.

The inspector ran through Silbermeister's accounts, initialled them as correct, and then took a receipt for the money which he brought with him. Silbermeister proceeded to lock the money up in the safe in his own room, and then checked the packing-cases which had just been stored in the baggage-room. Among these cases was a somewhat gruesome object, a coffin sent up by the Company from Castleton in order that the victim of the late accident might be decently buried on Sunday morning.

Another receipt was signed for the cases, and then the inspector told the engine-drive he was ready to return. Before doing so, however, he turned to Silbermeister and said:

"Do you feel quite safe here with all that money? Shall I leave you a man to spend the night here with you?"

Silbermeister shrugged his shoulders, and with a smile declined the offer. He said that the police looked after the navvies' camp, that he and his negro servant had spent many nights together at the station, and that he had no fear of burglars. He had, he said, his revolver beside him, and the money would not remain with him more than that one night. The two men shook hands, and the inspector departed as he had come.

Silbermeister then rechecked the books, re-counted the money, saw that the doors were properly locked, sent away his negro servant for the night—the man had been getting the table ready for his supper while he was escorting the inspector back to the engine—and, after locking the door leading to the platform, occupied himself with some small duties now that his day's work was done. There was no further possibility of being rung up from Castleton, so he took this opportunity of cleaning and readjusting the telegraph instrument which stood on a table by the wall, and had not been working quite satisfactorily that morning.

For this purpose, he disconnected the instrument, and being a fairly skilled electrician—though of an old-fashioned school, Torrens said—he did nearly all that was needed in a few minutes. Leaving the instrument as it was, he lit a pipe and started to get ready his supper. By this time the night had begun to fall in earnest, and he lighted the kerosene lamp on the table. More from habit than from anything else, as he knew that he was not likely to need it, he also lighted the bull's-eye lantern which, on most evenings in the week, he took with him on his final rounds.

Silbermeister then opened the cupboard and took down a loaf of bread, a tin of canned meat, and a pot of marmalade. His preparations for supper were simple. It was a cold night, and he meant to have some hot grog before turning in, so he lighted the spirit lamp and filled his kettle from a pitcher of water. While the water was boiling he opened the tin of meat, cut himself a German slice of bread, and arranged the table. By this time the sun had entirely set, and only the last reflections from the dull western horizon still found their way through the windows. For a moment he looked out through the windows across the platform and the wide level waste beyond. There was not a living thing in sight—not a tree, hardly a bush.

Then he shut up the house for the night, and fastened the shutters. He sat down at the table for his meal, propped up a book underneath the lamp, and made himself as comfortable as he could. The bully-beef was not a very appetising dish, and it occurred to him that he had a bottle of sauce put away in a box at the side of the room. He got up, opened the box, and, in order to find the sauce, turned out upon the floor with some noise most of the contents of the trunk. While doing so, he did not notice that the telegraph instrument on the further table ticked out a short and sharp message; at least, it was only the last few strokes that attracted his attention. He turned from the box, before which he was kneeling, to listen, but the message had already stopped. Leaving the sauce undiscovered, he rose to his feet and muttered:

"I'm sure the thing was talking," and went across to the table, to ask for a repetition from Castleton, only to discover, as he might have remembered, that he had himself disconnected the instrument while cleaning it. Dismissing the matter as an illusion, he returned to the box where the sauce was, and after a moment or two found what he wanted. He then resumed his seat at the table without thinking again of the telegraph instrument.

He began his reading, and was in the middle of an engrossing sentence when the telegraph instrument spoke again. This time there could be no mistake. Silbermeister, who knew that when he had left the machine three minutes before it was entirely disconnected, laid down his knife and fork and listened like a man in a dream. There was no doubt about it.

"E-N-T."

The signal for Enderton Station had been called up sharply, imperiously, unmistakably. He waited a moment, and then, in spite of the fact that he had not acknowledged the call, came the short message. He muttered the words as they were ticked out:

"Watch the box."

For one full minute Silbermeister sat immovable. There was no question of the fact, yet the man's common sense refused to believe in what his ears had heard. The room was dead silent except for the hissing of the spirit lamp which had just begun to boil. Silbermeister felt that he was the victim of some nightmare. He would not believe his own senses, and decided to test the thing once more. He rose from the table, went across to the instrument, and brought it bodily away from its position. He put it on the table in front of him next to the corned beef, and then, blowing out the spirit lamp in order that the silence might be more intense, he resumed his seat and waited, hanging over it with every sense on the alert. The lamp lighted up his angular jaw and deep-set eyes staring at the little contrivance of brass and wood. He had not to wait long. The instrument, with its connecting wires and plugs hanging over the side of his dinner-table, and still swinging to and fro beneath it, once again called out his station:

"E-N-T."

The sweat leapt to Silbermeister's forehead, but he made no sign. It went on. It was the same message, short, clear, and beyond all doubt:

"Watch the box."

Silbermeister passed a hand over his face and thought. Whatever the origin of this message was, the message itself was unmistakable. He reached for his bull's-eye lantern, saw it was burning well, turned out the lamp on the table, and rose silently. He moved across to the door that separated his living-room from the luggage-room, very quietly opened the door, and waited. One minute dragged its slow length along, then two, then three, and still Silbermeister stood in the darkness as motionless as the jamb of the door. There was no sound inside or outside the station-house. So still was the silence that, as Silbermeister said, a man could hear his blood circulating round the drum of his own ear—rather a good expression, Torrens thought.

At last, the tension was relieved. There was a sound, more like the sound of a gnawing mouse than anything else, and Silbermeister sank silently to his knee to listen more intently. A touch which, infinitesimal though it was, could only have been made by iron upon iron, betrayed the whole circumstance to him. There was a man in the coffin, and the man had so contrived the lid that he could get out of the coffin without attracting the notice of Silbermeister till it was too late.

There was at the same moment the sound of a cautiously planted footstep on the platform outside. Silbermeister acted at once. Some of the cases of railway material that had been sent up that evening contained steel tools, and were as much as two men could carry into the room. Silbermeister was a strong man, but he hardly knew how he managed unaided to drag down one of the packing-cases and set it on the top of the coffin with a crash that almost crushed it in.

The moment he had done so, all pretence was at an end, and the man within it shouted to his accomplice outside. The answer was a blow on the door like a battering-ram. The packing-case might hold down the man for some time yet, so Silbermeister leapt back into his living-room to meet the new danger, only to find the door on to the platform being battered through just above the bolt.

He picked up his revolver, and in order to make sure there should be no attack from behind, aimed at the coffin and pulled the trigger. There was no response. It was clear that treachery had been at work. His black servant had seized the opportunity while Silbermeister escorted the inspector to the engine, of opening and emptying it—an easy task, as it was lying on the table. There was no time to turn back to the baggage-room.

Seizing a small crowbar, Silbermeister had only just time to dash to the door, through the hole in which his negro servant's arm was now thrusting itself feeling for the bolt. He gripped the man's hand and pulled it into the room until the negro's arm-pit was forced up against the splintered hole in the door. He struck heavily with the crowbar, and the negro screamed in agony. He struck again, and again, and again. He hardly knows what happened during that awful minute. He went on striking blindly and mechanically at what had suddenly become a man's sleeve. In the baggage-room he had just left the tremendous exertions of the imprisoned man were making the room resound, and the packing-case on the top of the coffin rocked to and fro. Silbermeister paid no attention. He lost his head. Both lamps were now out, and all he could do in the darkness was to go on hitting at what he held.

Suddenly there was the whistle of an approaching engine. No train was due until the following morning, but Silbermeister admitted that at the moment he hardly regarded anything as unusual. A couple of armed men and the inspector leapt down on to the platform, collared the negro servant, who by that time was hanging half-unconscious from the hole in the door, and burst in just in time to intercept the man in the baggage-room who had at last overturned the packing-case above him and was crashing his way out through the lid of the coffin. It was an extraordinary scene.

The inspector pulled the negro servant, with his arm one pulp of splintered bone and blood, into the room and thrust him roughly aside. He fell without a moan into the corner. The two men then brought the burglar into the living-room between them. Silbermeister went back to the table, sat down, and put his head between his hands. The inspector looked at him for a moment in amazement as he raised his head and said: "Thank God!" After a pause he added: "Why did you come?"

The inspector answered:

"Your telegram caught us just before we left Castleton again. It was lucky, wasn't it?" he added grimly.

Silbermeister again raised his head from his hands, and as if he had heard nothing, said:

"But why did you come?"

The inspector, a trifle gravely, said:

"I told you, your telegram just reached us in time."

There was another pause of ten seconds, and then Silbermeister pointed to the disconnected instrument, and said once more:

"Why did you come?" His eyes turned in his head: "I sent no message"; and then he fell on the floor in a dead faint.

★★★★★★★★★★★★★★★★

That is all I know about it. That is the story that Torrens told me, and the story that undoubtedly Torrens believed.

LEONAUR

ALSO FROM LEONAUR
AVAILABLE IN SOFTCOVER OR HARDCOVER WITH DUST JACKET

MR MUKERJI'S GHOSTS *by S. Mukerji*—Supernatural tales from the British Raj period by India's Ghost story collector.

KIPLINGS GHOSTS *by Rudyard Kipling*—Twelve stories of Ghosts, Hauntings, Curses, Werewolves & Magic.

THE COLLECTED SUPERNATURAL AND WEIRD FICTION OF WASHINGTON IRVING: VOLUME 1 *by Washington Irving*—Including one novel 'A History of New York', and nine short stories of the Strange and Unusual.

THE COLLECTED SUPERNATURAL AND WEIRD FICTION OF WASHINGTON IRVING: VOLUME 2 *by Washington Irving*—Including three novelettes 'The Legend of the Sleepy Hollow', 'Dolph Heyliger', 'The Adventure of the Black Fisherman' and thirty-two short stories of the Strange and Unusual.

THE COLLECTED SUPERNATURAL AND WEIRD FICTION OF JOHN KENDRICK BANGS: VOLUME 1 *by John Kendrick Bangs*—Including one novel 'Toppleton's Client or A Spirit in Exile', and ten short stories of the Strange and Unusual.

THE COLLECTED SUPERNATURAL AND WEIRD FICTION OF JOHN KENDRICK BANGS: VOLUME 2 *by John Kendrick Bangs*—Including four novellas 'A House-Boat on the Styx', 'The Pursuit of the House-Boat', 'The Enchanted Typewriter' and 'Mr. Munchausen' of the Strange and Unusual.

THE COLLECTED SUPERNATURAL AND WEIRD FICTION OF JOHN KENDRICK BANGS: VOLUME 3 *by John Kendrick Bangs*—Including twor novellas 'Olympian Nights', 'Roger Camerden: A Strange Story', and ten short stories of the Strange and Unusual.

THE COLLECTED SUPERNATURAL AND WEIRD FICTION OF MARY SHELLEY: VOLUME 1 *by Mary Shelley*—Including one novel 'Frankenstein or the Modern Prometheus', and fourteen short stories of the Strange and Unusual.

THE COLLECTED SUPERNATURAL AND WEIRD FICTION OF MARY SHELLEY: VOLUME 2 *by Mary Shelley*—Including one novel 'The Last Man', and three short stories of the Strange and Unusual.

THE COLLECTED SUPERNATURAL AND WEIRD FICTION OF AMELIA B. EDWARDS *by Amelia B. Edwards*—Contains two novelettes 'Monsieur Maurice', and 'The Discovery of the Treasure Isles', one ballad 'A Legend of Boisguilbert' and seventeen short stories to cill the blood.

LEONAUR

ALSO FROM LEONAUR
AVAILABLE IN SOFTCOVER OR HARDCOVER WITH DUST JACKET

THE COMPLETE FOUR JUST MEN: VOLUME 2 *by Edgar Wallace*—*The Law of the Four Just Men & The Three Just Men*—disillusioned with a world where the wicked and the abusers of power perpetually go unpunished, the Just Men set about to rectify matters according to their own standards, and retribution is dispensed on swift and deadly wings.

THE COMPLETE RAFFLES: 1 *by E. W. Hornung*—*The Amateur Cracksman & The Black Mask*—By turns urbane gentleman about town and accomplished cricketer, life is just too ordinary for Raffles and that sets him on a series of adventures that have long been treasured as a real antidote to the 'white knights' who are the usual heroes of the crime fiction of this period.

THE COMPLETE RAFFLES: 2 *by E. W. Hornung*—*A Thief in the Night & Mr Justice Raffles*—By turns urbane gentleman about town and accomplished cricketer, life is just too ordinary for Raffles and that sets him on a series of adventures that have long been treasured as a real antidote to the 'white knights' who are the usual heroes of the crime fiction of this period.

THE COLLECTED SUPERNATURAL AND WEIRD FICTION OF WILKIE COLLINS: VOLUME 1 *by Wilkie Collins*—Contains one novel 'The Haunted Hotel', one novella 'Mad Monkton', three novelettes 'Mr Percy and the Prophet', 'The Biter Bit' and 'The Dead Alive' and eight short stories to chill the blood.

THE COLLECTED SUPERNATURAL AND WEIRD FICTION OF WILKIE COLLINS: VOLUME 2 *by Wilkie Collins*—Contains one novel 'The Two Destinies', three novellas 'The Frozen deep', 'Sister Rose' and 'The Yellow Mask' and two short stories to chill the blood.

THE COLLECTED SUPERNATURAL AND WEIRD FICTION OF WILKIE COLLINS: VOLUME 3 *by Wilkie Collins*—Contains one novel 'Dead Secret,' two novelettes 'Mrs Zant and the Ghost' and 'The Nun's Story of Gabriel's Marriage' and five short stories to chill the blood.

FUNNY BONES *selected by Dorothy Scarborough*—An Anthology of Humorous Ghost Stories.

MONTEZUMA'S CASTLE AND OTHER WEIRD TALES *by Charles B. Cory*—Cory has written a superb collection of eighteen ghostly and weird stories to chill and thrill the avid enthusiast of supernatural fiction.

SUPERNATURAL BUCHAN *by John Buchan*—Stories of Ancient Spirits, Uncanny Places & Strange Creatures.

www.ingramcontent.com/pod-product-compliance
Lightning Source LLC
Chambersburg PA
CBHW031121030726
47496CB00002BA/631